Rebecca Moving On

Mary Peters

Published by New Generation Publishing in 2017

Copyright © Mary Peters 2017

First Edition

The author asserts the moral right under the Copyright, Designs and Patents Act 1988 to be identified as the author of this work.

ISBN: 978-1-78719-592-9

All Rights reserved. No part of this publication may be reproduced, stored in a retrieval system or transmitted, in any form or by any means without the prior consent of the author, nor be otherwise circulated in any form of binding or cover other than that which it is published and without a similar condition being imposed on the subsequent purchaser.

www.newgeneration-publishing.com

New Generation Publishing

Cover design by Jacqueline Abromeit

Acknowledgements

A big thank you to my exceptional editor Linda Harris for being so supportive and a wonderful person to work with. I can't imagine doing this book without your assistance and patience. I thank you from the bottom of my heart.

Thank you too, to Jacqueline Abromeit who designed the cover for my book. What an amazing illustrator who I have had the pleasure to work with on my other novels. It has been an absolute joy, your work is superb.

Also by the author:

Marcie
Neither Use Nor Ornament
Betsy, The Coalminer's Daughter

Children's books:
Ollie the Orange Otter
Millie and Her Farm Friends
Patsy the Bag Lady

Rebecca Trapped

Rebecca Taylor is married, with eight-year-old twin daughters Amy and Mary. They live in Alysham, a market town in rural Norfolk, in a two-bedroomed semi-detached house. On the surface everything looked bliss, Rebecca's husband Jim worked as a builder and Rebecca had a part-time job in a salon called "Hair With Flair" in a nearby village. The family were very well respected by their elderly neighbours as Jim would often offer to cut their lawns or do odd jobs if asked, in the early days when they first moved into the property, but behind closed doors was an entirely different story. There were always arguments between Rebecca and her husband and things came to a head one morning over breakfast.

"Jim, will you take the girls to school? I want to meet Valerie for a catch-up – I'm phoning in sick."

"Piss off, Rebecca, you're having a laugh. I've got so much work on today, I've got an extension to do on a property and deadlines to meet – I *have* to complete the job by the end of the month."

Rebecca knew Jim had a nasty temper and he thought nothing of screaming at the top of his voice, so she sat silent and said nothing.

Jim kissed the girls good-bye, ignored Rebecca and walked out the door. Amy was more confident than her sister and asked her mum why their dad was always shouting.

"Nothing for you to worry about, Amy," her mum replied, "he has so much work on at the moment and is a bit stressed. Never mind that, would you please go and put your coat and shoes on – you too, Mary, or you'll both be late for school."

Rebecca dropped the girls off at school and got back into her car and rang her job to say she had a heavy cold and was taking the day off. June, who owned the salon, was very sympathetic and said she hoped she'd feel better soon. It was the first time Rebecca had taken time off work in two years so she didn't feel guilty and headed to meet her friend Valerie in the coffee bar on the high street. It was difficult parking the car as the car park was full, but she eventually found a space and hoped her friend was still waiting for her as she was running late, and more than ever she felt she needed a good natter. Her stomach was churning, the tension in the house with Jim was taking its toll and it was becoming unbearable. Valerie, her best friend since school days, never liked Jim and she'd stopped going to the house to visit the family as she found him to be an arrogant, impatient, selfish man – far too serious and harsh with the girls.

When Rebecca opened the café door she saw that Valerie was already there. As soon as Valerie saw her she jumped out of her seat and gave Rebecca a big hug.

"Gosh I was surprised you rang me, Rebecca, it's been ages since I last saw you – sit down and I'll get us two coffees."

"Thanks Valerie, I've missed you." When Valerie sat down she wasted no time asking Rebecca what the problem was. "Spill the beans, I know you too well, what's Jim been up to now?"

"We just seem to be rowing a lot lately. I can't seem to get through to him, Valerie, I know he has a lot of work on but it's having an effect on the girls – they spend most of their time in the bedroom, it's not right," Rebecca remarked, clutching her cup of coffee.

"To be honest," Val replied, "I don't know what you

ever saw in him, he's a miserable bugger and is trying to be something he's not, way above his station. Let's be honest, he comes from a council house like you and me, Rebecca, on a rough estate."

"There's nothing wrong with owning your own property, Valerie."

"I know that but never forget where you've come from and besides that he's a cold fish in the bedroom department, you've always told me that, Rebecca. What the hell do you see in him when you could have had your pick of blokes – remember what your nick-name was when we went dancing at the clubs? Audrey Hepburn, mine was fatty Arbuckle."

"I know but look at you now, Valerie, you're so pretty. I love your hair cut in a bob and look how slim you are," Rebecca smiled.

"I'm quite happy about the way I look, and anyway my Rob loves me fat or slim."

"How is he?" Rebecca asked.

"He's still working at the warehouse and I'm still cleaning pubs, we'll never be rich but we're happy. Our two boys are boisterous and can be a handful but I wouldn't change a thing – and how are Amy and Mary? They're the spitting image of you last time I saw them."

"Okay, doing alright at school but I think Jim is far too strict with them at times, Valerie."

"He's a bully, Rebecca, and possessive with you. I bet you never told him you were seeing me?"

"I did, I'm not going to lie, why should I? He wasn't too happy about it, I don't think he likes me having any friends at all; I only get to see my parents once a week if that." Rebecca spoke with tears in her eyes and Valerie held her hand across the table.

There was silence for a few minutes then Valerie took a tissue out of her handbag and handed it to Rebecca. "I was just thinking – how about you and the girls stay with me and Rob for a while, I think the break away from Jim would do you the world of good – what do you think?"

"Thanks so much but Jim will go mad and in the long run that won't solve anything. I admit I could pack my bags and leave right now the way I'm feeling but I'd rather face Jim and give him an ultimatum – if he continues his unreasonable behaviour I'm seeking a divorce."

"I just want you to be happy," Valerie replied in a sympathetic voice, "you and the girls deserve better. Listen, I have to love you and leave you, I have a couple of jobs to do today, Rebecca, but you know where I live – come anytime and I want you to know I'm here for you always. I must get going, give me a ring," and she kissed Rebecca on the cheek and hurried off.

Rebecca still had hours to kill before she picked up the girls from school so she took a walk down the high street to look at the clothes shops. She spotted a beautiful black double-breasted coat with silver buttons in the widow display in Marks & Spencer's and walked in and tried it on. An assistant came over and remarked how gorgeous she looked in it, being such a perfect fit.

"I can't see a price tag," Rebecca remarked, "how much is it?"

"It's £45 in the sale, it's reduced," the young assistant replied.

"Okay I'll have it."

When Rebecca left the shop she had butterflies in her stomach, what on earth was she thinking of? Jim will go berserk. In the past she always had to ring him at work to ask if it was okay to purchase any clothing for her and the girls; if it was only the food shopping she could choose whatever she needed and for which he gave her a fixed amount every week, not a penny more.

Rebecca popped in to see her parents on the way home, they had a beautiful bungalow which they purchased through an inheritance when her uncle

Thomas, on her father's side, died of bowel cancer. He never married and doted on Rebecca growing up and when she married Jim he gave them both a gift of £5,000 towards a mortgage to buy their own property.

"I must admit I'm surprised to see you, Rebecca, why aren't you at work?"

"I took the day off, Mum, I just fancied a bit of me time – where's Dad?"

"Pottering around in the shed making bird boxes, at least he's not under my feet. I'll make us both a cuppa and I have a chocolate cake I made the other day."

"Thanks, Mum, should I call Dad?"

"No leave him there in the shed, then we can have a good natter, you know what he's like he can talk for England I don't get a word in edgeways."

Rebecca chuckled, "You are horrible to him sometimes, Mum."

Grace made the tea in her china tea cups and called Bert, her husband. She felt a bit guilty not to, because he had been suffering from a bout of flu for a week and was only just on the mend.

"Dad, you look a bit peaky – are you okay?" Rebecca asked.

"It's nothing, just a rotten cold, lass, anyway when did you arrive?"

"Twenty minutes ago. Have your tea, Dad, it's getting cold."

"How's my son-in-law, has he finished the extension yet?"

"No he's a bit stressed at work."

"He's a grafter, I'll give him that. You have a good one there, my girl, such a gentleman – and how are my grandchildren?"

"The girls are fine, Dad, I'll bring them over next weekend. This chocolate cake is yummy, Mum, I wish I could bake like you."

"Don't be daft, Rebecca, of course you can, it's just that I've got more time on my hands since I retired."

Nellie the next-door neighbour and her husband Pete popped in for a chat, so Rebecca said her farewells to her parents and got into the car and headed home as it was still too early to pick up the girls from school.

On the journey home she felt a sadness inside, there were times when she longed to open up to her parents to tell them how controlling Jim was – not the perfect husband they both thought he was – but why worry them, they had been happily married all their lives. Her mum thought she was going through the menopause at forty-two when she found out she was pregnant; after failing to conceive over the years it was like a miracle had happened. They were elderly now and enjoying their retirement so there was no point in causing them any grief, it was her baggage to sort out and she felt such a failure.

Rebecca parked her car and went indoors but was shocked to see Jim sitting at the kitchen table eating a sandwich, thinking he would be at work.

"Where the hell have you been? I've been ringing you all morning, Rebecca."

"Why what's happened? I told you, Jim, I was meeting Valerie and I called in to see Mum and Dad."

"Oh good for you, some of us have to work. I was feeling ill – I think I have a virus or something and tried to ring you to make an appointment at the doctor's for me."

"Come off it, Jim, you could have done it yourself."

"Get lost, Rebecca, you're selfish. I'm working my bollocks off here, it's about time you showed some appreciation. I'm going to have a lie down – bring me a cuppa if it's not too much trouble."

Rebecca duly took a cuppa upstairs for Jim, put her coat on and went to collect the girls from school. She sat in the car for half an hour, it was still too early but she just wanted to get out of the house. She was furious with Jim, she felt suffocated and trapped.

Mary was the first one to get out of school, and five minutes later Amy arrived at the car. "Seat belts on, girls, have you had a nice day?"

"No, Mum," Amy piped up. "I didn't, I got told off by Miss Parker for talking in the lesson and it wasn't me it was Keiran – he kept pinching my leg."

"You're always talking in class and giggling, Amy, and you got a telling off by Mr Grimes our maths teacher last week."

"Shut up, Mary – that's not true, Mum."

"Stop arguing you two, I have a migraine – and your dad's at home, he feels unwell. I don't want you both causing him any upset, you know what your dad's like when he's feeling poorly."

Rebecca remarked, "I think he's grumpy all the time."

Amy commented, "He never plays with us and he always promises to take us to the pictures or the park but never does, Mum."

"You know your dad works so hard and he does his best. Never mind that, what would you like for your dinner – fish fingers and chips or sausages?"

"Fish fingers, please," Amy replied.

"What about you, Mary?"

"Egg, chips and beans."

"Okay, and if you're both good girls you can have ice-cream for afters."

Rebecca parked the car in the drive and noticed Jim was chatting to Paul their elderly next-door neighbour and his wife Brenda. "You've made a speedy recovery, Jim," she shouted and she and the girls went indoors.

Jim walked in the house ten minutes later with a look of anger on his face. He raised his voice, "Don't you ever show me up again like that, woman!"

"What do you mean, Jim, I was only joking," Rebecca replied. "Go up and change your clothes, girls."

She could tell they looked afraid and when they went out of the room she turned to Jim, "Do you have to start arguing in front of the children, what is wrong with you?"

"I went next door to see if they had any paracetamols."

"Okay I'm so sorry, Jim, can we call a truce – what do you want to eat?"

"Steak and chips if that's not too much trouble."

When Rebecca had cooked their meals they all sat around the kitchen table. "Where's the tomato ketchup, Mum?" Mary asked.

"I'll get it."

"No you won't, Rebecca, stay where you are – and you, turn your chair around and sit up straight, Amy, get your arms off the table and stop slouching."

Mary shrugged her shoulders and looked at her dad angrily as she went to get the tomato sauce. There was silence at the table; Jim didn't like too much talking when he was having his meal, only when he had finished eating.

"I was thinking, girls, would you like to watch a video tonight? Me and your mum can relax in the conservatory, we need to discuss where we want to take you both on holiday. I was thinking we could all go abroad to Malta instead of our usual holidays in Spain."

Amy couldn't contain her excitement, "Yippee!" she exclaimed, and Mary flung her arms around her mum.

Rebecca looked shocked, "I wish you'd discussed this with me first, Jim – can we afford it?"

"Let me worry about that, I just thought it would be a lovely break as a family to spend some quality time together. It's been two years since we've been away and I've been working my socks off – I thought you'd be pleased. I don't understand you at times, you're hard work, Rebecca," and Jim walked into the conservatory, not before he poured himself a large glass of red wine.

The girls watched their video enjoying a bowl of ice-cream, then it was their bed time and Rebecca tucked them up into bed and went downstairs to do the washing up. Jim walked into the kitchen and put his arms around her kissing her neck, he had drunk half a bottle of red wine.

"Can we talk, Jim, I need to tell you something?"

They sat at the kitchen table. "I want a divorce, Jim, we can't go on like this bickering all the time in front of the girls. We're not compatible and I feel I'm walking on eggshells, never knowing when you're going to erupt like a volcano, it's not good."

Jim sat with his legs crossed, looking so smug, "Don't be stupid, you're going nowhere, Rebecca, you love me and I love you. I admit I'm a pain to live with sometimes but we're here for the long haul – we can get through this, all couples have their squabbles."

"You're not listening to me, Jim, you're like Jekyll and Hyde, changeable like the weather. When you're good you're unbelievable, the kindest person you could ever wish to meet. That's what I loved about you when we first met – such a gentleman, considerate towards my feelings, a good listener, till you put the ring on my finger and we got married then everything changed."

"Enough, Rebecca, have you quite finished?" Jim remarked in a stern voice.

"What I'm trying to say, Jim, if you let me finish speaking, is that whatever happens you are the father of my children, I won't stop you from seeing them but I feel suffocated and need to find the real me. I'm being serious, I don't know who I am anymore," there were tears in Rebecca's eyes as she spoke, "living with you, Jim, is depressing – you're always so negative."

Jim didn't flinch an eyelid, he had heard all this before from Rebecca and put on the charm, "I love you more than anything, Rebecca, you and the girls are my world. I know we have problems but that will all change I promise you, just give me a chance. Do you really want to lose this beautiful home and end up bringing our girls up on a council estate? They've been used to a good lifestyle – how would you feel taking all that away from them, and to be perfectly honest what you earn at the hairdresser's part time is peanuts, it doesn't pay for the food shopping or all of the bills so stop talking nonsense."

Rebecca felt drained, all of a sudden the outside world looked frightening to her. Jim was right, how would she cope bringing her two girls up on her own.

The next morning Rebecca woke up and Jim had already left for work; he'd left her a note on the bedside table which read… *'Love you, give me a ring later* xx'. She sighed with relief, the tension in the house was getting too much she couldn't believe how insensitive Jim was asking for sex last night, but she gave in – anything to appease him. It was the usual, her getting on top of Jim, doing all the work while he came to a orgasm and him turning over to sleep, not even a cuddle. She felt it was like another job to Jim on his to do list; the sex lasted about fifteen minutes but she always put it down to him having a low sex drive and as her mum pointed out it wasn't the be all and end all. Jim was a good man, a good provider and she should thank her lucky stars to have met someone like that.

Rebecca took the girls to school and popped into the clothes shop before she went to work to get a refund on her coat she had purchased, saying it wasn't suitable. She had purposely left it in a carrier bag in the car knowing how Jim would react and felt guilty, but it was just a coat after all no big deal.

June was pleased to see her at work, she had become quite fond of her, "How are you feeling, Rebecca?"

"I'm fine thanks, feeling much better."

"This is a busy day today, I've got three perms to do and you have lots of tints and blow-waves."

The clients were mostly elderly – it wasn't a big shop, but a busy one.

"Phew! Let's have a cuppa, Rebecca, my next client Mrs Brown won't be in for another hour."

"I'll make the tea," Rebecca replied, "and there are some ginger biscuits in the tin and some fig rolls."

"I'll join you in a minute, Rebecca, I'll just give the floor a quick sweep," June replied.

When June and Rebecca sat down drinking their tea at the small area at the back of the shop, June got straight to the point about what was on her mind. She was a mature straight-forward woman who spoke her mind, "I've noticed, Rebecca, you've been very quiet lately, withdrawn – is everything alright at home? I don't mean to pry but I've known you a long time and I know how private you are but you can tell me anything, I promise you it won't go any further, I like to think we've become friends."

"Jim wants us all to go on holiday to Malta."

"That's lovely, Rebecca, and if you want time off that's not a problem – my sister can come in for two weeks and help. She's just qualified as a hairdresser at college, we'll work something out I'm sure."

"Thanks, June, but to be honest I'm not sure I want to go. Things haven't been good between Jim and me lately, he has a nasty temper and won't listen to reason he's so stubborn."

"Oh I see, I'm so sorry to hear that, have either of you thought of going to see a marriage counsellor? I divorced three years ago as you know and I have never been so happy living on my own. I hung around for years mostly for the children's sake, fed-up with my husband's affairs but the kids were unhappy like me, so what was the point.

Jim seems a nice guy but I've only seen him when he picks you up from work on the few occasions. Maybe a holiday will do you both good, but mark my words life is too short – if you both can't work things out, it's time to go your separate ways. Has Jim put his hands on you – is he violent?" June asked.

"No," Rebecca replied, looking awkward, "he doesn't hit me," but she knew in her heart that wasn't strictly true, he had slapped her face and punched her in the past, but not anywhere that was noticeable.

"Look, anytime you want to talk I'm here, pet, you're a good worker, Rebecca, and the clients love you. Now I'm afraid it's back to work."

"Thanks for listening, June."

"Don't be daft, us women have to stick together."

Rebecca finished work; she had seen another side of June which she liked – maybe she was a bit of a loud-mouthed no-nonsense kind of a person in her eyes but it felt good talking to her. Maybe they weren't so different after all, still she had to be on the side of caution – June loved a good gossip to the customers and if Jim knew she was discussing her marriage problems to anyone, all hell would be let loose.

Malta

Summer had arrived and the last two months living with Jim had been easier, only because threatening Jim with a divorce seemed to do the trick even though every time she said those words she had to be more convincing. It was hard work, he controlled the finances at the moment and she could see no light at the end of the tunnel.

They were now getting ready for the two-week holiday to St Paul's Bay in Malta; Jim had organised everything, booking them in at the Dolmen Resort Hotel and Rebecca felt quite excited. More than anything she wanted the girls to have a good time, and remembered the last holiday they had in Spain. Jim looked much more relaxed, less stressed.

Rebecca had done all the packing and the girls were tucked up in bed. Jim poured her a Bacardi and Coke and himself a beer and they were relaxing in the sitting room when the phone rang and Jim answered it. "Hello! Just ringing to say have a lovely holiday, Jim – is my daughter there?"

"I'll put her on – it's your mum," said Jim as he handed the phone to Rebecca.

"Hi Mum, is Dad okay?"

"He's fine, give the girls my love and we'll check on the house while you're away, I have the spare key. Give me a ring when you get there so we know you've all arrived safely."

"I will, Mum, take care – bye," and Rebecca put the phone down.

"Why don't you give your mum a ring, Jim, it can't be

easy her looking after your dad with his arthritis and we haven't visited them in months."

"She's a pain in the arse, nothing I do is ever good enough for her, and my dad doesn't have much to say for himself."

"Jim, they're still your parents, that's in the past."

"I know what you're saying, Rebecca, but Lee is their favourite son – he's mum's blue-eyed boy, him with his three rental properties and his posh job working at the bank. Do you know he's just paid for Mum and Dad to go on holiday to Cornwell and booked them in an expensive hotel – bloody show-off, he's always boasting, and his wife Lesley isn't much better, snobbish cow."

"I think you're both as bad as one another, so competitive, good luck to your brother – he works hard, maybe he felt he had to prove himself to your parents with their high expectations, whereas you were the more rebellious one. I don't see what your problem is, Jim, I quite like him. He's always been very generous with the girls on their birthdays and at Christmas – it's just I never know what to buy their children, they seem to have everything."

"Precocious boys Adrian and Jack. What the hell was Lee thinking of sending them to a private school?"

"Shush, Jim, stop moaning. What they do is their business, anyone would think you're jealous."

"Don't talk stupid, Rebecca, I've got everything I want apart from another cold beer – will you get me one and a few crisps while you're at it."

"I'm going to bed soon, I'm starting to feel a bit tired. I think we'd better have an early night, we've got to get up at six to get to the airport on time, Jim. I just hope we haven't forgotten anything."

"Stop worrying, Rebecca, I gave you the list didn't I? Do I have to think of everything around here?"

Rebecca put her arms around Jim and gave him a big

kiss, she didn't want him kicking off just when they were about to go on holiday.

When they woke up, Rebecca saw to the girls, getting them dressed and Jim helped by making the beds. He put the suitcases downstairs in the passage ready to be put into the car and then got himself ready.

"Do you want a cuppa, Jim?"

"No I'll have a glass of milk, you go and get dressed, Rebecca, I'll see to the girls. Do you two want some toast?"

"Yes please, Dad," Mary said excitedly.

"What about you, Amy?"

"No thanks I'm not hungry, I'm tired."

The taxi had arrived. "Rebecca, are you ready?" Jim shouted up the stairs.

"I'm coming in five minutes, Jim, just make sure all the windows are locked and the back door."

Jim opened the front door and helped the cab driver put the suitcases in the car. "You're early, I booked the cab for seven-thirty, it's only just seven o'clock."

"Sorry, mate, the girl in the office who took the call must have got the wrong information, nothing to do with me," and he went to sit back in his taxi.

As soon as Jim had checked that the house was secure, they all got into the cab.

The journey to the airport was straightforward; there was hardly any traffic on the road and Jim paid the cab driver but didn't give him a tip – he was a miserable sod Jim thought, and the cigarette he was smoking was a disgusting habit to have, especially in a confined space.

There was a long queue to book in for departure and the girls were very tired. Rebecca felt stressed and was relieved when they eventually boarded the plane. The girls fell asleep and Jim held Rebecca's hand, "You look stunning, Rebecca, very smart and beautiful," he remarked.

"Thanks, it's only an old dress you bought me three years ago for my birthday."

"I can't remember," Jim grinned, "I've bought you that much."

"Very funny, anyway if we're fishing out compliments you look very handsome – I love your shirt and cream trousers."

"Is that all, what about my smart shoes?" Jim asked, kissing Rebecca on the cheek.

"Them too, you silly bugger. It's lovely seeing you smile Jim, and relaxed. I can't wait to see the hotel."

"Me too, I hope it's up to standard – all the money I've shelled out, Rebecca."

"I'm sure it will be great, it has a four-star rating so I don't see why not. You look tired, have a snooze while I read my magazine."

"Now who's being bossy," Jim smiled.

They finally arrived at their destination at the hotel and booked in at the reception desk. Then they all took the lift to the second floor and were shown to their en-suite double connecting bedrooms by the porter Manuel. Rebecca thought what a handsome man Manuel was with his olive skin, jet-black curly hair and the most gorgeous muscular body she'd ever seen on a man.

"I hope you all enjoy your stay," Manuel politely remarked, shaking Jim's hand and was just about to leave the room.

"Hold on a second," Jim said and took his wallet out of his pocket to give Manuel a tip.

"Mum, look!" Amy shouted. "There's a balcony overlooking the swimming pool! I love it here, Dad."

"Me too," Mary said jumping up and down.

"What do you think, Rebecca?"

"It's gorgeous, Jim, the girls are going to have a fabulous time."

"I think we should start unpacking otherwise the clothes are going to get creased," Jim remarked, but the girls had other ideas and started to undress and put their swimming costumes on to go into the swimming pool.

"First things first, girls, help your mum put your clothes in the drawers and we'll go downstairs to have something to eat – I'm starving, we should all have a healthy meal."

"Your dad's right, you girls, you've hardly eaten a thing apart from them crisps and chocolate bars you had on the plane."

"Alright, Mum, I'll help you," Mary replied but Amy, who was the stubborn one, walked into her bedroom and sat on the bed with a face like thunder.

"Rebecca are you ready? Let's go." Jim had done his bit and emptied his suitcase, had put his clothes neatly away and put the toiletries in the bathroom. Finally they were organized and went to the lift to go to the ground floor.

"Blimey it's so hot, Jim, I should have put some sun tan lotion on the girls."

"Stop fussing, Rebecca, let's just find a café to eat – the main restaurant is closed," and they strolled over to the snack bar by the pool. "I don't fancy eating here, look on the board they're serving hot dogs and doughnuts and chips in some kind of cheese sauce, bloody awful," Jim commented, "let's go out of the hotel and take a walk along the sea front, we're bound to find a decent place to eat – I quite fancy a nice juicy steak with a salad."

"Let's hope the restaurant meals here in the hotel are good, Jim, we're on half board – we don't want to be eating out all the time on our budget."

"Let me worry about that, Rebecca, we're here to have a good time," and he put his arms around her and kissed her on the cheek.

They eventually found a small restaurant that had a large varied menu, but the girls were taking too much time choosing what they wanted and Jim was getting impatient so ordered them all steak, chips, and salad. Jim gulped it down, he was starving and Rebecca was the same.

"Mary, you've hardly touched your meal, just the chips."

"I don't like it, Mum, I hate steak and salad."

"Leave her," Jim remarked, "she's always been a fussy eater. I can see you enjoyed your meal, Amy, you've cleared your plate good girl."

"Can we go swimming now, Mum?"

"I think we should head back to the hotel," Rebecca suggested, "and let the girls swim in the pool, Jim, it's becoming so hot."

Jim called the waiter and paid the bill.

When they arrived back at the hotel they went up to their rooms where the girls changed into their bathing costumes and Rebecca put some suntan lotion on them. It was boiling, the temperature was 80F.

Rebecca changed into her bright red bikini. "Wow, you look stunning," Jim commented.

"Thank you, kind sir – what are you wearing, my gorgeous husband?"

"This white T-shirt and navy blue shorts, or maybe the red shorts – I'm not sure…"

"Hurry up, Dad," Amy piped up, "we're waiting for you, you're so slow like a snail. Can Dad not meet us downstairs, Mum?"

"Hey you cheeky monkey, you have no patience at all. Amy don't be so bloody rude."

"Calm down, they're both excited, Jim, you can't blame them," Rebecca remarked in her quiet voice. "Oh

I've just remembered something – Mary, will you get them two plastic bags off the bed in your room, there's one each for you and your sister with a T-shirt and shorts in and a small towel. You're both responsible for them so don't lose them."

"Well I'm ready now, let's go," Jim replied in a stern voice, so they all went downstairs in the lift, Rebecca carrying her large basket which had two large beach towels in plus suntan lotion, a large bottle of water, two sun hats for the girls and her small shoulder bag with her purse in.

Unfortunately all the sun-beds had been taken when they got to the pool so they sat on the lawn area nearby. There was a pretty spot here surrounded by lush palm trees and there were other couples with their children sitting on the lawn too.

"I think the hotel must be fully booked, Rebecca."

"Looks like it but I'd rather be lying on a sun-bed by the pool, Jim."

After thirty minutes they were approached by a young pretty girl with long brown hair tied back in a ponytail. "Hi my name's Rowena Rosso," she said, showing her name badge which was pinned to her short-sleeved cotton blouse, "would the girls like to come to the kids' club? We're doing activities in the pool for an hour."

"Please, Mum?" Amy said excitedly.

"I don't see why not," Jim remarked, "but how big is the pool, Rowena? They both can't swim."

"Don't worry, we only use the shallow pool next to the club house and we provide arm bands or rings for the non-swimmers. We've got three qualified staff and me in the pool with them at all times – they'll be in good hands. No problem. How long are you staying here for?"

"Two-weeks," Jim replied.

"Well here's a brochure of all the children's activities – we have disco nights, painting and drawing, and dancing classes, and exercises in the pool. We also have games for the kids – the times are on the back."

"Interesting – thank you, Rowena, my girls can be a bit of a handful," Rebecca remarked, "they are so competitive."

"I can swim a little bit," Amy said.

"So can I," Mary replied getting annoyed.

"You stay here, Jim, and watch our belongings, I won't be too long. Let's go, Rowena, you're a life saver," Rebecca remarked, "they're getting bored. Girls, you'd better take your clothes with you to change into when you come out of the pool."

Jim spread the beach towels out on the lawn and put some suntan lotion on and Rebecca came back ten minutes later. "The girls are fine, I have to pick them up in an hour at the club house later on – do you fancy a beer at the bar near the pool?"

"Okay. I'd put some suntan lotion on, Rebecca, if I were you but put some on my back first. I think tomorrow morning we ought to get down to the pool early to make sure we get some sun-beds, I don't fancy sitting on the lawn the whole fortnight."

"Neither do I, you know how I suffer with back pain from time to time, Jim, ever since I had the twins."

Jim packed everything into the basket and they walked down to the pool bar area, it was busy but they managed to find a small table in the corner. The waiter came to take their orders and Rebecca was surprised it was Manuel the porter.

"Blimey, how many jobs to you do in the hotel?" Jim asked.

"It's a family-run business, my uncle owns it."

"Oh I see. It must be fully booked – how do we manage to secure a sun-bed?"

"I'm afraid you have to get to the pool very early and put your towels on the sun-beds before you go to breakfast. What would you like to order?"

"Two beers please and two bags of crisps – salt and vinegar."

Manuel looked at Rebecca with a glint in his eye and a big cheesy smile on his face.

"Do you work out in the gym, Manuel? Gosh you look so fit," Rebecca remarked smiling.

"I swim in the sea early every morning before I start work at the hotel," Manuel replied. "I'll fetch your drinks."

"Please pack it in, Rebecca, you're with me," Jim said irritably when Manuel went back to the bar, "you were flirting with him."

"For god's sake, Jim, I was only being friendly – you're ridiculous, what do you want me to do, look at the floor when anyone is talking to me? I'm going to find the loo – is that alright with you or is that a problem?" and Rebecca got out of her chair and walked away.

When she returned, Jim apologised, "I'm so sorry, pet, we're here to have a good time. I admit I overreacted, let's kiss and make up," and he put his arms around her to give her a kiss on the lips but Rebecca was so tensed up inside she pushed him away.

When they had finished their drinks and Jim paid the bill, they walked back to the same spot on the lawn and Rebecca put the beach towels out and lay there, hardly saying a word.

"Look, I've said I'm sorry, Rebecca, speak to me."

"Fuck off, Jim, you make my blood boil."

"It's only because I love you so much, Rebecca."

"Bullshit, Jim, you're embarrassing and I'm fed up with your insecurities."

"Maybe you're right, I am a little insecure. Can we forget about what's just happened and move on, we don't want to be upsetting the girls arguing all the time do we?" and he bent over to give Rebecca a kiss on the cheek.

"That's where you have me by the balls, Jim, I want the girls to have a good time but I'm warning you if you persist in this childish behaviour when we're back home after the holiday I'm leaving you."

Jim tried everything to bring Rebecca around by stroking her hair and telling her how beautiful she was and how lucky he was to have her in his life.

She finally let her guard down, "You really do test my patience, Jim."

"I know, my darling, but you wouldn't change me for the world, Rebecca," he said and gave her a passionate kiss on the lips, but she felt so angry inside.

When it was time to pick the girls up Rebecca told Jim to stay and relax and went to fetch them on her own. She was pleased to get a little break away from him. When she went inside the club house Mary was the first one to run towards her, "It's great here, Mum. Amy and me have made a new friend – he's called Tommy – he's over there with his mum and dad."

Rebecca walked over to say hi, "I'm Rebecca, I'm the twins' mum – they seem to be having a good time today playing with your son Tommy, what a handsome boy he is I love his blond curly hair."

"Thank you, as you can see he takes after me – oh sorry, this is my husband Ben and I'm Linda, lovely to meet you. Your girls are little beauties, they're the spitting image of you, I can tell the difference though – Mary is slightly taller than Amy."

Rebecca smiled, "I can't believe they're not tired, we had an early start this morning, I feel shattered."

"Where have you come from?" Ben asked.

"Alysham in Norfolk."

"Never!" Linda had a big grin on her face, "You won't believe this, we live in Wroxham not far away from you and we often go to the big market in Alysham."

Rebecca looked surprised, "Goodness me, small

world, we're only about twenty minutes' drive away from you. My husband Jim has done a lot of jobs there, he works for a building firm."

"I'm a self-employed electrician," Ben commented, "maybe our paths have crossed."

"When did you arrive?" Rebecca asked.

"We came four days ago. It's a nice hotel but the food isn't brilliant, nothing like my Linda's home cooking—"

"Where's Dad?" Mary interrupted.

"He's on the lawn sunbathing, we'd better get going he'll wonder where we are."

"Oh do we have to, can't we stay here a little longer, Mum?"

"No you can't, Amy, don't start, we'll come another day – where are your swimming costumes?"

"Over there on the chair," Mary pointed to them.

"I'll get them for you," Tommy said.

"Thank you," Rebecca smiled, "you're a little gent."

"My boy can be a little treasure when he wants to be," Linda grinned. "He has enjoyed playing with the girls – he's a bit shy and was bored on his own, Rebecca. Perhaps we'll see you all around the pool tomorrow, bye girls," and Tommy gave both of them a hug.

"God where have you been, Rebecca?"

"Sorry to be so long, the girls had such a good time."

Amy sat on her dad's lap, "We have a new friend, his name's Tommy."

"That's great and how old is he?"

"The same age as us," Mary butted in, getting excited.

"You obviously both had a good time."

"They did, Jim, and you won't believe it – Tommy's parents Ben and Linda come from Wroxham near us, they're a lovely couple. Ben is self-employed and works as a electrician…"

"Tell me later, Rebecca, right now I need a shower and

a cold beer. I'm sweltering in this heat, let's go up to the room."

Jim decided they should all have an early night, it had been a long day and they were all tired, so he looked at the menu and ordered room service.

After they had eaten their vegetarian pizza and chips, Rebecca bathed the children and put them to bed. Jim had a shower and a cold beer from the mini-bar and Rebecca did the same; thirty minutes later they climbed into bed and it wasn't long before they were fast asleep.

The following morning the girls woke up, bright and early. "Mum, I'm hungry, are we going down for breakfast?" Mary asked.

"Give me a minute, I'll put your clean clothes on the bed, girls, and you can get yourselves ready. Jim, are you getting up, we don't want to miss breakfast."

"Give me five-minutes, Rebecca. Will you get me my blue T-shirt out of the drawer and my green shorts?"

"Bloody cheek! Get them yourself, Jim, while I see to the girls and get myself dressed, it's like having three kids."

Finally they were all ready and went down in the lift for breakfast. There was a queue and Rebecca noticed Linda, Ben and Tommy were at the front so she went over to speak to them. "This is Jim my husband."

Ben shook Jim's hand, "Pleased to meet you, Jim, get in front of us, we'll grab a table and sit altogether."

"Thanks," Jim remarked smiling.

When they went into the restaurant Ben put two tables together and Linda and Rebecca took the children to the self-service area which was serving a full breakfast, they didn't fancy cereal or a healthy option of fruit, and when they sat down at the table Jim and Ben went to get theirs. Tommy sat in between the girls and they both had big beams on their faces. Rebecca felt relaxed and was pleased she had met the family, Linda was someone who was very friendly easy to talk to.

"How long have you been in the building trade?" Ben asked Jim.

"Since leaving school as an apprentice, it's hard graft – long hours sometimes but it pays the mortgage."

"I have a few builders that work for me when I need them," Ben commented.

"You're an electrician – Rebecca mentioned."

"That's my trade, I advertise in the local papers – Ben Sharp electrician – but me and the wife also own two more properties which we bought cheap at auction and we've done them up to a high standard which are rented out. That's what I love doing, we've had them valued by the estate agent and made a profit. I do all the electrics myself but the building work is not my forte, I leave that to the professionals like you, Jim."

"You two stop talking about work, we're on holiday," Linda remarked, "the kids are getting bored."

They'd all finished their breakfasts by now, and the children were eager to leave the restaurant.

"Okay," Ben grinned, "got the message, that's telling us, Jim, we should make a move I don't want to upset the missus."

Beer and Tapas

Rebecca and Jim and the girls enjoyed spending time with their new friends and they were having a wonderful time. Ben hired a car to go to the water park thirty minutes away and sometimes took Amy and Mary with them, giving Rebecca and Jim a break on their own to sunbathe.

They were all around the pool one morning after breakfast, Rebecca and Linda were relaxing on the sunbeds and Ben and Jim were in the water playing with the children. Tommy was a good swimmer but the girls wore armbands.

"Are you working, Rebecca?"

"I'm a part-time hairdresser. What about yourself, Linda?"

"I work for the council in the housing department but I'm thinking of changing my job, it can be stressful especially when you have difficult problems to sort out. My Ben wants me to work from home doing the clerical work for his business but last time I did that I felt trapped and we did nothing but argue, Rebecca."

"Ben seems an easy-going bloke, Linda."

"He's so laid back when he's away from work, but he's a perfectionist when it comes to his job."

"I wish my husband would relax a bit more, he's always worrying about nothing and can lose his cool at the drop of a hat, Linda."

"Do you two socialise much, Rebecca? The reason I'm asking this is Ben and me both worked our socks off when we first got married and never had any quality time together and were growing apart for a while, so we both decided no matter what happens once a week we'll invite all our friends around and have a dinner party and sometimes we go to their houses."

"I would love to do that, Linda, but I can't see Jim being up for that, he wants me all to himself."

"I can't believe that, Rebecca, he seems to be getting along great with Ben, it's like they've known each other for years. I think Jim is a charming man and great with the children. I think we're both lucky – we have two good men there – Jim loves the very bones of you, anyone can see that."

Rebecca smiled, she could see Jim had worked his magic on Linda and Ben and wished she hadn't opened up to Linda about her feelings, after all they had only just met.

Jim came out of the pool, "What are you both talking about, my ears are ringing?"

"You're right," Linda remarked, "we were singing your praises, saying what a gorgeous hunk of a bloke you are with striking good looks."

Jim laughed, "Well what can I say, you both know good looks when you see it I have to agree, I love me."

"Who do you love, Jim?"

"Myself of course, Linda!"

The holiday had flown by for the Sharp family. It was the day they were going home, so they met up with Rebecca and Jim and the girls for breakfast in the restaurant to say their good-byes and exchange their telephone numbers. They were catching an early flight so they hardly touched their breakfast. Mary and Amy were getting upset to see Tommy leave.

"Don't be silly," Rebecca remarked, "you'll see Tommy again when we get back home."

"This was one of the best holidays my boy's ever had," Ben remarked.

"I have to agree," Linda commented. "Tommy has had a lovely time playing with your two girls, Rebecca, and it was lovely meeting you both."

"Thank you," Rebecca replied, "we'll definitely be in touch, Linda, when we get back to the UK. Have a safe journey."

Jim shook Ben's hand. Mary and Amy hugged Tommy and gave him sloppy kisses on the cheek. He became all shy and was blushing, with a frown on his face – that was his mum's and dad's cue to leave.

"Finish your breakfast, girls," Linda remarked, "and I hope you all enjoy the rest of your stay, we'd better get going – bye."

"What a lovely couple they are, Jim, don't you think Linda is really pretty?"

"She is but I don't know what she sees in Ben – he's short, stocky and bald, you wouldn't say he was a handsome bloke, Rebecca, would you?"

"I think he's like a cuddly teddy bear and has a lovely smile and a good personality. I think they're well matched, Jim. They're both easy-going and besides, looks aren't everything. I think they've got a few bob owning two rental properties and they both have good jobs. Ben said if we ever do an extension on our house he'll do the electrics cheaply for us."

"He's a nice bloke, we'll keep in touch with them, Rebecca."

"Good luck to them I say, they both work hard."

"So do I, Rebecca, I work my socks off but what we both earn is never enough to do the things I want to do, it's frustrating at times."

"What do you mean, Jim, we have a lovely home."

"I know that but it would be great to have more money in our bank account to do the extension on the house. I'd love to have two holidays a year and buy a new car instead of always buying second-hand ones."

"Christ," Rebecca replied looking agitated, "you're full of doom and gloom, Jim. I'm contented – we're all healthy, surely that's the main thing?"

"Can I go to the kids' club, Mum, they're painting and drawing today – Tommy told me yesterday."

"Alright, Mary, what about you, Amy?"

"Suppose so," she replied in a sulky voice.

"Let's go then and I want you both to stay in the building with Rowena, not run around outside playing catch up."

"We won't," Mary said in a grumpy voice. "Can we go now, Mum, you're getting on my nerves."

"Don't be so rude to your mum, Mary, otherwise you both won't go, simple as that."

"Please Dad, I don't think Mary meant to be so mean, she was just copying you, Dad, that's what you say to Mum sometimes. Can we still go to the kids' club?"

"Alright, Amy, but none of your nonsense either. Jim, stop being so horrid – they're children – you would think you were in an army camp," Rebecca commented.

"You're far too soft, Rebecca, I was never rude to my parents when I was growing up."

"Are you quite finished, Jim, you've said your piece," Rebecca said in a soft voice, "I just want to end the holiday on a high with the girls having a good time, okay?"

"Let's drop the girls off at the kids' club and we'll go for a walk along the beach, Rebecca."

"Sounds good, Jim, I'd like that."

The girls were excited when they reached the kids' club and ran straight inside. "I'll pick you up in an hour and if you're both good I'll buy you some ice-cream," Rebecca remarked.

"Oh thanks, Mum," Amy replied.

"This beach is beautiful," Rebecca said wistfully, "I wish we'd hired a car, Jim, we could have done a few trips around the island."

"I just didn't fancy driving, Rebecca, I do enough of that at home – how about we go back to the room and make love while we have this time together without the girls."

"I'm too hot, Jim, and I don't really feel like it."

"Charming I must say, what about how I feel?"

"I can't just turn my feelings on like a tap, Jim, when you've been in a bad mood since you got out of bed this morning, me and the kids had to tiptoe around you."

"I can't do right for doing wrong – forget it."

"Please don't go in a sulk, Jim, I feel like a big hug," and Jim held Rebecca tight and kissed her passionately, and they sat on the beach enjoying the sunshine. "I just had a thought, Jim, you haven't rung your parents."

"They can wait till I get back home, I won't be taking them a present back that's for sure."

"I don't think your mum likes me, Jim."

"My mother doesn't like anyone, she's hard work, no one comes up to her standard apart from my brother Lee. She's critical about everyone, Rebecca."

"What do you think made her like that, Jim?"

"Who knows, she never talks about the past much – all I know is that she worked as a housekeeper when she left home at an early age and her father was an alcoholic."

"That's sad, Jim, her life must have been tough – what about your dad?"

"Never says much, we were never close growing up, Mum rules the roost – she's the one that controls him, he just goes along with anything she says, he's a weak shite."

"Jim, don't take this the wrong way but sometimes I feel you have to prove something to them, especially your mother, and you don't."

"Utter rubbish, Rebecca, I only visit them because

you've always encouraged me to, telling me it's my duty. They're the girls' grandparents, otherwise I wouldn't bother."

"I had a lovely upbringing with my parents, Jim, we're quite close but it's common some of the older generation were reserved in them days and kept their feelings to themselves. They were hard times for some people, it wasn't the done thing to talk about your business. My mum and dad had their struggles but they just got on with it, they're very positive people."

"Good for you," Jim said sarcastically. "All this chatter has given me a thirst – I fancy a beer, Rebecca, and tapas – let's go."

They walked for ten minutes and found a nice little tapas bar, La Vida, along the sea-front. The waiter came up to them when they sat down, "Two beers please and a Serrano ham roll," said Jim.

"I thought you wanted tapas?"

"I've changed my mind, my stomach feels a bit dodgy, sometimes they're swimming in olive oil."

"I hope you're not coming down with something, Jim."

"Nah, I'm alright – have you got any paracetamols in your bag?"

"I have but don't be daft, Jim, you can't take them drinking beer," Rebecca advised.

"Suppose not, but I had diarrhoea this morning."

"You never told me, Jim."

Just then the waiter brought the beers and the roll which was the size of half a baguette, "Bloody hell! I don't fancy it now – do you want it, darling?"

"No, Jim, just leave it or wrap it in a tissue and I'll put it in my bag – the girls will eat it later on."

Jim paid the bill but now he started to feel rough. "Let's call in the chemist's on the way back," Rebecca suggested, "and get you something, Jim. Then I'll pick the girls up from the kids' club."

"Good idea, I do feel lousy. I may have a lie down when I get back to the room, sorry pet."

"It's not your fault, Jim, it can't be helped."

The chemist's was packed with customers and Jim was getting impatient, "Can I leave you here, Rebecca, I'll have to put my head down."

"You go, Jim, I'll talk to the pharmacist to advise me what to get, then I'll pick up the girls. Have you got the card to get into the room?"

"Yes stop fussing, woman."

Rebecca explained Jim's symptoms to the woman behind the counter and she handed her a box of Dioralyte, "Tell him to take one or two sachets dissolved in water, that will settle his stomach down and drink lots of fluids with light meals." Rebecca paid the cashier and thanked her.

When Rebecca arrived at the kids' club the girls were waiting outside with Rowena, "Where have you been, Mum?" Amy asked, looking worried.

"Why? Am I late, Rowena?"

"Yes, about fifteen minutes but no worries I've been having a lovely chat with the girls."

Rebecca looked at her watch, "Oh goodness, it's stopped! I'm so sorry, Rowena," and she explained to her she had to go the chemist's for Jim as he was feeling under the weather.

"I hope he feels better soon, bye girls – I have to shoot off, it's my break time. I'll see you tomorrow, we're doing activities in the pool."

"Thank you for looking after my girls, Rowena."

"Where are we going now?" Mary asked.

"To the room, your dad's not feeling well."

"Bother," Amy moaned, "You said you would buy us an ice-cream, Mum."

"Alright I'll get you both one but we have to go and see if your dad's okay after that."

Jim was lying in bed holding his stomach when she entered the room. "Have your pains got worse, Jim?"

"No I just like holding my belly – what do you think? Ouch! It hurts right across here, did you get me something from the chemist's, Rebecca?"

"Yes, Jim, I did – just give me a minute while I see to the girls. What I want you both to do is get your new drawing books out and pencils out of the drawer and you can sit outside on the balcony, no fighting you two."

"Do we have to?" Mary complained.

"Not for long, Mary, just till I see to your dad."

"I'm hungry," Amy remarked.

"I'll bring you an orange juice and a ham roll in a tick – do as you're told, Amy, and you Mary."

"I'm a nuisance Rebecca, aren't I?"

"No you're not, Jim, but it's a stomach bug – you're not dying, you're worse than the kids. Just have a rest, you'll be fine in a couple of days."

"Bloody great, we'll be going home then, Rebecca."

"Well if you keep moaning like this, Jim, thank heavens for that. Please drink this, it'll settle your stomach – and just try to relax."

Jim was in a strop, being his usual demanding self; it was the last few days of their holiday and Rebecca took the girls to the beach and to the water park while he stayed in bed ordering room service. She was so pleased when it was finally the morning of their departure, trying to keep the girls occupied and running around after him was getting too much.

"Have we packed everything?" Jim asked, "look in all the drawers and the wardrobes, make sure we don't leave anything."

Rebecca felt exhausted, "Can we just go, Jim, we have to hand the key in to reception and pay the bill, the taxi's been ordered we don't want to keep him waiting."

"I'm ready, let's go, sorry I spoke. Come on, girls, your mum is such a bossy boots."

The journey to the airport was a nightmare, there was so much traffic on the roads and the cab driver had the music on full blast so when they arrived at 'Departures' they got out of the cab and Jim didn't give the driver a tip, just a dirty look.

"Mum, can you buy me some sweets?" Mary asked.

"No but I'll buy you a sandwich and you Amy, you both must be really hungry – they've had no breakfast Jim."

"For god's sake, they can wait till we board the plane, Rebecca, it's expensive eating here – their prices are ridiculous."

"Whatever, Jim. I think you're the one being ridiculous, you never thought of that when you ordered room service for yourself – look at the bill you've just paid."

"I was ill, Rebecca, I had to have lots of fluids and light snacks."

"Does that include replacing all the drinks in the mini-bar which you drank? You seem to have made a remarkable recovery this morning."

"That's the sympathy I get," and he took out twenty pounds from his pocket and threw it on the ground, "Here's the bloody money, Rebecca, now piss off."

"Jim, lower your voice, people are looking at us."

Amy bent down and picked up the money and handed it back to her dad and Mary just stood there clutching her teddy.

When they went through Customs and eventually boarded the plane, Rebecca sat in her seat and took out her magazine and ignored Jim – she was seething inside.

"Can we call it a truce, Rebecca?"

"I'm reading, Jim, and I have nothing to say."

"Please yourself – now who's being childish," and Jim closed his eyes and slept most of the journey.

The drinks and snack trolley came around, so Rebecca bought the girls a sandwich and some biscuits and drinks, choosing still to ignore Jim. If he wanted anything he could buy his own, how dare he think he could treat her this way, switching on and off like a light bulb whenever the mood took him.

Everything went smoothly when they got off the flight and they went through Customs and Security and collected their baggage off the carousel and put it all onto a trolley. Jim parked the trolley in a bay once they were outside and they managed to get a cab at the taxi rank straight away.

The girls were tired when they arrived home; Jim paid the cab driver and they went indoors.

Jim took the cases upstairs and Rebecca put the kettle on, "Do you want a tea, Jim?" she shouted up the stairs.

"Yes if it's not too much trouble and a corned beef sandwich, I'm famished."

"Jim, I'll have to go to the corner shop for a loaf of bread, I won't be long."

Jim put a video on for the girls in their room while he started to unpack his suitcase. Rebecca came back from the shop and made a pile of sandwiches for Jim and the girls but they weren't hungry and he managed to scoff the lot.

"Gosh your appetite is back, Jim, you must be feeling better."

"Are you trying to be funny, Rebecca?"

"I don't want any arguments, Jim, just drop it."

Rebecca put all the dirty washing in the machine and Jim ran a bath for the girls.

Richard

The next few days things went back to normal, nothing had changed, Jim still made her feel she was walking on eggshells and she was pleased to get back to work.

"Great to have you back, Rebecca, you look lovely. I'm like a milk bottle compared to you – what a gorgeous tan you have!"

"Thanks, June, mind you I didn't do much sunbathing, I tan quite easily. How's it been here – have you been busy?"

"I've been run off my feet. My sister was useless, she turned up when she felt like it so I had to get a friend of mine to come in and help me."

"Sorry, June, I'm just happy to be back."

"Oh dear, things didn't turn out well then with Jim? I thought a break away would bring the spark back into your marriage."

"Shush, June, I think Mrs Brown is ear-wigging. I'll talk to you later."

Rebecca finished doing her cut and blow wave.

"I'm dying of thirst, put the kettle on I haven't got another client for another hour and you can give me all the juicy gossip," June grinned.

When they both sat down drinking their tea, Rebecca burst into tears. "Blimey, I wasn't expecting this – was the holiday that bad, Rebecca?" asked June as she handed her a box of tissues.

"It wasn't all bad, June, we met a lovely couple and their son Tommy, the girls got on well with him. It was Jim with his mood swings which spoilt it for me, it's not fair on the girls."

"You know what they say, Rebecca, a leopard never changes its spots. Anyway, forget about him – how about coming out with me and my friends tonight, it's my birthday."

"Oh I forgot, June, I'm sorry."

"Don't be daft, you can buy me a drink – are you coming or what?"

"I'd love to but Jim will kick up a fuss, June, he can be very controlling."

"Bugger him, Rebecca, I think you deserve some fun. Just tell him it's my birthday or I'll speak to him on the phone myself."

"Please don't do that. I'll talk to him, June, he'll just put the phone down on you, he can be a nasty bugger when he wants to be. You're right though, I can't remember when I had a girls' night out. I can't see I'm doing any harm – he has his friends."

"I've got a few male friends that are coming, Rebecca, but you don't need to tell Jim that, he sounds a bit possessive to me. Thank god I don't have to put up with that aggravation anymore, being on your own with the kids has got its advantages."

"Where are you thinking of going, June?"

"Do you know the Stag pub on the high street opposite Asda?"

"Yep, me and Jim used to go in there."

"Well, meet me there about eight o clock. You'll love my friends, Rebecca – they're down-to-earth, a good bunch of people, you'll have a lovely time I'll make sure of that. You'd better get off."

"I still have twenty minutes to go, June."

"I've looked at the appointments book, there's only two more clients to do, so I can see to them, no worries."

"Thanks, June, hopefully I'll see you tonight."

Rebecca climbed in her car and drove home, she was

dreading asking Jim but was determined to get her own way and started to think about what she was going to wear, feeling a little excited.

The phone rang and she picked it up, "Hello who's speaking?"

"It's Mum, did you enjoy your holiday?"

"It was okay, the girls had a good time. Jim was ill the last few days with a stomach bug but he's back to work now – how's Dad?"

"He's fine, pottering around in his shed."

"I'll pop up to see you Saturday morning – the girls have missed you both. Is there anything you want me to bring you?"

"No, pet, give my love to Jim, see you soon."

Rebecca put the phone down thinking if only her parents knew what kind of a man Jim really was but he had always been charming and kind to them, she just wished she had a marriage like theirs and in some ways envied them.

By the time Rebecca had done all the housework and she decided to run herself a bath, Jim walked in the door. "You're home early, has something happened?"

"I'm not skiving if that's what you think, Rebecca. What's happened – the window suppliers, bloody idiots, phoned me to say they can't make the delivery until tomorrow so we can't get on with the job."

"I'm just going for a bath, Jim, put the kettle on I won't be long – there's two pasties in the fridge if you're hungry, just warm them up."

Rebecca had her bath and got dressed and came downstairs.

"I might go out for a pint with Charley tonight, his missus is still in hospital having a hip operation."

"I'm going out tonight, Jim, it's June's birthday. I haven't been out in ages on a girls' night out and I've already told her I'm coming."

"Why didn't you ring me and ask me first, Rebecca?"

"I don't need your permission to go out with my friends, you go out and I don't say anything."

"Alright, go if you must but just don't make a habit of it. I'm not babysitting while you're out on the town getting pissed."

"That's a bit of an exaggeration, Jim, when do I ever get drunk?"

Jim threw his cup of tea Rebecca had made him in the sink, got a beer out of the fridge and went into the conservatory to read his paper with an angry look on his face.

Rebecca went to pick the twins up from school and explained to them in the car on the way home she was going to a friend's birthday celebration and told them both if they were good girls for their dad she would buy them a treat from the toy shop on Saturday before they went to visit Nanna and Grandad.

Jim was still in a mood when she got home but Rebecca just ignored him and put the beef casserole in the oven to cook. "Mum, can we play in the garden on the swing and slide?" Amy asked.

"Not until you both go upstairs and change your clothes. Jim, do you want any carrots with your casserole or just garden peas with roast potatoes?"

"That's fine – what time are you going out?"

"I have to meet June at eight o'clock at the Stag pub so I'll leave here about seven-thirty. I'd better order a cab, I don't want to drink and drive, Jim."

"Christ, more expense," he muttered, "and what time will you be home?"

"I don't know, for goodness sake June is my boss it would be rude of me not to go. Now can I have a hug, Jim, I hate the tension in the house, I promise I won't be too late coming home."

Rebecca put the dinner out on the table for Jim and the girls; she wasn't hungry and went upstairs to get changed. When she looked in the mirror with her make-up on and her low-cut black dress she was shocked – it had been a long time since she really took a good look at herself and approved of her appearance. She had to admit at this moment she did look attractive and felt happy inside, with a tinge of sadness at how long she had been feeling a lack of self-worth.

"Your cab's here, Rebecca, are you ready?" Jim shouted up the stairs.

"I'm coming," she answered and when she hurried downstairs to get her coat off the stand in the passage and her handbag, Jim kissed her on the cheek.

"Bye girls, be good," she called out, and went outside and climbed into the cab.

When Rebecca arrived outside the pub June was stood there waiting for her. "I knew you'd come, my friends are waiting inside."

When Rebecca walked into the pub they were all sitting at the table. "This is Sarah and Josh her husband, Ella and Gordon who have been living together for five years, and not forgetting Richard who is single and looking for his soul mate – but he's very fussy and promiscuous!"

Rebecca felt out of her depth, it had been a long time since she was socially with a group of friends but they all made her feel at ease. "You're a beauty," Richard commented, "where have you been all my life?"

"Don't embarrass my friend, Richard, you're full of bullshit," June remarked.

"He's right," Gordon butted in, "you do remind me of Audrey Hepburn – she had very classy looks, a beautiful lady."

Rebecca was blushing. "I think you're pissed, Gordon."

"Hey, I might have had a bit too much to drink but I know beauty when I see it." Josh gave a toast to June, "Happy birthday to a wonderful friend," and they all lifted their glasses and cheered.

Rebecca felt tipsy, the drinks kept coming and she wasn't used to that. Richard went outside for a cigarette and asked Rebecca to join him. "Lovely fresh air, I'm not used to drinking, Richard."

"Would you like a cigarette?"

"No thanks I don't smoke, I stopped three years ago when I had a bad bout of bronchitis, Richard."

"You don't mind me smoking do you, Rebecca?"

"Don't be daft. How long have you known June?"

"We were at school together, then I was there when she went through her divorce – I'm proud of her, she's a gutsy woman and a good friend. She told me you were going through a difficult time with your husband…"

"She had no right, Richard, it's my business – I told her in confidence."

"I'm like her brother, she was just worried about you, Rebecca, there's no malice in her, she admits she's not good at keeping secrets."

"I know that, Richard, she's a gobby cow," and they both started laughing.

"That's better, Rebecca, you have a gorgeous smile."

"Are you married, Richard?"

"I was till my wife did a runner with my best friend."

"I'm so sorry, Richard, that's awful."

"It wasn't her fault. I was young and stupid, drinking far too much and out with my mates all the time, anyway that was years ago I'm over it now."

"Have you any kids?"

"Nope. Nancy my wife was adamant she never wanted any, I don't think there was a maternal bone in her body.

Never mind me, what about you?"

"Jim my husband is a control freak, my marriage is just a disaster. I don't know who I am anymore. I'm fed up with going through the motions and if it wasn't for my twin girls I would have left him a long time ago."

"Do you still love him, Rebecca?"

"I honestly don't believe I do. I have so much ill feeling towards him what he's put me through and the children, it breaks my heart. I do sometimes feel sorry for him, I think he's carrying a lot of baggage from his past."

"What do you mean?"

"I just think he was brought up with a dominant mother with ridiculously high standards who crushed his self-confidence growing up. She's as hard as nails and never showed him any love or affection. I feel he's got so much anger inside he punishes me like he was punished himself, nothing I seem to do pleases him, Richard. My girls shouldn't be putting up with his outbursts."

"I think he's a fool, Rebecca, and I think there's more to the story than what he's telling you, mark my words, call it gut feeling," Richard put his arms around her. "Listen to me, if ever you need to talk to someone give me a ring," and he took his business card out of his wallet and handed it to her.

"Car salesman – Richard, I know that garage it's near Greenlands Primary School where my kids go."

"That's right, but don't let your husband see it – we'll keep it between ourselves. I love June she's a good friend, Rebecca, but as you say she is a gobby cow and with her working at the salon it doesn't take long before rumours spread."

Rebecca put the card in her bag and gave Richard a kiss on the cheek.

June came out of the pub holding onto Ella and Gordon's arm, she was as drunk as a skunk. "We're taking her home, Richard, she's spewed her guts out all over the table. Sarah and Josh have ordered a cab, they said they're going your way if you want a lift."

"I'd better pop in the pub and see them, Rebecca, we can drop you off first – I know what their intentions are, to come to my house and hang out and still party. I have a bar and a pool table indoors. I don't mind though, they're good friends of mine, I've crashed out at their place on many occasions worse for wear."

The cab driver arrived and Rebecca was dropped off first at her house and Richard was a real gentleman and got out of the front of the cab and opened the back door for her and gave her a peck on the cheek. "Goodnight, Rebecca, don't forget what I said, ring me anytime."

"I'll keep in touch, Richard, bye."

Rebecca walked up the driveway and saw the sitting room light on and the net curtains twitching and when she was about to open the door Jim opened it and stood there with a face like thunder. "Who was that guy Rebecca?"

"He's a friend of June's – can I take my coat off please." She pushed him aside and went into the kitchen to switch the kettle on.

Jim came up behind her and grabbed her arm, "I want answers, what's going on?"

"Are you crazy? They're just friends of June, it's the first time I've set eyes on them and they kindly let me share the cab to come home. You're being ridiculous as usual, Jim, overreacting when I haven't done anything wrong."

"We could have found a babysitter and I could have come with you, Rebecca, if there were blokes there – I thought it was just a girls' night out."

"I'm glad you didn't the way you are, Jim. You're a party pooper, always asking questions, it's like being in a court of law with you sometimes – you've got no sense of fun, you're far too serious."

"Is there anything you like about me, Rebecca?"

"The way I feel at the moment, Jim, I can't stand the sight of you, you're so arrogant and obnoxious, a control freak. You know something – tonight for the first time in years I felt attractive and respected, not like a piece of property like you see me."

"You're my wife, Rebecca, and you will listen to me."

"Piss off, Jim, get out of my sight," and at those words Jim lost all self-control and gave Rebecca a punch on the face. She felt disorientated and fell backwards against the work surface, but after a few minutes she composed herself, and without saying a word to Jim she went up to her bedroom, locked the door and burst into tears.

It was morning and Rebecca hadn't slept all night, tossing and turning, with thoughts running around her head about what to do, when she heard Amy shouting, "Mum!" trying to open the bedroom door.

"I'm coming," and she climbed out of bed and unlocked the door.

"I heard shouting last night, Mum, are you alright? You've got a nasty bruise on your face – who did that?"

"No one, child, I knocked it on the kitchen cupboard. Now I want you to get dressed and tell your sister to do the same – you don't want to be late for school."

Rebecca went downstairs and Jim had already gone off to work. "Thank god," she breathed a sigh of relief. Some of the cushions were on the floor from the settee where he had slept. When she looked at herself in the mirror on the sitting room wall she was in shock – there was a huge black and blue bruise on her cheekbone and her right eye was swollen.

Mary came downstairs and ran to put her arms around her, "I heard Dad shouting last night – I got up to go to the toilet and I could hear him on the landing Mum."

"Nothing to concern yourself about, Mary, you know

your dad has a favourite watch – like you have a favourite toy – well he broke it, what happened was that it fell off the work surface onto the tiled floor in the kitchen and made him very cross."

"Did you fall on the floor, Mum? Your face is a funny colour…"

"Why don't you eat your breakfast, your favourite egg with soldiers – and you, Amy, while I get your packed lunches ready."

When Rebecca had given the girls their breakfast she drove them both to school. Her head was all over the place because she had to go into work and knew the make-up she had put on didn't disguise the bruise she had on her face. June and her regular clients would ask her a lot of questions, how embarrassing.

Rebecca parked her car and walked to the salon. She had butterflies in her stomach but took a deep breath and walked in, took her coat off and hung it up on the peg.

"What on earth has happened to you, Rebecca?"

"I'll tell you later June, it's not as bad as it looks. "Hello Mrs Morgan, it's a cut and blow wave today is that right?"

"Yes my dearie, tell me who gave you that shiner?"

"Oh no one, my husband accidently threw the ball and it hit my face when we were playing out in the garden with the girls," Rebecca replied.

"My Bert always came back from the pub with one of them, he was always pissed out of his head getting into fights – I used to put frozen peas on his eye. I bet you gave him a black eye yourself."

"Mrs Morgan, tell the truth," June giggled.

"I'm not too old at eighty-two to put you over my knee and smack your arse, June, you're a cheeky little monkey," Mrs Morgan grinned.

"I have a hangover from hell, Rebecca," said June, grimacing. "I feel dreadful, I'm going to make a few phone calls to my clients and rebook them in for another time and shut up shop. Will you put the kettle on and make us both a cuppa. I'll take a paracetamol, Rebecca."

"That's awful, why don't you go to bed when you get home June, at least for a couple of hours before the kids come home from school. I'll even pick them up myself for you and drop them back at yours – if that's any help?"

"What a sweetheart you are, Rebecca, but I find it difficult to sleep during the day because if I do I'm up all night long watching telly. Don't worry about me, honey, what I have is self-inflicted brought on myself with all the booze I had to drink last night. What I want to know is what happened to you?"

Rebecca gave June her tea and poured herself one and they sat at the table at the back of the shop where there was a small kitchen area. "Okay, I'm listening Rebecca, did Jim do that to you?"

"He went into a frenzy, June, and totally lost control when I gave him a few home truths and he punched me on the face."

"Bastard! What set him off, Rebecca?"

"He saw me getting out of the cab and Richard kissing me on the cheek saying goodnight."

"So he was waiting up for you, what a creep. I don't know how you can stand living with him Rebecca, you both can't go on like this."

"I know, I just don't know what to do apart from moving in with my parents till I can sort myself out. I can't see Jim moving, June."

"I think it sounds a good option to me, Rebecca, but if you need any help to move your stuff just say the word."

"I'm scared, June. He'll make sure he makes my life a misery."

"It's your choice, Rebecca, but it's not good for the kids living in that environment. In my opinion I'd get the hell out of there and start afresh. I feel tired Rebecca, I'm not trying to be funny or anything but I'm going to take your advice and head home to have a kip for an hour – my head is still spinning and I feel rough. Just give me a ring if Jim gives you any more aggravation – I feel like ringing him myself to give him a piece of my mind."

"Don't worry about me, June, if he starts again I'm straight out the door with the girls – he makes me feel sick to my stomach."

"Get off home, Rebecca, I'll lock up and see you tomorrow."

Rebecca got in her car and drove straight home and when she was just about to open her front door the next-door neighbour called her to have a chat over the fence. "Hi Brenda, are you alright?"

"Not really, dear, what was all that commotion I heard last night – screaming and shouting?"

"I apologise Brenda, me and Jim had a row, it won't happen again."

"Look, it's none of my business, Rebecca, you're both a lovely couple but I suspect it was more than just a row – look at the state of your face." Rebecca burst into tears. "Why don't you pop into my place, I'll put the kettle on and we can have a chat."

"Thanks, Brenda, I don't want to be any trouble…"

"Hush, I insist. Come on then, lass, it's freezing out here."

Rebecca sat in Brenda's living room, it was so neat and tidy with cream carpets – she wished she'd wiped her feet on the mat before she entered.

Brenda brought a tray in with china cups and saucers and two small tea plates, and one with a selection of biscuits on.

"Where's Paul, is he in the shed, Brenda?"

"At the pub having his usual pint. I don't begrudge him that – we're both in retirement and we can get under each other's feet, it's good to have your own space at times."

"I wish Jim understood that, Brenda, he hates me having any friends and is so jealous."

"Jim never struck me as that kind of person, he's done a lot of favours for me and Paul over the years – so kind and considerate, a very easy-going man, warm and friendly – I find that hard to believe, Rebecca."

"You've seen his good side, Brenda, but he's got a nasty streak and a vile temper."

"I can't tell you what to do my love, all I can say is try to be patient with him. I can see why he must get stressed – he's a hard grafter and a good provider and you don't find many men like that, but I don't condone a man hitting a woman – I presume he gave you that bruise on your face, Rebecca?"

"He lashed out and punched me, Brenda."

"How dreadful! Maybe you both need to seek help from a marriage guidance counsellor, sometimes you have to work hard at the marriage especially when children are involved."

"I have to collect the children from school, Brenda – I must go. Thank you for the tea and chat but please don't tell Jim I've spoken to you, he'll be cross."

"I won't, my dear, just try not to stress and keep calm," and she kissed Rebecca on the cheek.

Rebecca hurried indoors, she felt she wanted to shut herself off from the world and she felt her life was falling apart now her neighbours knew her business and also her boss June. She felt such a failure, it was too overwhelming – the perfect marriage she dreamt of when she married Jim had turned into a nightmare. If only she had shut her mouth, she thought to herself, for the kids' sake it was all too much. How would she cope on her own with the children with her small wage? But there was no turning back now, she would have to leave Jim, she couldn't pretend any longer.

It was nearly time to collect the children from school but before she did that Rebecca threw some clothes in a large suitcase, some for her and the girls and left the house and put the case in the boot of her car.

The girls were waiting in the playground with their friends and their mums chatting in a group. Rebecca didn't stop to speak to them, she hurried the girls to the car as she wasn't in the mood for gossiping.

When Rebecca was driving along the road Amy, who was the more intelligent one of the two girls and never missed a trick, noticed her mum was driving in a different direction, "Mum, where are we going?"

"We're going to Nanna and Grandad's to stay for a while; Grandad is feeling poorly, Amy."

"What about Dad, is he coming too?" Mary asked.

"No, he'll be looking after the house, but I want you both to be on your best behaviour."

"We will," both girls said in chorus getting excited.

Rebecca parked the car outside her parents' home and rang the bell. Grace her mum opened the door, "This is a surprise, I was expecting you to come Saturday."

"I know, Mum, but I need to talk to you."

Grace could see the anguish on her daughter's face and told the girls to go and see their grandad who was in the garden planting some bulbs.

When Rebecca took off her coat she sat down in the sitting room and her mum joined her after she had put the kettle on. "Have you had an accident, Rebecca – your face is bruised?" Grace asked.

"Not exactly, Mum. Jim did it to me – we had an argument and he punched me and it wasn't the first time."

"I thought things were fine between you two," Grace remarked looking shocked.

"I didn't want to worry you and Dad," and Rebecca started to cry.

"Goodness me, you're our daughter – you should have told us, not kept all this stress to yourself my darling."

"I know, Mum, but you and Dad have had a wonderful life together, I just felt a failure and blamed myself in many ways."

"Such nonsense, you're a brilliant wife and mother and always have been in my eyes, but I did wonder if Jim was too good to be true."

"What do you mean, Mum?"

"He was always willing to please, I'll give him that, but your dad thought he had a dark side – do you remember when he was fixing the fencing one weekend for us, Rebecca?"

"Yes I do, Mum."

"Well, my neighbour Nellie walked over to her side of the fence to have a chinwag with Jim and he abruptly told her to stop being so nosey and get about her business."

"I can believe that, Mum, he can be a nasty piece of work. Can me and the girls stay with you, Mum – till I get on my feet?"

"Don't be silly, of course you can – does Jim know you're staying?"

"No, I never left him a note, but he might have guessed. I'll ring him later, I don't think he'll be too pleased."

"I expect he'll come over here and plead with you to go home, Rebecca."

"I'm not going back, Mum, but I know I will have to sit the girls down and talk to them – I just told them that Dad wasn't feeling well. Amy is as bright as a button but she's not stupid, anyway we'll just have to play it by ear for now."

"I know what your dad will want to do, go over to your house and give him what for."

"Mum, don't let him. Jim has a nasty temper – I don't want Dad landing in hospital – he's capable of doing anything pushed over the edge."

"I think I'll make us both a cuppa but first come and give your mum a cuddle," Rebecca knelt on the floor with her head in her mum's lap, cuddling her felt so good.

"I was waiting for my tea, Grace – it's about that time."

"Sorry, Bert. Your dad, Rebecca, is so set in his ways he's like a blooming alarm clock. Where are the girls, Bert?"

"They're alright, they're playing in the garden, how about giving your dad a big hug, Rebecca, and telling me what's going on – Amy told me she's staying with me and your mum for a little while because I'm poorly."

"I'll make your dad a cuppa and you can fill him in about what's happened, pet."

"Dad, I'm sorry to tell you I've left Jim."

"That idiot, I'm not shocked."

"I thought you liked him, Dad?"

"It wasn't my place to say anything or your mum's, it was your choice, Rebecca, who you chose to marry and we had to make him welcome into the family. But I'll tell you this for nothing, I never liked the way he disciplined my grandchildren – they're good kids – it was totally unnecessary the way he spoke to them, telling them to sit up straight at the table, don't speak when he's eating, don't laugh too loudly. I felt like knocking his block off but your mum told me to hold my tongue and say nothing, it's none of our business, and that's what I did. There's something about him I don't trust, Rebecca, he's sly and devious."

"Why didn't you tell me how you felt, Dad? I would have listened."

"Ditto, why didn't you, Rebecca? In the era your mum and me grew up in we were taught by our parents not to wash your dirty linen in public and keep things to yourself. Both our families were private and quite reserved and we were taught to just get on with it without a fuss. I wish I had spoken to you, Rebecca, I could see at times you weren't happy – what does that say about my parenting skills?"

"Dad, you and Mum gave me a fantastic childhood, marrying Jim was my decision."

"When your mum and me got married and you came along, our miracle baby, Rebecca, we never thought it would happen and I'm so proud of the young lady you have turned out to be. We all make bad choices from time to time but I want you to promise me one thing – you will leave that evil violent man of a husband and if he ever touches a hair on your body again I swear to god I'll kill him. He's nothing but a coward and a bully. Did you think I hadn't noticed the bruise on your face when I sat down, Rebecca?"

Grace brought Bert a mug of tea and the doorbell rang, "Dad, that might be Jim – I'll answer it."

"No you won't – I will, Rebecca, I'll tell him to clear off."

"Dad, stay there, I can handle him," so Rebecca opened the front door; "I'm not coming home Jim, the girls and me are staying here with Mum and Dad."

"Don't be so stupid. I want to see the girls Rebecca – get your coat and we'll talk back home."

"You're not listening Jim, I'm never coming back. I want a divorce, I've had enough."

"You'll be running back to me in a couple of days, I know you Rebecca…"

"Just go please and I'll collect more of my stuff tomorrow when you're at work…"

"You're making a big mistake Rebecca."

"No, Jim, the biggest mistake I ever made was marrying you," and Rebecca closed the door.

When she went into the sitting room she sat down and wept. "Did he threaten you Rebecca?" her dad asked.

"No, Dad, I just feel so much hatred and anger for

Jim, what he's put me and the girls through."

"Save your tears, he's not worth it and you don't want the girls to see you so upset, you'll be just fine my darling given time."

"I know, Mum. I don't know what I'd do without you and Dad – thanks for having me and the girls stay."

"Oh we do have our uses," Bert grinned.

Linda and Ben

After a few weeks had passed, Jim finally gave up ringing Rebecca and calling at the house. Bert had to call the police on one occasion when Jim was swearing and shouting, and the police came out and warned Jim to stay away from the property otherwise he would be nicked for disturbing the peace. That scared the life out of Jim, and Rebecca realized he wasn't the big man after all. She had started divorce proceedings against him on the grounds of unreasonable behaviour; Jim went along with it and the girls seemed much happier but missed their dad, so she agreed he could have them once a fortnight for the weekend and some summer holidays so long as he carried on paying maintenance for the children.

It didn't take Jim long to find a new girlfriend called Christine White who was a young student nurse. The information came from the girls after staying at their dad's one long weekend. It was good news for Rebecca, she was pleased to get shot of Jim; this Christine was welcome to him as far as she was concerned. The only good thing that she would never regret was having her two beautiful daughters.

The house was put on the market and Jim agreed to divide the money between them, when it was sold, after paying the mortgage off. His intention was to move back in with his parents for a while, whereas Rebecca couldn't wait to find her own place – it was lovely living with her mum and dad but she needed to have her own space.

The girls were at their dad's for the weekend and she had arranged to meet the couple she'd met on holiday – Linda and Ben – and when she told Linda she had left

Jim and the reason why, Linda was surprised but they both were looking forward to seeing her again.

"What a lovely dress Rebecca, you look beautiful – what time are you going out?" asked her mum.

"Around about seven, Mum, I've still got another forty minutes, I've ordered a cab."

"I'm going for a nap for half an hour; you have a nice time and don't forget to take your key with you."

"I will, Mum, where's Dad?"

"He's in the garden probably having a sly cigarette, he thinks I don't know where his hiding place is but I do!"

Rebecca laughed, "Where is it, Mum?"

"In a drawer in the shed last time I looked, but he keeps hiding the box somewhere else. Just don't let on I know, pet. He keeps telling me he has stopped, so next time he has a heavy bout of flu I'll give him what for and stick them on his lap."

"It's only an occasional ciggy he smokes isn't it Mum?"

"I know, but all the same it's not good for him Rebecca, it's a disgusting habit."

Grace went upstairs and Rebecca went out to the garden, "Hi Dad, do you not feel a bit chilly out here?"

"No lass, I don't feel the cold – you look pretty."

"Thanks, do you want me to make you a cuppa before I go out?"

"No I'll just have a beer from the fridge – where's your mum?"

"Having a nap, she must get tired having me and the girls living here, she never stops."

"Don't worry about that, she's in her element, it makes us feel young my dear. Nellie and Pete our neighbours are popping in later on to have a game of cards with me and your mum."

"I'll get your beer, Dad, do you want some crisps?"

"No thanks, I've got to watch my weight – I'm piling

the pounds on."

The doorbell rang, it was the taxi, and Rebecca opened the door, "I'll be with you in a tick." She gave her dad his beer, put on her coat and grabbed her handbag off the chair, and hurried out the door. As she climbed into the cab, the driver asked, "It's the Stag pub you're going to – is that right?"

"Yes please," Rebecca replied.

When Rebecca arrived at the pub Linda and Ben were sitting at the bar stools having a drink, "Gosh it's lovely to see you both," Rebecca remarked and kissed them both on the cheek, "let's sit at the table, these stools give me backache, Linda."

"What would you like to drink?" Ben asked Rebecca.

"A glass of red wine please, thanks Ben."

"How are your two beautiful girls?" Linda asked.

"They're great, they see their dad every other weekend and it's working out."

"What happened Rebecca, I thought you and Jim made a lovely couple?"

"As I explained to you on the phone, Linda, he was so controlling and jealous. When I think about it we weren't compatible at all, he was so regimental."

Ben brought the drinks to the table and sat down and held Rebecca's hand. "I'm so sorry your marriage didn't work out, Jim's an absolute fool, he wants his head testing. Linda told me bits and pieces what you've been through – what was he thinking about?"

"My Ben is right, Rebecca, what an idiot," Linda commented.

"You haven't room to talk," Ben remarked.

Rebecca felt tension between the two and when Ben went to the loo she asked Linda if there was a problem as Ben looked uptight.

"I was having an affair at work with Andrew a

colleague of mine for months and Ben found out about it, a friend of ours spilled the beans. Rebecca, we are trying to work things out but it's been hard. I love him so much but I don't know whether he'll ever forgive me. The problem was that he was working long hours on another property we bought recently at auction; he was working every hour God sends, late nights painting and doing the electrics – that's besides his other job he does during the day. I missed the attention and felt neglected and lonely."

"I see. I don't know what to say to you Linda, I thought you wanted to work with Ben and were getting stressed with your job working for the Housing Department."

"I was, Rebecca, but they gave me a pay rise and a promotion so I decided to stay… watch out, Ben's coming… talk about something else."

"How's Tommy?"

"He's fine, he's staying at his friend's house overnight. I was thinking, Rebecca, would you and the girls like to come and stay at ours next weekend – we would love you all to come wouldn't we, Ben?"

"That would be lovely. Tommy had a great time playing with the girls on holiday, you're more than welcome Rebecca."

"Are you sure, Linda? The girls can be a handful at times, they're full of energy."

"No problem, we're used to a full house. They'll have a smashing time, we have plenty of room."

"Okay Linda. I can't wait to tell the girls, thank you both so much."

"Linda told me Jim's got the house on the market – has it had any interest yet?"

"No Ben, I think the market is slow at the moment and as much as I love living with my parents I can't wait to find me and the girls our own home. My parents are retired and they never complain but I'm sure they want their own space, like me. They both should be slowing down, taking things easy."

"I'm sure you'll get a buyer soon, Rebecca. I'll get the drinks in…"

"No Ben, it's my shout."

"Sit down, Rebecca – a glass of red wine again?"

"Thanks, you're so kind – what are you drinking Linda?"

Ben pretended not to hear Rebecca's question and gave Linda a dirty look and walked up to the bar.

"See what I mean, Rebecca? He's being funny."

"I feel awkward Linda, maybe it's not such a good idea coming to stay with you next weekend."

"Shush, it'll be fine I promise, Rebecca. I haven't many friends now – when they found out about my affair they turned against me."

"I'm sure you'll work things out with Ben. Is Andrew still working with you?"

"No he left the job when Ben walked into the office and gave him a punch. It was awful. Andrew was cheating on me as well with someone else at the office. I don't feel proud about what I've done and I regret not talking to Ben about how I was feeling at the time."

"Don't beat yourself up, Linda; hindsight is a wonderful thing, we all make bad choices."

"I feel shattered, Rebecca, after this drink I'm heading off – do you mind?"

"Of course I don't."

Ben came back from the bar and hearing that Linda was feeling tired, understood it was time to go.

"I'll order a cab and drop you off first Rebecca, and I look forward to seeing you and the girls next weekend."

"You two just go, there's a friend I've just seen at the bar I haven't seen for a while. Thanks for the drinks, Ben."

"I'll give you a ring Monday morning, Linda, give

Tommy all my love," and Rebecca gave them both a hug and they left.

"Hello Richard."

"Oh my god, where did you spring from Rebecca?"

"I just had a few drinks with friends of mine, they've gone home – what about you, are you with anyone?"

"The woman I'm waiting for didn't turn up and I can't get her on the phone, it keeps going to voice mail."

"She stood you up!" Rebecca grinned.

"Nothing like that, she wanted to talk about buying a car I have for sale – she's an old customer of mine. Do you want a drink?"

"I'll have a red wine please. I shouldn't really – I'll be pissed, alcohol goes straight to my head. I'll grab the table over there, Richard. I've never seen the pub so busy."

Richard brought the drinks to the table and Rebecca noticed how dashing he looked in his black suit and white shirt and tie.

"What are you staring at, young lady?"

"I was thinking how smart you look, Richard."

"Never mind that, I have a bone to pick with you Rebecca, you never rang me. I couldn't ring you because you didn't gave me your telephone number. I didn't want to ask June, she's interfering and thinks she's got a monopoly on who I can or cannot see."

"That's weird, Richard, she told me you were just good friends – did anything happen between you two, sexually?"

"Give over, Rebecca, I don't see her in that way. I think it's because we've always hung around together with a tight group of friends. She likes to be in charge, she's good-hearted and has been there for me in the past – but trust me, she's not my type. I'm very fond of her but that's all."

"I believe you and I'm sorry I didn't ring you, Richard,

there has been so much to deal with. I'm living with my parents at the moment and waiting for my final divorce papers to come through from my solicitors. Jim agreed on the divorce, the more I think about it he wanted me as a trophy on his arm – someone he could manipulate and bully, he's such a coward."

"June did say something, but I didn't realize the marriage was so bad. You should have rung me, Rebecca, a shoulder to cry on, I would have been there for you and helped in any way I could."

"Thanks Richard, what a lovely thing to say but I'm fine now and so are my girls."

"I'm starving, do you fancy going for some fish and chips?"

"Why not, Richard, but only if I pay – my treat."

"You're on, Rebecca, let's go."

They got their fish and chips, and sat on a bench in the High Street eating them. "Have you ever been in love with anyone, Richard?"

"I was with my wife, and after it ended I've had a lot of short relationships that finished for one reason or another. Maybe it's my fault, I'm a selfish bugger – I enjoy my own space living on my own, Rebecca."

"I don't believe that, Richard. I think you're scared stiff of the responsibility, even though you put up a good front."

"You're getting deep now, Rebecca, now you're going to tell me it stems from my childhood with over-protective parents."

"There may be some truth in that, Richard."

"Bollocks, Rebecca. I had an idyllic childhood spoilt rotten with one sister and very supportive parents who live in Yorkshire, pretty normal stuff."

"Would you ever get married again, Richard?"

"Who knows, I just take life as it comes, if the right person came along I would never say never. I believe in fate, what is meant to be will be."

"Thank you for tonight, I've enjoyed your company Richard, but I must head home. My parents will be waiting up for me knowing them, that's why I'd love to find my own place. I promise I'll give you a ring tomorrow."

Richard called a cab for Rebecca and gave her a passionate kiss on the lips and she responded. Ten minutes later the taxi arrived and she told the cab driver her address, climbed into the back seat and waved Richard goodbye.

When the cab driver dropped her off at the bungalow, Rebecca noticed the downstairs lights were still on and her mum opened the door. "You haven't been waiting up for me, Mum?"

"Don't be silly, you're a big girl now. I came downstairs to get a hot water bottle and saw the cab pull up from the landing window. Did you have a nice evening Rebecca?"

"I enjoyed myself Mum, it was good to meet up with friends – where's Dad?"

"Where do you think – in bed fast asleep. Can I get you anything, pet?"

"No thanks Mum, I'm off to bed, goodnight."

It was Sunday morning and Rebecca couldn't stop thinking about Richard while she was lying in bed; she had enjoyed his company and it would be lovely to go out with him again, but she knew whatever happened she wouldn't rush into anything. It was early days, and Jim had left her feeling scared and mistrusting of men.

"Rebecca, are you awake?"

She could hear her dad's voice outside her bedroom door, "I'm getting up, Dad, I'll be down in a minute."

"Your mum is cooking breakfast, bacon and egg – is that alright?"

"That will be lovely, I'm hungry!"

Rebecca quickly got dressed and went downstairs, "Good morning, Mum, can I give you a hand?"

"No I've done it, sit at the table – and you, Bert – and I'll bring the plates before the food gets cold," and when they all sat around the table eating breakfast Grace started to rub her back.

"Are you alright Mum?"

"I have pains everywhere this morning, down my legs and in my lower back."

"Oh dear," Bert remarked, "it could be arthritis, take some pain killers."

"I'll be alright, it's old age – it comes to all of us. What time are you picking the girls up tonight, Rebecca?"

"The usual time, Mum, eight o'clock. I need to give them a bath before school in the morning and wash their hair."

"Do you want to come with me and your dad to the garden centre? He wants to buy some more plants, we can have a coffee there and cake and when I come back I'll cook a roast dinner for us all."

"You two go, Mum, I'll just relax and read a book. I've got a couple of phone calls to make."

"You know you can invite your friends here anytime," Bert commented.

"I know that, Dad. As a matter of fact, Linda and Ben invited me and the girls to spend next weekend at their house, but I'm not sure."

"I think the girls would love it," her mum remarked, "they never stopped talking about their son Tommy when they came back from holiday."

"It's just they're going through a bad patch at the moment, Mum. Linda did something stupid and went out with a guy from work."

"That's terrible, what on earth was she thinking of? The young generation of today, they have too much freedom, in my day you got married and stayed together through thick and thin."

"Thanks Dad, don't remind me."

"I'm not talking about you, Rebecca, you were just unlucky to meet an arsehole like Jim."

"Bert, watch your language," Grace scolded.

"I'll wash the breakfast dishes, Mum, and thanks – that filled me up."

Rebecca finished washing the dishes and said ta-ra to her parents who were leaving to go to the garden centre. It was lovely to have the place to herself for a few hours, so she went into the garden and took her phone with her and rang Richard, "Hi it's me."

"Bloody hell, it's early Rebecca, is something wrong?"

"No, I just wanted to say thank you for a nice evening, Richard."

"You did last night, what are you doing today?"

"Nothing much, I have to collect the girls this evening, what are you doing?"

"I have to deliver a replacement car for one of my mates, his has conked out and it's in the garage to be fixed. They kindly invited me for lunch, I didn't like to say no – it's been a while since I've seen them and the kids."

"That's okay Richard, I wasn't hinting for you to take me out or anything, maybe we can meet up sometime next week for a drink?"

"I'd love that, Rebecca, I'll have to go now – someone's ringing the bell – speak to you soon."

Rebecca felt Richard was a bit abrupt on the phone but dismissed it, it wasn't as if they were in a relationship. She rang Linda and Ben to say she would love to spend a weekend with them with the girls after all, it wasn't like her diary was full of invites – what could possibly go wrong, at least the girls would have a good time.

Grace and Bert came back from the garden centre with a load of plants. "My god, Mum, it's like Chelsea flower show in London, how many plants have you and

Dad bought?"

"That's his hobby, he loves gardening, Rebecca, different strokes for different folks. He enjoys it, that's all that matters."

Rebecca helped her dad carry the trays of plants into the garden and left him in peace spending the rest of the afternoon planting them, and joined her mum in the kitchen to help cook the Sunday roast dinner.

"Where do you get your strength from, Mum? You're so strong and never get too stressed, you take things in your stride."

"I do, my darling, life's too short but it does help when you have a wonderful person like your dad around, he has his faults don't get me wrong but I always knew I could trust him. We've always been honest with each other through thick and thin; no secrets, that's the key and never go to bed on an argument."

"I envy you, Mum, I hope I can find someone like Dad."

"I'm sure you will one day, Rebecca, but never let your heart rule your head – if something seems wrong it probably is – go by your own gut instincts and remember, it's not so much about the sex which is important but does your partner respect you."

"You're a wise woman, Mum, I love you."

"I love you too, pet, but them potatoes you've mashed are as lumpy as hell – did you put any butter or milk in them? Here give them to me, let me mash them."

They sat down for their meal at the kitchen table and Rebecca hardly ate a thing. "That's not like you," her dad commented, "what's up with you?"

"It's lovely, Dad, but it would have been me and Jim's wedding anniversary today – ten years we would have been married, it's sad."

"All the more reason to enjoy your grub, good riddance to bad rubbish I say, Rebecca, he's moved on and you must do the same."

"I know, Dad, I'm being silly, it's just not what I thought would ever happen to me."

"You're putting me off my food, Rebecca, stop being stupid. I wouldn't give him a second thought, he had his chances and blew it, you deserve much better than him."

"Leave her, Bert, she's bound to be upset from time to time, it's natural – she was with Jim a long time and they have children together," Grace reminded him.

Bert got up from his chair and went into the garden. He was vexed, even the mention of Jim's name brought his blood pressure up.

"Mum, Dad's upset."

"Leave him, Rebecca, he'll calm down – he gets himself worked up for nothing. I'll cover his dinner with a plate and he can finish it off later on."

Rebecca finished her meal and went out into the garden, "I'm sorry, Dad, I didn't mean to upset you," she said as she gave him a hug and a kiss.

"I just want you to be happy, Rebecca, and the girls."

"I know, Dad, stop worrying about me so much, I'm fine. You and Mum have been fantastic but you do know as soon as the house is sold I want to find my own place, hopefully not too far away from you both."

"I know that, my darling. "Will you get me a cigarette, Rebecca? You know where I put my stash in the shed, but don't let your mum see you."

"She's in the kitchen washing the dishes, Dad. I'll keep watch – you're a sly devil, she'll be so annoyed if she catches you." Rebecca looked in every drawer in the shed but she couldn't find them, "Sorry, Dad, I can't see them anywhere – have you put them somewhere else?"

Grace appeared behind Rebecca, "Is this what you're looking for?" and held up the packet of cigarettes.

"Oh bother! I just want one, Grace, hand them over."

"Mum, you used to smoke."

"Yes I did, Rebecca, but I gave up after I kept coughing. They're not good for your dad either, he's always having colds and flu but if he wants to kill himself let him."

"I am sitting here, Grace, don't I have a say in the matter?"

"You're a stubborn bugger, Bert," and Grace handed him the packet.

It was soon time to pick the girls up from their dad's and Rebecca climbed into her car feeling slightly nervous. The conversation with Jim was always amicable but she remembered how he used to make her feel and there was still fear inside her when she saw him.

When she arrived at the house she waited in the car with the window wound down and tooted the horn. Jim came to the door and waved to her, and it wasn't long before Amy and Mary appeared and climbed into the car.

"Do you want a cuppa, Rebecca? I want to discuss the house sale, I think I may have found a buyer."

"Sorry, Jim, Mum's not well so I have to get back. I'll ring you."

"Okay, no worries," Jim replied and blew a kiss to the girls.

"Would you both put your seat belts on, how many times do I have to tell you?"

"Mum is Nanna not well?" Amy asked.

"You don't miss a thing Amy. She's fine, I just didn't fancy a cuppa with your dad, I have far too many things to do."

"Like what?" Mary asked.

"Never you mind – what did you do at the weekend with your dad?"

"He took us to the park, and we went shopping, he bought me and Mary a pair of trainers, and then we went for a hamburger – Christine was working, she didn't come with us. Oh, I nearly forgot, Dad bought us two videos as well."

"That's good, Amy, it sounds as if you both had a good time."

"I did," Mary giggled, "Dad bought us ice-cream, and loads of sweets."

"Shocking! I hope you both cleaned your teeth before you went to bed?"

"We both did, Mum," Amy assured her, "you can ask Dad."

"Good girls, I believe you."

Rebecca was pleased to arrive home as the petrol tank was nearly on empty. "I want you both to take off your coats and go upstairs to have a bath."

"Do we have to?" Amy groaned, pulling a face.

"No you don't, but then you won't go to Tommy's house and stay next weekend with Linda and Ben."

"Yippee!" Amy jumped up and down in excitement and Mary did the same. That did the trick and both girls hurried upstairs to have their bath.

"Where's Mum, Dad?"

"She's resting, Rebecca, I think I may have to take her to get a check-up at the doctor's this week if I can get an appointment. She seems more in pain than she's ever been; I know she suffers with a bit of arthritis but I'm concerned her symptoms seem to be getting worse."

"Leave Mum rest, Dad, it will do her the world of good. I'll get the girls sorted out and put them to bed and make you something to eat."

Grace came downstairs later on and was surprised how long she had slept, "I wanted to say goodnight to the girls, Rebecca, what must they think of me?"

"Don't be silly, Mum, they understand. I'll make you a cuppa and Dad – do you both fancy a sandwich?"

"No thanks, pet, your dad and me like a few crackers with a little cheese on top and pickle."

After supper they all relaxed and watched some television programmes, and then went to bed.

Jealousy

The next morning Rebecca got up, feeling energetic. She got dressed and went downstairs, and made some scrambled eggs on toast for the girls and bacon sarnis with tomato for herself and her mum and dad.

"Blimey that was delicious, Rebecca," her dad remarked, "we've all got clean plates and the girls ate everything as well."

Rebecca got the girls dressed, leaving her mum to do the washing up and came downstairs. "Put your coats on girls and don't forget your school books – put them in your red bags. I want you, Mum, to take it easy today – do you want me to get you anything from the supermarket after work?"

"No thanks, I'll make us all a casserole tonight, I've got some stewing steak in the fridge."

"You're a star, Mum, thanks," said Rebecca and kissed her on the cheek.

"Please will you both get in the car, it's chilly, and Mary where's your coat?"

"On the car seat, Mum."

Rebecca climbed into the car and stopped at the nearest garage to buy some petrol and dropped the girls off at school. "Have a good day, you two, and go straight into the classroom."

"We will," Amy replied and gave her mum a hug.

Rebecca then drove further down the road and parked her car. As she walked down the high street towards the salon, she bumped into Richard, "Fancy meeting up with you, where are you off to?"

"Work of course, I don't always take the car – I need

some exercise. By the way, June rang me last night and I told her we had a drink together in the Stag pub."

"So what? We're free agents, what's wrong with that, Richard?"

"Nothing, but she told me to watch my step, you've got a lot of baggage."

"Bloody cheek, how dare she make a remark like that!"

"Don't worry, I told her what a lovely person you are and who I choose to see is my business and she put the phone down on me."

"I think she's besotted with you, Richard, and is jealous of me being on the scene."

"No, I think you're wrong, Rebecca, she's just possessive about our friendship; there's no way she fancies me, otherwise I would sense it."

"I think you're lying to me – you did sleep with her Richard – now tell me the truth."

"Alright, I put my hands up, Rebecca, it was only a few times when I had a party at my place and we were both drunk; in the morning I told her we were better off staying just friends, it was a big mistake."

"More fool you, Richard. I'm a woman, believe me I think she still does have feelings for you but she has no right to tell you or me how to live our lives. But you don't get off the hook that easily – how could you have lied to me like that, Richard? It's unbelievable. I'm not arguing with you right now, I have to get to work I'm late already I'll give you a ring later on."

Rebecca walked through the doors of the salon and June was stony-faced. "You're late, Rebecca."

"Sorry June, I'll make up the time."

They both did their job in silence, talking to their clients rather than having banter with each other until it came to having a break. Rebecca put the kettle on and made them both a cuppa at the back of the salon in the kitchen area. "Have I done something wrong, June, you seem in a mood?"

"Actually I'm pissed off with you, Rebecca. I warned you what Richard was like and you chose not to take my advice as a friend."

"Surely that's my decision, June, not yours. I don't know what you're making such a fuss about, we only had a drink together."

"Please yourself, Rebecca, but don't come running to me when things go wrong. He isn't the settling-down type – I know him much better than you, and if you persist in seeing him and he screws up I don't want to hear about how he let you down, because mark my words he will and if you want to continue working here in the salon I suggest you do as I say, or look elsewhere for other employment. It's your choice, Rebecca."

"June, you know how much I depend on my wages, jobs are scarce to find in the area and the hours suit me."

"I've got to go to the bank – you can sweep the floor and put the towels in the washing machine, time is money, I'm trying to run a business here. There's no shortage of people out there looking for work, Rebecca."

'What a cheek!' Rebecca thought to herself, 'how dare she tell me what to do in my personal life, what a nasty piece of work, such a jealous bitch.'

The atmosphere was awful in the salon and Rebecca was pleased when it was time to go home, "Bye Rebecca, if you're ever late again I'll dock the money out of your wages."

Rebecca said nothing to June and walked out of the salon.

On the journey home Rebecca tried to comprehend in her mind what the problem was with June and came to the conclusion she must be in love with Richard, and so if she couldn't have him no one else would. But she knew she couldn't afford to lose her job till the house was sold, her mum and dad didn't ask for any rent but with her wages and maintenance she received from Jim she managed to help towards the cost of the food and some bills.

When she got indoors her phone rang, "It's me – Richard – do you fancy going to the pub tonight or for a meal?"

"I'm busy, Richard, but thanks for asking. I must go, Mum's calling me," and she switched the phone off.

"Who's that?" Grace asked.

"Richard, a friend of mine, he wants to take me out for a drink tonight Mum."

"I'll see to the children – you go, Rebecca."

"No, Mum, I'm fine but thanks for offering. How are you feeling today?"

"I've got an appointment to see the doctor tomorrow morning, your dad insisted."

"I think you should, Mum, they may give you some blood tests…"

"I know what's wrong with me, Rebecca, it's arthritis."

"Yes but it doesn't hurt to be thoroughly checked over so they can give you the right prescription, Mum."

"I know you're right, pet, I just hate troubling them. There's a lot of people worse off than me; the surgery is usually packed full of people and besides that sitting there on a hard chair for ages does my back in."

Rebecca smiled, "That's exactly why you're seeing the doctor, Mum; if Dad had his way he'd call the doctor out to you. Let's face it, the other day you were really struggling to move your joints, you were in a lot of pain."

"I'll pick the girls up today from school, Rebecca, you go and make yourself a cuppa and there's a ginger cake in the tin."

"Are you sure, Mum?"

"I'm sure. Your dad's next door talking to Nellie and Pete – he'll want a cuppa when he comes in, he says Nellie makes tea like treacle but never refuses. He doesn't like to offend her, he reckons that's why he sometimes suffers with stomach problems drinking her bloody tea for years."

Rebecca laughed, "That's Dad, he's set in his ways Mum, daft as a brush."

Grace went to collect the girls from school and Rebecca made herself a mug of tea and went out into the garden. She was just about to sit down when she heard the doorbell ring, 'who the hell can that be?' she thought, and when she opened the door Richard was standing there.

"How did you find my address, Richard?"

"I heard you tell the taxi driver when you got into the cab after the passionate kiss you gave me."

"You're stalking me," Rebecca remarked with an angry look on her face.

"I wanted to surprise you – aren't you going to invite me in?"

"No, Richard, I'm not. You had no right to turn up like this out of the blue, I'm still going through a divorce remember? My parents won't be happy seeing you here. My mum is bringing the children back from school any minute now – will you please go."

"Will you ring me later on, Rebecca?"

"No and don't ring me either, Richard, this was a bad idea me and you getting together… Dad's coming, just go," and Rebecca closed the door in his face.

Rebecca felt awful being rude to Richard as she was just beginning to feel a bit of chemistry towards him. She thought he was handsome and kind and considerate and good company; still, she had to keep focused on the children that was the her top priority. Last night lying in bed she dreamt she was having sex with Richard and woke up in the middle of the night after having an orgasm and felt wet with muscular contractions in her vagina. She missed not having a partner, her sex life was non-existent but knew she couldn't afford to rush into a relationship with Richard or any other man for that matter; the time wasn't right, she still felt vulnerable and fragile.

Grace and the children walked into the bungalow, "Goodness me, Rebecca, the children have run me ragged! I took them into the pet shop after I picked them up from school but Amy started to get upset and then Mary they wanted me to buy them a rat so we came to a compromise and I've bought them a hamster and a cage for it. There's also food in the other carrier bag – they're in the car."

"Mum, you should have said no, you spoil them."

"All children love pets, Rebecca, you had one as a child."

"Alright, Mum, but where are we going to put it? How about in their bedroom?"

"They'll soon get sick of it when it makes a noise all night, spinning around on the wheel."

"Mum you're absolutely right, but they must look after it and take on the responsibility to give it clean water and food."

"I expect me and you, Rebecca, will have to clean the cage out but I don't mind, pet."

Amy's face was beaming and Mary's, waiting for their mum's approval… "Okay girls, the hamster can stay," Rebecca said grinning, "but I want you, Amy, to carry the cage up to your bedroom and put it on the chest of drawers; and you, Mary, give the hamster fresh water and food, and I'll get it out of the car."

"Mum, is it male or female?"

"The assistant behind the counter said it was male, Rebecca. Your dad isn't keen on rodents, still the girls are happy that's the main thing – where is your dad?"

"He's in the shed Mum. I haven't seen him to make

him a cuppa, he must have gone straight to his shed after having a chat with the neighbours. I heard him hammering wood and the radio was on when I popped into the garden but I didn't disturb him, I think he likes his own space pottering around."

"Leave him be, he'll call me if he wants anything Rebecca, especially when it's coming up to meal times – your dad loves his grub."

Rebecca helped her mum to cook the dinner while the girls played in their bedroom with their toys. "Your dad loves lambs' liver and onions Rebecca, and I know you do too – what about the girls? I was thinking of cooking that for tomorrow's meal."

"No, Mum – they love fish fingers, sausages, and hamburgers, but they do love stewing steak. Are you putting dumplings in the casserole, it smells delicious?"

"I am, sweetheart, and we're having carrots and peas with gravy and mashed potato to go with it."

"You're a good cook, Mum, I'm starving."

Dinner was soon ready and they all sat around the kitchen table. "Grandad, do you know what Nanna bought me and Mary?"

"Some sweets or some comics, Amy?"

"No – a hamster, Grandad," Amy chuckled.

"Oh my god! Bloody smelly rodents, what were you thinking of Grace?"

"Be quiet Bert, don't spoil their fun."

"I like them, Grandad," Amy remarked. "You're being horrible."

"What are you going to call the hamster?" Rebecca asked the girls.

"Goldie, Mum," Mary replied. "Can we please go upstairs to play with him?"

"I think they sleep through the day and are more active at night but I can see you've both finished your meal, I don't see why not – just be careful handling him, be very gentle, he may bite until he gets used to it."

"We will, thanks Mum."

"Do you think he likes carrots?" Amy asked.

"No, I think hamsters like apples – just go before I change my mind," Rebecca remarked, "let Grandad and Nanna finish their dinner in peace."

Bert looked annoyed, "You're far too soft with the girls, Rebecca, and you Grace – they run rings around you both."

"I know you're right, Dad, but I love to see them happy knowing what they have been through."

"You're grumpy, Bert, I think you look tired – go and have a lie down," Grace remarked.

"I think I will, I enjoyed my dinner – that stewing steak was so tender, is there any left Grace?"

"Sorry that's it Bert, you had a big plate full, surely you're not still hungry?"

"No, I thought I'd finish it off tomorrow."

"You're a greedy bugger Bert, go and have a rest."

"Trying to get shot of me, woman? Don't worry, I'm going."

Rebecca washed the dishes and made a mug of tea for her and her mum who was relaxing in the garden.

"I was thinking, Rebecca, would you make an appointment for me to get my hair done? I could do with it cut and blow-waved."

"I'll do it for you here Mum."

"No, pet, I'd rather go to the salon, it's good to get out from under your dad's feet."

"When was the last time you went to the hairdresser's, Mum? You normally just put it up in a bun."

"I can't remember, I just fancied a treat and besides it will be nice to see where you work and meet your boss Rebecca – what's her name again?"

"June, Mum, but you won't like her."

"Is there something you're not telling me? I thought you enjoyed working in the salon."

Rebecca hesitated to speak then blurted everything out, the whole story. Grace was shocked, "What's wrong with you Rebecca, I would have walked out right there and then. Who the hell is she to tell you how to live your life?"

"I know, Mum, but I'm not exactly in a position to do anything, I need the job."

"Rubbish, Rebecca, tell her to go and get stuffed. We can manage, I have a few bob in the bank, I can give you a loan till you get back on your feet."

"I have never seen you angry like that, Mum, but you're right – I'd love to give June a piece of my mind. She's a controlling bitch, likes her own way just like Jim. I seem to attract those sort of people Mum."

"I wish you would stop putting yourself down, Rebecca. There are some nasty evil people out there, the trouble is you have a heart of gold and always see the good in everyone."

"I love you so much Mum."

"I love you too, and I'm glad you told me, now go upstairs and see what the girls are up to – it's their bedtime."

Rebecca kept her head down at work all week, not to annoy June, till it was Friday when she was finished for the weekend.

"You're off Rebecca, here are your wages."

"Thanks for nothing June, I won't be coming back, you can find someone else. You pay me peanuts and I think you're a pathetic sad bitch and just for the record I could have Richard in a heartbeat. I chose not to see him again, he doesn't fancy you at all, I think he just feels sorry for you. Bye," and Rebecca walked out of the salon smiling, it was worth it to see the look on June's face, she looked devastated.

On the journey home she felt excited, her mum was picking up the kids from school and they were all going to spend the weekend with Linda and Ben. She had her case ready packed in the boot of the car.

Grace was pulling in the driveway and the girls got out of the car, "Thanks Mum, the girls can get into my car and I'll give you a ring later on. By the way, I took your advice and told June to stuff the job and gave her a piece of my mind."

"Good for you, Rebecca."

"Girls, are you coming or what – stop messing about and get into the car."

"What about Goldie, Mum?" Mary asked.

"I'll look after him," Grace replied, "and I hope you all have a lovely time."

"Thanks Nanna, bye."

Rebecca drove to the house and parked the car in the street. Ben was in the front garden mowing the lawn, "You found us alright Rebecca? Lovely to see you again. Tommy's out the back, girls – he'll be delighted to see you both – go through."

"Where's Linda, Ben?"

"In the kitchen cooking the dinner," Ben replied.

"I'll go and give her a hand…"

"I think she's got everything under control, you go in and relax – I'll be with you in a minute, Rebecca."

Linda shouted from the kitchen, "I'm here Rebecca, come and have a glass of wine."

"Blimey, this is a beautiful big house Linda, how many bedrooms has it got?"

"Four, so I have a cleaner that comes in once a week for four hours – she's worth her weight in gold – otherwise I wouldn't be able to find the time to clean it with working full-time since I got my promotion."

"What can I do to help, Linda?"

"Nothing, the dinner is all done. I hope the girls like chicken and roast potatoes with vegetables?"

"They love chicken, just with peas, though it smells delicious – do you want me to set the table, Linda?"

"No that's okay thanks – the dining room is down the hall; we just use the kitchen table for breakfast."

Just then, Ben walked into the kitchen, "Are you ready to dish up, Linda? I'll give you a hand."

"Thanks Ben, but before you do will you ask the children to sit at the table, and Rebecca you can take your glass of wine to the table with you, you're our guest. Ben will bring the meals on the food trolley. I hope everyone is hungry, I think I've cooked far too much as usual."

They all sat down eating their meal, "I told Tommy about the hamster, Mum."

"Mary, eat your dinner, please don't talk with your mouth full."

"Sorry, Mum," she replied, pulling a face.

"Have you heard anything about the sale of your house Rebecca?"

"Not yet Ben, but as much as I like staying with my parents I'd give anything to find my own place. It's not fair on them, Mum is suffering with arthritis and she never complains but having the children around all the time must make her feel tired and Dad."

"Does Nanna not like having us?"

"Amy, I didn't say that, she loves having us live with her and Grandad does, I just think it would lovely to have our own home. Now eat your dinner, young lady."

"What would you be looking to buy, Rebecca?"

"I'm not sure what I could afford – maybe a small two-bedroomed house or a flat, Linda. My house is in a good sought-after area near the train station and shops, but by the time you pay all the solicitor's and agent's fees and Jim takes his share, I won't have a great deal of money left over."

"We've just finished renovating a property we bought at auction to sell, Rebecca, it's a bit small but with a large garden not far from here."

"How many bedrooms has it got, Ben?"

"Two, but they're not a bad size; we were going to rent it out but changed our minds – I'll sell it to you if you like it at a reasonable price."

"You can't do that Ben, surely you want to make a good profit on it?"

"I think we should discuss it first, Ben. What makes you think Rebecca would live around here anyway? You forget she lives near her job at the salon."

"Not anymore Linda, I left today and I'm not going back. I'll tell you about it later, Amy doesn't miss a trick," she added in a whisper.

"That's settled then. I'll show you around the house tomorrow Rebecca."

"The trouble is Ben, it takes a long time for the process to go through, even if I have got a buyer."

"No worries, just have a look at the house and see what you think – now who wants a dessert of apple pie and ice-cream?"

"I'll have some, Dad," Tommy piped up, "and Amy will."

"What about me?" Mary sulked, crossing her arms.

"You too, Mary, we wouldn't forget you," Rebecca said, giving her a hug. "Let me at least do the washing-up Linda."

"You don't have to, I have a dishwasher, you just relax in the garden and I'll bring you a coffee – me and Ben will clear the table, Rebecca – and Tommy, go upstairs and show Mary and Amy where their bedroom is and you can play with your new video games I bought you the other day."

"Thanks Mum," said Tommy as he got up from the

table and the girls followed him upstairs.

"Did you bring a case with you Rebecca?"

"I did Linda, it's in the boot of the car."

"I'll go and get it, give me the car keys Rebecca, and I'll take it up to your room."

"Thanks Ben, you're such a gentleman."

"He must like you Rebecca, he never does anything like that for me these days," Linda remarked.

"Maybe because you don't deserve it."

"What do you mean by that remark? Don't start, Ben."

"Hey you two, you're not going to have an argument are you?" Rebecca smiled, feeling slightly awkward.

"Don't be daft, I'll go and get your case, Rebecca. You'll be alright to do the dishes on your own, Linda? I'm just going to wash the car at the garage and fill it with petrol."

"Go on then Ben, bugger off and leave us in peace," Linda replied, giving him a dirty look.

Rebecca helped clear the table and when everything was cleaned up they both sat in the garden drinking coffee. "Are you and Ben alright now, Linda? I still sense tension between you two."

"He thinks I'm having another affair, Rebecca, but I'm not. Alex, my new boss who is fantastic, rings me if has any queries at work and we get on so well. He's come from another office in Cambridgeshire and moved down here, so he's still finding his feet. We've had a few lunches together but that's all."

"Oh dear, I can understand why Ben feels insecure, Linda."

"That's his problem, Rebecca. I'm getting fed up with his sarcastic remarks and him mistrusting me, anyway let's hear the gossip – why did you leave your job?"

"Nothing much to tell really. I had a drink at the pub with Richard, who my boss first introduced me to saying he was just a good friend, and to cut a long story short she turned nasty when she found out and made my life hell at work and warned me off him, so I told her to get stuffed and I wasn't coming back."

"I think she liked him more than she was letting on, Rebecca."

"I do too. I think she was besotted with him but I know for a fact he didn't fancy her, Linda."

"Have they got history together? It sounds to me Richard wasn't telling you the whole story or why would she feel that way."

"He admitted he did sleep with her on a couple of occasions but he told me they were both drunk."

"There's nothing like a woman's scorn – are you still seeing Richard?"

"No I did like him, I found him handsome and funny, but I have too much on my mind at the moment… I think your phone's ringing, Linda."

"I'll be back in a minute, it's probably Alex – he's just moved into a flat after living in a hotel for a while and needs my advice about something. Men – honestly they're useless on their own, Rebecca."

Ben came into the garden, "I've put your case in your bedroom, Rebecca, here's your car keys. Where's Linda?"

"She's on the phone, Ben."

"I bet it's her boss, what a bloody cheek ringing on the weekend, I wonder what he wants now. Do you want another drink, Rebecca? I need a cold beer."

"No thanks, Ben, I'm fine."

Linda walked into the garden with a big smile on her face. "Who the hell was that on the phone," asked Ben, "not your boss again?"

"Shut up Ben, yes it was Alex – he wanted to know if there were any good Indian restaurants in the area."

"Has he got no friends?"

"What is your problem Ben? Christ, he's my boss – you didn't complain when I brought that expensive bottle of brandy home he gave me the other day."

"I'm saying no more, I'm keeping my gob shut – will you get me a cold beer, Linda, if it's not too much trouble?" and Ben gave her a look of annoyance.

"I think I'll go and unpack my case Ben."

"Okay Rebecca, it's the bedroom at the top of the stairs on your right – oh how rude of me, I'll show you where it is."

"No need Ben, stay where you are and have your beer, I won't be long."

Rebecca went upstairs and when she walked into the bedroom, which had an en-suite, it was sheer luxury and had a small leather settee in the corner of the room and a beautiful dressing table with a vase of fresh flowers on top and a king-size bed with a lovely floral pattern cover on it. 'Blimey,' she thought, 'how beautiful the walls look,' as they were covered in pictures of the family in silver frames. She put her clothes away, had a quick shower and got dressed and went back downstairs into the garden.

"The room is gorgeous, Linda."

"Thank you, we both chose the décor and furniture – that's something we did agree on. We've spent a fortune on the property but I must admit I love it Rebecca."

"I don't blame you, Linda, it's amazing, you both should feel so proud, I could never afford this."

"I was just thinking, Rebecca, you could always rent our property till you get yours sold, that's if you like it."

"Ben, you're jumping the gun – Rebecca hasn't even seen it yet, she may not like it."

"Alright Linda, I'm just saying it makes no difference to me either way, it's a lovely property and we will get a buyer I'm sure of that."

"I think it's Tommy's bedtime Ben – it's funny we haven't heard a squeak out of him since dinner time. The girls must be tired too, Rebecca."

"I'll come upstairs with you Linda, and put them to bed."

The children were finally settled and tucked up in bed for the night. Ben opened a bottle of red wine and Rebecca and Linda joined him in the sitting room.

"I was thinking I may do mobile hairdressing, there's a new residential home for the elderly opened up near the high street; it's in Elm Street – they're advertising for someone to go and work in the home twice a week. Do you know it Linda?"

"Not really, but it's not a bad idea. If I were you I'd apply for the job Rebecca, or you can always pop into the place and ask to see the person in charge."

"Do you do unisex hairdressing Rebecca?"

"I do, Ben. I've worked in a couple of unisex hair salons in the past; but I know the money won't be that great, the elderly are not going to pay top prices and I also think there will be a lot of people applying for the job, especially if they have school children the hours would suit them."

"Do you want another glass of wine Rebecca?"

"No thanks Ben, I feel a bit tired – it must be the wine. I'll say goodnight to you both and thanks for the lovely dinner Linda."

"You're welcome Rebecca. Do you want a tea to take with you upstairs?"

"Oh no, I'm fine Ben, when my head touches the pillow I'll be fast asleep. I can't keep my eyes open."

The next morning Rebecca woke up after having a sound sleep and had a shower, got dressed and went downstairs to the kitchen where Linda and Ben were busy making breakfast.

"You should have called me, Linda."

"What for? It's only scrambled eggs and sausage and

baked beans with toast. Rebecca, will you tell the girls to come downstairs – breakfast is ready, and Ben tell Tommy to get a move on, he'll sleep for England."

They all sat at the kitchen table having breakfast. "Are you playing golf today Ben?" Linda asked.

"I'm only going for a couple of hours after I've shown Rebecca and the girls around the property. You're coming aren't you Linda?"

"I have some emails to send – you and Rebecca go and I'll look after the children Ben."

"I don't want to go, Dad," Tommy piped up.

"And neither do I," Amy joined in, jumping up and down.

"Girls, I want you both to see it – that house may be our new home."

"Mum, I want to stay here with Tommy."

"Alright Amy, calm down – what about you, Mary?"

"That's boring, I'm staying here too Mum."

"So long as you don't mind, Linda."

"Don't be daft, it's no bother Rebecca, they're good kids."

After breakfast Rebecca climbed into the car with Ben and he drove thirty minutes up the road to see the house; it was in a quiet cul-de-sac and had a garage attached to it. "What are your first impressions Rebecca?"

"Looks lovely on the outside Ben, I can't wait to go in and see the inside of the property."

They walked in the front door, there were stairs in front of you and a glass door on the left-hand side leading into the sitting room.

"It's quite small Ben, but I love the bay window – where's the kitchen?"

"Through that door there Rebecca…"

"It's quite a good size and I can see you've done it to a high standard – I love the cream tiles and wooden floors."

"Let's go and take a look upstairs Rebecca…"

Ben showed Rebecca around the upper floor, which she admired, "I like the two bedrooms with fitted wardrobes, they're much bigger than I thought Ben, and the bathroom is quite large – is there another toilet besides this one?"

"No there was no room to put one in. I tiled this bathroom myself, but not everyone likes green – Linda hates the colour – maybe it was a mistake, but I got a cheap deal with the tiles."

"I think it's lovely Ben, I would have chosen that colour myself; just one thing, is there an airing cupboard?"

"In the passage Rebecca, and you can see the house is central heated throughout. Would you like to see the garden? It's all fenced off so you have plenty of privacy."

"I like the kitchen leading into the garden, it's gorgeous – not too big to cope with, Ben – and there's room to put a table and chairs out here on the patio area and that's a reasonable size lawn for the children to play out in. I love the property and I think the girls will too, and they won't have to change schools."

"Exactly, Rebecca, the only thing is it needs some furniture and curtains."

"Jim and me discussed all that, Ben; he doesn't mind what I take from the house when it's sold."

"Let's cross that bridge when it comes Rebecca, the house is yours if you want it."

Rebecca reached over to Ben and kissed him on the cheek, then he put his hands on her cheeks and kissed her passionately on the lips. Rebecca pushed him away, "What the hell do you think you're doing Ben?"

"Oh god, I'm so sorry Rebecca!" he said, putting his hands over his face, "that was stupid of me, I'm an idiot. It's just that me and Linda have been at each other's throats for weeks and being with you is like a breath of fresh air – that didn't give me the right to take advantage of you."

"Look Ben, I know all about the affair Linda had, she told me, and I can see you're both going through a bad time together, but I have my own shit to deal with. Let's just forget this ever happened Ben, let's go."

They got back into the car and Ben dropped Rebecca off at the house and drove straight off to the golf course. Rebecca walked into the house and saw Linda in the passageway laughing and giggling on the phone to someone and when she went to pass her to go into the kitchen Linda quickly put the phone down.

"Who was that?" Rebecca asked.

"It was Alex, it's his birthday today and he's bored out of his mind – he said he wants us all to come to his flat and have a party! I said that was a bad idea. The silly bugger made himself a cake and it has burnt, I think he sounds pissed – did you like the house Rebecca?"

"It's beautiful, it's small but meets my needs, but I'm not sure. I'll have to think about it – where are the children?"

"They're in the garden playing on the trampoline; let me make you a cuppa…"

At that moment, Rebecca's phone rang, "Hi Dad, what's up?" It was always her mum who rang her.

"I'm at St George's Hospital with your mum, Rebecca – she had a fall in the kitchen and banged her head on the tiles."

"Oh my god Dad, I'm coming – I'll be with you soon – is it serious?"

"Stop panicking my darling, she's sitting up in bed having a cuppa. You just drive carefully. I'll wait for you outside the hospital, Rebecca."

"I'll be with you in about forty minutes Dad, bye."

Rebecca quickly packed her case and said her goodbyes to Linda, who understood, and told the girls to climb into the car.

When Rebecca reached the hospital she parked the car and found her dad was waiting outside the hospital for her. "Is Mum alright, Dad?"

"She's fine thank goodness, they did an X-ray on her head and it was normal. She's got some bruises but nothing to worry about."

When Rebecca saw her mum lying on the bed in the ward she rushed over to her and flung her arms around her, "Mum, you gave me such a shock when Dad rang me, how are you feeling now?"

"I'm fine, pet. It was my fault, I tried to reach the top cupboard in the kitchen and felt a bit dizzy and fell backwards. I couldn't stand up."

"You have a small bump on your head, Mum."

"Hush, sweetheart, it was shock more than anything. The doctor just wants to keep me in hospital overnight to make sure I'm alright. It's a lot of fuss over nothing, the hospital is busy and I'm taking up a bed that could be used for someone else, but I suppose they have to do their job properly Rebecca."

"I'll take Dad home, he looks tired Mum and I'll come back in the morning. Is there anything you want?

"Nothing I can think of, pet, just give your dad something to eat, he must be starving. The girls are very quiet?"

"Ignore them, Mum, they didn't want to leave Tommy, they're both sulking." Rebecca kissed her mum and so did Bert. "We'll see you tomorrow, have a good night's sleep – bye, Mum."

Rebecca got back to the bungalow and put a children's video on for Mary and Amy to watch in their bedroom and went downstairs. "Would you like something to eat, Dad?"

"Just a ham sandwich please, I'm not very hungry. I'm sorry to have spoilt your weekend Rebecca, it's just I didn't know who to call. Nellie and Pete were staying with family for the weekend."

"Don't be silly Dad, you did the right thing. Mum will be okay, so stop worrying, we'll go and see her first thing in the morning and bring her home; they're only keeping her in overnight."

Rebecca went into the kitchen and made some ham sandwiches for the girls and her dad and called to Mary and Amy to come downstairs.

"Do we have to Mum?" Mary replied, "we're playing with Goldie."

"If you two don't come down right now, Mary, the hamster is going straight back to the pet shop tomorrow."

"Alright Mum, we're coming, I'll just put him back in his cage."

At that moment the phone rang and Rebecca picked it up. "Rebecca, it's me Ben, sorry I missed you to say goodbye – how is your mum?"

"She's staying overnight in hospital just for observation, but the scan they did on her head looks fine so me and dad will probably bring her home in the morning when the doctor has done his rounds."

"That's good. Rebecca, I meant what I said about the house – it's yours if you want to rent it, you can move in anytime you want."

"That's so kind of you Ben. Where's Linda?"

"She's popped round to see Alex to take him a birthday gift, a bottle of wine. I'm bloody furious, what is she playing at?"

"I can't talk right now Ben, I have to see to the children and put them to bed. I'll give you a ring tomorrow."

"Okay I'll speak to you soon, bye Rebecca."

The following morning Rebecca gave the children their breakfast, and her dad who was suffering with a migraine. "Dad, why don't you stay at home and keep an eye on the girls for me and I'll go and collect Mum from the hospital."

"If you don't mind, Rebecca – my head is splitting."

"Take a paracetamol, Dad. Maybe you need an eye test at the optician's, when was the last time you had your eyes checked out?"

"I can't remember, don't worry about me. I'm going into the garden to have a ciggy, mum's the word Rebecca."

"Girls, go and get dressed and be good for Grandad, I'm going to pick Nanna up from the hospital."

"Can we come, Mum?" Amy asked.

"No, you both can keep Grandad company, I won't be long."

Rebecca arrived at the hospital and when she went up to the ward her mum was all dressed, waiting on the bed for her with her few belongings in a carrier bag.

"Hi Mum, has the doctor seen you?"

"Yes, I'm good to go. He thinks the dizzy spell I had was a bit of vertigo which I've suffered with in the past. Let's go, pet, I'm dying for a good cuppa at home – the tea in here is like dishwater and the food is appalling."

There was no traffic on the road and Rebecca was relieved to bring her mum home; she knew her dad would be lost without her, he was useless on his own and they were never apart for too long.

"How are you feeling, Grace?"

"I'm much better Bert. You stink – you've been smoking again, I can smell it on your clothes."

"I was worrying about you Grace, see what you drove me to."

"Rubbish," said Grace smiling, "I'll let you off this

time but I wish you'd give up that filthy habit of yours."

"Where are the girls, Dad?"

"Playing in the garden. I'm parched, I'd love a cup of tea Rebecca."

"I'll make it Bert, the poor lass is not your skivvy."

"It's alright Mum, I'll make it, stay where you are."

When they were all sat down drinking their tea, Rebecca explained about Ben and Linda's house she'd viewed. "It was lovely, Mum, not too far away from here and they both said I could rent it and move in any time."

"I thought you wanted to buy a property Rebecca. You don't want to waste your money on paying rent," Bert remarked.

"I know, Dad, but it's not a bad idea to rent it and get to know the area first to see if I like it, and Ben said I could buy it later on when my house is sold."

"How do you know this bloke Ben won't change his mind Rebecca, and how much rent is he charging? He seems to putting himself out quite a bit, you haven't known the family that long."

"Dad, they're lovely they have other properties and besides I want my own space – I can't stay here forever."

"Bert, it's Rebecca's decision, she knows what she's doing."

"Alright Grace, I'm just saying I find it odd that's all."

The phone rang and Rebecca picked it up. "It's me Rebecca, I have a buyer for the house but I need you to make an appointment to see your solicitor and sign some papers for it to go ahead. We got a good price for it."

"That's good news Jim, I'll ring her tomorrow."

"Can I speak to the girls?"

"No Jim, you can't. You'll be having them next weekend and I don't want you unsettling their routine."

"Okay if that's what you want," and Jim put the phone down.

New Beginnings

A few months passed and Rebecca had applied for the job hairdressing at the Residential Care Home; she was pleased to hear she had got the job which entailed working twice a week. The money wasn't good but she hoped if word got around she might pick up some work privately, and she was looking forward to starting work the following day.

The sale of the house was going through nicely and she made the decision that Jim could have most of the furniture; she just wanted a writing desk which her mum and dad gave her and two sofas, plus two single beds and other personal belongings. Jim had more or less chosen most of the furniture – he was still always in control. So it was a fresh start, new beginnings for her and the girls and she felt a sense of freedom. There were not many happy memories to look back on in the house, so the material things didn't bother her but she had to be practical – she needed every penny she could save. Ben had rung her and was over the moon that she'd decided to take up his offer of renting the house she viewed, but she had the feeling when she spoke to Linda that she was not as enthusiastic as him.

The girls were at their dad's and Rebecca was having a cuppa with her mum in the garden, "I can't believe you and the girls are leaving next weekend, Rebecca."

"Don't be sad Mum, I'm not that far away and it will be nice for you and Dad to have the place to yourselves, the girls can be tiring – they're so energetic and noisy at times."

"Don't be daft, I've loved having you all here, it made

me feel young again."

"Dad has been in his shed all morning Mum, it's the best thing you ever bought him."

"I know it was a birthday gift three years ago but it gets him from under my feet. I don't know how many bloody bird boxes we've got – I could open up a shop! Rebecca, are you looking forward starting your new job tomorrow?"

"I feel a bit nervous Mum. I'll probably get some awkward fuddy-duddy ladies who like their hair done in a certain way but I'll cope."

"You'll be fine Rebecca, you have a lot of patience and you're so caring – they'll love you."

"Mum, will you do me a massive favour?"

"What's that, Rebecca?"

"Ring the removal people up tomorrow and see if you can find a man with a van to come Wednesday morning early, so I can take him to the house and get my furniture and he can take it all straight to Ben's property. God knows what it's going to cost."

"I said I'd help and I will, Rebecca. I'll pay for the removals and if you need some money I told you I'd give it to you – I have a few bob put away."

"Thanks Mum, I think I'll take you up on that one. I'll have to give Ben a ring to make sure I have access to the house when the removal man arrives. It's getting stressful Mum, I have so much to think about – the girls know it's happening and they seem alright but I haven't really sat them down and talked to them properly… I'll do that tonight."

"I think you need something stronger to drink Rebecca – how about a glass of red wine?"

"That's a good idea Mum."

Bert came into the garden looking a bit annoyed, "If you two have stopped gossiping, Grace, I want something to eat – I'm bloody starving!"

"Sorry Bert, I forgot the time. I have three nice pieces of sirloin steak and we can have a jacket potato with it and a salad. I don't feel like cooking a roast dinner today."

"I'll come and give you a hand Mum, and you Dad sit down and I'll bring you a cold beer."

When dinner was cooked they sat out in the garden to eat. "I'm not keen on salad, it's just rabbit food," Bert complained.

"Dad stop moaning, you *are* in a grumpy mood today."

"Take no notice Rebecca, he's always like that when he's hungry. I think he loves his grub more than me."

Bert grinned, "Not the rabbits' food I don't. Is there another jacket potato?"

"No there isn't but I have sponge cake and custard for afters, and you ate four ginger biscuits with your tea earlier on, Bert – you're piling on the weight."

"Hush, Grace, leave me be."

When dinner was over Grace and Bert went upstairs for a nap and Rebecca washed the dishes and mopped the kitchen floor. The phone rang it was Ben, "Hi Rebecca, how's your mum?"

"She's fine now. I was just about to ring you – I'm coming up to the house Wednesday, not sure what time, with a removal van. Will you be around to let us in? The trouble is I don't know long the move will take, Ben."

"No worries, I'll stick around and give you a hand Rebecca, it's about time I took a day off work."

"Are you sure, Ben? It's really good of you."

"What are friends for – I'll even make some sandwiches and a flask of tea for us both, will cheese and ham do?"

"Sounds lovely, I'll pay you for your time and trouble."

"Don't be stupid Rebecca, you can buy me a pint sometime."

"How's Linda, I hope she doesn't mind me moving into the house?"

"She's a worry bead that's all, and she can't complain – it's extra money for us you moving into the property, it's not as if you're getting it rent-free."

"We didn't really discuss the rent much, are you sure £500 a month is alright Ben?"

"I told you Rebecca, that's fine. I'll have to go now – Tommy's calling me. Linda's out drinking with friends from work, no change there. See you Wednesday, bye."

Rebecca had her suspicions about Linda especially having an affair before, but she thought it was none of her business and next time Ben talked about his situation she would have to be up front and tell him straight she isn't getting involved. She had enough on her plate to deal with, that was the last thing on her mind coming out of a bad marriage herself, she didn't need the aggravation of their problems.

A little later, Grace came downstairs. "Have you had a good sleep Mum?"

"I did, pet, I left your dad snoring away… crickey, is that the time! You should have woken me up Rebecca, it's nearly time to pick the girls up from their dad's – do you want me to come with you?"

"No stay here Mum, enjoy the peace and quiet while you can. Will you do me a favour and put some fresh water and food in the cage for the hamster, I forgot to do it."

"Your dad says you're taking that vermin with you when you move, he can't stand any rodents."

"I'll have to Mum, otherwise the girls would be so upset. I'm off now to pick the girls up – see you later Mum."

Rebecca dreaded seeing Jim, she would have to have a civil conversation with him talking about the move whereas in the past she picked up the girls and drove off. When she parked in the drive of their house he came out, and she got out of the car, "Where are the girls, Jim?"

"They're coming Rebecca."

"I'd like to come Wednesday morning with a removal van to pick up some furniture. I have the key to get in Jim, I'll put it through the letterbox when I'm done."

"No need, I'll be here making sure we agreed on what you said you're taking."

"Piss off, Jim, I don't want you there – be reasonable. Here's the list of what I'm taking…" and she handed him a piece of paper. "Trust me, all I want is to get you out of my life and collect my belongings."

"I'm not arguing with you Rebecca, if that's what you want."

"I do Jim, let's not cause a scene in front of the kids," and she got back into the car.

The girls came out of the house and climbed into the back seat, "Put your seat belts on, girls," Rebecca urged as they waved goodbye to their dad.

Rebecca drove home with a sadness in her heart; the girls adored their father and she spent years trying to make her marriage work with Jim, which was impossible, so why did she feel such a failure? When she arrived at the bungalow she parked the car in the driveway. The girls quickly took off their seat belts, anxious to get out of the car when they saw their nanna at the door, and ran indoors.

Rebecca sat there on her own and burst into tears. Grace saw her crying and walked up to the car and opened the car door and sat in the front seat with her, "My goodness, has Jim upset you my darling?"

"No not really Mum, it's just hit me it's over between us. I'm glad I have closure but I think at least for the girls' sake maybe I should have tried harder."

"Listen to me Rebecca, a leopard never changes its spots; you can't stay with Jim because of the children, you have a right to be happy. Jim had his chances and he blew it, you deserve someone who loves you for who you are. Now wipe your eyes, pet, and let's go indoors – you don't want the children to see you upset like this. Try to stay strong, I'm very proud of you my beautiful daughter."

Rebecca hugged her mum, she was right, she wasn't happy with Jim and couldn't go on living a life of pretence, it was time to move on.

Back inside the house, Rebecca tried to regain her composure as she thought about the children; "Where are the girls, Mum?"

"Where do you think! They've run upstairs to play with the hamster."

"I'm going up, I need a word with them... girls, put your pyjamas on."

"Mum have you been crying?" Amy asked. "Your eyes are red."

"I have, Amy, they're tears of joy – it's exciting us three moving into our new home next weekend, what do you think?"

"I think it'll be fun living near Tommy but I'll miss living here with Nanna and Grandad, will they be lonely on their own Mum?"

"They'll be fine and you can come and see them as much as you like, Amy."

"Can we have school friends stay with us?" Mary asked.

"I don't see why not, or we can invite them to have dinner with us."

"Great!" Mary replied, "I'd like that, but what about Dad?"

"What about him, Mary?"

"Will we still stay with him some weekends?"

"Of course, don't be silly, your dad loves you both very much and that won't ever change. Now come downstairs with me and I'll make you both a sandwich –

it'll be bedtime soon, you both have school in the morning."

"Mum, is Goldie coming with us to our new home?" Amy asked.

"I think Grandad might be upset if I take him, you know how much he loves hamsters." The girls giggled.

"I don't think so, Mum," Mary replied.

The next morning Rebecca woke up and got dressed in a smart black suit and felt nervous about her first day at work. She washed her face and hands and put some make-up on her face, brushed her hair and went downstairs to the kitchen to make breakfast. "Mum, you beat me to it, I was going to do it."

"No worries, I've called the girls and made them some scrambled eggs on toast – sit down and eat yours, Rebecca, before it gets cold."

Five minutes later the girls came down and sat at the table. "Where's Dad, Mum?"

"Having a lie-in, just leave him be, I'll sort him out later on. Girls, drink your milk up and here's your tea Rebecca."

"Mum you're a gem! I've got butterflies in my stomach, I can't think straight. Thanks for making breakfast."

"It's nothing, now stop worrying – you'll be just fine Rebecca."

Grace got the girls dressed for school and Rebecca washed the breakfast dishes up, "Mum," she called up the stairs, "are the girls ready? I'm running late."

"They're coming, Rebecca…"

All ready for school, the girls then climbed into the car. "Bye Mum, see you later."

"Good luck my darling, but you won't need it," said Grace, and Rebecca drove off.

When she parked the car at the school she noticed a

familiar figure walking down the road, it was Richard. She got out of the car and kissed the girls goodbye and they ran into school. "Long time no see, Rebecca, how have you been?"

"Fine, Richard, and you?"

"Not too bad, but I've missed you even though you gave me the brush-off on our last meeting. I wasn't sure if I should ring you or not, so in the end I didn't bother."

"Don't be daft, I had a lot on my mind at the time. Do you still see June?"

"I keep well away from her, she's nothing but trouble Rebecca."

"I start my new job today, hairdressing at the new Residential Home, so I had better go. I don't want to be late on my first day."

"Can I give you a ring sometime and maybe we can arrange to have a drink together?"

"I'd like that, Richard, see you soon," and Rebecca climbed back into the car.

She drove a few miles down the road and parked the car at the car park of the Residential Home, walked up to the large building and rang the bell. A middle-aged lady opened the door: "Hello, I'm Margaret Dunn the manager, but everyone calls me Maggie – you must be Rebecca," she said and shook Rebecca's hand, "Come in and I'll show you around the salon – it's this way."

They walked up the corridor, "This is it – what do you think Rebecca?"

"Goodness, it's quite small and basic, Maggie, only one sink and two salon chairs."

"I know, but you can see it's well stocked. You can put some pictures on the walls to brighten it up if you want to. Jenny worked here for two weeks but I'm afraid I had to let her go Rebecca, the prices she was charging were ridiculous and I had a lot of complaints from my residents. There's a wholesale supplier on the high street who sells hairdressing products, and it's up to you to order anything you need; but the way it works it's your responsibility to pay them. Remember to keep all the invoices of your customers' payments, stating who had what done and how much it costs; the home will collect the money from the residents or it's added to their monthly account. I get paid directly from the nursing home and I'll pay you once a month – but I'm sure you'll get your head around it, given time. I'll have to leave you now; I have a resident who's been taken ill and I may have to call the doctor in – anything you need to ask me just come into my office, it's further up the corridor."

"Thanks Maggie, I'll be fine."

Rebecca had quite a few customers, mostly wanting cut and blow-waves. Rosie stood out in her mind, such a character telling her stories about how she was a stripper in her youth living and working in Soho in London and earned good money. Rebecca enjoyed her first day at work and swept the floor and cleaned the sink and said goodbye to Maggie before she left.

On the journey home she stopped at the supermarket to buy some groceries and bumped into June. "You look like you've put on weight Rebecca."

"Contentment June, I've never been so happy. Oh by the way, I bumped into Richard earlier – we've arranged to go out for a romantic meal this week, it's good to keep up with old friends don't you think?"

"More fool you," muttered June and walked away.

Of course Rebecca was lying through her teeth, but couldn't resist the look on June's face and chuckled to herself.

When she arrived home her mum was sitting in the garden with Nellie her neighbour, "How was your new job Rebecca?"

"It was lovely Mum, and the manager Maggie is so nice."

"I told you you'd be fine my darling, sit down and I'll make you a cuppa – would you like another one, Nellie?"

"No thanks Grace, I'll head off, Pete will be wanting his lunch soon. I must say you're looking very smart, I love the suit Rebecca."

"Thanks Nellie, it's too good to wear for work and I forgot to take my overall with me this morning – silly me, but one of the cleaners kindly lent me one of hers. I'll see you later, Nellie. Where's Dad, Mum?"

"He's next door talking to Pete, he's been in there for hours but if Nellie is serving lunch he'll hang about. I don't know where he puts all his grub, he's a gannet. Are you hungry Rebecca?"

"I am a bit, Mum, but I've bought us a cooked roast chicken for tonight's dinner – is that alright? We can have that with some new potatoes and vegetables."

"That's grand, Rebecca. I've got some fresh ham in the fridge, so I'll make us both a sandwich for now – I'm famished."

The phone rang and Rebecca picked it up, "Rebecca speaking."

"It's me – Valerie – I thought you'd left the country, you never got back in touch Rebecca."

"I'm so sorry. I'm going through a divorce, Valerie – I've been staying with Mum and Dad with the girls but I'm renting a house from a couple I met on holiday and moving in next weekend."

"I'm not surprised you've left Jim, but why did you leave the house? You should have thrown him out."

"It wasn't worth staying and putting up with the aggravation Valerie."

"My bus is coming Rebecca – we can meet up tonight at eight o'clock in the Stag pub near you, if you like?"

"Okay, I'll get Mum to look after the girls, see you then – bye."

"Who was that Rebecca?"

"It was Valerie, Mum, she wants me to have a drink with her tonight, you don't mind looking after the girls for me do you?"

"That's okay, you should get out, it will do you good Rebecca. Now drink your tea and I'll pick the girls up from school for you."

"I'm dreading moving, Mum, you do everything for me and the girls – it's a scary thought being on my own."

"If anyone can cope you can, just think positive. I'd better make the most of my time with the girls while they're living here."

"Don't be daft Mum, we're close by; they can have a sleep-over and maybe have a weekend with you and Dad occasionally."

Grace went to pick the girls up from school and Rebecca had a bath. She was looking forward to going out to the pub and seeing Valerie; if she'd known earlier she could have asked Richard to come…

"Is that you upstairs Grace?"

"No it's me, Dad, Mum's gone to pick the girls up from school. I'll come down and make you a cuppa."

Bert went out to the garden and Rebecca took him a tea, "Have you eaten, Dad?"

"Nellie gave me some lunch – a bacon sarni."

"Do you fancy a currant bun?"

"No thanks, I'll eat later. Tell me, how did you get on at work today?"

"Fine Dad, but I don't think the wages I get are going to cover all the bills, I'll probably have to look for extra work elsewhere. I'll feel much happier when I get the money from the sale of the house in my bank account."

"Make sure Jim gives you your fair share Rebecca, I don't trust that snake – he needs a good kicking the way he's treated you but I wouldn't soil my boots."

"My solicitor deals with all that Dad, so don't worry about me."

Grace arrived back at the bungalow with the girls and they ran straight out into the garden. "Have you had a good day at school, girls?"

"No Mum," Mary remarked, "I had a horrid day, Amy kept bossing me around in the playground, she wouldn't let me play with her and Katy."

"That's not true, Mum," Amy piped up, "Mary spoilt our game taking the skipping rope off us."

"Will you two stop arguing and go upstairs and change your clothes, I want you to be nice to one another – you're sisters."

"I see you found your way home, Bert, I've hardly seen you all day," said Grace.

"Shut up Grace, you complain if I'm under your feet. I'm going to the shed to get some peace and quiet, just call me when dinner's ready."

"You're not fooling me, Bert, you're going for a sly ciggy and I bet Pete is the culprit who gets them for you."

"You're like Miss Marple, it's my money I'll spend it as I wish, Grace. Now leave me be," Bert replied, grinning from ear to ear like a Cheshire cat.

Rebecca cooked the dinner and they all sat around the kitchen table; "What time are you going out?" Grace asked.

"I was thinking about seven-thirty Mum – is that alright? I'll bath the kids first."

"Don't be daft I'll do that, Rebecca, and wash their hair."

"Where are you going Mum?" Amy asked.

"To meet a friend at the pub so I want you both to be good for Nanna and Grandad."

"Have you any money on you, lass?"

"I have, Dad, but I won't be drinking much – I can't afford to."

Bert took £20 out of his pocket and handed it to

Rebecca, "Thanks – are you sure, Dad?"

"I had a flutter on the horses and won £60."

Grace's eyes lit up, "That's the first I knew of this, you're a sly devil Bert."

"I was going to buy you a couple of plants from the garden centre Grace, but I'm not sure now."

"I bet they would be lilies, the ones you were going to buy for yourself – you're a crafty old bugger."

"Watch your language Grace, we have two children sitting here," he said and gave her a wink.

"You're as daft as a brush, Bert," said Grace and gave him a cheeky grin.

Rebecca was ready to go out – she felt excited, it had been such a long time since she had seen Valerie. She kissed the girls goodbye. "I have my key, Mum, but I won't be that late; however, I don't want you waiting up for me, you need your beauty sleep. Bye Dad, the taxi's here," she called out and hurried outside and climbed into the back seat.

Twenty minutes later she arrived at the pub and when she walked in Valerie was already sitting at a table. "I'm so glad you could make it, Rebecca, I'll go and get the drinks in."

"I'll have a glass of red wine please, Valerie."

Valerie soon returned from the bar with their wine, "I don't think I'll be coming back to this pub Rebecca, the price they charged for two glasses of red wine is daylight robbery."

"Enjoy it Valerie, I'll get the next round in. How have you been?"

"The boys are well, Rob still works at the warehouse and I'm still cleaning the pubs but I'll have to give it up – I'm four months' pregnant."

"That's wonderful Valerie, congratulations!"

"I'm not happy about it Rebecca, we can barely pay

the bills as it is. We're just about managing and we're in arrears with the rent."

"I wish I could help you Valerie, but my mum and dad are giving me a loan till I get my money from the sale of the house. I work at the Residential Home, the one on the high street, a couple of days a week hairdressing but the money isn't great."

"Life sucks, Rebecca, where are you moving to?"

"Glendale Close, it's in a cul-de-sac."

"I know it Rebecca, it's quite a posh area – who are this couple?"

"I met them holiday, they've got a son called Tommy the same age as my girls. You'd like them Valerie, they own a few properties, Linda works for the council and Ben's an electrician by trade. I think they have issues though, that's my only reservation – I think she's cheating on him with her boss."

"How do you know, Rebecca?"

"Well it won't be the first time, she's done it once before. I have the feeling Ben hasn't forgiven her but he's trying to work things out."

"What's Ben like?"

"Really friendly and kind, I feel sorry for him – he's too good-natured. Mind you, he kissed me once full on the lips, unexpectedly, when I was viewing the house – that was a shock."

"My god Rebecca, be careful – he might fancy you. I would have slapped his face."

"Don't be silly Valerie, it's only because his head's all over the place worrying about Linda. He apologised and it's all been forgotten about – a stupid mistake."

"If you say so Rebecca, but I'd watch myself, you're far too soft for your own good."

"I'll get the drinks in – same again Valerie?"

"Yes please, but no more – my Rob doesn't want me drinking too much when I'm pregnant. He's picking me up in the car in half an hour – I hope you don't mind Rebecca, but I get tired easily these days, this pregnancy is taking its toll on me. I feel like a beached whale! We can drop you off at home if you like."

"Don't be daft, you're going the other way, I'll get a taxi. Who's looking after the boys?"

"They're staying at their friend's house tonight."

They had just finished their drinks when Rob walked into the pub, "Hi Rebecca, lovely seeing you again."

"You too, Rob, you're looking well. I hear congratulations are in order – can I buy you a drink?"

"No thanks Rebecca, are you ready Valerie?"

"I'm knackered, let's go. Keep in touch Rebecca, and when you're settled in your new home I'll come and see you."

"I hope so Valerie, take care – bye."

Rebecca phoned for a cab and waited outside the pub; it arrived fifteen minutes later and it started to rain so she quickly climbed into the cab.

Arriving back at the bungalow she was pleased to see the lights were all off, so her mum was in bed – she was the one who always waited up for her, worrying till she came home. When Rebecca got indoors she went straight upstairs to bed and slept like a log.

It was Wednesday morning, the day she had to collect her furniture from Jim's, and the removal van was coming early to pick her up. She dreaded the thought of Jim being at the house even though he agreed not to be, he could have easily changed his mind; she knew how interfering he was and she didn't need all the aggravation, it was always stressful being around him.

Grace took the girls to school and Rebecca got dressed and made a cuppa for her dad, "I hope that bugger doesn't give you trouble Rebecca."

"I know, Dad, I'm hoping Jim's at work and keeps his

promise to stay away, it will make my life easier. I just want to get in and out of the house as quickly as possible." Just then the doorbell rang. "I'm off, Dad, it must be the removal guy – see you later."

Rebecca opened the door. "Hi, I know you – doesn't your daughter Daisy attend Greenlands Primary School?"

"She does, I recognise you too – I'm Todd, nice to meet you."

"I'm Rebecca, we'd better get going," and Rebecca climbed in the van. "You've got the address, Todd?"

"Yes, I have it written down; if I go wrong you can give me directions, Rebecca, I've only been doing this job for a few months."

"You'll be fine, I haven't much furniture to take out but how are you going to carry it on your own, Todd, the sofas are heavy?"

"I'm meeting my mate there, we'll manage fine between us."

"I hope my husband isn't at the house Todd, we're going through a divorce."

"Oh dear, I'm sorry to hear that, Rebecca."

"Don't be sorry, getting rid of him was the best thing I ever did. I've never seen your wife at the school Todd, you always take Daisy to school and pick her up."

"Stephanie my wife died two years ago of breast cancer Rebecca, I bring up Daisy on my own."

"I'm so sorry, that's awful Todd, I take my hat off to you, it can't be easy."

"It's not, but we manage and my parents help out a lot – you just get on with it."

"How old is Daisy?"

"Seven, she's quite shy till you get to know her, but she's my princess, we're very close. You have twin girls Rebecca don't you? They're lovely, they often play with my daughter in the school yard."

"Amy is the more confident one and Mary is the shy

one. I can't complain, they're both good kids."

Arriving at the house, Todd reversed the van into the driveway and Charley his friend was waiting outside to give him a hand. "You found the place alright Todd?"

"The roads were quiet Charley, shall we get started – oh, this is Rebecca…"

"Hi, have you got the key? I rang the bell but there's no one in."

Rebecca opened the door, "Todd, could you take the two brown sofas in the sitting room and the oak writing desk in the corner – I'm going upstairs to sort some sheets and duvets out and pillows."

After Todd and Charley had put the furniture into the van they went upstairs, "What are you taking up here Rebecca?"

"The two single beds, Todd, and all the bedding on top – I'll find a black sack to put it in – and the two lamps. You can put the two chests of drawers in the van… oh I forgot, take these two rugs as well."

"What about the pictures on the wall?"

"Just leave them Todd, I never bought them – they're Jim's, I hate them."

It took the whole morning to remove the furniture and bits and pieces; the van was full, Rebecca hadn't realized how many things she needed to take with her.

"I'm off now, Todd," said his mate.

"Thanks Charley, we'll have a pint tonight, meet me at the pub around nine o'clock – bye."

Rebecca and Todd climbed into the van. "Where to now Rebecca?"

"Glendale Close, Todd."

"I know it, I've done a delivery there once before, it's a lovely area."

"Ben, a friend of mine who owns the property, will be there to let us in, he'll give you hand to unload the van Todd."

"I was going to ring the office for them to send someone round to the property but I won't bother now – we're short staffed at the moment and there's one of our vans at the garage getting fixed. Have you been living with your mum and dad, Rebecca?"

"Yes they've been great, Todd, but they're elderly and retired and I'm used to having my own place where I can entertain friends and let the children's friends come over for sleepovers, you know what I mean."

"I do. My parents are the best but they're set in their ways, it's just a different generation Rebecca."

"When I get settled in the house you can come over with Daisy for dinner Todd, the girls would love that."

"Ditto Rebecca, you can come to my place too – it's just a two-bedroomed ground floor flat with a shared garden in Lime Close, near St Helen's church."

"I used to attend that church with Mum and Dad when I was a child, Todd, it's beautiful."

Todd parked the van outside the house and Rebecca rang the doorbell. Ben opened the door and kissed Rebecca on the cheek, "Come in."

"Oh this is Todd – we both could do with a cuppa Ben!"

"No worries, I've got a flask of tea here."

"I brought more stuff than I intended to bring, Ben, I bet I get some grief off Jim."

"Bugger him, Rebecca, let's get started."

The three of them didn't waste any time and soon the van was empty. "Thanks Todd, I'll see you at the school."

"More than likely. Give Daisy a big hug from me."

"I will Rebecca – bye."

"Do you know him Rebecca?"

"Todd's daughter attends the same school as my girls, Ben, he's such a nice guy. Now where's my sandwiches you said you would bring, I'm starving, and is there any more tea?"

They both sat on the settee having their lunch. "Phew! I'm glad that's all done Ben, I was dreading today. It's a gorgeous house, the girls are going to love it here."

"I'll have to shoot off Rebecca, I have a job to do – will you be alright? There's the keys."

"I'll lock up the house and get a taxi to Mum's bungalow; we'll move in tomorrow. I need to pack the girls' stuff and my clothes. Thank you so much Ben, and give my love to Linda and Tommy, I'll catch up with them soon – bye."

Rebecca rang her mum to ask her to pick up the girls from school and phoned a taxi to take her to the bungalow. She waited half an hour for it to arrive and when she climbed into the cab she felt exhausted.

Back at her parents' bungalow, she found her dad sitting in the garden, "How did it go Rebecca?"

"Jim wasn't there, thank god, he stayed away like he said he would. I think I've remembered everything, Dad. I just feel so tired, do you want a cuppa?"

"No thanks Rebecca, why don't you go upstairs and have a rest."

"I feel like it, Dad, but Mum will be bringing the girls back soon and I need to start dinner."

"What are we having?"

"Pork chops, chips and peas."

"My favourite and what's for afters?"

"Dad you eat like a horse! I don't know, you'll have to ask Mum, I'm going to make myself a cuppa."

Before long, Grace walked in with the girls. "Thanks Mum, I was worried I'd be late picking them up from school, and I think I'm coming down with something – I feel a bit rough."

"Oh dear, go to bed Rebecca and I'll see to the dinner. Was Jim at the house?"

"No he wasn't, Mum. I was just telling Dad I don't

know what I was thinking about – there was a lot more stuff to take than I thought, which I'll need."

"You're probably feeling stressed Rebecca, go and have a rest, I'll call you when dinner's ready."

"I think I will Mum, but don't let me sleep too long otherwise I won't sleep tonight – and you, Amy and Mary, go and get changed and help Nanna set the table."

When dinner was ready, Grace called Rebecca to come downstairs to eat. "These pork chops are tough as old boots Grace," complained Bert.

"No pleasing some people Rebecca, your dad is a misery guts sometimes."

"I'm just saying, woman…"

"Don't talk with your mouth full Bert."

"You two – honestly, you're like children!" Rebecca remarked.

It was the day of the move. Rebecca got up early and packed two suitcases of clothes; she was feeling excited but nervous at the same time. After she'd got dressed she went downstairs and Grace was in the kitchen, "Do you feel better Rebecca?"

"I do, Mum. I've packed the clothes – are you coming to the house with me, Mum?"

"Yes I will, but we won't take your dad with us, he'll just get in the way – he can see the house another day."

"I must remember to take the hamster cage Mum."

"Don't worry, your dad will remind you, that's the first thing he'll put in the car," Grace replied smiling.

"I'll just have some toast Mum and a cuppa."

"What about the girls?"

"They'll have the same; we must get off early as I have to make the beds when I get there and empty a few boxes."

"You're worrying over nothing Rebecca, if you forget anything here I can always bring it to the house for you."

"I don't know what I would have done without you and Dad, Mum – you've both been amazing."

"That's what parents are for – now I'll see to the girls, you just see to yourself."

Rebecca put the cases in the boot of the car and Grace got the children washed and dressed and made them some toast in the kitchen.

"Should I wake Dad up, Mum?"

"Just leave him be, I'll ring him later on, Rebecca. You know how grumpy he is when you wake him up, besides he'll just get under our feet."

"Amy, bring the hamster cage down from upstairs."

"It's too heavy Mum, you do it."

"Okay but we need to make a move, you and Mary get into the car."

"Are you ready Mum?"

"I'll just get my coat Rebecca, just give me five minutes."

They all climbed into the car, Grace with the hamster cage on her lap sitting in the front seat. There was no traffic on the road and they got to the house in no time at all. "The journey's not that far Rebecca, I could do the drive here."

"You're a good driver Mum, I told you it's not too far away for you and Dad to visit."

"I love the area, the house looks beautiful from the outside Rebecca."

They all got out of the car and walked up the driveway. Rebecca opened the door, and once inside the girls ran straight upstairs to see the bedrooms.

"It's really lovely Rebecca, I love the wooden floors and the cream kitchen units and black granite work tops are great."

"Just put the hamster cage on the floor in the corner for now Mum, let's go upstairs and make up the two single beds. I'll be sleeping on the sofa bed in the sitting room for now till I buy a double bed."

"Why didn't you bring your double bed with you Rebecca?"

"Do you really want me to answer that question Mum? Jim's welcome to it – out with the old and in with the new quite literally."

"Oh I see, Rebecca, understandable. I can't believe how you took very little furniture from the house, I think Jim is so lucky – you were far too generous."

"I don't care about the material things Mum, I'll get them eventually. I'm just happy to get rid of him."

"That's my girl Rebecca, I'm so proud of you – now let's get started."

Finally the house looked more like a home and the girls loved it.

"Mum, I'll make you a cuppa."

"You're lucky to have fitted wardrobes Rebecca, they would have cost you a fortune if you had to buy them."

"I know Mum, but I want you to go home and have a rest after you've had your tea – you look so tired."

"I am a bit, but it's been worth it to see you and the girls sorted out, and I think you made a good choice moving here – I feel it in my bones, you're all going to enjoy living here."

Grace got a taxi home and Rebecca rang Linda, "Hi it's me, Linda, we've moved in and the girls love the house, me too."

"I'm so glad. We're having a barbecue tomorrow Rebecca, come over and bring the girls – say about one o'clock."

"Thanks Linda, we'll be there – bye."

The next morning Rebecca made the girls their breakfast and they were so excited they were going to see Tommy again. Rebecca spent most of the morning emptying boxes while the girls played in the garden with their skipping rope or upstairs with Goldie the hamster which had been placed on a chest of drawers in their bedroom.

"When are we going to see Tommy, Mum? Me and Mary are very bored."

"We're going now so you can put your coats on."

"Yippee! I will Mum," Amy replied getting excited.

Rebecca took a bottle of red wine out of the cupboard and put it in a plastic bag, "We're off now, girls, get in the car."

When she arrived at the house Ben was sitting in the front garden on the bench, "Lovely to see you Rebecca."

"Where's Tommy, is he here?" Mary asked.

"In the back garden – go through, girls, he's expecting you. Linda's in the sitting room Rebecca."

"This is for you Ben, it's only a cheap bottle of wine."

"Thanks, I'll pour you a glass, let me take your coat Rebecca."

"Who else is coming Ben?"

"No one, Linda and me just thought it would be nice for a catch-up."

"Hello sweetheart, lovely to see you again."

"You too Linda."

"How was your first night in the house?"

"I love it Linda, it's so peaceful and homely. How are you getting on with your job Linda?"

"It's a bit stressful but the money is good, what about you Rebecca?"

"The money is crap but I love working there, I love the elderly but I'll just have to find other work."

"Have you sold your house yet?"

"The sale is going through Linda; it will be nice to see money in my bank account, but don't worry – you'll get your rent on time."

"I wasn't worrying about that Rebecca, I can assure you," said Ben. "Would you like a glass of red wine, Linda?"

"Yes please Ben."

"Here's yours Rebecca, and there's a few nibbles on the coffee table – I'm going outside to do the barbecue."

"What about my drink Ben?"

"On second thoughts, you can get it yourself Linda, you've been sitting on your fat arse all morning like a pampered poodle."

"Charming I must say!"

Ben went out to the garden, giving Linda a dirty look. "Is everything alright between you and Ben?"

"Not really, there's not much action in the bedroom department, he's either bored or he's gone off me, but I know he still mistrusts me since the affair I had Rebecca."

"I'm sorry to hear that, Linda."

"Thank god I have Alex to talk to, he understands me. It's been hell living with Ben, he just bites my head off when I try to discuss anything with him…"

They carried on chatting, and a little while later Tommy walked in the room, "Dad wants you two to come and eat, it's ready Mum."

"The master has spoken Rebecca, we'd better go outside – bring your glass of wine with you."

They all sat around the table – there were sausages, chicken, spare-ribs and a salad. "This is lovely, Ben."

"Tuck in and help yourself Rebecca."

"I want a hamburger in a roll," Tommy remarked.

"There aren't any," Ben replied, "you can have a sausage instead – there's some tomato ketchup, now sit down Tommy and eat. I'll pop around the house tomorrow Rebecca, there's a few jobs I want to finish off – is that alright?"

"That's fine Ben, but I'll be at work, what needs doing?"

"The kitchen door is sticking and the bathroom needs a lock put on, and also the shed in the garden."

"This wine tastes like vinegar Ben, it's bloody awful," Linda remarked.

"That's what Rebecca brought, don't be so rude."

"I didn't know, Ben, I'm sorry Rebecca."

"That's okay Linda, it is a bad wine – cheap plonk I bought from the supermarket," she said chuckling.

"Do you fancy a gin and tonic? I'm having one, Rebecca?"

"I will Ben, but only one as I'm driving."

"Do you want one Linda?"

"No I'll have a Bacardi and Coke please – on second thoughts this pampered poodle will get it herself Ben."

"Don't you start Linda, you do my head in," and he walked indoors.

"Honestly, you can't say anything to Ben, he's so touchy Rebecca, I was only joking. Girls, go and play now if you've finished eating – and you, Tommy, show them your new video game I bought you."

"I'm not being funny, Linda, but kids pick up on everything. I feel sorry for Tommy, he must feel the tension in the house between you and his dad. I think you ought to talk to each other, it's not good."

"I know, Rebecca; we used to have a lot of dinner parties but that's all stopped now because he embarrasses me in front of my friends and we end up arguing…"

Ben came back into the garden and sat down, "Can I get you anything else Rebecca?"

"No thanks Ben, I'm heading off. I promised to pop in to see Mum and Dad, but thanks for the meal it was lovely." Rebecca called the girls to put their coats on, they were both upset they couldn't stay longer to play with Tommy but politely did as they were told.

"I'll see you out," Linda remarked, "and thank you for coming, it's been lovely seeing you Rebecca, give me a call and we can go out together for a drink sometime – preferably without Ben. Bye girls, see you soon."

Rebecca and the girls climbed into the car, "Are we going to Nanna's house?" Amy asked.

"No we're not, Amy, blimey you never miss a trick."

"I heard you tell Linda we were going Mum."

"I've changed my mind. Now put your seat belts on, you two. When you get home you can watch a video and have an early night, it's school tomorrow."

The following morning Rebecca got dressed, went downstairs to the kitchen and made herself a cuppa. She heard the girls were up so she put bowls of cereal out on the table and two glasses of milk for them.

"Good morning Mary, has Amy finished getting ready?"

"Yes Mum but she's playing with Goldie."

"Go and tell her to come downstairs right now and have her breakfast."

On the journey to school Rebecca remembered she had left her phone on the kitchen table but it was too late to go back and get it. She parked the car outside the school gates and the girls ran into the playground. "Have a good day, you two, be good."

"We will Mum," Mary replied, "bye."

Rebecca was just about to start the car up when she saw Todd walking towards her so she pulled the window down, "Hi Todd, how's Daisy?"

"She's great, she loves school and goes in no bother at all Rebecca – where are you off to? I was going to the café for a coffee before I start work, do you fancy one?"

"Why not," Rebecca replied. "I have a customer who cancelled her appointment so I'll be alright this morning – get into my car Todd, there's a coffee bar just down the road."

Rebecca parked her car outside the coffee bar. They got out of the car and walked in, it was empty and the waitress rushed up to them to take their order when they sat at the table. "We have a full breakfast with black pudding, sausage, eggs, beans and mushrooms and toast."

"No thanks, just two coffees please," Todd replied. "Have you settled in the house Rebecca? It's a lovely street," he remarked.

"I'm not sure it's going to work out, Todd. The owners, Linda and Ben, are my friends but they're at loggerheads with each other constantly, and it makes me feel uneasy."

"What's that got to do you with you Rebecca? Surely it's their problem not yours."

"I know what you're saying Todd, but they did me a favour letting me move into the house and I kind of feel responsible for them both."

"Rubbish, just keep your distance and pay the rent on time – simple as that, nothing to do with you. It's their relationship and their problem; I would just keep a distance between them."

"I agree with what you're saying Todd, but Ben makes me feel uncomfortable."

"Has he come on to you Rebecca?"

"No not really, but he kissed me once on the lips when I was viewing the house and I pushed him away, but I let it go and nothing's been said about it since."

"Be careful Rebecca, don't be so naive – he's a bloke, and to be honest you're a gorgeous beautiful woman – any man would fancy you. Just put him in his place next time and be firm, don't let him take advantage of you."

"Now you're making me feel worried Todd."

"Don't be daft Rebecca, any time you need someone to talk to just give me a ring…" and he took a card out of his wallet and handed it to her. "I'm in most nights with Daisy but it's a bit more difficult during the day when I'm working – I don't always get a signal on my phone."

"Todd, I'd better get going."

"I'll pay for the coffees Rebecca, and see you in the

car." Five minutes later Todd came out of the café and Rebecca dropped him off outside the school. "Cheers Rebecca, don't forget what I told you – bye."

Rebecca drove to work and parked her car in the car park. She was surprised to see Mrs Jones waiting outside the salon, "I thought you cancelled your appointment last week?"

"Oh dearie me, my memory isn't what it used to be, Rebecca. I'll go home."

"Don't be silly, Mrs Jones, it was a cut wasn't it? Come and sit down in the salon and if you don't mind waiting, I'll see to my other lady first then I'll see to you."

"What a sweet girl you are, thank you Rebecca."

The morning went quickly. Rebecca had five customers, mostly wanting their hair cut, and she made some good tips but she knew it wasn't enough to pay all the bills and the sooner she found a second job the better.

Rebecca was shocked when she got to the car park to find someone had hit her wing mirror and it was hanging off – she was furious.

She got into the car and was glad when she arrived home. She went straight into the kitchen to put the kettle on to make a cuppa and heard a noise coming from upstairs – she went to the bottom of the stairs and called out, "Who's there?"

"It's me Rebecca, I'm fixing a lock on the bathroom door."

"Ben, you gave me a bloody shock! Do you want a cuppa?"

"I won't say no – milk and two sugars please."

Rebecca took her coat off and made the tea and sat at the kitchen table with Ben. "Oh by the way, some guy rang you Rebecca."

"Who was it Ben?"

"I don't know, I just said you were out. I'll have to come back and do the kitchen door, but you now have a lock on the shed. There's the spare key, Rebecca."

"Where's my phone? I left it on the kitchen table…"

"Silly me, it's in my pocket," and Ben handed it to her. "Thanks for the tea Rebecca, I'm off now – anything you need just give me a ring – bye."

Rebecca gave Todd a ring and he picked up the phone. "Sorry to bother you Todd, did you ring me?"

"No, why? Are you alright Rebecca?"

"Ben was here when I arrived home – he gave me the shock of my life – he was upstairs fixing a lock on the bathroom door. I thought I had burglars, I forgot he was coming; I don't want him popping around anytime he wants."

"You'll just have to tell him straight – after all, you're paying the rent. I have to go now Rebecca and get some shopping in before I pick Daisy up from school, I'll give you a ring tomorrow – bye."

The phone rang, it was Grace, "Hello my darling, how's things?"

"I'm fed up Mum, someone has hit my wing mirror it's hanging off."

"Take it round to the garage and I'll pick the girls up from school, they can stay with me for the night and I'll take them to school in the morning. You can't drive the car like that, it's pelting down with rain."

"Thanks Mum, just explain to the girls what's happened – love you Mum, bye."

Rebecca put her coat on and grabbed her umbrella from the stand in the hallway and her bag. She locked the door and climbed into the car and drove to the garage which was just up the road. As she parked the car, an elderly guy came out, "Can I help you?"

"Yes, it's my wing mirror, it's hanging off. I left the car in the car park at work and somebody has knocked it."

"We're very busy, I can't do it right now for you – not until tomorrow morning. I'm John by the way."

"I'm Rebecca – that's okay John, I'll pick the car up tomorrow, can you give me a time?"

"Say about ten-thirty."

"Thanks, I'll see you tomorrow John," and handed him her car keys. Rebecca put her umbrella up and started walking away from the garage when she noticed Richard standing outside the car showroom talking to someone, "Hi Richard."

"Hello Rebecca, what are you doing here?"

"Someone has knocked my wing mirror, I've just left it at the garage."

"This is Clive, he works with me," announced Richard.

"Pleased to meet you. I have to catch a bus Richard, I'd better get going."

"Don't be daft Rebecca, I'll give you a lift home."

"Are you sure? You're working, I don't want to put you out Richard."

"No trouble at all, my car's over there, Clive can keep an eye on things."

Rebecca climbed into the car and Richard drove her home. "Do you fancy coming in for a cuppa Richard?"

"I won't say no Rebecca, the vending machines at the car showroom aren't working."

Rebecca took off her coat and went into the kitchen to make two mugs of tea, and she and Richard sat at the kitchen table.

"It's a lovely house Rebecca."

"My friends own it, I'm just renting it out with a view to buying it if I like it."

"Good idea, try before you buy. I think the house is great, Rebecca."

"To be honest, Richard, I miss living with Mum and Dad, it's scary on my own. I don't know many people yet, not even the neighbours."

"Takes time Rebecca to settle anywhere – do the girls like it here?"

"They love it, children are so adaptable though and the good news is they didn't have to change schools so that's one consolation."

"I rang you yesterday – who was that man I was speaking to on the phone, he was so abrupt?"

"I thought it might be you who rang me, oh that was Ben you spoke to – his wife Linda is nicer, they own this property – what did he say?"

"I just asked to speak to you and he said 'she's not here, mate,' and put the phone down on me before I could leave a message Rebecca. What's his problem?"

"He's creeping me out, Richard, he is a bit weird."

"What do you mean?"

"I can't put my finger on it – he's jealous of his wife who had an affair quite a while ago, but keeps putting her down in front of me and I feel awkward. She reckons the only person who really understands her is her boss Alex – they seem to be quite close Richard."

"This bloke Ben had better watch out, it sounds to me he's pushing her away and she's turned to the other chap for comfort. I bet she's having an affair with him, still it's none of your business, Rebecca. I'd keep well out of it if I were you, don't get yourself involved."

"My mum has the children and I'm on my own – how about coming over? We can get a takeaway, Richard, and a bottle of wine – or am I being too presumptuous?"

"Not at all Rebecca, good idea. I'll come around about seven-thirty tonight and head off now, I need to get back to work to see what Clive's been up to."

Rebecca kissed Richard on the cheek and when she stood at the door and watched him get into his car she waved him goodbye. Ten minutes later the doorbell rang – 'it must be Richard,' she thought, 'he's forgotten something' – and opened the door.

"Hi Rebecca, I've come to fix the kitchen door."

"Sorry Ben, I'm on my way out to do some shopping,

can you come back another time?"

"I suppose so but I can do it now while I'm here and lock the door when I've finished Rebecca."

"I'd rather you did the job another day Ben, I have loads to do today."

"Fair enough, I'll leave you to it."

"Tell Linda I'll give her a ring."

"I will do, bye for now."

Rebecca put her coat on and walked down the high street to the off licence and bought two bottles of red wine and six cans of beer. Then she went to the florist further down the road and bought a bunch of carnations. It started to pour down from the heavens so she hurried straight back home. She was drenched through, so when she got indoors she took off her coat and put the flowers in a vase of water and placed them on the kitchen table, then went upstairs and to run herself a bath. It was lovely to have quality time to herself and she went downstairs and poured herself a glass of wine. The phone rang, it was Grace, "Hi Mum are the girls okay?"

"They're playing with their new Barbie dolls I bought them. Did you get the car sorted Rebecca?"

"I did, Mum, it'll be ready tomorrow... oh bugger I've got to go mum – I'm running a bath, I'll speak to you later."

Rebecca had a good soak in the bath, then put on her jeans and T-shirt and went downstairs. She made herself a cuppa and did a pile of ironing and put clean sheets on the beds.

The doorbell rang so she went downstairs and opened the door. "You look very smart Richard!"

"You look gorgeous Rebecca."

"Give over – in my old jeans and T-shirt? Let me take your coat, there's beers in the fridge and I have some red wine."

"I brought you a bottle of white wine and some

nibbles Rebecca," he said and handed her a carrier bag. "I'm hungry, what do you fancy to eat – Indian, Chinese, or a pizza your choice?"

"It's ages since I had a margarita pizza takeaway, Richard, or am I being boring?"

"No, that's fine if that's what you want. I'll have the same, Rebecca, but next time I want to take you out for a meal – there's a new Indian restaurant opened on the high street and it's had some good reviews."

"You're on, Richard, I'd like that – now what's it to be, a cold beer or wine?"

"I'll have a glass of red wine and a few crisps please."

Rebecca poured Richard a glass of wine, rang the Pizza Hut and ordered two margarita pizzas. "Would you like a small, medium or large?" the guy on the phone asked. "Hold on a tick – Richard, do you want a large pizza?" – "No a medium one is okay."

"Can I have two medium pizzas please," she replied and gave her address.

"I wondered if you could do me a massive favour Richard?"

"Depends what it is," Richard replied, grinning from ear to ear.

"You know my car won't be repaired till ten-thirty tomorrow and I have a customer's hair to do at nine o'clock – could you pick it up for me and bring it here? Otherwise I'll have to cancel the appointment. I'll give you the spare keys."

"Of course I will Rebecca, no bother, I'll put them in my coat pocket now in case I forget to take them with me."

"You're an absolute star, thank you so much – I owe you one, Richard. Let's take the bottle of red wine and our drinks into the sitting room, these kitchen chairs are so hard to sit on – oh by the way, have you seen June recently?"

"You asked me that once before Rebecca, I told you I have nothing to do with her now. I bumped into Josh at the pub and he told me she has a chap on the scene, poor bloke he has my sympathy, she's nothing but a possessive interfering cow."

The doorbell rang and Richard opened the door; the pizza man stood there and handed over the takeaways with the bill. "Thanks mate," said Richard and took out his wallet from his pocket and paid him.

Rebecca went to get two plates from the kitchen and took them into the sitting room, "I'm starving," Rebecca remarked, "but I don't think I can eat all of this, I feel slightly pissed, I'm not used to drinking much, Richard."

"Relax, I feel you're tensed-up Rebecca," and he kissed her passionately on the lips and she responded. After the meal they both went up to Rebecca's bedroom, got into bed naked and Richard made love to her. The wine had an effect on both of them and they soon fell fast asleep.

Rebecca was the first one to wake up in the morning. She crept into the bathroom and looked in the mirror and tears streamed down her eyes out of sheer joy and delight. She had experienced for the first time in her life what love-making should be like, having a sex partner who is caring, kind and considerate and Richard met all of her needs. She felt bitter at the thought of what she had missed out on all of those years, emotionally with Jim; he was always a selfish lover, a cold fish void of emotion who looked upon sex as if it was on his to-do list and she had no comparison to go by – Jim had been her one and only boyfriend. Was she a fool to think Richard might be the one or was she deluding herself because of the fantastic sex she had just had with him?

Rebecca had a shower and got dressed. "Wake up, Richard, you sleepy-head."

"What time is it Rebecca?"

"Eight o'clock."

"Christ!" he exclaimed, jumping out of bed, "I'd better get going, I'll be late for work. I need to get home to get changed."

"Don't you want some breakfast?"

"I don't eat breakfast, Rebecca, I'll just have a glass of milk."

"How about you come here tonight for dinner – you'll meet my girls?"

"Whoa, Rebecca, it's a bit too soon don't you think? I can't see you tonight anyway, I have to meet a client in the pub – he's interested in buying one of the cars in the showroom and if I can clinch the deal the commission will be good. I'll ring you later and I'll collect your car from the garage and leave it in your drive and put the keys under the plant pot outside the door."

"Thanks Richard," Rebecca said and kissed him on the lips.

"I'm going to shoot off now, Rebecca."

"What about your milk?"

"Don't worry, I'll grab a coffee when I get to work – speak with you later," and he hurried down the stairs and out of the door.

Rebecca went downstairs into the kitchen and made herself a cuppa and a slice of toast. She was feeling a little disappointed Richard couldn't stay for breakfast but she knew how his work was important to him. She drank her tea and phoned the taxi office and ordered a cab to take her to work. Fifteen minutes later the taxi arrived and she heard the cab driver tooting his horn, so she grabbed her coat and hurried outside and climbed into the cab.

When she arrived at work Maggie was outside the building talking to a lady. "Good morning Rebecca."

"Morning Maggie."

"Will you go to my office, I'd like a word with you, I'll be with you in five-minutes."

Rebecca walked down the corridor and into the office and sat down on the chair; she felt nervous, maybe some of her customers had made some complaints.

Maggie walked in the room and sat down behind her desk. "I was just wondering how are you getting on with your job, have you settled in?"

"I love it Maggie, the only thing that worries me is the money is not great, I'm a one-parent family now."

"Oh I see Rebecca, well if you don't mind being flexible with your hours, the staff here would like their hair done including me – you only do two days a week so you can fit us in on the other days and that way you can still pick the children up from school. I've had glowing reports about your work – the elderly people here are quite fond of you and I'd hate to lose you."

"I'd love that, Maggie, I could do with the extra cash."

"That's settled then, and if ever you need any advice about anything Rebecca, you know you can come and talk to me."

"Thanks so much, Maggie."

Rebecca had a difficult customer who none of the residents liked, Miss Pendleton, who wanted a cut and blow dry. "I don't want you to use boiling water on my hair, Rebecca, you nearly burnt my scalp last time."

"Sorry Miss Pendleton, I'll be careful," Rebecca replied, gritting her teeth.

After Rebecca had washed the lady's hair, she started to trim the ends. "You stupid girl, you're taking far too much off – watch what you're doing with them scissors. Are you sure you have trained in hairdressing?"

"I would say it was highly unlikely, Miss Pendleton," Rebecca answered, a little sarcastically, "now will you uncross your legs please, then it's much easier for me to cut your hair – you're moving from side to side."

"You're very rude, honestly the youth of today have

no manners whatsoever and I won't be giving you a tip."

Rebecca chuckled to herself when Miss Pendleton left the salon. Maggie had previously warned her about the lady – she was a nightmare, arguing with all the other residents in the home. A headmistress in her former days, she was a formidable woman, a force to be reckoned with by all accounts.

Rebecca had four more customers and when she finished work she phoned a cab to take her home but changed her mind and asked the cab driver to stop on the high street near the shopping precinct. She needed to get a few bits of food shopping in before she picked the girls up from school. She paid the cab driver, climbed out of the cab and walked down the high street and into a café/bar to have a coffee.

She sat at a table the near the window and the waitress came over to take her order. She was shocked to see Richard on the other side of the road holding hands with a tall pretty young lady who was dressed so stylishly. 'My god!' she thought to herself, 'I've been taken for a fool – who the hell is she?'

Rebecca paid for her coffee and went to the supermarket next door to buy some fish fingers and frozen chips for the girls and a leg of lamb, and hailed a taxi to take her home. When she saw her car was in the drive she was relieved, at least Richard had kept his promise and the keys were under the plant pot outside, so she opened the door and went inside but she felt fuming and gave him a ring.

"Hi Richard – it's me Rebecca – thanks for collecting my car."

"It was expensive Rebecca; I paid the bill and have the receipt…"

"I saw you on the high street earlier on Richard, with a woman, holding hands – who the hell is she, and don't you lie to me."

"You're paranoid Rebecca, she's my sister Rose who stays with me sometimes – she's an air hostess."

"How come you've never mentioned her to me before, Richard?"

"I don't believe we're having this conversation Rebecca," he said and put the phone down.

Half an hour went by and Rebecca rang Richard again. "I'm sorry, I bet you think I'm pathetic."

"Don't be daft, but remember not all blokes are arse holes, Rebecca. Speak to you soon, I'm busy right now – bye."

Rebecca put the phone down and felt like an idiot, what on earth must Richard think of her, a stupid jealous cow overpowering and possessive.

It was time to pick the girls up from school so Rebecca quickly put her coat on, grabbed her car keys and dashed out the door. She liked to get to the school early to park her car otherwise she had to keep driving around the block till she could find a space.

The girls were waiting in the playground when she arrived and ran to her, "Mum, look what Nanna bought us," Mary said excitedly.

"That's a lovely Barbie doll, your nanna spoils you two. Let's get into the car, it looks like it's starting to rain – wait a minute, where's your coat Amy?"

"I left it in Nanna's car, I'm sorry Mum."

"Never mind, climb into the car and put your seat belts on, girls."

"Did you feed Goldie, Mum?"

"I did, Mary, and I gave him some fresh water – I think he's very cute."

"What's for dinner Mum?"

"Fish fingers, chips and beans."

"Yummy! Can we watch a video?"

"Yes Amy you can, just calm down – don't scream in my ear I'm driving."

When they got indoors the girls ran straight upstairs to play with Goldie, and Rebecca took her coat off and made herself a cuppa and started to peel the potatoes. After she had cooked the meal she called the girls to come down to eat, and they all sat around the kitchen table.

The phone rang and Rebecca picked it up. "Hi Rebecca, it's me Jim – would it be alright to have the girls this weekend? I'm going to visit my parents and want to take them with me."

"That's fine Jim. I don't think the girls will be bothered much, they are hardly grandparents – they were never interested in them before."

"I didn't ring to have an argument Rebecca."

"That makes a change. So have you heard anything more about the house Jim?"

"Not yet, but I'm sure it will be all done and dusted soon; the couple who are buying it are desperate to move in. I'll pick the girls up from school tomorrow and see you Sunday – bye."

When the meal was finished Rebecca washed the dishes while the girls watched a video in their bedroom. She went to have a shower and then the doorbell rang so she quickly wrapped a towel around her head and body and went downstairs and opened the door.

Ben stood there with his toolbox in his hand, "Hi, have I caught you at a bad time Rebecca? I've just come to fix the kitchen door, it won't take long."

"Come in Ben, the sooner you get the job done the better, but I wish you would ring me when you're going to come around, it's not on. I'm going upstairs to get dressed."

"Have you got a cold beer Rebecca?"

"There's one in the fridge – help yourself," Rebecca replied, looking cross.

Thirty minutes later Rebecca came downstairs and Ben was sitting on the settee in the living room having his beer. "I've sorted the door out for you Rebecca; you have the house really cosy."

"Where's Linda?"

"We had an argument so she went to the pub with her friends. Why don't you come and sit by me, Rebecca?"

"I'm alright sitting here," so Ben went over to her and bent over to kiss her.

"Fuck off Ben, what are you playing at?"

"Come on, don't be like that," and put his hand up her dress.

"Get the hell out of here Ben, you have no right to touch me like that – you're disgusting."

"Okay I'm going, but just remember Rebecca it's my property not yours and I can decide whether you stay or go," and he walked out the door.

Rebecca got straight on the phone to Linda, "Hi it's me."

"Rebecca you sound upset, pet, what's wrong?"

"Your husband, Linda, has turned up at my house and made a pass at me – he's a slimeball and I don't want him coming here again – I thought you should know."

"The filthy bastard! I'm sorry Rebecca, I'll call around your house in half an hour. I'm in the pub, I'll just finish my drink and say goodbye to my friends – is that alright?"

"Okay fine. I'll see you then, Linda," and Rebecca put the phone down, trembling.

She heard the doorbell ring after half an hour and opened the door in tears, "Come in Linda."

"Hey come here, pet," and Linda put her arms around her, "I've brought a bottle of wine, get some glasses and we'll have a chat."

They both sat in the sitting room, "Did Ben try it on with you Rebecca?"

"Yes he did, Linda, he put his hand up my dress."

"What a pig and a hypocrite, putting me through hell all those months accusing me of all sorts. I'm going to be honest Rebecca, I always suspected Ben couldn't be trusted."

"Why did you think that, Linda, has he had an affair in the past?" Rebecca asked.

"We went through a period where he was telling me one lie after another but I could never prove anything, it makes my blood boil when you think the one affair I had how many friends I lost because of it – they took Ben's side and felt sorry for him, he was good at flashing the cash, buying his friends drinks when we went out together. The truth is Rebecca, I really wanted my marriage to work; Tommy adores his dad, they have a good relationship."

"I did too, Linda, with Jim. I thought we'd grow old together but when he put the ring on my finger as far as he was concerned he had me and stopped trying. I always felt lonely with him. Thank god I had the children, that's the only good thing that came out of my marriage which I will never regret. We had very few friends he was so bloody controlling."

"Ben's friends' wives think I'm an ungrateful spoilt cow, Rebecca, because we own properties and are comfortably well off and can afford to have expensive holidays abroad twice a year."

"They're just jealous bitches Linda."

"I know, Rebecca, and if I have to be honest I did love the lifestyle we had, but I feel different now – I can't bear Ben near me and I intend to leave him soon and move in with Alex for a while."

"Do you love him, Linda?"

"Alex? You're joking, no way – he's gay. I class him as one of my best friends Rebecca."

"Why did you never tell Ben?"

"It was none of his business, he mistrusted me with him and that was Ben's problem not mine. Why did I have to prove myself? I was doing no wrong."

"Now I feel awful, Linda, I thought the same as Ben – that you were having an affair with Alex."

"All I know, is you should never judge a book by its cover Rebecca. I admit Ben is charming, polite, and well-mannered and everyone likes him. He fooled me for years, buying me expensive gifts – he thought he could buy anyone."

"I'm so sorry Linda, I wish you'd spoken to me sooner. Are you taking Tommy with you?"

"I can't believe you asked me that question Rebecca – he's my son, he stays with me."

"Ben mentioned he could throw me out of the property."

"Let him try, it's actually in both our names Rebecca, so stop worrying."

"I have to put the girls to bed, Linda."

"No worries, I have to get going myself, I'll give you a ring tomorrow Rebecca."

"Thanks for coming over, Linda, I class you as a good friend," and she kissed her on the cheek, "I'll speak to you soon," and Linda walked out the door.

Second Thoughts

Rebecca poured herself a glass of wine and sat at the kitchen table. She felt bitter-sweet about the house and wished she'd stayed with her parents till the money from the sale of her property was in her bank account and had thought things out more clearly. She had rushed into the idea of having a home of her own with the girls too soon.

She could hear the girls arguing upstairs so she went up and told them to put their pyjamas on and read them a bedtime story, *Millie and her Farm Friends*. "Goodnight you two, sleep tight."

When she switched off the light she went downstairs and the phone rang, it was Grace, "Hi Mum, I've just put the girls to bed."

"What's up my darling, you sound fed up?"

"Nothing for you to worry about, Mum. How's Dad?"

"He's in bed with a cold and a cough. I blame them cigarettes he smokes but he won't listen to me Rebecca."

"I'll pop up to see you and Dad Sunday morning, Mum."

"Great, I'll cook Sunday lunch for us all. I'd better go, Rebecca, I can hear your dad calling me – he's got me run off my feet."

"Love you, Mum, give Dad a big hug from me."

"I will, pet, see you Sunday – bye."

Rebecca went upstairs to bed, it had been an eventful day and she was glad it was all over. She climbed into bed feeling shattered and slept like a log.

The following morning she heard the girls chatting in their bedroom and got dressed and went downstairs. She made the girls' breakfast, scrambled eggs on toast and made herself a bacon sarni. She called them to come downstairs – Mary was the first one to come down, "Mum, I'm not hungry."

"You must eat something, even if it's a bit of toast. By the way, your dad is picking you up from school today Mary."

"Why can't you, Mum?"

"I thought you liked going to spend the weekend with him?"

"I do Mum, but he gets cross if I don't make my bed."

"Don't be silly, and eat your breakfast."

Amy appeared in the kitchen looking grumpy, "What's the sour face for, Amy?"

"Mum, I don't like Mary touching my toys."

"I think you both should share, you have to be kind to one another. Your dad told me he's taking you to visit Nanna and Grandad Taylor."

"I don't like them, Mum," Amy complained.

"Why not?" Rebecca asked.

"They tell us off all the time and they never play with me and Mary, Mum."

"You'll have your dad with you, just be good girls for me – now finish your breakfast and go and brush your teeth."

When breakfast was over Rebecca washed the dishes and put her coat on and so did the girls. She grabbed her bag from the hall stand and they all climbed into the car.

Arriving at the school she parked her car and took the girls into the playground and kissed them both goodbye. On the way out she bumped into Todd with Daisy when she was going out of the gate, "You look pretty Daisy, I love your shoes," Rebecca commented.

"Daddy just bought them for me."

"Well I think they're lovely! Mary and Amy are in the playground…" so Daisy hugged her dad and ran off to play with them. "You must feel so proud of Daisy, she is a such a sweetheart Todd."

"I know Rebecca, she has her mum's traits, she was shy, affectionate, kind and beautiful... but I am biased, Daisy is my daughter. I've got the day off Rebecca, do you fancy a coffee?"

"I'd love one, Todd, I'm doing nothing myself – I have no customers booked in at the salon."

"I'm glad I've seen you Rebecca, it's Daisy's birthday on Sunday and I wondered if you'd like to bring Amy and Mary?"

"Oh, I'm sorry Todd, I can't – they're at their dad's on Sunday otherwise I would have brought them to the party, they would have loved it."

Todd got into Rebecca's car and she drove to the high street and parked outside the coffee bar. They both climbed out of the car and walked in and sat at the table nearest the window, "My treat, Rebecca, do you want a full breakfast?"

"No thank you Todd, I had a bacon sarni earlier on – I just want a coffee please."

"Fair enough, two coffees it is," and Todd went up to the counter and ordered them.

Rebecca felt uneasy; maybe Todd fancied her but she didn't feel that way towards him and didn't want to mislead him in any way so when he sat down at the table she started to bring up the subject about Richard who she was seeing, and when she had finished singing his praises Todd held her hand across the table.

"I hope he appreciates you Rebecca, you are a beautiful woman with a good heart and I'm happy to call you a good friend of mine."

"How sweet Todd, thank you. It must be difficult bringing Daisy up on your own."

"It hasn't been easy since her mum died, Rebecca. I have just about learned how to plait her hair and put suitable clothes on her without her looking like little orphan Annie, so it's still a learning curve for me."

"I understand, Todd. Now let me pay for the coffees…"

"No way Rebecca," and Todd went up to the counter and paid the bill. "I want to buy some clothes for Daisy for her birthday – do you fancy coming with me to Marks & Spencer's, Rebecca? I wouldn't know what to buy her, I don't have a clue what's in fashion."

"Of course I will Todd. I'll leave my car here though, it's difficult to park further down the road where all the shops are. We'll walk there, it's not far. My girls love the colour pink – what does Daisy like?"

"She likes pink too; she's very girlie, she loves bright colours and sparkly dresses Rebecca."

"Similar to my two, Todd. Who's going to Daisy's birthday party?"

"I've invited a few friends from her class. My mum is making her a birthday cake and she's organizing the food for me."

"I'm sure she'll have a lovely time Todd."

They walked into Marks & Spencer's and headed for the children's department. The shop had a large selection of dresses and a bright pink one caught Rebecca's eye, "Todd, look at this dress, it's beautiful – what do you think?"

"I think Daisy would love that one Rebecca, and I quite like the purple one on the rail beside it with the white bow on it."

"Me too Todd, just buy Daisy a few sparkly accessories to go with the dresses – all kids her age love them – they sell them next door in the toy shop."

Todd went up to the counter and paid for the two dresses and then Rebecca followed Todd into the toy shop where he picked a basket up at the entrance of the shop. Rebecca browsed around the shop on her own leaving Todd to look around himself and she noticed a large selection of Barbie dolls on the shelves and picked one off.

When she caught up with Todd his basket was full, "I've gone a bit mad Rebecca, I've bought Daisy a teddy bear, a selection of games, some glittery accessories and a school bag."

"She'll be over the moon, Todd. I've bought this Barbie doll for her – I'll put it in your basket and I'll give you the money for it," and Rebecca got her purse out of her bag and handed the money to Todd.

"Thanks so much, I'm all done now – how about we go for a coffee and grab a sandwich? I'm a bit peckish Rebecca."

"Good idea, but first I want to pop into the stationery shop further down the road to buy a birthday card for Daisy. I can write the card out while we're in the café and you can give it to her."

Todd sat in the café while Rebecca nipped in the stationery shop and bought a card. When she came into the café Todd ordered two coffees and two meat pasties.

"You're a gem Rebecca, thanks for coming with me."

"It's been my pleasure Todd, I've enjoyed myself, and this pasty tastes delicious." Rebecca took a pen out of her bag, wrote on the card and put it back in the envelope. "Here Todd, give that to Daisy from me and the girls."

"I can't believe Daisy will be eight Rebecca, time seems to fly by, they're not babies for long."

"I have double trouble having twins Todd, they can be a handful at times but I wouldn't change them for the world. Can I ask you something personal Todd?"

"Yep, ask me anything you want Rebecca."

"Have you never been out with anyone since your wife died?"

"I have, she was called Jenny. She was a one-parent family like me who had two boys aged ten and twelve, but she was a party animal she loved going to clubs having weekends away with her friends. Our outlook on life was completely different Rebecca."

"How long were you going out with her?"

"Only for a couple of months, but to be fair we both agreed it wasn't working and I wish her well, that's life. Anyway, enough about me, are you ready to go Rebecca? I'll pay for this."

"No you won't Todd, I'm paying this time," and she walked up to the counter and paid.

"You're a bossy boots, Rebecca!"

"Have you just noticed Todd? You're not very astute are you," and she chuckled.

"Cheeky bugger you are – listen, I have to go to the supermarket and I don't want to drag you around there Rebecca. I'll leave you now and thanks for going shopping with me," and he kissed her on the cheek.

"Give me a ring any time you want Todd, and give Daisy a big hug from me – bye."

Rebecca walked up the road and climbed into her car and drove home. When she got indoors the phone rang, "Hi it's me Richard – I've been trying to get hold of you."

"Sorry, I was out shopping and I put my phone in the bottom of my bag – sometimes I don't hear it."

"I was thinking of coming to your place tonight, have you got the girls?"

"No, they're at their dad's, but it would be a nice change to go to your place Richard."

"My sister Rose is staying with me Rebecca, I told you."

"I'd love to meet her Richard."

"Maybe another time, she's not feeling too well at the moment. What time should I come over Rebecca?"

"Anytime you want, Richard, we could go out for a meal at that new Indian restaurant you were telling me about."

"Oh, I'm not staying at yours tonight Rebecca, I have to drive to Leicester to pick up a car from a client so I can only stay with you for a couple of hours. I'll take you out next week, I promise."

"Okay Richard, I'm a little disappointed but I understand – will you get some cod and chips at the chippy before you come?"

"I'll do that and see you about six o'clock – bye."

Rebecca went upstairs and ran a bath; she went into the bedroom and took a pair of clean pyjamas out of the drawer, there was no point in getting dressed up she wasn't going anywhere and felt a bit fed up. It would have been nice to go out even if it was just to the pub. After she'd had a bath, she put on her pyjamas, and came downstairs and went into the kitchen and made herself a cuppa. Not long after, the doorbell rang and she opened the door.

"Were you having a kip Rebecca? You're not dressed."

"Why would I Richard? It's not as if I'm going out."

"Are you in a bad mood Rebecca?"

"I'm alright, I'll get some plates and cutlery…" and they both sat at the table eating their fish and chips. When they'd finished their meal, Richard took a receipt out of the pocket of his coat that he'd hung on the hall stand, and handed it to Rebecca.

"Bloody hell! That's an expensive job, £100 – Christ, more than I was expecting Richard. Do you want the money now?"

"I'm short of cash, I need it Rebecca."

So she took it out of her purse and handed it to him, "I'll have to ask Mum to lend me some money on Sunday. I don't understand why you can't travel to Leicester tomorrow Richard – why tonight?"

"The couple whose car I'm looking at are flying to Spain on holiday, early morning, and I want to get the deal done before they go."

"Oh I see. We can go out tomorrow night, Richard."

"I'm working tomorrow and meeting my mates in the pub; it's Tony's stag do – a guy who used to work with me."

"Great and what am I supposed to do here on my own Richard?"

"I don't know, go and see a friend. Blimey, all you women are the same – you think men can drop everything just like that. My work is important to me, it pays the bills and I don't see my mates that often Rebecca."

"I don't want to argue with you Richard."

"Neither do I," and he got up from his chair and kissed her passionately, and lifted her up and carried her upstairs into the bedroom. He undressed himself and she took off her pyjamas and they got into bed. Richard made love to Rebecca for an hour, she noticed because he kept looking at the clock on the wall.

"You were putting me off, Richard, you're all tensed up – I could feel it."

"What's wrong with you Rebecca? There's no pleasing you," and he got out of bed and got himself dressed.

"Richard, I'm sorry – come back to bed and give me a cuddle."

"I have to go now," he said and bent over and kissed Rebecca on the cheek.

"Drive carefully Richard, and I'll give you a ring tomorrow.

"See you soon, I'll let myself out – bye."

Rebecca got out of bed and went downstairs and made herself a cuppa and rang her friend Valerie. "Hi it's me – Rebecca, sorry I left it so long to ring you."

"I was waiting for an invite to your place Rebecca, have you moved in yet?"

"Yes I have but I'm not sure I've made the right decision, Valerie."

"Why's that hun?"

"It will take too long to explain, do you fancy meeting up at the Stag pub tomorrow night at eight o'clock?"

"It'll be good to have a catch-up, Rebecca, I could do with a good night out. Rob will look after the boys for me; right now we're watching a video and having a pizza."

"You must be quite big now with the baby on the way Valerie."

"I'm huge and get tired easily, but so far I've been fine – touch wood. Rob and the boys are dead excited. I just want it all over with so I can fit into my clothes, I'm like a beach whale."

"Are you sure you want to go out tomorrow, Valerie? You must get shattered."

"Don't be daft, it'll be good to have a catch-up Rebecca, but I'll be drinking orange juice. I have to go now, the boys are playing up – they're driving me mad they are so competitive. I'll see you tomorrow, looking forward to it. Bye hun."

Rebecca put the lights out and went to bed. She felt Richard was a bit on the selfish side and wanted things his way and next time she saw him she would have things out with him, otherwise she was wasting her time. She had a gut feeling that told her he was hiding something, but she was feeling tired and dismissed it from her mind and climbed into bed and fell fast asleep.

The following morning she woke up and got dressed, went downstairs and made herself a cuppa and a slice of toast. She was still sitting at the kitchen table ten minutes later when the doorbell rang and she went to open the door. An elderly lady was standing there.

"I'm so sorry to bother you, I live next door – I'm gasping for a cup of tea and have run out of milk."

"Why don't you come in and I'll get you some… sorry, my name's Rebecca – what's yours?"

"I'm Mrs Thomas, but you can call me Irene. It's lovely and homely here, Rebecca, very cosy; don't think I'm a being a nosey parker – I've seen your twin girls play in the garden but I've never seen your husband."

"I'm on my own with the girls, we're going through a divorce Irene."

"I'm sorry to hear that, dearie, it's a shame. My husband Harry died fifteen years ago, he had a massive heart attack. I can't complain though, we had many good years together."

"Did you have children, Irene?"

"I've got a daughter who lives in Scotland; she's married and has two daughters – Tilly and Gemma – I don't see much of them, maybe once a year. She has to make an appearance sometime, she knows she'll inherit my house when I die – I've got no other living relatives. My daughter's a selfish person, she only thinks about herself; my fault in many ways, I spoilt her rotten growing up."

"That's sad, Irene, let me make you a cuppa."

"That's kind of you Rebecca – no sugar, just milk please. I hope I'm not taking up too much of your time?"

"No you're not Irene. Would you like a biscuit with your tea?"

"No thank you. Where are the girls?"

"They're at their dad's, I pick them up Sunday evening. How long have you lived here Irene?"

"I can't remember – it must be about thirty years. Me and my hubby used to live in Newcastle-upon-Tyne, that's where we both come from originally, but the jobs were scarce in the north east in them days. My hubby was a postman and I worked for Marks & Spencer's in their offices. Are you working Rebecca?"

"I work at the new residential home for the elderly

down the road – as a hairdresser."

"Oh that's wonderful, you can do my hair Rebecca one day, it needs a good cut – I like it kept very short, it's more manageable."

"I'll do that for you Irene, no problem. Just let me know when you want it done."

"I must go now, Bob will want his breakfast."

"Who's he Irene?"

"My cat, he's ten years old, a bit scruffy and very independent – goes missing for weeks on end but turns up on my doorstep wanting a good feed and somewhere to put his head, down just like most men!"

Rebecca chuckled, "You're funny, Irene, here's a mug of milk to be getting on with and if you ever need my help in anyway just knock on my door."

"You're a sweetheart Rebecca, thanks for the tea, lovely meeting you – I'm sure we're going to be good neighbours." Rebecca showed her to the door and gave her a big hug.

Irene left a good impression on Rebecca – a down-to-earth person with a cheery disposition, small and chubby with a round face, clear skin with very few wrinkles, beautiful big blue eyes which matched her thick short silver-grey hair with a fringe. Rebecca thought she must have been quite a beauty in her younger days.

Rebecca spent the rest of the day cleaning the house till it was time to meet Valerie in the pub and went upstairs to get herself changed and put on her black dress and black boots, a tiny bit of make-up and brushed her hair into a ponytail. She went downstairs and grabbed her coat and bag from the hall stand, hurried out the door and climbed into the car; she knew Valerie hated to be kept waiting, especially sitting in a pub on her own.

When she arrived at the pub she parked her car and walked in; it was packed with customers and she looked around the room and saw Valerie at a small table in the corner, "Gosh it's lovely to see you Valerie, you're looking well."

"I feel uncomfortable. I need to go to the toilet but I was afraid if I left the table someone would take our seats, now you're here I'll go."

"You go Valerie, I'll get the drinks in when you come back."

When Valerie came back and sat down at the table, Rebecca remarked, "Blimey, you are big – how far on are you?"

"The baby's due in October, so I've still got a while to go yet but I think he or she is going to be a big baby. I'm sick of talking baby talk, Rebecca, I get that all the time at home with friends and family. I want to know the juicy gossip about you Rebecca, what's been happening to you since I last saw you?"

"What are you like Valerie! What you see is what you get, straight to the point with you, but let me get the drinks in first – what would you like?"

"I'll have a glass of red wine and then I'm on orange juice, Rob would go mad if he thought I was drinking alcohol."

Rebecca went up to the bar and ordered two glasses of red wine and brought them back to the table. "Tell me about Ben your landlord, has he tried it on again Rebecca?" asked Valerie.

"Yes he did, the dirty bugger and I rang his wife Linda and she came around to my house. She was lovely Valerie, she said she was leaving him and apparently her boss Alex, who I thought she was having an affair with, it turns out he's gay."

"Why didn't she come clean and tell her husband, Rebecca, and perhaps he wouldn't have given her such a hard time?"

"I don't blame her, why should she have to prove herself. I feel sorry for her, she worked just as hard as him to achieve what they had and it just goes to show money isn't everything Valerie."

"I don't know about that Rebecca, it does help a bit. Me and Rob are just scraping by, I don't know what it's like to have money in a bank account, we just manage from week to week."

"Are you still in arrears with the rent, Valerie?"

"I was, but my mum helped me out and paid it off for me."

"I'm still waiting for the money from the sale of the house Valerie, and then I'll think about moving somewhere else. Ben gives me the creeps, I don't feel settled living there. Linda his wife tried to put my mind at rest and told me she owns half the property and I more or less have nothing to worry about Valerie, but I just feel I want to move on."

"I would if I were you Rebecca. How do you know if they get a divorce whether it goes in your favour, they both may decide in the settlement that Ben keeps his rental properties and Linda stays in the house she lives in now. You don't need the aggravation, I would start afresh and move on."

"You're right, Valerie, too much water has gone under the bridge. I honestly don't trust Ben and I'd still like to buy a small flat or a terraced house if possible when the money comes through."

"I think what you need is a good man in your life Rebecca."

"Funny you should say that, Valerie, I've been seeing this guy called Richard – he's a car salesman."

"Okay spill the beans, what's he like Rebecca?"

"I think he's good looking; he's tall, dark and handsome. I have goose bumps in my stomach when we're together but I'm not sure if he feels the same way about me Valerie."

"You're gorgeous Rebecca, I don't see why not."

"He prefers to come to my place when the children are not around. We have great sex together and he's good company but he always makes excuses he has to be somewhere – it's either his job or seeing his mates. He told me his sister Rose is staying with him at the moment – she's an air hostess. I'd love to meet her but I get the impression Richard doesn't want me to, Valerie. I haven't even seen his place yet."

"I think I would be cautious Rebecca, if I were you. He could just be using you for the sex – I'd have it out with him. It sounds to me he doesn't want any commitment – he knows you have two children. Surely he must realize you're looking for a serious relationship. Has he got any children of his own?"

"No, he told me he was married once but his wife never wanted children. I really don't know that much about him, he's quite evasive when I ask questions Valerie."

"I know what you're like Rebecca, you're far too soft for your own good. Jim was very controlling, you felt trapped in your marriage and you don't want another bloke like him. I'd put your foot down and let him know you're not going to be messed about with, try to be more assertive like me… right now Rebecca I'm bloody thirsty with all this chatting, will you get me a drink?"

"I'm sorry Valerie, what do you want to drink?"

"An orange juice please – I was only joking, pet, look at your face. I'll pay for this round…"

"Don't be daft, I will," and Rebecca went to the bar and ordered a glass of red wine and an orange juice and sat back down at the table. "You look tired Valerie, you're yawning. We'll have these drinks and we'll go – is Rob picking you up?"

"Yes he is. I hate being pregnant, I keep wanting to pee all the time. I hope you're taking precautions Rebecca, you don't want to get yourself pregnant."

"Shut up Valerie, you're scaring me now. There was only once Richard didn't use a condom."

"It only takes the once – be careful, you don't want to bring up three kids on your own."

"That's really cheered me up, Valerie. Never mind that, when would you like to come to my place?"

"I'll give you a ring next week and we can arrange something… Rob's just walked in the bar to take me home – I'd better get going Rebecca, he hates hanging about. I promise I'll ring you soon, bye."

Rebecca left the bar and climbed into her car and drove home. As soon as she got indoors she took her coat off and locked up, and went straight upstairs to bed.

About ten minutes later the phone rang by her bedside and she picked it up, "Sorry I can't hear you, can you speak up?"

"It's me Richard, my darling."

"I'm in bed, what the hell are you phoning me for at this time?"

"What are you wearing Rebecca, are you naked? I was just thinking about you…"

"You're pissed, Richard. I'm putting the phone down, don't ring me again." But shortly after, the phone rang again; this time Rebecca ignored it and fell asleep.

The next morning Rebecca woke up, feeling angry inside, and thought to herself the next time she saw Richard she would tell him to piss off – enough was enough, what was he playing at? She got dressed and went downstairs and put the kettle on for a cuppa. Her head was all over the place.

The phone rang and it was Richard, "You've got some nerve, what are you playing at Richard?"

"What's your problem Rebecca? I admit I was a bit drunk last night when I rang you, I'm sorry, but you take things far too seriously – you need to lighten up a bit."

"Bloody cheek! I have responsibilities, don't take me for a fool Richard. I'm not your bit on the side."

"It's you that's the problem Rebecca, you're suffocating me; I'm not your husband. Why can't we just take things slowly, what's the hurry? I work hard, I'm entitled to see my mates."

"Bollocks Richard, you're afraid of any commitment – me and my girls come as a package. I'm not wasting my time on you anymore, you need to grow up, you're full of bullshit."

"If that's what you really think of me, Rebecca, there's nothing more to say," and he put the phone down.

Rebecca was furious and upset at the same time. She put her coat on and took her car keys off the kitchen table and went outside and climbed into the car. She drove to her mum's bungalow and opened the door with her spare key and found her mum in the kitchen.

"You're early Rebecca, I was expecting you much later – your dad's still in bed. You look worse for wear, are you coming down with something?"

"I'm alright Mum, it's because I have no make-up on."

"I'll make us both a cuppa and you can tell me what's really wrong – I know you better than you think Rebecca, you can tell me anything – I'm a good listener."

"I just hate living in my house Mum, I don't feel settled and can't wait to move out."

"I thought you liked it Rebecca."

"I did, but let's just say I don't like Ben the landlord, he's a nasty piece of work Mum, I don't trust him."

"Do you remember the old boy Mr Jackson who lived in the bungalow opposite on his own?"

"I do, Mum, he was a sweet elderly gentleman – his wife is in a home with dementia isn't she?"

"That's right. Well, he has his property up for sale – he's moving in with his son and daughter-in-law. I was talking to the estate agent the other day who's handling the property and he told me it's going very cheap. He kindly showed me around the bungalow and I was a bit in shock – it was quite neglected Rebecca. The garden was overgrown, it needs a new bathroom and kitchen and a good lick of paint, but it's spacious."

"How many bedrooms has it got Mum?"

"Three, the layout is similar to ours. It needs money spent on it but I think it would be nice when it's been renovated."

"That doesn't bother me – the renovation, Mum. It would be fantastic living opposite you and Dad but I haven't got the deposit money to put down till my money comes through from the sale of house."

"It must be due to come through soon Rebecca. Me and your dad were talking and if you like we could lend you the deposit money and you could pay us back when your money comes through."

"I can't ask you both to do that, Mum."

"Now you're being silly Rebecca, it's just sitting in the bank, and besides it would be lovely to have you and the girls living close by. I've got the estate agent's card…" and Grace took it off the shelf and handed it to Rebecca, "…give them a ring as soon as you can, I don't think it will stay on the market for too long."

"I'll ring him Mum."

"He's a lovely young chap, the estate agent, he's called Andrew Clifford – ask to speak to him – his name's on the card."

"Thanks Mum, how exciting! You've cheered me up."

"Do you want some bacon and eggs and toast? I'm making some for your dad."

"Yes please Mum, I am a bit peckish. I'll set the table and make a fresh pot of tea."

"Call your dad Rebecca – he's a lazy sod, he wants me to wait on him hand and foot since he was unwell with the flu – tell him to get downstairs pronto otherwise his breakfast is going in the bin."

"You're hard as the hobs of hell Mum."

"He's stubborn as a mule your dad, Rebecca. I was taking his meals upstairs on a tray to him when he was under the weather but he's stringing me along, he's much better now and the exercise will do him the world of good to come downstairs," Grace commented with a chuckle.

Rebecca called upstairs to her dad and it wasn't long before he came down and they all sat at the kitchen table having their breakfast.

"Bert, I was telling Rebecca about the bungalow up for sale."

"Yep, I think it's a good idea Rebecca, it's going cheap. I think it's better to own your own property than pay rent."

"I agree Dad, but if I do buy it I don't know who will do the work for me – there's a lot of cowboy builders about, I have to be careful."

"We'll cross that bridge when we come to it, Rebecca. Give the estate agent a ring tomorrow."

"I will Dad, I'll make an appointment for a viewing and when it's over I'll pop in for a cuppa and let you know if I like it or not. Just think, if I do decide to put an offer in and it's accepted, I'll be living across the road – I can keep an eye on you and Mum."

"Give over, we're not past our sell-by date yet, my girl."

"I know that, Dad, but I still worry, it's natural – you're my parents, you're no spring chickens."

"I'm going into the garden to stretch my legs Grace."

"I give up, go and have your ciggy Bert – if you get lung cancer be it on your head, you're a stubborn old bugger."

"You see how your mum treats me Rebecca, with a rod of iron."

"I'm saying nothing Dad," Rebecca remarked smiling.

"I wish you'd sit down in the sitting room and relax, Mum, and leave the washing-up to me."

"I think I will, pet. I'm going upstairs and having myself a long soak in the bath, my arthritis in my knees is giving me gyp – I feel as stiff as a poker."

Rebecca washed the dishes and her phone rang and she took it out of her bag. "It's me Richard – don't put the phone down."

"What do you want?"

"I was thinking we could go out for a meal tonight. I have been acting selfish, I'm sorry – can we start again? You must know how much I care about you Rebecca."

"I'm with my mum and dad, then I'm picking the girls up later on."

"Alright, how about tomorrow night?"

"I'm not sure, I'll have to think about it… I'll let you know, Richard. I have to go now, bye."

Grace came downstairs and noticed Rebecca looking in a pensive mood. "Is something troubling you Rebecca? I heard the phone go – who was that?"

"To be honest Mum, I've been seeing this guy called Richard – he's a car salesman – I think I mentioned him to you before, he was June's friend from the salon I worked at."

"The name doesn't ring a bell, Rebecca, I can't remember him," Grace remarked.

"Well, we have been seeing one another, Mum. He's fabulous company and I have feelings for him but I don't think he's the settling-down type, maybe I'm expecting too much too soon."

"I know what you mean Rebecca, but remember you have two children which is a big responsibility and any mature man that you meet must know that you're not a teenager anymore, and you're not looking for just a fling. If things don't seem right they probably aren't, as my mum used to say."

"I know what you're saying Mum, I just wish I could have what you and Dad have – you're devoted to each other."

"You will find the right person one day, my darling. I must admit me and your dad have had our fair share of ups and downs over the years but the secret is you talk things out and never hold your feelings in, whatever the outcome. Then you know where you stand. Honesty goes a long way in my book."

"You're a wise woman, Mum, and I think you're right."

Rebecca sat in the sitting room reading a book while her mum prepared the vegetables for dinner. The doorbell rang and Grace answered the door – it was Pete, the next-door neighbour. "I'm sorry to trouble you Grace, my Nellie is baking a cake and she's run out of self-raising flour – have you got any and I'll replace it tomorrow?"

"No bother, Pete, I'll get you some. Bert's in the garden, go through – do you want a cuppa?"

"No thanks Grace, I'll just have a chat to Bert... Hello Rebecca, I'm on the cadge again – how are your girls?"

"They're fine Pete, I'm picking them up tonight from their dad's."

"The trouble is children grow up so fast, Rebecca, they don't stay babies for long. I'll just pop into the garden – I need to pick your dad's brains about my apple tree, he seems to have green fingers, I could do with a few tips from him. Give the girls my love and tell them when they're here next time to pop in next door and see my Nellie, she's very fond of them."

"I will Pete, thanks," Rebecca replied.

The phone rang and Grace picked it up. "It's me – Nellie – did you have you any self-raising flour Grace?"

"I have, I'll give it to Pete and send him home – he's having a chinwag with my Bert in the garden, you know what them two are like when they get together – he must have forgotten."

"Thanks Grace, my Pete can talk the hind leg off a donkey. I'll catch up with you later."

Rebecca helped her mum in the kitchen to cook the dinner and set the table. "That smells good Mum I love roast beef and Yorkshire puddings."

"I get fed up cooking chicken, but I know your dad will complain – the beef is too tough, it's not the best I've bought, it was going cheap in Sainsbury's. I like it sliced thinly in a sandwich with lots of mustard on."

"Me too, Mum, delicious!"

"Dinner's ready, tell your dad Rebecca to come and eat now before it gets cold."

After being summoned by Rebecca, Bert eventually appeared in the kitchen. "Bert, go and wash your hands – they're filthy, you've been digging in the garden."

"Shush woman, they're fine – a bit of dirt doesn't hurt anyone, you fuss too much."

"Dad, I think Mum's right."

"Don't you start Rebecca, can a man not have a bit of peace eating his dinner."

"What's the roast beef like, Bert?"

"It's tough like leather, Grace."

"Do you want something else?"

"I'm eating it aren't I? Have you any more Yorkshire puddings?"

"There's none left Dad, I don't know where you put it all – you can have mine."

"That's my girl, looking after your old dad – what's for afters Grace?"

"Fruit salad and cream."

When the meal was over Bert went upstairs for a lie down. Grace washed the dishes and Rebecca made them both a cuppa.

"Jim has a girlfriend, Mum."

"I pity the poor woman, you're well shot of him my girl. Have you met her?"

"No Mum, I don't particularly want to but the girls quite like her."

"I suppose that's a blessing – what time are you picking the girls up?"

"Usual time. He'll always be in my life Mum, so I have to be civil to him for the girls' sake – he's their dad."

"Have you still got Goldie the hamster, Rebecca?"

"Yep, I wish I hadn't Mum, it smells musky in the children's bedroom – not the best present you have ever bought the kids, Mum, but they do love him."

"I should have bought them a puppy," Grace remarked grinning.

"Don't you even think about it Mum. I have no time to walk a dog, it's too much responsibility and a huge tie. I think the hamster was a better option. I feel a bit tired Mum and slightly dizzy – you don't mind if I go upstairs and have a lie down?"

"Don't be silly, of course not – I hope you're not coming down with something Rebecca?"

"Me too Mum, I have work tomorrow."

Rebecca went upstairs to bed and slept for three hours. When she woke up she went downstairs and found her mum and dad sitting in the garden, "I can't believe I slept that long, Mum, you should have woken me up."

"What for? You must have needed it, pet. I'll go and make you a cuppa."

"Thanks Mum, the trouble is I probably won't sleep tonight. Just lately I've been feeling so tired, no energy whatsoever, I must be lacking in vitamins or something."

"I would go and see the doctor, you may have a virus of some sort Rebecca."

"I might just do that Mum. Have you got two paracetamols?"

"I have, I'll make the tea first – do you want one Bert?"

"Yes please and a slice of that fruit cake, my love."

"Christ, Bert, you eat me out of house and home – you're a greedy bugger."

"You look after me well, Grace, I don't know what I'd do without you," Bert remarked with a huge grin on his face.

Rebecca put her coat on, "I'm going to collect the girls, Mum, and head home. Thanks for the lovely dinner, I'll give you a ring tomorrow."

"Take care my girl," Bert remarked and Rebecca gave her dad a kiss on the cheek.

When Rebecca arrived at the house, Jim was sitting in the front garden with the girls, "I have some good news, Rebecca, the buyers are moving in next week and you should contact your solicitor – your money should be put into your account soon," Jim remarked.

"Great, I'm pleased, but I need to get home Jim. I'm feeling unwell – have the girls got their belongings together, I'm not in the mood for small talk."

"Bloody hell Rebecca, you're so fucking annoying."

"Don't start, Jim. Get into the car, girls, it's time to go home."

The girls climbed into the car but Amy looked annoyed, "Why were you angry with Dad, Mum?"

"I'm sorry Amy, I just feel unwell. I'll be alright once I get you two home and have an early night – it's nothing for you to worry about."

Rebecca arrived at the house and when they went indoors the girls did what they always did and went upstairs to their bedroom to see Goldie the hamster. Rebecca wasted no time in making them both a sandwich and a glass of milk and telling the girls to put their pyjamas on. Mary was in a strop, "Mum can we watch telly in our bedroom? It's still early – me and Amy aren't tired yet – you're being so unfair."

"Okay, anything for a bit of peace. I'll bring you up a tray with your sandwich and milk and when I say lights out, Mary, I mean it."

Rebecca felt awful not giving the children the attention they deserved, but all she wanted to do at that precise moment was to go to bed herself.

Finally she got the girls into bed and read them a bedtime story, *Ollie The Orange Otter*, and went downstairs and made herself a cuppa. It had been a long day feeling the way she did, she felt exhausted and glad it was all over.

The phone rang but she ignored it. She locked the door, turned the lights out and went upstairs to her bedroom. She got her dress out of the wardrobe and placed it on the chair ready to wear for work in the morning, got undressed and put on her pyjamas and climbed into bed and fell fast asleep.

The alarm clock went off and Rebecca was still out for the count; it wasn't until Mary jumped on the bed she opened up her eyes, "Wakey! wakey! Mum, I'm hungry."

"Gosh I've slept in! Tell your sister to get ready for school and you too, quick sharp and don't forget to put your school books into your satchel and remind Amy to do the same."

Rebecca quickly got dressed and went downstairs into the kitchen and put two bowls of cereal out for the girls and two glasses of milk and made herself a cuppa. When breakfast was over she told the girls to put on their coats quickly and collect their satchels off the chair and to get into the car.

Amy was moaning on the journey to school, "Mum, my teacher is going to tell us off for being late."

"Don't worry, Amy, I'll explain it was my fault – now what have I told you before about putting your seat belt on…'

Rebecca arrived at the school and parked the car. The children were already in assembly and one of the English teachers approached Rebecca, "I'm sorry we're late Miss Penfold, it was the traffic on the roads."

"Not to worry, you go, I'll see to the girls."

Rebecca hurried back to her car, she hated lying but she was normally punctual so no harm done.

The first customer Rebecca had was Mrs Brown for a cut and blow wave but she had phoned the salon to cancel her appointment due to ill health; just as well as Rebecca wasn't there, she arrived half an hour late and was just about to phone her to apologise but thought it best to say nothing and made another appointment for her.

Rebecca was disappointed; another client phoned in to say she had to cancel her appointment so she only had two customers who wanted a cut and blow wave. When she had finished, she decided to phone the estate agent Andrew Clifford to make an appointment to view the property he'd shown her mum around. He was very helpful and friendly and booked her in for a viewing for the following week.

A New Life?

Rebecca loved her job but knew it wasn't financially giving her a good income and she would have to look elsewhere but brushed it from her mind; there were other things to think about, her divorce for one and getting her share of the money from the sale of the property.

On the drive home she stopped at the supermarket to get a few groceries and had a brief fainting spell in the aisle and fell on the floor. One of the staff members rushed over to her and took off her cardigan and folded it like a pillow and put it under her head and kept her flat on her back. She soon came to and insisted she was okay, and with the help from two customers holding each of her arms she managed to get to her feet and a chair was brought from the staff room for her. One of the ladies who helped her was a student nurse at the local hospital and insisted she rang for an ambulance to take her to the hospital to get a thorough check-up. Rebecca finally agreed after a lot of persuasion; she hated all the fuss and attention, being rather shy, and when the ambulance arrived she was put into a wheelchair and taken outside and put straight into the ambulance. She thanked everyone for all their help and soon after she arrived at the hospital which was only ten minutes away.

Rebecca felt like a fraud, she was feeling much better; there were other people in A&E on beds in the corridor who needed attention more than her but it wasn't long before the nurse wheeled her into a cubicle and told her to lie on the bed. The nurse asked her some questions and wrote all the details down on a form and soon Dr Wilson arrived and introduced herself and examined her. When she had finished the examination she was given a bedpan by the nurse so she could have a urine test done and also had other tests done by the nurse – an E.C.G. and her temperature and blood pressure were taken also a blood sample. The doctor was called on her bleeper so she left the cubicle and Rebecca lay on the bed for what seemed to be hours before she came back.

"Mrs Taylor, tell me are you in any kind of pain?"

"No," Rebecca replied. "I have had a lot of stress lately though," and she explained to the doctor she was waiting for her divorce papers to come through; she also told her she got tired very easily and was lacking in energy.

"What's your appetite like?"

"Not good Dr Wilson, I'm always skipping meals. I haven't eaten anything this morning."

"I'll go and get the nurse to bring you a sandwich and a cup of tea."

Thank you Doctor, I'm feeling a bit peckish," Rebecca replied smiling.

Rebecca lay on the bed thinking whether to call her mum or not, as she may have to pick the girls up from school for her later on, but she thought she would hang on for a bit longer because she was sure it was just stress and not eating very much that caused her to faint, and as she was such a worry bead the doctor would probably give her a prescription to calm her down and vitamins to build her up and let her go home.

Rebecca was getting worried; how long had she been waiting? So she gave her mum a ring, "Hi it's me, Mum, I'm in A&E – don't panic – I fainted in the supermarket and I've seen the doctor, I'm just waiting for her to come back and see me, I'm fed up here."

"My goodness Rebecca, what on earth caused that to happen?"

"I'm not sure, but I feel okay now so don't worry about me – would you do me a favour Mum and pick the girls up from school and I'll ring you later and let you know what's happening. I have to go now Mum, the doctor is waiting to have a chat with me – I'll speak to you later, bye."

The doctor pulled up a chair and had a quiet chat with Rebecca, "Do you know when you had your last period?"

"I can't remember, I'm always irregular – why?"

"The tests showed you are pregnant, and as you say you have a habit of skipping meals I'm not surprised you had a fainting spell Mrs Taylor."

Rebecca burst into tears, "Oh no, that's the last thing I need. I don't want a baby!"

"I have a letter here to give to your GP; I looked at your notes, it's a Dr Judith Roberts you see at the medical centre in Medway Road. Make an appointment with her, she will keep an eye on your progress and in the meantime I suggest you eat properly and look after yourself."

"Thank you Doctor, can I go now I feel fine?"

"I don't see why not, your tests were normal; try not to stress too much, it's not good for you or the baby."

Rebecca ordered a taxi to pick her up outside the hospital to take her to the supermarket to get her car. The journey home was horrendous, she was in a state of shock, how would she explain to Richard – he had made it plain he wasn't keen on getting to know the twins just yet or did he even like children? How stupid to put herself in that predicament, what a nightmare and how was she going to explain to her mum and dad and the girls she was pregnant?

When she arrived indoors she made herself a cuppa and sat at the kitchen table trying to take everything in. She felt she had to talk to someone, her head was spinning and just then the phone rang and she picked it up. "It's you Mum, I was just about to ring you."

"What did the doctor say, Rebecca?"

"I'll tell you when I see you Mum, when you pick the

children up from school bring them over to me."

"Now you're getting me worried Rebecca, tell me now."

"Alright Mum, you're going to find out anyway. Do you remember me telling you about Richard I've been seeing? Well, the doctor told me I am pregnant – Richard's the father."

"Dearie me Rebecca, I don't know what to say. I'll pick the girls up and I'll be with you soon."

Rebecca paced up and down waiting for her mum to arrive. When the doorbell rang, she opened the door and flung her arms around her mum, in tears.

"What's wrong Mum?" Mary asked.

"Go upstairs and change your clothes, you too Amy – your mum is feeling unwell, she'll be fine soon it's just a migraine, nothing to worry about."

Grace sat with Rebecca on the settee. "I don't want the baby, Mum."

"Hush, you're in shock my girl, don't talk like that. What do you think Richard will say?"

"He'll run for the hills Mum, I told you I don't think he's much of a family man."

"Never mind him, you have to concentrate on yourself and the baby."

"The doctor told me I have to stop skipping meals, that's how I had a brief fainting spell."

"Rebecca you make me so cross, I've told you about this before – you eat like a bird, you could do with building up. Now I want you to promise me you'll eat healthily."

"I will Mum. I'm sorry I cause you so much worry and Dad."

"Look my darling, the way I see it what's happened has happened, you just have to get on with it. The twins will be over the moon to have a brother or sister and me and your dad will be grandparents to three children – how exciting is that?"

"Mum you amaze me, you are always thinking positive."

"I don't always Rebecca, but when you can't change things you have to make the most of the situation. What's done is done, you have to deal with it the best way you can. I think I'll take the girls home with me Rebecca and give you a break, you can collect them from school tomorrow. You need time on your own to take everything in and maybe you can talk to Richard and see what he has to say."

"I'm not sure I will today Mum, I'm shattered, but I wouldn't mind time on my own; it's not fair on the children if I keep getting upset in front of them."

Rebecca called the girls down from upstairs and they were both happy to go with their nanna to her home, she always spoilt them – they got to watch a lot of videos and have lots of treats. Rebecca said goodbye to her mum and the girls and thirty minutes later she plucked up the courage to phone Richard.

"Hello, it's me Rebecca."

"It's lovely to hear from you, so you decided to ring me after all – do you want to go out for a drink tonight Rebecca?"

"I'd rather you came to my place Richard, say about seven o'clock. I'm not feeing too well so I won't be drinking but we can get a takeaway when you come."

"Sounds great to me, see you then Rebecca. Where are the twins?"

"Staying at their nanna's – is that convenient enough for you?"

"What do you mean by that remark Rebecca? I was only asking you."

"Never mind, see you later Richard," and she put the phone down.

Rebecca was having a lie down and had slept for a few hours when the doorbell rang. She went downstairs and opened the door, Richard gave her a kiss and had a bottle of wine in his hand.

"I told you I didn't want a drink Richard."

"You don't but I do Rebecca, I've had a busy day at work. You look terrible Rebecca – is it the flu? Your eyes are all puffy…"

"Come and sit down in the sitting room Richard, I need to talk to you."

"Blimey you sound serious, what's happened?"

"I had a fainting spell and went to the hospital and, to cut a long story short, they told me I'm pregnant."

"I think I need that drink Rebecca. You're saying it's mine?"

"For god's sake Richard, who else's could it be? You're the only man I've been with since I've been separated from Jim."

"How do I know you haven't been seeing someone else before me?"

"Get lost you bastard, I want you to leave right now."

"Calm down Rebecca, I was only asking, it's a lot to take in. You know you have options – you can get rid of it."

"I always knew you were irresponsible Richard, and I don't intend to get rid of it as you put it. I don't believe in abortions, the only reason I'm telling you this is I know for a fact you are the father and every child should know where they come from."

Richard bent over and put his hands over his face, Rebecca felt a bit sorry for him. "Listen, I admit I have got feelings for you Richard and I know it's a lot to take in. I just want to hear from you there's a future for me and you – or am I kidding myself?"

"If you insist on keeping the baby Rebecca, I'll give you my support in any way I can, but I have to make a confession to you."

"What's that?" Rebecca asked.

"Rose isn't my sister, she's my girlfriend, we live together but things haven't been working out between us and she's moving out next week. My head's all over the place."

"I can't believe you want me to feel sorry for you, are you mad? I was always suspicious you were up to something, that's why you never invited me to your place – and tell me, how long has she been living with you?"

"Three weeks before I met you."

"What a slimeball you are Richard, a compulsive liar. Now get out of my house and don't even think of ringing me, I can't trust you as far as I can throw you – you're pathetic," and Rebecca stood up and gave him a big slap on his face.

Richard walked out the door and Rebecca locked it and sat at the kitchen table in floods of tears. She took the bottle of wine that Richard had left, opened it and poured herself a large glass, she felt like drowning her sorrows. She vowed never to trust another man again.

The next morning Rebecca woke up with a splitting headache and was pleased she didn't have to go into work. She put her dressing gown on and went downstairs to the kitchen and made herself a cuppa and a slice of toast and took two paracetamols. The phone rang, it was her mum.

"I've just dropped the girls off at school Rebecca, how are you? Did you speak to Richard?"

"I did Mum, he told me he's been living with Rose who he told me in the beginning was his sister, the lying cheat."

"Don't upset yourself Rebecca, if I were you I'd concentrate on yourself and the girls, at least you know where you stand. Would you like me to come over?"

"No Mum, I'm fine, stop fussing. I'll give you a ring

later, thanks for having the girls. Did you tell Dad I'm pregnant?"

"I did but you know what he's like, he worries about you, he keeps things to himself, he probably doesn't know what to say. I just want you to stay strong my girl."

"I will Mum, I love you."

"Me too Rebecca – I'll speak to you later on, your dad's calling me."

Rebecca got herself dressed and picked up the car keys from the kitchen table. She had to go shopping and would have to make an appointment to see her GP at the medical centre.

When she parked the car outside the medical centre she got out of the car and walked in; it was packed with patients in the waiting room and she went up to the desk and got an appointment for a few days' time. She hurried back to her car and drove it to the supermarket car park. All she felt like doing was to go home and to stay in bed, burying her head under the covers, but she knew she had to face up to what was happening and there was no running away from it.

When she was walking around the supermarket she bumped into Todd, "Long time no see, how is Daisy?"

"She's fine Rebecca, and how are the twins?"

"Still bundles of mischief. Do you fancy a coffee Todd – in the café next door – I can't remember what I've come in here for."

"I will have one with you Rebecca. I'll meet you in the café, I just need to put my groceries through the check out, I've done all my shopping."

"Okay Todd, I'll see you in there."

Rebecca ordered two coffees and sat at the table near the window, and it wasn't long before Todd came in and sat with her. "What have you been up to Rebecca?"

"Well for a start I'm pregnant Todd."

"You don't look happy? I was just about to congratulate you."

"The guy I was seeing was living with someone else unbeknown to me."

"What a swine! Some people have no morals. I'm sorry to hear that Rebecca."

"You're so sweet Todd, I'm surprised you haven't met anyone yourself."

"Probably because I haven't been looking."

"Thanks a lot Todd."

"Don't be daft Rebecca, I didn't mean you, I meant I don't have the time with looking after my girl. Being a one-parent family it isn't easy to find babysitters; my parents are great but I can't always ask them, they have loads of hobbies and they have a life of their own."

"I understand Todd. My parents are great too but they're quite elderly, do you think you'll ever meet anyone Todd?"

"Of course I do, one day; but I think when you have a child to think about you have to be careful, me and my daughter come as a package. Before my wife died I promised her I would give Daisy a good life so she will grow up confident and happy."

"You're amazing Todd, a fantastic father."

"Thanks Rebecca, you can only do your best. I wouldn't change anything, my Daisy is my world. Why don't you give me a ring anytime you want, you have my number Rebecca – you may just need a chat. I'll have to go now I have chores to do at home – the joys of fatherhood!"

"I'll give you a ring, bye Todd."

Rebecca went back into the supermarket and did all her shopping. She loved talking to Todd, he was an inspiration; how he lost his wife to cancer and looked after his daughter, the two were very close.

Rebecca put her shopping in the boot of the car and drove straight home and when she arrived, her next door neighbour Irene was standing on her doorstep. Rebecca stepped out of the car, "Are you alright Irene?"

"There was a lady called Linda came to see you not long ago, you've just missed her, she said she will ring you."

"Thanks, do you want to come in for a cuppa?"

"I don't want to put you out Rebecca."

"Don't be silly, I'll just get the two bags of shopping out of the boot of the car."

When Rebecca had put her shopping away and made the tea, they sat at the kitchen table. "You look tired," Irene remarked.

"I am a bit, do you fancy a ginger biscuit or can I make you a sandwich?"

"Oh that's kind of you, but I'm fine Rebecca, I'm set in my ways – I have my porridge oats for breakfast every morning, and at lunch time I have a sandwich and a light evening meal."

"I wish I was like you Irene, I'm always skipping meals."

"You shouldn't, young lady, what have you eaten today?"

"I've had a slice of toast."

"Well I'll make myself useful and make you a sandwich Rebecca."

"If you insist, I'll have a cheese and ham one thanks Irene. I'm eating for two now, you may as well know – everybody else will when I get bigger."

"Is the father that handsome man that comes to see you?"

"You nosey bugger Irene, you don't miss much do you."

"I'm sorry Rebecca, I hope I haven't upset you."

"I'm only joking Irene, but you're right, it is him. I told

him to sling his hook – I just found out from him he's living with someone."

"His loss Rebecca, I believe he did you a favour telling you when there is no trust. You're better off without him, and if you need anything just knock on my door Rebecca. I don't mind babysitting any time."

"Thank you, you're a star Irene, I'm so lucky to have you as a neighbour."

"The same goes for me – if you need shopping or any help, just let me know. I'll go now and thank you for the tea. I meant every word I said Rebecca."

"I'll catch up with you another time – bye… wait a minute Irene, why don't you have a bite to eat with me and the girls tonight, I'm going to collect them from school soon, it won't be much maybe just a chicken salad."

"If you're sure Rebecca, but I've made a cottage pie – there's enough for us all, I always tend to make far too much and freeze the rest."

"Sounds delicious Irene, you're on. I'm not in the mood to cook, let's say about six o clock? I'll do the salad, so I'll see you later."

Rebecca made a salad and put it in the fridge. She put on her coat and picked up her car keys and climbed into the car. When she arrived outside the school gates the girls were waiting for her and they climbed into the back seat.

"Have you both had a good day at school?"

"Boring," Amy remarked. "I hate PE and the teacher kept telling me off for talking to Lilly."

"You're a little chatterbox Amy, I don't blame the teacher, you have to pay attention otherwise you won't learn anything."

"Alright Mum, don't you start. Mary does the same but she never gets told off, I think she's the teacher's pet."

"No I'm not, take that back!" Mary shouted at Amy

with a face like thunder.

"You two stop arguing. Irene is having dinner with us and I want you both to be on your best behaviour."

When they arrived home Rebecca told the girls to get changed and give Goldie some fresh water and food. Meanwhile she made a phone call to Linda who answered the phone; she was pleased it wasn't Ben her husband.

"I heard you called around my place today, is everything alright?"

"I just wanted a catch-up Rebecca, and to tell you face-to-face Ben has moved out of the house and agreed to a divorce. I'm on my own with Tommy, what a relief! He said I can have the house and everything in it but he wants me to sign over the rentals to him and I agreed. Tommy loves living here, he has all his friends nearby and his school and it makes life easier for us both. So Ben will be your landlord and I'll have no say in anything he does. I know I told you not to worry about him putting you out of the property, you only have to deal with me and I meant it Rebecca, but I have to think about what's best for me and Tommy. I hope we can still stay good friends Rebecca?"

"Don't worry about it Linda, I intend to move out just as soon as possible and if the worst comes to the worst I will move back in with my mum and dad till I get myself sorted. I'm pleased things turned out okay for you though, I'm really happy for you. We'll meet up sometime soon, I'll give you a ring – I must dash now I'm in the middle of cooking dinner," and she put the phone down. That was a lie, she felt a tinge of jealousy, why was her life so complicated? Apart from struggling with money she felt trapped. Linda had her freedom, ready to move on with her life and a beautiful house in the bargain. She knew Ben would always give financial help for Tommy, he adored him being an only child. She got the feeling Linda would always fall on her feet and could never imagine she went through hard times like herself. But reality set in when she thought of Ben her husband, what a disgusting man, he was such a creep who had the nerve to try it on her – god knows what he was like to live with, so she felt guilty being envious about her friend. Who was she to judge? Linda had worked hard for what she had and if she was put in that situation herself she would put her girls first, anything for a peaceful life. She hoped Ben didn't give her any aggro like before and turn up at the house uninvited, the thought gave her shivers up her spine having him as the landlord…

Mary interrupted her thoughts, she was crying at the top of her voice. "What on earth is going on?" Rebecca shouted up the stairs.

"It's Amy, Mum, she pushed me and I've hurt my arm," Mary replied sobbing.

"I want you both to come downstairs, you can play in the garden and get some fresh air. I'm going to take the TV out of the bedroom tomorrow – you're always sitting in the room watching cartoons which is not good for you both."

"Mum, please don't do that, you're being horrid and it's your fault – you're always telling us to go to our room."

"You have a point, Amy. Well things are going to change around here, and say sorry to your sister, no fighting, you know how sensitive she is, Amy."

The doorbell rang and Rebecca opened the door – it was Irene, she was holding a large casserole dish, "I've heated the cottage pie up. I'll put it on the work surface Rebecca and leave you to dish up."

"It looks delicious Irene, sit at the table and I'll call the girls, they're in the garden."

When they were all seated around the kitchen table eating their dinner, Rebecca was surprised how the girls were tucking in and enjoying it without talking.

"This is delicious Irene, you must give me the recipe.

Did you put grated cheese on the top?"

"I did, Rebecca, I'm glad you like it."

"My mum can't cook," Amy grinned.

"I doubt that," Irene smiled, "but I'll tell you a secret – I love baking fairy cakes the best. Perhaps your mum will let you two come to my house one day after school and we can make some, girls."

"Yes please," the girls said in chorus.

"I don't see why not," Rebecca grinned, "but I'll warn you Irene, they will tire you out – they have loads of energy."

"Now let me wash the dishes, you put your feet up, Rebecca."

"No Irene, you've done enough – now can I make you a cuppa?"

"No thanks, I have to go and feed Bob. I have a memory like a sieve, I forgot to feed him earlier."

"Can we come with you Irene, we'd love to see your cat?"

"Of course you can, Amy and Mary."

"Alright, only for one hour Irene and tell them to come straight home, they both need a bath, and you two be good."

"We will Mum," and they both held Irene's hands and walked out the door.

Rebecca washed the dishes and made herself a cuppa and sat on the settee and put her feet up. It had been a long day and she was pleased it was nearly over. There was a knock at the door, 'Bloody hell,' she thought, 'it must be the girls, that hour went quick,' but when she opened it there was a smart young man standing there with a briefcase in his hand.

"Can I help you?" Rebecca asked.

"I hope you don't mind me calling at this time of the evening – here's my card, I was seeing a client in the area."

"Oh I see," she said when she looked at the card, she

recognised the name Andrew Clifford.

"You're the estate agent I briefly spoke to on the phone, what can I do for you? I've already made an appointment with you to view the property in a few days' time."

"I know, I tried to ring you Mrs Taylor but couldn't get through. The client I was supposed to show around the property you're interested in tomorrow has changed her mind so I thought I could show you around instead if you are available."

"Blimey, you're very keen, do you always call on your clients when you can't reach them on the phone?"

Andrew smiled, "Not really, let's just say I'm enthusiastic. I love my job and I had the pleasure of meeting your lovely mum."

"You're lucky, I'm not working tomorrow but I have to take my two girls to school – is nine thirty any good to you?"

"That's fine, I'll meet you here Mrs Taylor and we'll take my car and I'll bring you home, or you can follow me in your car."

"Sounds great to me, I can pop in and see my mum and dad. Thanks Mr Clifford."

"Please just call me Andrew. I'll see you tomorrow, bye for now."

'That's strange,' Rebecca thought to herself, her phone had been working all day, maybe Andrew wrote the wrong number down?

She closed the door, but it was not long afterwards that the doorbell rang again. Rebecca opened the door, "You're a sweetheart, thanks Irene for having them, you must be tired. What do you say girls?"

"Thank you Irene. Can we have a cat Mum?" Amy asked.

"No you certainly can't. Now I want you both to go upstairs, it's bath time. I hope they behaved themselves Irene?"

"They're a pleasure to have, lovely company and very polite. Goodnight Rebecca, I'll collect my casserole dish tomorrow when the girls come to my house to make some fairy cakes."

Rebecca bathed the girls and put them to bed. She went downstairs and put the telly on, but she couldn't concentrate on it so she switched it off. She stretched her legs and dozed off on the settee and when she woke up it was pitch black outside, so she drew the curtains, locked up and went straight upstairs to bed. She was glad the day was over; she got undressed, climbed into bed and fell fast asleep.

The next morning she woke up and switched the alarm clock off and climbed out of bed. "Please God," she muttered to herself, "make this a good day, give me strength." She wasn't religious but always felt there was a higher being up there somewhere and she needed all the help she could get.

She got dressed and went downstairs and went into the kitchen and made herself a cuppa. She noticed there was a little drop of wine left in the bottle in the fridge so she poured it down the sink; what was she thinking of drinking wine and being pregnant? What a stupid thing to do. She decided to take her mum's advice and eat healthily and made herself a bowl of porridge and put some cereal out for the girls and made some toast with honey on it.

Amy was the first one to walk into the kitchen. "Do I have to go to school today Mum? I don't feel well."

"Let me feel your brow, you haven't got a temperature, but okay you can have the day off. So you won't be making fairy cakes with Irene after school, just Mary, and I was thinking of taking you both out on Saturday to buy you both some new shoes and maybe popping into the toy shop – but I can see you're not up to that, Amy."

"I think if I drink my milk and eat my breakfast I'll feel much better Mum."

"Good idea Amy, now where is your sister?"

Rebecca shouted up the stairs and Mary came down and glanced out of the window and could see the postman coming up the driveway.

"Mum it's the postman."

"I'll get it, you go and sit at the table Mary."

Rebecca opened the door, "Good morning Frank, it's chilly today."

"I think we may have some rain later on, have a good day," and he handed Rebecca a letter. When she closed the door she went to sit at the kitchen table and opened it. Finally, she thought to herself, some good news – it was from her solicitor – her money from the sale of the property had been transferred into her bank account which put a smile on her face.

"I want you to finish your breakfast, girls, you don't want to be late for school. I'm just going to put some make-up on, I'll be back in a tick."

Rebecca collected the girls' school bags from upstairs and came down and washed up the breakfast dishes and tidied up the sitting room. "Chop! chop! Come on, girls, let's go or we'll be late." They hurried out the door and the girls climbed into the back of the car.

There was hardly any traffic on the road. Rebecca dropped the girls off at the school entrance, kissed them goodbye and watched them walk into the school yard, then drove straight back to her house. Five minutes later, Andrew drew up in his car and opened his car window, "Are you ready for the off, Mrs Taylor?"

"I am, I'll follow you Andrew."

When they arrived at the property Rebecca was shocked to see the garden so overgrown. "Blimey, it needs some work on it Andrew!"

"You have to look beyond that, it's a good size garden. Anyway, let's go inside."

"I can see the potential. They are good size rooms similar to my mum's bungalow; the kitchen needs gutting out and the bathroom also needs replacing which will cost me but I love the property Andrew."

"To be honest that's why the client has put down the price already Mrs Taylor."

"For goodness sake, call me Rebecca. I can imagine you have a lot of buyers after this property – it's perfect for me and my two girls. How much is he asking for it?"

"£135,000 which is a steal; it's got three bedrooms and this is a good area so it's a good investment for the future Rebecca."

"I'm sold Andrew, and the good news is I'm a cash buyer – my money from the sale of my property has come through but I would like you to try and get the price down to £125,000 so I can have some money left over to do the work on it."

"I'll ask my client. I can't make any promises but I'll be in touch soon Rebecca. Lovely meeting you."

"You too Andrew, and thanks for your help. Just one thing though, you said yesterday you couldn't get me on the phone, but it was working perfectly okay."

"It's my fault Rebecca, I put the wrong number down in my diary, I noticed when I called into the office this morning. Sorry about that."

"No worries, I guessed that. I'll speak to you soon Andrew – bye."

Rebecca walked over the road to her parents' bungalow and her mum was pleased to see her.

"I've been viewing the property across the road Mum and have made an offer."

"That's wonderful! Let me put the kettle on and you can tell me all about it."

"Where's Dad, Mum?"

"He's next door talking to Pete."

"I dread seeing him, I bet he thinks I'm a stupid cow getting myself pregnant."

"You know your dad, he doesn't say much, he just worries about you. Never mind him, what do you think of the bungalow?"

"I love it Mum and the girls will. I've put an offer in for £125,000 – it's £10,000 under the asking price, let's just see what happens."

"I think that sounds a bit low Rebecca, but I may be wrong."

"Mum the property needs a lot of money spent on it, it's been quite neglected. I'm not going to worry, I'll see what Andrew says but I'll be disappointed if I don't get it as I told him I'm a cash buyer. My money has been transferred into my bank account – I got a letter from my solicitor this morning Mum."

"That is fantastic Rebecca, let's just keep our fingers crossed and think positive."

Bert walked into the kitchen, "I thought I could hear your voice Rebecca, come and give me a hug."

"I thought you would be cross with me, Dad."

"What on earth for?"

"You know why Dad, because I'm pregnant."

"I would much prefer you to be married and settled down with someone, to put my mind at rest, but what's done is done – now where's my tea Grace, and I'll have a slice of ginger cake."

"Yes sir, what did your last servant die of?"

"Shush woman, I'm going outside to sit in the garden."

"I'm so lucky to have parents like you two, you're both my rock."

"We're quite close as a family Rebecca, but you're our daughter and you have given us two beautiful grandchildren, and the one on the way we'll love just the same."

"I don't want Richard to have any part in bringing up the baby Mum."

"I think it's early days to talk like that, he may have a change of heart when the baby arrives."

"I don't want anything to do with him."

"I'm not saying you do Rebecca, but you do know he has his rights being the father. Anyway let's just forget about him, it's more important you take good care of yourself. Do you want a sandwich?"

"Can I have a ham and tomato one, Mum, with a few crisps on the side?"

"I'll just take your dad his tea and cake out to him in the garden and then I'll make you one. Go and relax in the sitting room and put your feet up."

"You're spoiling me, Mum."

"You know me, I hate sitting around doing nothing, it makes my joints stiff. I must admit you're looking a bit pale Rebecca."

"Give over, I'm always white as a ghost Mum, that's my colouring. I'd better go and see Dad in the garden."

"I'll join you in a minute, he's probably having a sly ciggy."

Rebecca went out into the garden and had a chat with her dad. "The garden is looking beautiful, you'll have to do mine if I buy the property across the road Dad."

"You've seen it Rebecca?"

"Yes I just viewed it and I've put an offer in Dad."

"How much Rebecca?"

"£135,000 but I'm trying to get it down to £125,000 because the garden is in a terrible state and the bungalow needs updating."

"I wish I was up to doing the garden for you Rebecca, if you are lucky enough to get it, but I'm finding this garden too much for me lately."

"Don't be daft Dad, I wouldn't dream of asking you, I was only joking. I'm sure there's plenty of gardeners out there looking for work… oh by the way, my money has been put into my account Dad."

"I'm pleased for you my girl, but just watch the pennies. Your mum told me the bungalow needs a lot of work doing to it."

"I'm not stupid, I know that, Dad. Money will still be tight even if I do purchase the property, my job hardly pays the bills. I'm going to look for another job which pays more; it would be ideal if I can get one working from home but that's just wishful thinking."

"You know me and your mum will help you in any way we can."

"I know that but I shouldn't have to depend on you two, I'm sure things will be fine."

"Now stop stressing and go and get your dad another tea."

"Mum waits on you hand and foot Dad, you're spoilt."

"I know, but you must admit she's looking fit, that's all down to me," he said chuckling.

"I heard that," Grace commented when she walked into the garden, "how about you getting fit Bert? I must find you more jobs to do, like tidying the shed out for a start."

"My back is playing me up and my knees; you have enough to do Grace without nursing me. I prefer to take things steady."

"If you get any more laid back I will be wondering if you are alive or dead Bert, you're getting a lazy bugger."

"You two, what are you like the pair of you!" Rebecca laughed, "You're always having a go at each other."

"I just put it in one ear and out the other what your mum says, Rebecca, she loves spoiling me really."

"I'm going to shoot off, Mum."

"Have you got the girls at the weekend?"

"I have, I've promised them I'll take them to buy them some new shoes and buy them a treat at the toy shop, it's not often I can afford to do that. It's you who spoils them Mum."

Bert took £30 out of his pocket, "Here take this Rebecca, and buy them something nice."

"Dad what are you like, you don't have to."

"I was just going to spend it on more plants at the garden centre which I don't need."

"Thanks Dad, I'll tell the girls you bought them their shoes. I'm off, speak to you later Mum."

On the journey home Rebecca decided to treat herself and have a wash and cut at the hairdresser's near her, she didn't have an appointment but she thought she'd try her luck if the salon wasn't busy. Some salons would fit you in, so she parked her car outside the salon "Turning Heads" got out of the car and walked inside. She went to the reception area where there was a young girl on the desk, "Can I help you?" She spoke in a friendly voice.

"I haven't got an appointment, I just wanted a wash and cut – can you fit me in?"

The hairdresser that was seeing to a customer overheard, "If you take a seat I'll be with you in five minutes."

"Thanks," Rebecca replied and took her coat off and hung it on the coat stand. It wasn't long before she was asked to go through to the back of the shop and the trainee young girl who was on the desk washed her hair. Then she was introduced to Sally, the stylist, who showed her where to sit.

"I just want about an inch cut off," Rebecca commented.

"You have a good head of hair, it's so thick, you're lucky – mine is so blooming fine."

"Thanks, but it's hard to manage sometimes. Have you

been working here long?"

"Me and my partner Ian own the salon, we've had it for about five years. I'm sure I've seen you somewhere before, what's your name?"

"Rebecca Taylor."

"Do you ever go to the Stag pub?"

"I do sometimes, I live just up the road from there and I used to work in 'Hair with Flair'. I'm a hairdresser Sally, you may know June who was my boss."

"Oh her, yes I knew June who owns the salon, she was friends with my sister – I can't stand her. She's a real bitch, a nasty cow to her customers but I have heard through the grapevine the shop is closed down. Oh sorry, trust me to open my big mouth – was she a good friend of yours?"

Rebecca grinned, "Don't worry, I couldn't stand her myself. I left the salon because of her bitchy ways."

"Where are you working now?"

"I'm currently working at a Residential Home for the elderly, Sally, but the money isn't great so I'm thinking of leaving."

"I'm closing the salon down in a few weeks' time to have a refit done but I'll be looking for more staff, so if you're interested Rebecca, give me your number and I'll be in touch."

"Thanks Sally, have you got a pen and paper and I'll write it down."

"Hold on a tick," and Sally brushed the hairs off Rebecca's clothes, "I haven't cut too much off your hair, is that okay Rebecca?"

"That's lovely Sally, it's ages since I had my hair done; the ends were getting so split, it looks great, thanks."

Rebecca paid at the desk and left her number and when she looked at the clock on the wall above the desk she panicked and hurried to get into the car. She had forgotten the time and was running late to pick the girls up from school.

There was a lot of traffic on the road and when she finally arrived at the school gates and climbed out of the car, she saw Amy and Mary were waiting in the school yard with their class teacher. All the other children had gone, "I'm so sorry I'm late Miss Clark."

"Not to worry," she replied, looking annoyed.

Rebecca was pleased to get home with the girls, she had terrible back pain and felt a bit sickly, so she made herself a cuppa while the girls played on the swing and slide in the garden.

The phone rang and she picked it up, "Hello Rebecca, it's me, I've just received my decree nisi this morning in the post – have you got yours?"

"Not yet Jim. Is that what you rang to tell me?"

"No, I was just wondering if I could have the girls this weekend so they can go and visit their uncle and the family."

"I'm sorry Jim, no way. I've made plans to take them out and you can't just have the girls when you feel like having them. Let's just stick to what we're doing, otherwise they'll get confused."

"You're a hard woman Rebecca."

"I'm a realist and I'm not really bothered what you think of me Jim. I can't wait to get the decree absolute."

"I'm not going to argue with you Rebecca. Give the girls my love."

"Will do – bye," and Rebecca put the phone down.

The doorbell rang and she opened the door, "Come in Irene."

"Have I come at a bad time Rebecca, you look really fed up?"

"I'm alright Irene. I'll call the girls, they're in the garden. I hope you don't mind having them, they're looking forward to making fairy cakes."

When the girls walked into the kitchen they were excited to see Irene. "Can we go now Mum?" Amy asked.

"Yes you can, and be good you two. You should really have changed your clothes first, you both know the rules but I'll let you off the hook this time. See you later, girls."

Rebecca made a ham and egg salad for the girls for later on and put it in the fridge, and made herself a ham salad sandwich and went into the sitting room and put her feet up. Her back started to pain even more so she went into the kitchen and took two paracetamols with a glass of water. She hadn't been lifting anything so was baffled what it could be caused by, she had never been troubled with back pain like this before.

The phone rang, 'Christ,' she thought to herself, 'no peace for the wicked, who the hell is ringing me now?' and she picked it up.

"Hi Rebeca, it's me Andrew. I'm pleased to tell you my client has accepted your offer on the property and has taken it off the market. I would just like to know your solicitor's details."

"That's fantastic news Andrew, can I give you a ring in the morning if you don't mind?"

"No worries Rebecca, I'll speak to you then, bye for now – have a nice evening."

The pains in her back were getting worse so she filled a hot water bottle up and put it behind her back, and lay down on the settee. She had a little doze and when she woke up half an hour later she looked at the clock, 'Blimey, the girls must be hungry by now. I'll knock next door,' but she didn't have to as when she opened the door Irene was just about to ring the bell. She was holding a large cake tin, "They have enjoyed themselves and they made twelve fairy cakes Rebecca."

"Mum, they're yummy," Mary said, getting all excited.

"Thank you so much Irene, I'll catch up with you another time – oh wait a tick, I'll just get you your casserole dish. You girls must be hungry, go and sit at the kitchen table."

Rebecca gave them their salad and a glass of milk each, "I'm not hungry," Mary moaned.

"Neither am I," Amy said, pulling a face.

"No, because you two have been stuffing yourselves with cakes no doubt."

"We only had three each Mum."

"Disgusting, Amy, nothing for you to giggle about. Well you both must drink all of your milk and I'll make you a sandwich later on."

The evening was spent watching cartoons with the girls. Rebecca had watched the same videos over and over again with them and was pleased when they went upstairs to put their pyjamas on and were happy to read their books in bed, neither of them were hungry. So Rebecca went downstairs and made herself a cuppa and tidied up the kitchen, and did some ironing.

There was silence upstairs, not a peep out of the girls. She crept up the stairs and saw both of them were fast asleep, so she put their lights out and ran herself a hot bath. She had a good soak and then put on her nightdress, and it wasn't too long before she was tucked up in bed herself and was soon out for the count.

The next morning Rebecca climbed out of bed and looked out of the window, it was pelting down with rain. She didn't feel so good but she managed to muster up some strength to get herself dressed and went downstairs into the kitchen to make herself a cuppa and a slice of toast. It wasn't too long before the girls appeared.

"How about I make you both a boiled egg with soldiers, you two?"

"I just want cornflakes with banana on top Mum."

"Me too," Mary piped up.

"Okay, if that's what you both want. I was just thinking if I pick you both up from school tonight we could go for a burger and chips."

"Can we have ice-cream too, Mum?"

"Yes Amy you can, but not unless you both eat all your breakfast up, and then go upstairs and give the hamster fresh water and some food."

"He's called Goldie, Mum."

"I know that, Mary, you silly billy. I have some good news, girls – how would you both feel about moving in the same street as Nanna and Grandad? If everything goes well, the bungalow I've chosen is just directly opposite them."

"Yippee!" Amy said, jumping up and down.

"What about you Mary?"

"I'd like that Mum, but are we going to another school?"

"Don't be daft, of course not, everything will stay the same. It will take some time to move, it won't be for a long time yet, but now what I want you both to do is quickly go and get your school bags from upstairs and put your coats on and I'll take you to school."

Rebecca washed the breakfast dishes up and put her coat on and it wasn't long before they all climbed into the car. The journey took twenty minutes and when she dropped the girls off at school she headed straight back home. She had a few phone calls to make before she started work; her first customer of the morning was a Mrs Thomson who had booked a late appointment for a cut and blow wave.

When she got indoors she rang Andrew Clifford the estate agent and gave him the details of her solicitor and then rang her mum. "Guess what Mum, my offer on the bungalow has been accepted."

"That's wonderful my darling, your dad will be over the moon when I tell him, he's next door with Pete at the moment. Did you tell the girls?"

"I did Mum, they're excited only because they'll be living near you and Dad and you both spoil them rotten.

I think at their age though they are not so much bothered about seeing the bungalow, so I'll take them to see it when I get the work done on it which won't be for quite some time with my luck."

"What about the baby, have you mentioned anything?"

"Don't be ridiculous Mum, it's early days. I'm not going to say a word and I don't want you and Dad to either."

"You're right, pet. Are you off to work now?"

"I am, Mum, I'll speak to you later."

Rebecca put her coat on and grabbed her car keys off the kitchen table. She went to the front door to open it and noticed a letter on the mat; she opened it up and saw that it was her decree nisi so she put it in her bag. She didn't feel like going to work but knew every penny counted and she would just have to put up with the job for a while longer.

The journey to work was a nightmare, there had been an accident on the road and the traffic was diverted so it took much longer to get there and Mrs Thomson, her client, was waiting for her outside the salon. "Sorry I'm a bit late, the traffic was horrendous on the roads," and she took the key out of her pocket and opened up the salon.

"I haven't been waiting long Rebecca, you're here now, that's all that matters."

"How are you Mrs Thomson?"

"Not too bad, a few aches and pains, but at eighty-three I have to expect that. I mustn't grumble, only about the weather – it's shocking today, it puts me off leaving my bungalow, I was in two minds whether to ring you or not Rebecca to cancel my appointment today."

"Thank you for making so much of an effort to come, it can't have been easy for you Mrs Thompson, not with your hip problems."

"I'm just waiting to go into hospital to have an operation, god knows when that will be but there are plenty of people worse off than me. I have been lucky in life Rebecca, right up till last year before I had my nasty fall. I was in good shape so I can't complain."

Rebecca finished doing Mrs Thomson's hair and had three more clients after that. She was pleased when she was finished so she could make herself a cuppa and put her feet up before she swept the salon floor and cleaned all the mirrors.

Adam

Two weeks had passed since Rebecca's offer had been accepted on the bungalow, so she rang her solicitor to find out if it would be possible to take a builder into the property to get some quotes on various jobs that needed doing. Her solicitor said she would speak to the vendor's solicitor and would get back to her.

It was Friday morning, the girls were at school and their dad was picking them up from school to stay with him for the weekend. She was pleased about that because her back was still giving her pain; even Dr Roberts who examined her the week before at the clinic in Medway Road about her pregnancy didn't seem very concerned when she mentioned it, and she was told just to take two paracetamols for the pain. So she booked herself in for a further appointment, 'Get a grip,' she thought to herself, 'it's either something or nothing at all,' and her train of thought went when she heard the phone ringing and picked it up.

"Do you fancy going for a drink tonight, stranger?"

"Who's that?"

"Me, Valerie your friend who you haven't kept in touch with."

"I'm sorry Valerie, I meant to give you a bell."

"Don't be daft, I'm only kidding Rebecca."

"God you must be due to have the baby any time soon surely?"

"Not far off, but I've got cabin fever, I can't remember when I last went out with any of my friends they don't bother asking me now because I don't drink like them anymore. Not that I want to, being pregnant, my Rob would do his nut if he thought I was."

"You can't call them true friends Valerie, they should understand. I'd love to go out with you tonight, I'll meet you in the Stag pub – say about eight o'clock – will Rob be there?"

"No, he'll be looking after the boys."

"It will be great seeing you, we can have a good chinwag; I have loads to tell you Valerie."

"That's good, you know me, I love a bit of juicy gossip."

"You crack me up! I'll see you tonight, bye for now my dear friend."

Rebecca knew Valerie was a bit rough and ready, someone who speaks her mind but had a heart of gold; what you see is what you get with her. Valerie will get such a shock to know she was pregnant herself, she thought to herself, especially giving her advice when they last met up in the pub, to take precautions when she told her all about the way Richard was inconsistent and the way he had been treating her. She remembered her words: 'It only takes the once, Rebecca, to get pregnant, if you're not careful, you don't want to bring up three children on your own.'

It's funny how things had worked out; she always thought she was the lucky one who struck gold when she married Jim, owning her own house for a start, and a much better lifestyle than Valerie who had a holiday on a budget, while she was enjoying holidays abroad with the family, and had felt a bit sorry for her friend. Her life looked bleak; what kind of future did the family have? They were living on a rough council estate for a start, with a low income coming in. Her thoughts changed as time went by, noticing that Valerie and Rob were happy, so devoted to one another and always looked out for each other; having money wouldn't have made any difference to them, she thought they were so compatible and had the experience to take the rough with the smooth. It must be so wonderful to be in a relationship like that…

"Bloody hell, is that the time?" she gasped when she looked at her watch, "I must start getting changed to go out."

When she got dressed in a low-cut red dress and put on her make-up she was good to go, and took her black leather jacket out of the wardrobe. 'Should I drive to the pub or ring for a taxi?' she thought to herself, but soon realized there was no way she could drink much alcohol, not in her predicament, and took the car keys off the table and headed out the door and climbed into the car.

The journey only took about twenty minutes but when she arrived at the pub to park her car it was full. After driving around the block for five minutes, getting frustrated, she managed to find a spot to park it around the corner.

Rebecca walked into the pub and it was packed with customers and she saw Valerie sitting at a table next to the bar. She came up behind Valerie, and tapped on her shoulder and when Valerie turned around she stood up and gave her a hug.

"It's great to see you Rebecca, you look stunning."

"You look massive Valerie!"

"Oh thanks, remind me not to pay you a compliment again. You're right though, I am huge."

"I'll get the drinks in – what do you fancy Valerie?"

"I'll have a shandy. Hey, just check the barman out when you get the drinks – he's gorgeous, Rebecca."

When she went up to the bar and ordered a red wine and a shandy she could see what Valerie meant. Adam was a tall handsome man, slightly heavily built with a mass of blond curly hair and blue eyes. Rebecca blushed when he gave her a big smile. She paid for the drinks and took them to the table and when she glanced back at the bar she could see he was staring at her.

"Well, what do you think?"

"He's alright Valerie."

"Just alright? Christ he's so handsome – you need to go to Specsavers, Rebecca."

"You have your Rob."

"When I see a bloke so handsome I can look can't I?"

"What are you like! But yes, I agree with you Valerie, he is good looking. I've never seen him here before, he must be new," she grinned.

"Are you still seeing Richard?"

"No I'm not. His so-called sister Rose I was telling you about, Valerie, turned out to be his girlfriend he was living with. I certainly know how to pick them, what a deceitful liar he turned out to be."

"Good riddance to bad rubbish, I wouldn't give him a second thought Rebecca."

"Not as sorry as I am, I'm pregnant carrying his child."

"Holy Moses, Rebecca, does he know?"

"Yes he does but I told him to get lost, he's a piece of shit. I don't trust any man."

"Don't be foolish Rebecca, we all can make mistakes. Mr Right will come along one day."

"I hope so Valerie. You've done alright for yourself meeting Rob."

"I must admit he has his faults but I can never imagine my life without him in it."

"There is some good news to tell you – I put an offer on the bungalow opposite Mum's and it has been accepted, so I'm over the moon and the sooner I move out of my rental property the better, I have never really settled there knowing Ben was the landlord."

"That's great, but I think you have an admirer Rebecca – that bloke at the bar keeps staring at you."

"Would you like anther drink Valerie?"

"I'd love an orange juice please, and you shouldn't be drinking alcohol Rebecca."

"One more glass of red wine won't hurt and I'll check the barman out when I get the drinks," she said, winking at Valerie.

"You little minx, I don't blame you."

Adam smiled when she walked up to the bar. "One red wine and a glass of orange juice please. What are you staring at?"

"You – you're stunning, I can't keep my eyes off you. My name's Adam, what's yours?"

"Rebecca," she replied and took her purse out of her bag to pay for the drinks.

"These drinks are on me, I have a fifteen-minute break soon – you don't mind if I sit with you?"

"I'm with my friend but she won't mind," and she started to blush and went to sit back at the table. "Phew! Are my cheeks red, Valerie?"

"Blimey, I thought you'd gone off men Rebecca."

"Adam's his name; he's coming over in a minute to join us – is that alright?"

"Have I got a choice? I'm only kidding, look at your face! Did you notice if he was wearing a wedding ring Rebecca?"

"Shut up, I'm only having a bit of fun and anyway we got free drinks, I didn't have to pay."

Adam came to the table and Rebecca introduced Valerie and he sat down. "Are you married, have you any kids?" Valerie asked.

"Christ leave the poor man alone. I'm sorry Adam, you'll have to excuse my friend."

"That's alright and to answer your question – nah, I'm not married and as far as I know I have no kids out there," he replied with a grin on his face.

"How long have you been working here?" Valerie asked.

"I'm only filling in for a mate for a few days who I share a flat with. I'm a self-employed builder."

"That's interesting, I'll be looking for a builder soon. I've just had my offer on a bungalow accepted, but it needs work done to it – I need a refit on the kitchen and bathroom."

"I'll give you my card before you go, it's in my jacket pocket, and you can ring me Rebecca, anytime, no worries."

"How long have you been a builder for?" Valerie asked.

"I learned the trade from my uncle when I left school. I can give references to you Rebecca."

"Thanks Adam, I may do that."

"I'd better get back to the bar to finish my shift – would you two ladies like another drink?"

"No thanks we're fine."

"Okay Rebecca, I'll catch up with you later and give you my number."

"He put a smile on your face Rebecca, I could see you were flirting with him."

"You have a vivid imagination Valerie, no I wasn't."

"Bloody hell, I'd better make a move– my chauffeur has arrived, Rob's just walked in the door Rebecca. God the time went by quickly, listen I'll give you a ring tomorrow. I must dash, he hates hanging about waiting, you know what men are like they have no patience," and she gave Rebecca a kiss on the cheek.

Rebecca finished her drink and walked up to the bar, she caught Adam's attention and he came over. "Are you going now? Why don't you stay and have another drink, my shift will be finished shortly."

"No thanks I'm driving, Adam."

"Here's my card, I'd love to take you out for a meal sometime Rebecca."

"I have a lot going on at the moment; I'm going through a divorce and I don't think I'll be good company."

"Let me be the judge of that Rebecca, I'm a good listener."

"Have you got a pen and a piece of paper?"

"Yes I have," and Rebecca wrote her number down and she handed it to Adam. She was surprised when he bent over the bar and gave her a kiss on the lips. She turned around and walked out of the bar thinking she must be mad, but had a good feeling inside.

She walked to her car and climbed in. The weather was shocking, it was pouring down from the heavens and on the journey home she noticed one of her windscreen wipers wasn't working so she drove slowly and was relieved when she arrived at her house. She got out of the car and quickly went indoors. 'Bugger,' she thought to herself, 'one more thing I have to see to,' and took off her coat and made herself a cuppa and took it upstairs.

She got herself undressed and went to bed, and when she lay there drinking her tea she reflected on the evening. She had enjoyed herself with Valerie and Adam, but if he knew she was pregnant he would run for the hills and who could blame him. Still, there was no harm in going out for a meal if he asked her again. It had been a long time since she had felt good about herself and she turned the light off and snuggled under the covers and fell fast asleep.

The next morning she woke up and got dressed and went downstairs to the kitchen and made herself a cuppa and a bacon sarni. After breakfast she did all the housework from top to bottom and suddenly had to sit down, she felt painful cramp in her stomach which took her breath away. Just then, the doorbell rang and she opened it.

Irene could see she was doubled up in pain. "Dearie me, what's wrong Rebecca?"

"I'm not sure, I need to go to the toilet – come in Irene."

When she came downstairs she knew she was having a miscarriage. She had been with a friend years ago when she had one herself when they were having a day out at the fun-fair and went with her to the hospital.

"Irene, would you get my diary out of the top drawer over there please."

"Of course, what's wrong Rebecca? You look awful."

"I'm going to phone for the doctor to come out to see me," and when she rang she gave all her details to the receptionist and she confirmed she would have a home visit shortly.

"What do you want me to do?" Irene asked, looking anxious.

"Will you stay with me for a while, I need to put my nightdress on and go to bed."

"Let me help you Rebecca."

"Thanks Irene, there is a hot water bottle under the sink over there, will you fill it up for me – ouch!" she screamed out, "my stomach hurts."

Rebecca was tucked up in bed and Irene sat on the chair beside her and held her hand till the doctor arrived.

Sadly it was confirmed Rebecca had had a miscarriage and stayed resting in bed for ten days. Her mum and dad looked after the children and her mum informed Maggie her boss the reason why; she was very understanding and full of empathy. Irene was a good friend and there on hand every day to see to her needs till the doctor gave her the all clear and she could go back to work.

Rebecca felt a deep sadness in her heart but she knew she had to be strong for her girls who were told by their grandparents their mum had a nasty bout of flu. She was just coming around to the idea there was going to be a new arrival in the family and was relieved she never told the children she was pregnant. The doctor explained the pregnancy was not meant to be, but could not give her any explanation the reason why it had happened, only to say it would not stop her conceiving in the future and going on to have healthy children.

The doorbell rang and Rebecca opened the door, it was Irene, "Come in."

"How are you feeling Rebecca? It's good to see you up and dressed."

"I feel weak a bit but it's good to be out of bed. Thank you so much for all you've done for me Irene, I don't know what I would have done without you. I thought my mum had enough to do looking after the girls and my dad who can be a handful."

"I understand Rebecca, it was my pleasure. I'm just happy to see you're feeling better and if ever you need to talk I'm here for you."

"Thank you," Rebecca replied with tears in her eyes. "I'll put the kettle on, Irene, tea or coffee?"

"Tea please. I'm going shopping Rebecca, is there anything I can get for you?"

"You've done enough for me, I have to do things for myself now. I'm collecting the girls from Mum's tomorrow, I've really missed them and starting back to work on Monday."

"Are you sure you're ready Rebecca?"

"I just want to get back to normal otherwise I will have too much time on my hands to dwell on things."

"That's true but you still have to build your strength up Rebecca."

The phone rang, "That will be my mum," and she picked it up.

"Hello my darling how are you?"

"I'm alright Mum, how are the girls?"

"They're at the park with their grandad, Rebecca. Do you want me to tell them to ring you when they come home?"

"No don't worry, I'll be seeing them tomorrow. I'll come early Mum."

"What are you doing today darling? You know you still have to take it easy."

"Stop bloody fussing, Mum. Honestly I'm okay, I have Irene here – I have to go, sorry."

"I'll let you get off, your dad sends all his love."

"Me too, bye Mum," and she put the phone down.

"I'm going now Rebecca, I'll catch you later," said Irene.

"No Irene, you won't – you have a good rest, I'm fine, I have things to do."

Irene gave Rebecca a hug and walked out the door. 'Shit,' Rebecca thought to herself, 'why am I being so rude?' She needed some fresh air and went upstairs to get changed into some warmer clothes and came downstairs and put her coat on. She was just about to go out of the front door and the phone rang.

"Hi it's me – Adam. I rang you a couple of times Rebecca and this lady said you were in bed feeling unwell."

"That will have been my neighbour Irene you spoke to. How are you?"

"I'm alright Rebecca, I just wondered if you would like to go out for a meal tonight?"

"I don't think I would be good company Adam."

"Is it because you're still unwell?"

"I'm fine now, it was just a flu bug I had."

"Well then, meet up with me please – please, I'd love to see you again."

"Why not, it's not like I have anything better to do."

"Charming I must say Rebecca, don't get too excited. So I'll pick you up at your house – what's your address?"

"No Adam, I'll meet you outside the Stag pub at eight o'clock, there are plenty of restaurants nearby, is that alright?"

"Great! I can't wait to see you again Rebecca."
"Me too, bye Adam."

The weather had improved so instead of taking her car Rebecca thought the walk to the high street and back would do her good, so she set off with an umbrella in her bag just in case it started to rain. The Saturday market was on, so she headed there; it was packed with crowds of people and she wandered around the stalls till she spotted a stall that sold beautiful dresses. She spent some time browsing around looking at items on the rails and came across a gorgeous linen green dress. "How much is this?" she asked the guy behind the counter.

"£30, it's reduced from £40."

"I'll have it," and she took her purse out of her bag and paid for it. There was a bag stall opposite so she had a good look around and saw a black shoulder bag she quite liked.

"Can I help you?" the elderly woman behind the counter asked.

"How much is this one, there's no price on it?"

"It's real leather, good quality, the price is £45."

"I don't think I'll bother, it's a bit expensive."

"How about £40, I'll knock £5 off?"

"I'm not sure, I think £30 is all I can afford."

"Hey young lady, you must be joking, I'm trying to earn a living here," the lady remarked in an angry voice. It took Rebecca by surprise, "I'll take it thank you," and she paid for it. She felt a bit anxious and walked away from the market and headed to the nearest café she could find and was pleased to see through the window it was nearly empty. She walked in and sat down at a table in the corner; she was feeling guilty about her purchases, what on earth was she thinking of spending £70 just like that with money she could ill afford to spend.

A young girl came up to the table, "What can I get

you?" she asked.

"Just a tea please," Rebecca replied, "and a bottle of water." When she looked around the café she noticed how dirty it was – the tiles on the walls were filthy and the floor looked like it hadn't been washed in months, there were cigarette butts and rubbish everywhere. When her drinks came she drank the water but left the tea it was so strong, and the white mug was dirty around the rim, it looked like lipstick. She quickly paid at the counter and was pleased when she was outside breathing in the fresh air.

There was a twenty-minute walk home and she was thankful when she got indoors. She felt a bit tired and took her coat off and put her carrier bags on the chair and went straight upstairs to bed to have a lie down. Not long after she fell fast asleep and when she woke up and looked at her alarm clock on her bedside table she was shocked – she had slept for hours. She climbed out of bed and went to the bathroom and ran herself a hot bubble bath. When she climbed in she had a long soak, then got out and wrapped the towel around her body and went downstairs to get the carrier bags off the chair. She couldn't wait to try on her new dress.

Just at that moment the phone rang. 'Bugger, who the hell can that be?' She ignored it. 'Whoever it is,' she thought, 'can ring back later,' and she went back upstairs to get herself dressed. When she looked in the long mirror in the corner of the room she had a huge smile on her face, the dress was such a perfect fit. 'All I need now,' she thought, 'is just to put some make-up on and tie my hair back in a ponytail and I'll soon be good to go.'

She rang the cab office and ordered a cab to take her to the Stag pub and waited downstairs, looking out of the window behind the net curtains; within ten minutes it arrived and the driver tooted his horn. She put her coat on and grabbed her bag off the table, hurried out the door and climbed into the back seat of the car.

Rebecca felt nervous inside when she got out of the cab, after paying the driver, and saw Adam waiting there looking very handsome. "I'm so glad you could make it. You look beautiful, do you want a drink in the pub first before we go for a meal?"

"I'd like that," and they walked in the pub and Rebecca sat at the table.

"I'll get the drinks in, what would you like?"

"A large glass of red wine please."

"Coming up," and Adam went to the bar.

She saw him chatting and laughing with his mates who were behind the bar serving the drinks and thought maybe it was a bad idea meeting up with Adam. She wasn't quite ready to be sociable, it was too soon after having her miscarriage. There were guilt feelings, sadness and anger, but when he sat back down and they started chatting she started to relax.

"Have you always lived around this area Adam?"

"No, I lived with my parents in London. I left them to come and work here with my uncle who is a builder himself; he had a big job on at the time and I decided to stay in Norfolk when the job was finished, whereas he went back home to London. Me and my mate share a flat together, he's a self-employed builder like me."

"Are you an only child Adam?"

"No, I have a brother Mark who is the brainy one in the family – he's at university studying to be a Doctor of Engineering. What about you Rebecca?"

"I'm an only child and, as I told you before Adam, I'm going through a divorce – and I have twin girls, they see their father at weekends."

"How old are they?"

"It will be their ninth birthday soon. I must say I'm surprised you haven't got a girlfriend Adam, a good looking guy like yourself."

"Gee thanks! I was in a relationship for two years but she broke it off, she met someone else."

"I'm sorry to hear that, you must have been devastated."

"I was at the time. I thought we'd get married and have loads of kids Rebecca."

"How long ago was that?"

"About nine months ago, but I've moved on. You can't force someone to love you if they don't – forget about me, you must be hungry, I'm starving myself. Should we make a move?"

"Good idea, let's go."

When they left the pub and walked down the high street they both decided to try the new Italian restaurant, which had not long since opened, and walked in. But there was no atmosphere and it had very few customers.

"Do you want to try somewhere else Rebecca?"

"No Adam, I love pasta, this is fine," and the waiter came and showed them to their table and gave them both a menu, "What drinks can I get you?" he asked.

"A red wine and a beer please – sorry Rebecca, I didn't even ask you what you wanted."

"That's alright, I don't like mixing my drinks anyway. What do you fancy on the menu?"

"I'm not really a pasta person Rebecca, I'm normally a meat and two veg man. I'll just have a margarita pizza – what about you?"

"I fancy a carbonara pasta."

The waiter appeared ten minutes later and took their order.

"I can't stop looking at you Rebecca, you're gorgeous."

"Give over Adam, you're making me blush. I wasn't sure whether to turn up tonight or not, I've been through so much shit."

"What do you mean Rebecca?"

"For a start, as you know I'm going through a divorce

and I met a guy called Richard who I became quite fond of… and let's just say he turned out to be a compulsive liar. I was his bit on the side; I found out he was living with someone. I'm not sure whether or not to trust any man."

"That's daft Rebecca, not all blokes are the same, you had a bad experience."

"I know in reality that's true Adam, but it's left me feeling vulnerable and I'm not ready for a full-on relationship."

"I understand Rebecca, we can take it as slow as you want," Adam remarked, holding her hand.

The waiter brought the food to the table. "Looks good, but I don't know if I can eat all of this Adam."

"Eat what you can, they're massive portions, my pizza is huge – do you think I can take some away in a doggy bag for my flat mate Tim, he'd love this."

"I don't see why not, and he can have some of my pasta too, I can't eat all of this either."

They were both stuffed, and when they had finished eating there was loads of food left over on their plates. "Please allow me to pay half the bill Adam."

"I wouldn't hear of it Rebecca, I'm paying," and he took his wallet out of his pocket and paid the waiter who kindly brought the takeaways to the table.

"Thank you so much for a lovely evening Adam."

"You're welcome, my pleasure," and he rang for a taxi to take Rebecca home. They waited outside the restaurant and Adam gave her a passionate kiss on the lips. "I'll give you a ring Rebecca, I'd love a second date?"

"Me too Adam, thank you for a lovely evening." The cab arrived and she climbed into the back seat and gave Adam a wave.

The taxi driver dropped her off and she paid him and went indoors and took her coat off. It had been a lovely evening spending time with Adam, but there was no way she was going to tell him about her miscarriage, he didn't need to know. She hadn't come to terms with the loss herself but in time she knew it would get much easier, and having the girls back at home tomorrow brought a smile to her face. It would be the best tonic she could have, she had missed them so much. She went upstairs and got undressed and climbed into bed, tossing and turning, thinking positive thoughts about her future and then fell fast asleep.

After the Ordeal

Sunday morning Rebecca woke up feeling excited, she was collecting the girls from her parents' home. She put on her dressing gown and went downstairs into the kitchen and put the kettle on to make herself a cuppa, before she did the job she hated doing most – cleaning out the hamster cage. When she had finished drinking her tea she began to do all of her chores then quickly got herself dressed. She put on her coat, left the house and climbed into the car.

There was hardly any traffic on the roads so Rebecca soon arrived at her parents' bungalow and when she walked in the door the girls ran to her. "I've missed you Mum, are we going home now?" Amy asked.

"Not yet, I want to speak to your nanna and grandad, child, don't be so impatient."

"Mum, Nanna has bought us a doll's house to share and some games and books," Mary said excitedly jumping up and down.

"Calm down you two, you're both spoilt, now let me take my coat off please – now where's your nanna?"

"She's upstairs and Grandad is in the garden having a cigarette," Amy chuckled, "it really stinks!"

Grace came downstairs and the girls went back to playing with their new toys. "How are you my darling?"

"I'm okay Mum, thanks for looking after the girls for me, I must admit it's been a bit tiring."

"Rebecca they have so much energy! I'll put the kettle on, your dad must be ready for a cuppa."

"I'll come and help you Mum."

"I think you have been through a terrible ordeal my

darling, I wish I'd been the one looking after you."

"Mum you can't do everything, looking after the girls was a great help and besides I had Irene calling in every day."

"She sounds a good woman, I must thank her when I see her. Why don't you bring her with you next time Rebecca?"

"I will Mum, I think she gets a bit lonely living on her own."

Bert came into the kitchen and gave Rebecca a hug. "Are you alright my girl, how are you feeling now?" he asked, looking awkward, not knowing what to say.

"Look I'm fine, you two, honest. Now let's sit down and have our tea, you know what the girls are like earwigging they don't miss a trick. I don't want them to know about the miscarriage – anyway, changing the subject, I have some good news to tell you. I know a builder who is willing to give me a quote on the work that needs doing to the bungalow Dad, and if the estimate that he gives me is reasonable I might use him. His name's Adam. I went out for a meal with him last night, he's a lovely guy.

"Aye lass, you can't jump into something like that without knowing his credentials, he could be a cowboy builder, you have to be so careful Rebecca. Where did you meet him?"

"What's this, the third degree, Dad? I'm not a kid."

"I'm not saying you are, but you're a pushover when it comes to blokes – you let your heart rule your head."

"Thanks a lot Dad, you mean Richard?" and she started to get tearful.

"Now that's enough Bert, look what you've done, you've upset her, you and your big mouth. It's Rebecca's business who she chooses to employ to do the work on her property. We can only learn by our mistakes and by god you've made some in your time, so stop interfering," Grace said in a firm voice.

"I was only trying to help. I'm sorry if I upset you Rebecca," and Bert handed her his handkerchief and went back out into the garden.

"Ignore your dad, he's only worried about you. He's not tactful with his words sometimes but he means well Rebecca, he's only looking out for you. Now dry your tears and I'll make another brew."

"He's right Mum, look at my marriage to Jim, there's a part of me still feels I failed, and Richard – who, let's face it – used me."

"For goodness sake Rebecca, it doesn't matter how long you're married for but if you're not happy you can't waste your life away. Jim was happy with you on his terms and conditions – that was no life for you and the girls; and this Richard bloke, well as you said yourself he's a compulsive liar – you trusted him but he probably gave you no reason not to. We can only learn from our mistakes, that's life, don't be so hard on yourself my darling."

"Thanks Mum, I certainly know how to pick 'em, maybe I'm better off on my own with the girls."

"Nonsense, when you meet someone you just have to take things slowly and make sure you're both singing off the same hymn sheet. You will find Mr Right, I'm sure."

"Mum, you always think positive, I wish I was like you."

"I have no choice living with your dad, he can't make a decision without me – he is so indecisive he drives me around the bend at times," Grace chuckled.

"I think I'd better go into the garden and see Dad, I hate it when we fall out."

Bert was digging around the flower beds and Rebecca walked up behind him and put her arms around him.

"Sorry if I upset you my girl, I really am. I'm an old fool."

"You're only looking out for me, I know that, Dad.

Let's just forget all about it and if ever I'm unsure about anything I'll come to you for advice – I promise."

"It's a deal! Are you staying for dinner Rebecca?"

"No Dad, I'm shooting off – you and Mum need a rest, the girls are ready to go home now," and with that she went into the sitting room and picked up the toys off the floor. Grace helped her put them into small black sacks and they took them outside and put them into the boot of the car.

"Mum you must stop buying the girls so many toys, you would think it was Christmas, I have nowhere to put them at home it's ridiculous."

"You can leave them here Rebecca."

"You must be joking, I don't want the girls screaming in the car all the way home Mum."

"Alright, point taken. I just wish you'd stay for dinner and the girls – there's enough to go around, it will save you cooking when you get home."

"No Mum, stop fussing. You take it easy, you look tired to me and you've done enough. Now get into the car, girls, and put your seat belts on."

Bert stood at the front door with Grace waving goodbye.

On the journey home she got the girls some chicken nuggets and chips from a McDonald's drive thru and bought herself a cheese hamburger.

"You're very quiet, you two."

"Daddy always tells us we shouldn't talk with our mouths full."

"Amy that's correct, he's right, now try not to make too much of a mess in the back seat – there's a box of tissues there, wipe your mouth Mary, it's full of tomato sauce."

"Are we nearly home Mum? I want to see Goldie."

"Five more minutes and we're there. Did you enjoy

yourselves staying with Nanna and Grandad?"

"I did but I missed you Mum."

"And so did I," Amy said in a grumpy voice, "it seemed a long time – are you feeling better now?"

"It was flu and I didn't want you two catching it but I'm well now, fit as a fiddle."

They arrived home and the girls climbed out of the car and stood by the front door. "Hey girls, you can help me carry some of these carrier bags in."

"Do we have to Mum?"

"Yes Mary, they're your belongings; and you too Amy."

When Rebecca had got everything out of the boot of the car they went indoors and the girls ran straight upstairs to see Goldie their hamster. Rebecca took off her coat and put the kettle on, she was pleased to sit down and have five minutes' peace.

The phone rang and she picked it up, "Hi it's me Richard, how are you Rebecca?"

"You have some nerve, what do you want?"

"I'm just ringing to see if you're alright and maybe pop around to have a chat?"

"I have nothing to say to you Richard, what's happened has Rose left you?"

"Yes she's moved out. Anyway forget about her, you're having my child and I want to be there for you."

"Oh, so you finally accept the baby is yours? I'm afraid it's too late, I've had a miscarriage and even if I hadn't you'd be the last person who I would wish to be the father of my child. I want nothing to do with you, so there is no reason for you to ring me again, so piss off – you're a waste of space," and Rebecca put the phone down.

'Phew! Thank god that's over with,' she thought to herself. She had intended to ring him and let him know about the miscarriage as she felt it was the right thing to do but he saved her the job, now she would never have to have anything to do with him.

It was lovely having the girls home and Rebecca spent the evening playing games with them and watching videos. It was soon supper time, so when they put on their pyjamas she give them a glass of milk and made them a sandwich.

"Are we going on holiday in the summer Mum?" Amy asked.

"Maybe, where would you like to go?"

"Where you and Daddy took us to."

"We'll see. I may ask Tommy to come for lunch one day – would you like that, girls?"

"Yippee!" Mary said with a gleaming smile, "he was my best friend on holiday."

"No he wasn't, he was mine, he thought you were annoying Amy, you always wanted your own way."

"Stop it you two, be nice to each other. It's time for bed, I'll come upstairs with you and read you a bedtime story."

"Can we have *The Very Hungry Caterpillar*?"

"I don't see why not Amy, I think I'll let you read the book to me."

"That's not fair, what about me?" Mary protested.

"You can too, moany Minnie. Now upstairs girls before I change my mind."

The girls were soon tucked up in bed and fast asleep and Rebecca lay on the settee, reading her book, but before long she started to feel sleepy so she put the lights out and locked the door and went upstairs to bed. It had been a long day and she was soon in a deep sleep.

Rebecca woke up and climbed out of bed and she drew back the curtains. The sun was shining through, spring had arrived which put a smile on her face. She heard the girls chatting and told them to get washed and dressed and come downstairs for breakfast.

Mary was the first one to complain when she sat at the

kitchen table, "Yuck, scrambled eggs – I don't like it."

"Neither do I," Amy said pulling a face, "it's runny Mum, not how Nanna makes it."

"Honestly there's no pleasing you two, eat the toast and drink your milk – there's no cereal, I'll have to do some shopping today."

When breakfast was over, Rebecca washed up the dishes and the girls put their coats on. "Goodness me, you look like you've both been dragged through a hedge backwards! Mary, go to the bathroom and get a brush for me."

Finally they were ready, and the girls climbed into the back seat of the car.

Rebecca dropped them off at school and got back into the car to drive to work. She saw Maggie outside the building talking to the gardener when she parked her car, and before she opened the door she took a deep breath. She was dreading talking to her, having so much time off work and discussing the circumstances was something she didn't particularly want to do, even though her mum had rung in and informed Maggie of her absence from work and explained the reason why. She just wanted to try and put everything behind her and do her job.

"Hello Rebecca, lovely to see you – will you wait in my office I'll be there in ten minutes, I just need a word with you."

Rebecca sat waiting patiently until Maggie walked into the office and sat behind the desk. "I would just like to say I'm so sorry for your loss Rebecca, how are you feeling now?"

"I'm fine thank you Maggie."

"I was just wondering whether you should have taken more time off work, it's a lot to go through emotionally having a miscarriage."

"Honestly I'm alright, do I have many bookings?"

"I have a list here for you," and she handed it to

Rebecca. "I'll let you get on, you can come and talk to me anytime. It's lovely to have you back. The ladies were all asking after you – I explained to them you had a bout of flu, you know how inquisitive they can be, anything for a bit of gossip."

"Thanks Maggie, I'd better make a start."

Mrs Jackson was Rebecca's first customer, she wanted a cut and blow wave. "I hope you're feeling better? I heard you had a bad dose of flu."

"I did but I'm fine now Ruby, how have you been?"

"You know me, I don't like to complain, you just have to get on with it – not like certain people I could mention who moan for England, they depress me. When you come to our age group you have to thank your lucky stars, every day is a bonus. I'm a bit parched, I'd love a cup of tea."

"I'll make you one Ruby, just let me finish your hair."

Rebecca had another customer arrive at the salon so she started to wash her hair. Ruby was still sitting there sipping her tea, she was in no hurry to leave and made herself comfortable.

Miss Sharp was a sweet frail elderly lady, riddled with arthritis, and spoke in a soft voice.

Rebecca fussed over her, "You look so uncomfortable Helen, let me put a cushion behind your back."

"You're so kind Rebecca, how are you my dear?"

"I'm okay – do you want your fringe long or cut short?"

"I don't mind, I hate it coming over my eyes though, I suffer with corneal ulcers."

"You are in the wars," Ruby piped in, "you look like you need to put a bit of weight on Miss Sharp, you're a bag of bones."

Rebecca gave Ruby a dirty look, and Ruby took the hint and got out of her chair and said she had things to do and left the salon.

"What a cheeky bugger she is Helen, take no notice of her."

"I don't, she is a formidable woman – I heard she was a policewoman in her day."

"Makes sense," Rebecca said chuckling, "she's a force to be reckoned with."

Rebecca had two more customers who just wanted a trim and she was finished work. She rang Andrew the estate agent, "Hi it's me – Rebecca."

"I'm glad you rang, I was going to phone you Rebecca. I have the keys to Mr Jackson's property – you can collect them from the office."

"Can I pick them up tomorrow morning, Andrew, when I've taken the girls to school? I want to ring a builder I know who can come with me and give me a quote."

"No problem Rebecca, so long as you hand the keys back into the office before closing time."

"No worries. Thanks Andrew, I'll speak to you soon, bye," and she straightaway got on the phone to Adam.

"Hi it's me Rebecca, I need a big favour from you, I know it's such short notice…"

"Go on then, what is it?"

"Do you remember me telling you I've made an offer on a bungalow and I need a quote for the work to be done? Well I'm picking up the keys tomorrow morning from the estate agent's office and wondered if you can come with me to give me a rough estimate how much the work will cost me."

"I have a lot of work on but I can get away for a couple of hours – is that alright?"

"Thanks Adam, that will be great, we'll go in my car. I'll pick the keys up and meet you outside the Stag pub say about nine-thirty."

"No problem. Do you fancy going out for a drink tonight Rebecca?"

"I can't Adam, but when I see you we can arrange to go out sometime this week."

"See you tomorrow, sweetheart, looking forward to it."

"Me too Adam, bye."

Rebecca put her coat on and picked up her bag off the rail and was pleased her first day back at work went well. Things were slowly getting back to normal, her job was the best therapy she could have keeping herself busy.

On the journey home she parked her car down the high street and walked around the shopping centre and took a browse around the clothes shops where she bumped into her friend Linda. "I didn't expect to see you here, I thought you'd be working."

"It's my day off Rebecca – do you fancy a coffee in that café over there?"

"Why not – I'm sorry, I meant to ring you."

"I've been busy Rebecca, it was probably the other way round – my turn to ring you."

"How's Tommy?"

"He's alright, he's adjusting to his dad not living with us anymore but I'm loving him being out of our lives, it's the best thing I ever did getting shot of him."

They walked into the café and both sat down at the table over looking the square. The waiter came over and took their order.

"It's lovely in here Rebecca, quite upmarket, I love the décor."

"It's an Italian family who run it Linda, I've been here once before. I think the elderly couple behind the counter must be the owners. Just look at them yummy pastries and cakes on display."

"I'm not looking Rebecca, I'm on a diet."

"How have you been Linda?"

"Life is good. I'm seeing someone called Charlie, I met him in a country pub at my friend's birthday celebration, he's a bank manager and comes from good stock – his parents are quite well off and they are both solicitors Rebecca."

"Get you, you're a snob Linda."

"No I'm certainly not!"

"I'm only joking, does Tommy get on with him?"

"Obviously there's no one like his dad but they get on okay. I'm six years older than him."

"Ah, so he's your toy boy Linda!"

"You're a cheeky bugger, but I suppose he is," Linda grinned.

"What about Ben, is he seeing anyone?"

"Yes he is but every time I see him when I take Tommy to stay at his place there's a different woman – *every* time!"

"That must be awful for Tommy to see, he's not a good example as a father, poor lad how confusing."

"I want to know your news Rebecca?"

"Nothing much to say really, I'm hoping to move into a bungalow opposite my mum's. My offer has been accepted and I'm just waiting for the completion of the sale of the house."

"That takes time Rebecca, I've been through all that as you know it can be stressful and frustrating."

"I'm going with Adam tomorrow to get an estimate on the work that needs doing – it needs a new kitchen and bathroom Linda."

"Who's Adam? You're such a dark horse Rebecca – spill the beans."

"He's a builder I met in a pub, we've had one date and I quite fancy him but I want to take things slowly after all I've been through I—"

"Oh shit! I'm sorry to interrupt you Rebecca, I must dash I just remembered I forgot to shut the kitchen window, I'll have to go home. We've had several break-ins in our neighbourhood recently. I'll give you a ring later on."

"You go Linda, I'll pay for the coffee."

"Thanks – bye."

Rebecca paid for the coffees and when she left the café she went across the road to a small supermarket and bought some groceries and treated herself to a bottle of wine.

She walked further up the road and climbed into her car and drove home; once indoors she took off her coat and put the groceries away and poured herself a large glass of wine. It was early in the day, she thought to herself, but what the hell – one won't hurt – and she sat on the settee relaxing, but that was short lived. There was a knock at the door and when she opened it Irene was standing there looking tearful.

"What on earth has happened Irene? Come in."

"My Bob never came home last night and there's no sign of him this morning, that's not like him."

"I'm sure he will, you know what cats are like – they are so independent but when he gets hungry he'll make his way back home. Now sit down and I'll put the kettle on. Did you tell the other neighbours to keep an eye out for him?"

"I did. I'm lost without him Rebecca, he's my companion."

"I know, it must get lonely living on your own. Have you ever thought of going to a day centre for the elderly which involves outings and other activities? I'm sure there must be one somewhere around here Irene."

"Christ no, god forbid, it's not my cup of tea – a lot of old woman prattling on talking about their ailments."

"I don't think they're all like that. I've got elderly customers at work and some of them have really interesting stories to tell. You should give it some thought Irene, and I can make some inquiries for you."

"I'll think about it Rebecca, but I'm making no promises, I'm too set in my ways. I must say you make a lovely cuppa, aren't you having one yourself?"

"No I don't fancy one – would you like a biscuit?"

"No I'm going to make myself a salmon sandwich later on. I'm sorry to take up your time I know how busy you are with work and the girls."

"Don't be silly, I enjoy your company."

"I can't sit still, I must get back indoors. I can't stop worrying about Bob, thanks for the tea Rebecca."

"You're welcome. I'll keep a look out for him and I'll tell the girls to do the same, he sometimes comes into my garden."

"Thanks – cheerio."

It was time to collect the girls from school. Rebecca put on her coat and picked up her keys off the kitchen table and hurried out the door, she didn't want to be late again. She climbed into the car and drove to the school.

It was far too early when she arrived so she chatted to Todd who she met at the school gates. "Hi Todd, it's quite hot today!"

"Take your coat off Rebecca, you must be sweltering."

"I am! How is Daisy?"

"She's had a bit of a cold but she's fine now. I was thinking of taking her to the zoo at the weekend – do you and the girls fancy coming too?"

"I can't Todd, they're at their dad's."

"It was just a thought. Perhaps we can have a coffee one morning?"

"I'm very busy this week but I'll let you know Todd."

"Please yourself, no worries."

The girls came out of school and she said bye to Daisy and Todd. Blimey that was awkward, she thought to herself, Todd's attitude was quite stroppy – that was out of character with him. What was his problem? She saw him as a friend, nothing more, maybe she was reading too much into it.

She took the girls to the car and they climbed into the back seat and she drove straight home. Once the girls were indoors they went straight out to play in the garden, on the swing and slide.

"Honestly, you two make me cross. What have I told you before about changing your clothes when you come home from school?"

"Sorry Mum," Amy replied, "let's go upstairs Mary, otherwise we're in big trouble!" They both giggled and did as they were told.

Rebecca made some sausages and mashed potatoes with onion rings and gravy for dinner while the girls played with their doll's house upstairs. When the meal was ready she shouted upstairs for them to come down before it got cold.

When they all sat around the table, Mary noticed Bob sitting on the mat at the entrance of the open French doors, "Look Mum, there's Bob."

Rebecca turned around in her chair, "So it is, thank goodness, stay here girls I'll be back in a tick," so she picked Bob up and went outside and knocked on her neighbour's door.

When Irene opened up the door her face lit up like a Christmas tree. "Thank the lord – my Bob, he's been in the wars fighting no doubt, he's got blood on his front paw. Where did you find him Rebecca?"

"Sitting on the mat outside our French doors."

"You naughty boy Bob, I'm very cross with you. Before you go, pet, would you mind coming in to look at my telly – it doesn't seem to be working."

Rebecca went indoors and saw she had one of the leads loose at the back. "It's fixed, I have to go Irene – I'm in the middle of having my dinner, I'll catch up with you soon, bye."

When she got back indoors her meal was stone cold so she threw it into the bin.

"Mum I've eaten all my dinner, can I have some ice-cream?"

"Yes you can, good girl Amy, you too Mary. You can both watch a video in the sitting room and I'll bring you some, just let me do the washing-up first."

Rebecca sat watching the telly with the girls the rest of the evening until it was their bedtime. "You two sleepy heads, go upstairs and put your pyjamas on and don't forget to clean your teeth. I'll be up shortly to read you a story."

Rebecca went upstairs and was surprised to see they both had fallen asleep, so she put the lights out and went back downstairs. She made herself a ham sandwich and a cuppa and sat in the sitting room watching a film for two hours. But she felt tired then, so she switched the telly off and the lights and took herself off to bed. It wasn't long before she hit the pillow and fell into a deep sleep.

Rebecca woke up feeling excited, she was meeting up with Adam to go and see the bungalow so he could give her an estimate on the work that needed doing. She wanted to make a good impression on him and got dressed in her tight blue jeans and her favourite white blouse, but when she looked in the mirror she looked pale so she put on her make-up and brushed her hair back into a ponytail. 'Not bad,' she said to herself, 'it's not like we're going out on a date. Oh bother,' she thought when she looked at her alarm clock, 'look at the time I'm running late!'

The girls were already awake and dressed so she went downstairs with them and prepared breakfast of porridge oats for them and made herself a cuppa and a slice of toast with honey.

"I'm not very hungry Mum."

"Alright, just eat what you can Mary."

"Can I have some toast Mum?"

"No you can't, do as you're told Amy and eat your porridge. I'm going upstairs to get your school bags."

When Rebecca came downstairs, the girls had left the kitchen table and were in the garden playing on the swings. "You're both testing my patience this morning, get indoors – you haven't touched your breakfast. Will you put your coats on right now, I'm really cross with the pair of you."

Amy stuck her tongue out and Mary copied her.

"That's not funny, it's very rude. Now let's get you both into the car."

On the journey to the school the girls were very quiet in the back seat; they both knew their mum was in a bad mood. "There will be no watching videos when you get home from school you two, and no ice-cream."

"That's not fair Mum," Amy replied, "I'm sorry I stuck my tongue out, Amy told me to Mum."

"You are a liar Mary, I did not," and Amy hit her on the arm.

"Stop fighting you two, you're both as bad as one another."

Rebecca parked the car outside the school gates and got out of the car and gave them cuddles and kisses. "Be good girls and have a nice day – bye, see you later." She then got back into her car and drove straight to the estate agent's and picked up the keys from the lady at the desk who was expecting her.

When she drove to the Stag pub, Adam was there waiting for her and climbed into the car. "Hi gorgeous," and kissed Rebecca on the cheek.

"Thanks for coming Adam, I know you must be busy with work."

"No problem, do you want me to drive?"

"No I enjoy driving, I was stressed this morning I thought I'd be late picking you up – my girls were driving me mad – I was a bit bad-tempered with them but feel guilty now."

"I wouldn't worry, mornings are not my thing either till I have my first cup of coffee."

"Good to know, Adam, I must remember that."

"I think I would make an exception if I was with you Rebecca."

"You're a charmer Adam, I walked right into that one."

"What are you doing Friday?"

"Nothing, the girls are with their dad for the weekend."

"That's a shame, I thought we all could go out for a meal."

"That is so sweet of you Adam."

"My flat mate is away the weekend Rebecca, you can come to my place – it's a bit pokey and messy but I'm not a bad cook."

"I must be mad, but would you like to come to my house Friday night Adam? We can order a take-away…"

"That's an offer I can't refuse – are you sure about this, Rebecca?"

"Don't be daft, of course I'm sure."

"Great! I'll bring some beers and wine with me. Have we got far to go Rebecca?"

"Five more minutes, it's just around the corner Adam. It's a lovely area, the front gardens are kept neat and tidy."

Rebecca parked the car in the driveway of the bungalow and they climbed out. "Well, what do you think?"

"It looks a decent size but you can see it needs a paint job and the garden is overgrown, but that's nothing Rebecca, superficial jobs. Let's go inside and I'll have a better idea."

They went straight into the kitchen, "Blimey! I see what you mean Rebecca, the whole kitchen needs gutting out – removing the units and the old tiles and doing some plastering where necessary."

"Come through Adam, and have a look at the bathroom."

"I would say it's the same job needs doing as the kitchen, everything needs gutting out."

"How much will this cost me Adam?"

"Steady on, I'll have to come back to you with an estimate Rebecca, but I'll keep the costs down as low as possible. I think when the work's all done it will be a fantastic home for you and the girls, the room sizes are good, it has great potential but it's just dated and needs a make-over – purely cosmetic, no worries."

"Thanks Adam," and she gave him a sloppy kiss on the lips. "Do you fancy a cuppa?"

"Where should we go?"

"Across the road to my mum and dad's – look at your face Adam, they won't bite you."

"I'm not worried, I'd love to meet them," so they walked across the road and rang the doorbell.

Grace opened the door, "Where's your key Rebecca?"

"I forgot it – Mum, this is Adam who I told you about."

"Pleased to meet you Adam, come in. Your dad's next door Rebecca talking to Pete."

"I'll put the kettle on Mum and make the tea. Come through to the kitchen with me Adam."

"It's a lovely place you have here, similar layout to the bungalow across the road."

"Me and my Bert like it – sit down Adam, would you like a piece of my ginger cake? I made it myself."

"Looks delicious, thanks."

"It's going to cost an arm and a leg to do the bungalow up, you have your work cut out there Adam. I'm surprised it's been left in that state."

"Mum be quiet, Adam said it's just superficial and

when it's all finished it'll be great."

"Rebecca's right, I've seen much worse. The building itself looks in good nick."

"What do I know Adam, it just seems a lot of work to do and will take some time to finish."

"Only a couple of weeks I would say, Mum. I thought you wanted me to buy the bungalow…"

"I do honestly, just take no notice of me I'm just being silly, I worry too much. I'll just give your dad a call over the garden fence to tell him you're here."

When Grace came back from the garden, a few minutes later Bert walked in the door. Adam stood up from his chair and shook his hand. "I'm Adam, pleased to meet you."

"I'm Bert, let's sit in the garden – Grace make me a cuppa please," and they both sat at the table outside. "How long have you been in the building business?"

"I worked for my uncle when I left school, that's the only work I've ever done."

"You're not from these parts with your accent?"

"No my parents live in London, my dad's a carpenter and my mum's a primary school teacher."

"Are you an only child Adam?"

"No, I have a brother who's at university studying to be a Doctor of Engineering."

Grace brought Bert's tea out to him, "I hope he's not giving you the third degree Adam?"

"No, that's alright."

"Go and have a chinwag to Rebecca, woman, and leave us in peace."

"See what I have to put up with Adam," Grace said and tapped Bert on the head, but she took the hint and went back to the kitchen to have a natter with her daughter.

"Rebeca wants you to do the work on the property – is that alright with you Adam?"

"Yep I can do it, no problem Bert. A mate of mine is a kitchen supplier who does kitchens and bathrooms at a reasonable price. When it's nearer the time we can take some measurements and we can go along to the showroom and see him."

"I want you to keep me informed about all the costs on the kitchen – me and Grace are going to pay for it to be done. I know how expensive this will all cost Adam."

"That's good of you both, no worries Bert."

"I'm going to have a lie down now, it's been nice meeting you. Come and visit us anytime."

"Thanks," replied Adam, then got out of his chair and went into the kitchen.

"Where's Dad?"

"He went for a lie down Rebecca. I must get going, I still have some work to do."

"Mum we have to shoot off, I'll ring you later on."

"Bye my darling, give the girls a big hug from me. It's been nice meeting you Adam."

"You too Grace, bye."

On the journey home Rebecca couldn't stop smiling. "I think my dad has taken a shine to you Adam, you must have made a good impression on him."

"I don't know about that but he seems a good bloke and your mum is lovely. I think it's very generous of them both to pay for the kitchen."

"It's news to me Adam, is that what Dad said?"

"Yes, he wants to pay for everything. You're so lucky to have parents like them Rebeca. Don't get me wrong, mine are fantastic but not that generous, especially my dad – he can be tight when it comes to spending money."

"Being an only child I suppose I have been spoilt. I must give Dad and Mum a ring when I get home and thank them."

"I wish I could take the day off and spend it with you Rebecca."

"I still have the girls to pick up from school and I'm seeing you Friday."

"What time do you want me to come to your place?"

"Say about six o'clock? If you look in the dashboard glove box there's an old letter with my address on it, put it into your pocket."

"I must admit I admire you bringing up the girls on your own, it can't be easy."

"I do get help Adam, from my parents as you know, however the thing I miss the most about not having a partner is planning things together. It can get a bit lonely even though I have the girls for company. What do you do to relax Adam?"

"I like reading books, especially thrillers and having a game of pool with my mates in the pub, but with my type of work I'm normally knackered when I've finished work. I come home have a shower, get changed and eat a meal in front of the telly with a few cans of beer. I'm a bit boring I'm afraid."

"Don't be daft, nothing wrong with that. I think most blokes do the same… we're here, that didn't take long. Don't work too hard Adam, I'll see you on Friday."

Adam got out of the car and Rebecca drove straight to the estate agents and handed Mr Jackson's keys in, then got straight back into the car and headed home.

Feelings

The week flew by, it was Friday morning and Rebecca had taken the girls to school and was sitting at her kitchen table having a cuppa, all she could think about was seeing Adam at six o'clock. She wanted to make a good impression so she spent most of the day cleaning the house from top to bottom and when she had done all of her chores she had a bubble bath and glammed herself up, went downstairs and poured herself a stiff drink of Bacardi and Coke to calm her nerves.

When she had finished her drink she glanced at the clock on the wall – it was seven o'clock and she was getting annoyed. 'Where the hell is he?' she thought, 'what a nerve he has, he could have rung me.' She poured herself another drink and by eight o'clock she was just about to give up when she heard a knock at the door.

She opened the door to see Adam there, "You decided to come – what a bloody cheek, you're two hours late Adam, come in and explain yourself."

"Calm down, I had an emergency, Rebecca. I had to take my mate Tom to A&E – he was opening a can of corned beef and cut his finger really badly. I think he needs stitches, he's still waiting to be seen. I left him there but I rang his girlfriend and she's popping down to the hospital to sit with him. I'm really sorry I'm late."

"I've heard it all now, what a load of bullshit! You expect me to believe that? You were probably in the pub with your mates, and why didn't you give me a ring Adam?"

"Your address was in my jacket pocket Rebecca, I left it at the flat when I drove Tom to the hospital. It all happened so quickly I didn't think straight. I had to drive back to my place and get my jacket."

"If you think you can use me Adam, you can't. Don't take me for a fool."

"My god you do have mistrust issues Rebecca, if you don't believe me ring my mate. I'll give you the number and he'll confirm what I've just told you or I can drive you to the hospital and you can see for yourself… but on second thoughts, I'll just go. I don't need the aggravation," and Adam walked out of the door.

A few minutes later when Adam was just about to start up the engine of his car to drive off, Rebecca tapped on the car window, her eyes were filled with tears. Adam climbed out of the car and put his arms around her. "Listen to me, I was telling the truth Rebecca."

"I'm so sorry Adam, can we forget all about this and start again?"

"I will if you pour me a large beer, you feisty woman," and he took a carrier bag from the back seat and handed it to Rebecca. "Wine and beers as promised."

"I feel awful Adam."

"So you should," he replied with a grin on his face, and when they went back indoors Rebecca poured him a large beer and they sat in the sitting room on the settee cuddling and kissing.

"Do you feel hungry Adam?"

"I'm famished, but do you know what I fancy? Some cod and chips, I'm not over keen on Indian food or Chinese."

"I'll go and get it Adam, I fancy that too. It won't take me long, it's not far away, that's the very least I can do giving you so much grief. You just relax, I won't be long."

"Thanks my darling, there's money in my wallet in my coat pocket – take what you need."

"No worries, my treat Adam," and Rebecca took her keys off the coffee table and left Adam stretched out on the settee.

The fish and chip shop was empty, no customers at all, so when Rebecca got there she soon got served and hurried back to her car. When she arrived home, to her surprise Adam had set the table. "Goodness me, I see you managed to find everything in the kitchen, you're a star, and you've poured me a glass of wine!"

"Sit down and I'll get the plates, the only thing I didn't find Rebecca was any tomato sauce."

"I never use it much Adam."

"No worries, the cod looks delicious – it's a big piece. I must say you have a lovely place here, it's very homely and I love the décor. Won't you miss it when you move, Rebecca?"

"Not in the least Adam, I haven't really settled here."

"Why's that Rebecca?"

"I hate my landlord, he's a creep, and apart from my neighbour next door I don't know any of the others. I can't put it into words, maybe it's because it was the first time living on my own with the girls when I moved here. When my marriage broke down I lived with my mum and dad and they did everything for me."

"I understand, Rebecca. I had a mate when I lived in London who was bringing up his boy on his own, he used to tell me the evenings were the worst when he put his kid to bed he felt lonely and isolated."

"I sound pathetic Adam."

"No you don't. I think when you move near to your parents you'll be happier – we all need support from time to time especially when you have children and you're a one-parent family, but I think you're doing a grand job Rebecca."

"Thanks, I try my best. Blimey, you must have been

hungry, you scoffed that meal up quick. I'm stuffed, I can't eat any more – do you want this piece of fish Adam?"

"No I'm bloated, I'll do the washing up."

"Just leave it Adam and go and put your feet up in the sitting room. Do you want another beer?"

"Yes please."

"I must admit I have never met a man with such good manners."

Adam smiled, "That's my mother's influence Rebecca, she drummed it into me growing up to say please and thank you and always taught me to treat a woman with respect."

"Gosh I'd like to meet her, we would get on great."

"My dad is quite reserved, till you get to know him. He's from the old school of thought – you have to work hard for what you want and shouldn't have everything handed on a plate. He has no time for lazy people who are looking for handouts."

Rebecca got another beer for Adam and they sat in the sitting room. He began to kiss Rebecca passionately and she responded; his hands were all over her breasts. She was feeling excited as he kissed her neck and moved his hands up and down her thighs and then gently got on top of her, but she pushed him off.

"Stop Adam, I can't do this, I think you ought to go," and she sat up and straightened her clothing.

"What's wrong Rebecca? Crikey, you blow hot and cold, I don't understand you."

"I'm sorry, it's not you Adam it's me. I don't want to get myself pregnant again and go through… oh never mind, I just think neither of us are thinking straight, we're being irresponsible."

"You certainly know how to kill the moment Rebecca, what did you mean by pregnant again and go through what exactly?"

"Okay, I may as well tell you. Do you remember me telling you about Richard who I was seeing?"

"Yes I do."

"Well I got pregnant by him and had a miscarriage."

"Is that why you two split up?"

"Christ no, he was never into me, I was his bit on the side, he used me and when I told him I was having his baby, he even suggested it could be someone else's. That's why I'm afraid. I don't want to bring another child into the world unless I'm in a stable relationship Adam."

"Well we'll just have to take precautions and be sensible... and I'm sorry for your loss Rebecca."

"I'm glad you understand, Adam."

"I do, I'm just waiting for my John Thomas to go down," and they both laughed. "I was in the boys scouts when I was a kid, I'll just have to keep the motto in my head."

"What's that Adam?"

"Be prepared!"

"You're a daft sod – do you want another beer?"

"No I'm heading off, I have work tomorrow morning but I'm finished by one o'clock – if you like we can go and have some lunch at the Stag pub. I'll come here and pick you up."

"I'd love that, Adam. You drive home safely, but you know you can stay here if you like?"

"Nah, I have to get changed into my work clothes, it's easier if I get back home. Some of my tools I need are there as well. I'll see you tomorrow," and Adam gave Rebecca a passionate kiss on the lips and walked out of the door. As he got into his car Rebecca looked behind the net curtains and gave him a wave.

Rebecca washed the dishes and tidied up the kitchen and put all the lights out. She went upstairs, got undressed and climbed into bed. So many thoughts were running through her head, she felt relieved inside she had held back from having sex with Adam – it would have been so easy to. 'He's so handsome, charming, great body and the chemistry was there; still, tomorrow I'll be seeing him again for lunch,' she chuckled to herself and snuggled under the covers and it wasn't long before she fell fast asleep.

Rebecca woke up and got out of bed, and looking out of the window she could see a clear blue sky. She put her dressing gown on and went downstairs and made herself a hearty breakfast of bacon, eggs, tomatoes and toast and a mug of tea. She was just about to sit down at the kitchen table to eat it when the phone rang and she picked it up.

"Rebecca are you coming over today? Me and your dad are going out for lunch, you can come with us."

"I'm sorry Mum, I've got other plans – I'm having lunch with Adam."

"He seems a nice young man, your dad quite liked him, you must bring him over for lunch one day."

"I'll ask him Mum, and next week I'll bring the girls over but please don't buy them any more toys – my place is cluttered."

"Shush, what else am I going to spend my money on? I enjoy treating them."

"I know Mum, but I can't compete with you – every time I take the girls out they expect me to buy them something. I'm not having a go at you but I'd rather you and Dad spent the money on yourselves, you've both worked hard all your lives, and another thing you don't have to pay for the kitchen I'll find the money somehow."

"Sorry it's all been decided Rebecca, it's our pleasure, we want to."

"You're both stubborn, I just give up! Listen Mum I have to go, my breakfast is getting cold – love you."

"Love you too, bye."

Rebecca ate her breakfast and washed the dishes. She

went upstairs to get changed into her denim jeans and T-shirt. She felt full of the joys of spring and fancied taking a walk to browse around the shops and maybe buy herself some sexy underwear, so she took her bag off the armchair and left the house.

Irene was in the front garden removing some dead leaves off her hanging basket, "Good morning Rebecca, where are you off to?"

"I'm just taking a walk to the high street instead of taking the car, the exercise will do me good. There's a few bits and bobs I need to buy – do you want me to get you anything Irene?"

"You can get me an uncut white loaf of bread from the bakery and a pint of milk please – I'll go and get my purse."

"No worries, you can pay me later."

"Thanks Rebecca."

The high street was quiet, some shop owners were just opening up but Rebecca spotted an underwear shop which was open and went in. "Can I help you?" a young assistant asked.

"I'm not sure, they all look a bit skimpy to me. I like them but I also like comfort."

"I have some matching sets in the stock room, I can show you which might be more suitable – I'll get them for you."

A few minutes later the assistant produced three different sets for Rebecca. "What size are you?"

"I'm not sure, can you measure me?"

"Of course, just come through to the back, there's a cubicle there."

Rebecca undressed and the assistant took her bust measurements, "You're quite petite, I'll go and get you a few bras to try on – any colour preference?"

"I like black or white," Rebecca replied. She finally

found two sets of underwear she liked and got dressed and went to the counter to pay.

"That will be £40 please – is there anything else you want, we also have a large selection of sexy lingerie?"

"No thanks," Rebecca answered, blushing, "but thank you for your help."

She left the shop and thought to herself, 'That's it, I must stop treating myself,' and decided to go straight to the bakery to buy Irene some bread. When she had done that she called into Gino's café.

She ordered herself a coffee and sat down at her favourite table overlooking the square, and as she glanced out of the window she saw a familiar face looking at the shop windows so she went to the entrance of the café and called him, "Hi Todd, long time no see – do you fancy a coffee?"

"Why not," and when they both sat down the waiter brought her coffee and she ordered another one for Todd.

"Where's Daisy?"

"She's staying at my mum's so I thought I'd do some shopping. How have you been Rebecca?"

"Not too bad, my girls are with their dad for the weekend. What have you been up to Todd?"

"I've been working my socks off to try and save some money to take Daisy on holiday this summer."

"That's lovely! Where were you thinking of going?"

"I'm not sure, I'd like to go abroad somewhere – maybe Spain or Portugal."

"Have you ever been abroad before?"

"Nah, I could never afford it, I still can't but Daisy has set her heart on it as all of her friends at school have been."

"I think that's a great idea Todd, it's good to have goals."

"Do you fancy going for a drink tonight Rebecca? We

could have a meal afterwards."

"Are you asking me on a date Todd?"

"Don't sound so surprised Rebecca, you must know I've always fancied you."

"I think you must have a vivid imagination Todd, you have got to be joking – I never thought anything of the sort. I just see you as a good friend who I admire, being a one-parent family like myself. I could connect with you, but I'm seeing someone and even if I wasn't I don't see you in that way Todd, just as a friend."

"Well it certainly didn't take you long to find someone or is it the same guy you were telling me about who got you pregnant? I can't keep up with you Rebecca."

"Why are you being so fucking nasty? I'm not sitting here listening to this, what I do is my own business," and Rebecca picked up her bag and carrier bag off the floor and walked out of the café. She was fuming, but remembered she had to get some milk for Irene so she popped into a local store and bought a pint of milk and made her way home.

When she got to her front door Irene was still pottering around in the garden, "Did you enjoy your walk Rebecca?"

"I wished I'd never gone, some people make my blood boil – you think you know someone and then you find out you don't."

"Who's rattled your cage, pet?"

"This guy Todd whose child goes to the same school as my girls, who I thought of as my friend and had coffee with him on several occasions, has just been quite abusive to me Irene."

"You mean in the street?"

"Not exactly, I was sitting in the café and invited him to join me and he comes out with all this spiel about fancying me and I must have known, and then goes on to more or less tell me I'm some sort of man-eater when I declined his offer to take me out. Bloody cheek!"

"I wouldn't give it a second thought Rebecca, he's got a deflated ego because you turned him down, sounds a nasty piece of work. I wouldn't speak to him again."

"Don't worry Irene, I won't."

"Did you get my bread and milk?"

"I did, here in the carrier bag and don't worry about paying me, you've done enough for me in the past. I'm going indoors now to put my feet up."

"Thanks Rebecca, you're naughty though – you should let me give you the money."

"Nonsense, I'll catch up with you another time Irene."

Rebecca was pleased to be home, the incident with Todd had upset her, she was furious. How dare he speak to her like that! She put the kettle on and made herself a mug of tea and took it upstairs with her and the new purchases of underwear she had just bought, neatly wrapped in soft tissue paper. She decided she would wear the black matching set, not the white, and ran herself a hot bubble bath. While it was running she went to the bedroom and took her plain tight-fitting black dress out of the wardrobe and her red high-heel shoes.

After she had a long soak in the bath she climbed out and dried herself and put on her sexy underwear which fitted like a glove, then put her make-up on and got dressed. 'I feel fabulous, now what to do with my hair,' she thought to herself and decided to leave it hanging over her shoulders instead of the usual sweeping it back into a ponytail. 'All I need now is a small spray of Chanel perfume and I'm done.'

While she was waiting for Adam to pick her up she poured herself a glass of wine, and after ten minutes there was a knock at the door. When she looked at the clock on the wall he was spot on, the exact time he said he would pick her up, and she opened the door.

"Wow you look amazing Rebecca!"

"You don't look so bad yourself, you're so handsome Adam and I love your black shirt. Come in while I get my bag and find my purse."

"Hurry up Rebecca, let's go – I'm dying for a pint."

"I'm ready, blimey you are impatient!"

Rebecca climbed into the car and Adam drove to the Stag pub which wasn't very far down the road. He had a job finding a space to park in the pub's car park with it being lunch time but eventually he found a space. When they walked into the pub it was packed with customers, all the seats had been taken so they sat outside in the garden.

"I like it out here better Adam, it's too stuffy inside."

"I think the landlord could have made it more attractive, it's a bit neglected – the lawn could be cut and the table and chairs are falling apart. What do you want to drink Rebecca?"

"Red wine please. Are we eating here?"

"Let's just have a drink and go somewhere else more quiet – what do you think?"

"That's fine with me Adam."

Rebecca sat for ages waiting for Adam to bring the drinks and he looked annoyed when he sat down. "Christ you can hardly get near to the bar, they should have more staff on, it's ridiculous."

"Is your friend still working here?"

"Nah, he found another job, the wages are crap. I think it's a bit of a dump this pub."

"You're right, but it's busy Adam, they must be doing something right. Let's just drink up and go. What about going to the Steak House on the high street Adam? It's quite nice, I've been there once and we're nearer home – you don't want to get picked up for drinking and driving."

"Okay let's go, I'm famished," and they walked out of the pub and climbed into the car.

Adam drove to the restaurant and parked the car outside. They walked in and the waiter came over and showed them to a table and gave them the menus, "What would you like to drink?" he asked.

"Can I have a pint of lager and a glass of red wine please. I love it here Rebecca, it's very oldie-worldly. I love the décor, I think it's quite a romantic place. What a huge fireplace and the thick velvet maroon curtains are lush. You look gorgeous Rebecca, far too classy for a dump like the Stag pub."

"Give over Adam."

"It's true, and *I* feel under-dressed."

"You look very smart, I'm proud to be with you," Rebecca complimented.

"Now what do you fancy on the menu? I'm ordering the steak with the peppercorn sauce and French fries."

"Sounds delicious Adam, I'll have the same."

The waiter quickly came and took their order as the restaurant wasn't that busy.

"Are you staying at my place tonight Adam?"

"Do you want me to?" he asked with a twinkle in his eye.

"You know I do," Rebecca said shyly.

"That's an offer I can't refuse! Do you want another drink Rebecca?"

"Yes please, but you should be careful – you're driving Adam."

"I'll have another pint. Don't worry, it's not as if I have to drive far."

The waiter brought the meals and took their drinks order. "This looks yummy, it's ages since I had steak – it's tender and the sauce is so tasty Rebecca. I'm glad we came here, my type of food. I'll be coming here again."

"Have you got a lot of work on Adam?"

"I'm doing an extension at the moment but I always get work in from word of mouth, I don't have any complaints from my customers. I enjoy grafting, I can't understand how there's so many people on the dole or claiming benefits, I would do any kind of work if I had to. I'd get bored stiff doing nothing Rebecca."

"You have good work ethics Adam, your parents must be the same."

"They are and it hasn't done me any harm."

Adam soon polished off his plate of steak and French fries. "You were hungry Adam, you ate that fast!"

"I enjoyed that – look at you Rebecca, you eat like a bird. Don't tell me you've finished your meal?"

"I have Adam, I'm not a big eater."

"Do you want a dessert?"

"No I don't but you have one if you like – I have to watch my figure, I can easy put the pounds on."

"You have a gorgeous figure Rebecca."

"Thanks. Tell me, what do you look for in your ideal woman?"

"I suppose she has to be attractive, intelligent, honest, and ambitious – just like you Rebecca, but without the feisty temper!"

"You won't let me live that down Adam, cheeky bugger."

"Now I just may add 'sensitive' to my list," he said grinning from ear to ear.

"Shall we go Adam?"

"Yep," he replied. He called the waiter and paid the bill.

They left the restaurant and got into the car and it wasn't long before they were indoors back at Rebecca's house.

"Do you want a coffee Adam?"

"Yes please," and he went into the sitting room and took his jacket off and stretched out on the settee. Rebecca took two mugs of coffee into the room and found Adam was fast asleep, dead to the world. 'Never mind, he must be shattered,' she thought to herself, 'I'll just leave him there.' So she put all the lights out and took herself off to bed. She tossed and turned all night long but eventually fell asleep.

Rebecca woke up and put her dressing gown on and looked in the sitting room where Adam was still asleep on the settee, so she went to the kitchen and put the kettle on. She was just about to make a cuppa and he appeared, "Hello sleepy head, I didn't want to wake you last night – you were out for the count Adam."

"You should have woken me up, sorry about that."

"Do you want a cuppa?"

"Yes please, milk and two sugars. Come over here and give me a kiss, you sexy woman." Adam kissed her passionately and she responded; he picked her up and carried her upstairs. Rebecca pointed to the direction of her bedroom and he placed her gently down on the bed.

"Just a tick Rebecca, I've forgotten something," and he went back downstairs and took a packet of condoms out of his jacket pocket and hurried back upstairs.

"You remembered your boys scouts' motto Adam – be prepared!"

"How could I forget – better to be safe then sorry."

They both undressed one another and lay stretched out on the bed. Adam placed the condom over his penis and he got on top of her and kissed every part of her body. Her heart was beating fast with excitement, she had never experienced a lover like this before and stuck her breasts out so he could suck her nipples while he touched her sweet spot, the clitoris, and then entered her. He started rubbing his hands up and down her thighs and she screamed out in ecstasy and he came not long after.

"Are you alright Rebecca? I'm sorry, I couldn't hold back any longer."

"Me neither. I didn't have a wink of sleep last night

thinking of you sleeping downstairs Adam," and they snuggled up to each other.

"You have a beautiful body my darling," and he put his hands through her hair, taking it back off her face, "you are so stunning!"

"Thank you kind sir. Do you use the gym Adam? Look at your huge muscles, so sexy."

"Nah, it's just down to hard graft – where's the bathroom?"

"Down the corridor on the left-hand side. I can't move Adam, I'm too relaxed lying here but I do feel a bit peckish."

"Have you got any bacon and eggs, and perhaps sausages? I can cook us both a big breakfast."

"Look in the fridge, there's everything you need Adam."

"I'll just have a quick shower first, but stay where you are don't move – leave it to me."

Adam cooked a full English breakfast and put it on two plates which he then put on a large tray with some toast in a rack and took it upstairs to the bedroom.

"Sit up Rebecca."

"Wow! Thanks Adam, but I can't eat all of this, it's far too much."

"Just eat what you can and I'll eat the rest. Christ I forgot the knives and forks, I'll be back in a tick... shit the food is going to get cold Rebecca."

"Will you bring me some salt Adam."

When Adam finally climbed back into bed he tucked into his breakfast."

"You're a good cook Adam, this is delicious!"

"I don't mind cooking but not fancy food, just plain. I do a good roast though. What do you want to do today, I could take you out for lunch?"

"Why don't we go to supermarket Adam and buy two fillet steaks and new potatoes. I'll cook us lunch and maybe we can have a drink in the pub after, but I have to pick the girls up at their dad's at six o'clock."

"That's alright, I'll go and meet my mates in the pub for a game of pool. You've eaten hardly anything Rebecca, give me your sausage and bacon…"

"You're like my dad Adam, he loves his grub."

"Nought wrong with that."

"I need a shower. Leave the washing up to me, I'll do it later on – you've done enough. The breakfast was lovely Adam, thank you, you're spoiling me."

Rebecca went for her shower and Adam took the breakfast tray downstairs and washed the dishes. He also tidied up the kitchen and mopped the floor.

Rebecca had her shower and got dressed and came downstairs. When she walked into the kitchen she was surprised to see how spotless it was, "My goodness you have been busy! I wish you were here every day Adam, I love a domesticated man. Thanks a lot, but you should have left it for me to do."

"It didn't take too long but I've noticed one of your kitchen cupboard doors is loose, I'll sort that for you. Have you got any screwdrivers?"

"I have somewhere, but I can't remember where I've put them."

"Don't worry, I'll bring some with me next time I come."

The phone rang and Rebecca picked it up, "It's me – Linda – I was wondering if you fancy going for a drink? my boyfriend Charlie's away doing a course in London."

"Hold on a second…" Rebecca replied, turning to Adam, "Adam it's my friend Linda, she wants to go out for a drink with me – her boyfriend is away – can she join us in the pub, do you mind?"

"No worries."

"Hi Linda, I'll meet you in the Stag pub at one o'clock. Adam will be with me."

"Are you sure you don't mind Rebecca? Maybe you need time to yourselves."

"Don't be daft, I'll see you soon – bye."

Adam grimaced, "I thought we'd go to another pub, not that dump Rebecca."

"I said that one because Linda knows that pub, so it's easier to meet her there, anyway we're just having a few drinks – does it really matter?"

"I suppose not, now let's go to the supermarket and get some shopping – we'll go in my car, are you ready?"

"I don't need my coat, it's a nice day. You're not putting your jacket on Adam are you?"

"You must be joking! I'm sweltering now, I wish I'd brought my T-shirt and shorts."

So they both climbed into the car and Adam drove straight to the supermarket and parked the car. Rebecca picked up a basket from outside the store and inside they headed straight for the meat counter where she picked up two fillet steaks. Next they went to the vegetable section and she put some new potatoes in her basket.

"Do you fancy a dessert Adam? I quite like an apple pie and ice cream, but we'll have to go straight back home to put the ice-cream in the freezer."

Rebecca hurried around the store to get the items for dessert while Adam waited in the queue. When it was his turn to pay he was still waiting for Rebecca; the assistant behind the cash desk was looking fed up as there was a long queue behind him getting impatient. Rebecca finally appeared carrying two baskets full to the brim of groceries.

"You're a silly bugger, why didn't you get a trolley in the first place Rebecca?"

"Stop moaning Adam," she said, taking her purse out of her bag.

"Put it back, I'm paying," he said, and after they packed the groceries into carrier bags they left the store.

"Bloody hell Rebecca, we only went there for a few items and now we've got four carrier bags!" Adam put the groceries onto the back seat of the car and they climbed in and he drove them home.

When they went indoors Rebecca put all the shopping away and Adam took a lager out of the fridge and sat in the garden. Rebecca made herself a cuppa and joined him outside. "What time are we meeting your friend Linda?"

"I told her one o'clock, why?"

"I think I'd rather have dinner after we've been to the pub, I'm stuffed after that big breakfast I had. What's this friend of yours like Rebecca?"

"I think she's very attractive, clever, ambitious, and has a son called Tommy – he's adorable, he's a similar age to my girls. I met Linda and Ben on holiday in Spain. She's split up with him now and has a new boyfriend on the scene – a bank manager."

"I couldn't do that job, I love the outdoors. He must be earning quite a few bob?"

"I wouldn't know, Adam, but she has a gorgeous house and has a good lifestyle."

"Money isn't everything Rebecca, so long as you're happy."

"I agree, but you can't do much if you haven't got any. I was thinking Adam, let's walk to the pub instead of taking the car – shall we go now? It's a bit early but I need to stretch my legs, the exercise will do me good, let's go."

The pub was full of customers when they arrived and they sat at a table near to the bar. Adam ordered the drinks and paid for them; fifteen minutes later Linda walked in. Rebecca stood up and she gave her a wave and Linda came and sat down at the table.

"You must be Adam, pleased to meet you, I'm Linda."

"I know. Rebecca's told me all about you."

"Good things I hope!"

"Of course, what would you like to drink?"

"I'll have what Rebecca's drinking – a glass of red wine please."

Adam went up to the bar to get the drinks. "Blimey! you were right Rebecca, he is handsome."

"Hands off, he's mine – you have your boyfriend."

"I'm just saying he's a good catch, look at them biceps!"

"Behave yourself, Linda, he's coming..." and they both burst into laughter.

"What's so funny? My ears are burning – what are you two talking about?"

"About your fabulous sexy body Adam, and your handsome good looks."

"Shut up Linda, don't embarrass him."

"I think your friend Linda obviously has good taste in men Rebecca. I'm not going to disagree with her," and he gave Linda a wink.

"On a serious note Adam, can I have your advice – Rebecca told me you're a builder. I had an extension done on my house a while back but the rain is coming in from the ceiling now."

"Is it a flat roof or a tiled roof?"

"No it's tiled. I'd love you to take a look at it for me, the sooner the better before the problem gets much worse."

"No worries Linda, maybe it just needs a few tiles replacing. Give me your telephone number before you go and I'll bell you tomorrow. I just have to look at the dates in my diary when I get home and see which day I'm free to do the work."

"Gosh you have a good bloke there Rebecca, I'd hold on to him if I were you. I'll get these drinks in, it's my shout, are you both having the same?"

"Thanks Linda, we'll have the same."

When Linda went to the bar Rebecca turned to Adam

looking angry, "You're flirting with her, do you fancy her?"

"Piss off, what is your problem Rebecca? I'm only being friendly, I haven't done anything wrong."

"I want to go home, I feel uncomfortable."

"Honestly Rebecca, I know you've been through a lot with the miscarriage but be reasonable, if I had ignored your friend you would have been furious."

"Okay lower your voice, just leave it there Adam, she's coming with the drinks, please don't embarrass me."

Linda brought the drinks to the table, "This is my last one, I have to love you and leave you both after I've finished this drink. I'm picking up Tommy from his nanna's Rebecca."

"I'll give Adam your number Linda."

"Thanks a lot pet, I've no pen or paper on me."

"I'm sure he'll sort the problem out for you, and give Tommy a big hug and kiss from me. My god, you gulped that drink down quickly!"

"I know but you haven't met Ben's mum, she's a bloody nightmare if I'm late. It's been lovely meeting you Adam, don't forget to ring me."

"I always keep my word Linda."

"I'll ring you soon Rebecca, we can meet up for a coffee – I must say you both make a lovely couple! Bye."

Adam sat drinking his pint, giving Rebecca the silent treatment.

"Great, you're not talking to me Adam. Look I said I'm sorry, now you're being childish."

"I'm bloody angry with you Rebecca, there's no need for all that, you're so full of insecurities. I wasn't flirting."

"Okay it just looked like that to me Adam."

"Why because Linda asked me to look at her bloody roof? I was only being helpful because she's your friend, and besides small jobs are as important as bigger jobs. I get my work through word of mouth I told you that."

"I know that, anyway you'll be working on my bungalow soon."

"You just don't get it Rebecca do you? I can't stand your jealous streak."

"Please Adam let's not argue, I said I'm sorry. Let's go home and I'll cook us both some lunch."

They left the pub and Rebecca put her arms around him, "Please forgive me for being so stupid."

Adam took her hand and they walked home, and when they got indoors Rebecca kissed him passionately and he responded. "You can wrap me around your little finger, but you do get me riled up Rebecca. I hate aggravation for no reason."

"I know, Adam, I can be a bit of a nightmare. I don't know what comes over me."

"I'm hungry, do you want me to cook, Rebecca?"

"If you don't mind, Adam, I'm not the best of cooks as my children are always telling me. Do you want a beer?"

"No, just make me a strong black coffee with milk and two sugars. How would you like your steak cooked?"

"Medium rare please. I don't deserve you Adam, you're far too good for me."

"Absolute nonsense, I wouldn't be here if I thought that. You're just too distrustful Rebecca, which would drive anyone away. You need to chill out a bit more and stop taking things too seriously."

Rebecca set the table and Adam served the meal.

"Looks yummy Adam, who taught you to cook?"

"My mum – she loves cooking; my dad isn't interested."

"This meat is so tender Adam!"

"When I cook steak, if it's quite tough I rub a little olive oil on it with black pepper and salt, and when I've cooked it both sides I leave it to rest for a few minutes."

"I must admit I do a good spag bol," Rebecca

mentioned, "but I'm not all that keen on cooking. Remind me to give you Linda's number before you go Adam."

"Are you sure you can trust me to go to her house?"

"Point taken, give it a rest please Adam, of course I can trust you."

"Well I'll give her a ring then, it's probably just a small job."

"What are you doing tonight?"

"I told you, I'm going to have a game of pool with my mates; if not I'll stay in and watch the telly. We can go to the pictures or for a meal in the week Rebecca."

"I'd love to, it's just finding a babysitter, but my neighbour Irene might watch the kids for me – when I think about it, she's always offering."

"Have you not heard anything more about the bungalow?"

"I'm hoping I hear something this week from my solicitor, it's just the waiting game. I can't wait to move, Adam, I hate living here."

"That's a shame, it's a lovely house – much better than my pokey flat. That meal was delicious, even if I say so myself, and you have a clean plate Rebecca."

"It was tasty, thanks Adam."

"I'll do the washing up and I'll get going; you don't want to be late picking the kids up."

"You're right. Christ look at the time! Leave the dishes to me Adam, for god's sake, just go – I'll stick them in the dishwasher."

"They're a waste of space them machines, I prefer to wash the dishes myself. It's only a couple of plates and a few utensils."

"Yes I know but I have the twins who keep me busy and my work, so it does save me time – oh before I forget, there's Linda's telephone number."

"Thanks I'm off," and Adam put his jacket on and he gave Rebecca a passionate kiss and a cuddle.

"Bye sweetheart, drive carefully I'll give you a ring tomorrow."

When Adam left she felt sorry for him. How could she have been so stupid? She wouldn't have blamed him if he'd said he never wanted to see her again. It made her cringe just thinking about the way she treated him, she had never seen him so angry. But she pushed her thoughts to the back of her mind – she had to focus on collecting the children from their dad's house. She was running late so she picked up her bag from the table and walked out of the door and climbed into her car.

The journey seemed to take forever; there was a lot of traffic on the roads and construction workers, and there were long tailbacks where the traffic was diverted. When she finally got to the house and parked her car, she waited a few minutes before Jim came out of the house and walked to the car.

"Where's the girls?"

"They're just finishing their meal – come in Rebecca."

"You knew I was collecting them Jim, they should be ready."

"What's the rush? I can make you a cuppa while you're waiting."

"Is your girlfriend indoors?"

"That's over with, it's just me on my lonesome."

"Oh I see, she probably couldn't put up with your controlling ways."

"No it was me who finished with her as it happens. How about you, are you seeing someone Rebecca?"

"I am but it's none of your business Jim. Now tell the girls to hurry up please."

"You can't just be civil to me can you? We had some good times in our marriage Rebecca, it wasn't all bad was it?"

"I don't want to discuss it. As far as I'm concerned it's

in the past Jim."

"I'll go and get the girls, you miserable bugger," and ten minutes later they came out and climbed into the back seat of the car. "Bye girls, see you soon. Drive carefully Rebecca."

"I always do, bye Jim."

Rebecca drove home and the girls were quiet in the back seat, they both looked tired.

"Did you have a nice time with your dad, girls, what did you do?"

"Nothing much, it was boring. We went to the park and to the shops to buy some food and watched videos all night."

"What time did you go to bed Mary?"

"It was very late; we went the same time as Dad," Amy replied.

"No wonder you're both tired, you are having an early night tonight – it's school in the morning."

When they arrived home Rebecca noticed Irene's door was wide open which was unusual, she was always careful to lock it at night as she had been burgled in the past, so she quickly got out of the car and let the girls indoors. Rebecca knocked on Irene's door but got no answer, so she went into the sitting room and found her on the floor.

"What happened Irene? Let me help you up," and Rebecca sat her in the chair.

"The key broke in the lock. I came in here to ring a locksmith and felt dizzy, next thing I know I fell on the floor."

"I'll call an ambulance, Irene."

"Don't be silly, I'm fine. It's just I didn't have the strength to pick myself up off the floor."

"Listen, let me see to the girls and I'll come straight back and make you a cuppa and ring a locksmith."

"Thanks dearie, I'm sorry to be so much trouble."

"Now you're being daft – I'll be back in a few minutes."

Rebecca explained to the girls what had happened and told them to go upstairs and put their pyjamas on. Then she went next door to ring an emergency locksmith and told the guy on the phone all the details and to knock at her door when he arrived. She then made Irene a mug of tea.

"You're going to have quite a few bruises tomorrow morning Irene."

"It's my own fault, I haven't been taking my tablet like I should – I suffer with Meniere's disease of the inner ear."

"You never told me Irene. You must remember to take it – will you be alright for a little while?"

"I'll be fine. You go, you have things to do."

"When the guy comes I'll bring him in, you don't need to be worrying about strangers coming into your home. I'll be here till he leaves."

"You're a sweetheart Rebecca, now go."

When Rebecca went indoors she called the girls to come downstairs and they sat the kitchen table while she made them a ham sandwich and poured them a glass of milk.

"Is Irene ill? She's very old, have you seen her walk – she looks funny," and Amy got off her chair and showed her mum, "she's like a penguin."

"No she'll be fine Amy, she just had a nasty fall and I think you're being unkind – don't let her hear you speak like that, it may hurt her feelings. Now eat your sandwich, and you too Mary."

"Can we watch a video, Mum?"

"No I told you Amy, you're both having an early night."

"That's so unfair, Dad lets us stay up late."

"I'm going to have a word with him next time I see

him, now go upstairs and brush your teeth – you too Mary, no arguments."

Rebecca washed the dishes and went upstairs. She told the girls a bedtime story and tucked them up in bed and put the lights out.

When she came downstairs there was a knock at the door and she opened it

Hello, I'm the locksmith – here's my card."

"It's my neighbour next door, her key has broken in the lock – I'll take you in there…"

"It's only me Irene, the locksmith's here."

The job didn't take long to do, and Betty the new neighbour who recently moved into the house across the road called in to see her. "Are you alright Irene?"

"I'm fine thanks to Rebecca. You can go now Rebecca, Betty will look after me."

"Nice meeting you Betty, bye Irene, let me know if you need anything."

"You have enough to do looking after your girls, don't worry about me – cheerio."

Rebecca went indoors, she was pleased Irene had become friendly with the new neighbour; they were both of a similar age and she knew how lonely Irene got living on her own. She put the kettle on and made herself a cuppa and the phone rang so she picked it up, "Hi, it's me Rob."

"Is Valerie okay?"

"She's fine, she told me to ring you – we have a baby girl! We've named her Ruby; she weighed in at 8lbs 6oz."

"Congratulations to the both of you, when was she born?"

"Six o'clock this morning."

"That's a good weight Rob. I bet the boys are over the moon having a sister. Give Valerie all my love and I'll give her a ring tomorrow."

"I'll tell her Rebecca, I have to go now – bye."

Rebecca took her mug of tea off the kitchen table and went upstairs to check on the girls. They were fast asleep so she went into her bedroom, undressed and put her nightie on. She lay on the bed feeling sleepy and dozed off and when she woke up and looked at the clock it was 2am. She remembered she hadn't put the lights out downstairs or checked the doors were locked, so she crept downstairs worried she might wake the girls up, and checked everything was okay. Before long she was back in bed, making sure she set the alarm clock on her bedside table and was soon fast asleep.

Friends and Family

Two weeks had passed and Rebecca had her decree absolute and she felt she was finally moving on. The house purchase had gone through and she exchanged contracts, so now she could get the work started on the bungalow.

It was Saturday morning, she was having a lie in bed as the girls were staying at their nanna and grandad's house. Adam was in London visiting his parents and she had arranged to meet Linda for a coffee at the Italian coffee bar on the high street.

She climbed out of bed and got dressed, went downstairs into the kitchen and made herself a cuppa. The phone rang and she picked it up, "Hi sweetheart."

"Blimey Adam, you're ringing early."

"Are your parents keeping well?"

"My dad's full of flu, otherwise they're alright."

"I'm missing you Rebecca."

"Ah that's sweet of you to say, I miss you too – are you staying there tonight?"

"Yep, my parents don't see me that often, but I'll see you Monday morning and I'll bring a mate with me to get a start on your bungalow."

"I can't Adam, I'll be working. You go and when I've finished work I'll drive up there."

"Okay, no worries if you're busy, we can always meet up in the evening and maybe go out for a drink."

"I'll see. I have the girls Adam, anyway I'll speak to you later on, bye darling." Rebecca put the phone down and picked up her bag off the armchair and walked out of the door. She thought she'd have a stroll to the high street instead of using the car as it was a beautiful day.

Linda was already sitting in the café when she arrived. "I've ordered a coffee, do you want one Rebecca?"

"Yes please."

So Linda went over to the waiter to order Rebecca's coffee, then sat back down. "Where's Adam?"

"I told you on the phone Linda, he's visiting his parents. I'll see him Monday."

"That's right, I forgot. I have another job for him to do."

"What's that Linda?"

"I want him to lay a brick wall at the bottom of my garden; he did such a good job putting the tiles on my roof."

"Why can't Charlie do it for you?"

"He's no good at manual things and besides I think he's going off me."

"What makes you say that Linda?"

"He's not as thoughtful or affectionate as he used to be, maybe his job stresses him out."

"I think you might be overthinking it, you know what men are like – when the honeymoon period is over they can get more complacent and take you for granted. Talk to him about how you feel."

"I don't think it's that, Rebecca, he still talks on the phone to all his ex-girlfriends, he doesn't see he's doing anything wrong."

"What! You must be joking, I wouldn't put up with that, Linda."

"I've had it out with him but he says they're just good friends and one of them is still very friendly with his mum and dad. Charlie mixes with a lot of snobs – he's got a circle of friends who do lavish parties."

"Good for him, but that wouldn't be my scene. I'm happy with my Adam. What are you going to do Linda?"

"Nothing. The sex is good, I enjoy his company and our social life and he takes me to decent restaurants, otherwise I'd be sitting at home every night on my own when Tommy goes to bed. I do get a bit lonely. I'll just see how it pans out between us, but never mind him – will you ask Adam if he can do the job for me?"

"I think you should look for someone else. Adam's working on my bungalow on Monday and that will take up all of his time Linda; on the other hand maybe one of his mates can do it for you. I'll ask him."

"Cheers, I'd appreciate that."

"I have to ring Ben next week Linda and give him a month's notice; when you see him you could tell him instead? I don't really want to talk to him."

"No it's better coming from you Rebecca, he owns your property, I have nothing to do with it."

"Okay, I'll ring him."

"What if the bungalow isn't finished in a month's time Rebecca?"

"Me and the girls can move in with my mum and dad for a while, that's not a problem and I'll be close on hand to oversee the work. Do you want another coffee?"

"Why not. I don't know what to do with myself today – Tommy is staying with his dad and Charlie is with his mates, he is going to a stag do tonight."

Rebecca ordered two more coffees at the counter and sat back down at the table. "Why don't you come back to my place – I'll buy a bottle of wine and I'll cook us something to eat, it won't be much just a spaghetti Bolognese, Linda."

"Thanks, sounds good to me. I hate my own company."

"I'm the opposite – I sometimes love my own space, I don't like being in crowded places."

"The trouble is, a lot of my friends have moved on. I miss all the parties me and Ben had, we used to entertain a lot in those days."

"I remember you telling me, but surely you don't miss being with Ben – he's a creep, not being funny or anything."

"Christ no, I'd never take him back, it's all my old friends I miss; it's strange when you split up from your partner how many close friends you lose."

"They're hardly close friends Linda, otherwise it should have made no difference either way."

"True Rebecca, I'm just being stupid."

"I'll pay for the coffees – shall we go?" Rebecca paid at the counter and they walked down the high street and came to Marks & Spencer's.

"Do you fancy looking around the store Rebecca?"

"Nope, I always end up spending money I can't afford and besides I don't need any more clothes. Let's just go back to my place, we can call at the off-licence on the way and buy two bottles of red wine."

"You can be a bossy boots Rebecca. I thought you must be loaded with the sale of your property!"

"You're talking rubbish Linda. I have to pay for the work to be done and the bungalow needs a new bathroom and kitchen – God knows how much all that's going to cost me."

"Surely Adam will do the work cheaply for you?"

"Come off it, he might be my boyfriend but he still has to make a living – he's not loaded, he's just an ordinary working-class bloke."

"I've known some self-employed builders in the past who earn a bomb Rebecca, it's a good trade to have."

"Adam isn't interested in making big bucks, money isn't everything."

"That's where we differ Rebecca, I like men to be ambitious and have goals."

"I suppose your Charlie has all of them qualities? Well at least I can trust my Adam. It seems to me you're selling yourself short going out with someone who builds up his ego talking to his ex-girlfriends on the phone. I would find that demeaning. I'd get shot of him."

"I'm sorry Rebecca, I can see I've upset you. I didn't mean it the way it came out."

"Yes you did. Deep down you're a snob, but I won't hold that against you Linda. Let's forget about it and you can pay for the wine."

They walked to the off-licence and Linda paid for the wine, but as they walked further up the road Rebecca hardly spoke to Linda till they got indoors.

"Blimey Rebecca, the place is looking lovely, it's ages since I've been in this house. I remember when me and Ben bought it we did a lot of work on it, the garden was like a jungle."

"I agree it's a lovely house but I'll be happy when I move into the bungalow. Now do you fancy a cuppa?"

"Not really, can I have a glass of wine?"

"It's a bit early to be on the booze – pour yourself one, I'm having a tea."

They both sat in the garden with their drinks. "Gosh it's so quiet here you can hear a pin drop."

"The neighbours are mostly elderly, Linda. I don't mind the peace and quiet."

"I'd hate it – it's like a cemetery. My road has families with young kids."

"I'm going into the kitchen to make the spag bol – you must be hungry, do you want some crisps?"

"Yes please and another glass of wine."

"You're going to be pissed Linda."

"No I'm not – why don't you have one yourself?"

"I need to eat something first Linda. I can't drink on an empty stomach."

Rebecca set the table and served the pasta dish into two bowls and called Linda from the garden to come and eat.

"Looks delicious, you're a good cook Rebecca."

"Not really, this is the only thing I can cook well – oh I forgot, do you want some grated parmesan cheese on it?"

"Yes please. I must say the décor is lovely Rebecca, it's very homely and you keep the place spotless."

Linda poured Rebecca a large glass of red wine. "Jesus! Steady on, we'll both be pissed."

"Lighten up, Rebecca, you worry too much."

"It's not that, I'm not much of a drinker, I enjoyed the meal but I'm stuffed."

"Rebecca, you've hardly eaten a thing."

"Go in the sitting room and relax and I'll just put the dishes into the dishwasher."

"I'll take the bottle of wine with me and the two glasses."

Rebecca cleaned the kitchen and went into the sitting room. Linda was stretched out on the settee.

"You're tired Linda, it's the drink – don't have any more – I'll make you a coffee."

Linda sat up smiling, "Don't be daft, I'm fine – pour me another glass."

"Crikey, you're knocking it back quickly, I've only had one glass of wine and the bottle's nearly finished."

"You're so stuffy at times Rebecca, can't you just relax?"

"I am but I'm worried about you Linda, I know you enjoy a drink but I've never seen you like this."

"What are you getting at Rebecca?"

"When I met you in the café earlier on, I noticed you were not your usual confident bubbly self."

"You're quite astute Rebecca, I'm not. I've been suffering with depression and drinking like a fish."

"How long have you felt like this?"

"For a long time, I just feel numb and I'm not sleeping well."

"Have you been to see the doctor?"

"I have and he's given me some sleeping pills."

"That's okay but you need to talk to someone who is qualified, maybe a counsellor."

"To be honest my drinking is getting worse, Rebecca."

"How much do you drink?"

"At least a bottle a day."

"Christ that's serious. You've always been an upbeat person, full of self-confidence – have you any idea what sparked this off Linda?"

"I have thought about it, I think it's because I've set myself high standards most of my life and now with my marriage broken up and my job in jeopardy, I feel such a failure."

"What do you mean about your job? I thought you were doing well and been given a promotion…"

"I have but I'm on a warning because I keep turning up late and forgetting to book appointments."

"I'm so sorry Linda, I think you need to talk to someone – go and see your doctor again and I'll come with you for support. Just ring me and let me know when the appointment is."

Linda had tears streaming down her face. Rebecca went over to the settee and hugged her, "Shush, you'll be alright. I wish you'd told me all this before."

"I always put up a good front Rebecca, but I know I need help."

"You look shattered, why don't you go upstairs to bed and I'll bring you up a cuppa."

"I'm sorry to give you all my troubles…"

"Look, depression could happen to anyone. There have been times when I've felt worthless and so low myself, believe you me. Now will you please go upstairs and have a rest and I'll be up in a minute – you know where my bedroom is, it's the large one along the corridor next to the bathroom."

Rebecca made a cuppa and took it upstairs – Linda was out for the count, so Rebecca went quietly back downstairs and sat in the garden and drank the tea. 'Poor Linda how awful,' Rebecca thought to herself, 'she must be going through hell.' Of all the people she knew she thought she'd be the last person to suffer with depression, she had always been so confident and self-assured.

The phone rang and Rebecca went into the kitchen and picked it up, "Hi Rebecca darling, what are you up to?"

"I was just relaxing in the garden, Adam. I've got Linda here – she's a bit worse for wear and sleeping upstairs."

"Are you two tipsy?"

"Don't be daft, I've only had one drink – it's a long story, I'll tell you when I see you."

"I'm coming back tonight, my mum and dad have some friends staying so I don't want to hang about here. My brother was supposed to come but he's gone to visit his girlfriend's mum instead – typical of him."

"What time are you coming Adam?"

"I'll be at your place about eight o'clock."

"Fantastic! I can't wait to see you – should I cook something for you?"

"Don't bother, Mum's cooking me a dinner now and I'll have a sandwich later on. I'll have to go – see you soon sweetheart, love you."

"I love you too, bye," and Rebecca put the phone down.

Rebecca sat in the garden reading her book; hours had passed and Linda was still sleeping, she had gone upstairs to check on her but she was dead to the world so she closed the door and left her to sleep.

When she went downstairs into the kitchen to make herself a cuppa, she heard a knock at the door and opened it. "Adam! I wasn't expecting you for ages."

"I know, but I was bored stiff. Mum and Dad have Patrick and Jenny to keep them company – they're alright but drive me mad, they want me to play cards with them and all they talk about is the good old days."

"I see. Well don't just stand there, come in and let me take your coat."

"Where's Linda?"

"She's sleeping in my bed, I'll have to wake her up soon she's been there for hours. I feel sorry for her, Adam, she's suffering with depression."

"I thought she was the girl who had it all?"

"Shush, keep your voice down, don't let her hear you. She's drinking like a fish, I said I would go with her to the doctor's – she needs support. Why are you smiling? It's not funny Adam."

"Sorry, I just think you're taking it far too seriously Rebecca. She's probably just feeling fed up and letting her hair down by getting pissed."

"Honestly, you men have no idea when it comes to women's emotions, she's ill and needs help."

"Okay I get it, calm down Rebecca. I'm thirsty – have you got a beer?"

"There's two left in the fridge, help yourself – I'm having a coffee."

Just then, Linda came downstairs, "Hi Adam."

"You look rough Linda."

"Shut up Adam! How are you feeling, pet?"

"I'm sorry Rebecca, I wasn't much company, you should have woken me up."

"Don't be daft. Do you want a coffee Linda?"

"No thanks, I'd better get going – can you order a taxi for me please?"

"Oh, there's no need to order a taxi, Adam will take you home."

"Do I have a choice?"

"Just ignore him Linda. I'll give you a ring tomorrow."

Adam put his coat on and Linda gave Rebecca a big hug. "See you soon and thanks for everything, you're a good friend."

"I won't be long Rebecca, will you make me a ham and tomato sandwich – I'm starving."

"Yes Adam I will, just drive carefully. Bye Linda, take good care of yourself."

Rebecca went into the kitchen and made two rounds of sandwiches and it wasn't long before Adam came back. "Is she alright Adam?"

"Yep, I saw her to the door."

"Sit down and eat, I'll make you a cuppa."

"Has Linda lost weight? She's so thin Rebecca, like a skeleton."

"I noticed that. I don't think she's looking after herself properly but I think you could have been more tactful Adam – telling her she looks rough. I think she's worried about becoming an alcoholic – she drinks a bottle of wine a day."

"Bloody hell, that's far too much. How does she manage to hold her job down?"

"God knows, I couldn't function drinking every day like that. She said she's had her first warning at work and if she's not careful she'll lose her job."

"There's nought you can do Rebecca, she needs professional help."

"I know that, I'm not stupid, but it's not nice going through all that on your own – she's my friend."

"By the way, my mum and dad said next time I visit them to bring you and the girls with me, I've told them all about you."

"I'd love to come but I think you should come here one evening and have dinner with me and the girls."

"I'd love to meet them Rebecca, we could always go out for a pizza or go to McDonald's or Burger King."

"Great idea Adam. Have you done the costings on the

bungalow? You'll need me to give you some money up front."

"I normally charge £120 a day, plus materials, but I won't charge you that."

"Thanks, I'll give you £500 in advance Adam on Monday when I see you."

"That's fine. I don't know what my mate will charge you to fit the kitchen and bathroom, you'll have to discuss it with him but he's pretty reasonable with his prices. Remind me to give you his number."

"How long do you think your work will take to do?"

"Hopefully no more than ten days; I have a skip coming on site on Monday for the rubbish."

"Fantastic, Adam! I'm getting so excited something is happening. I'm going to look at kitchens and bathrooms with my mum and dad next week."

"That's good. I feel tired with all the driving I've done today, let's go to bed," so they went upstairs to the bedroom.

Adam undressed, showing his toned body, and Rebecca undressed and they both got into bed. Soon they were getting there via more kisses, and Adam's hand sliding between her legs, he was approving she was wet. Rebecca was disappointed when Adam stopped playing with her nipples, that was her weak spot, and she tried to experiment by touching his body all over and his shoulders and upper arms. Adam thrust into her and they became as one, the feeling was electric between them and they both came together.

"Phew! Adam, that was fantastic, it took my breath away."

Adam kissed Rebecca passionately, and soon they fell fast asleep in each other's arms.

The following morning Adam was the first one to wake up. He climbed out of bed and went to the bathroom for a shower, leaving Rebecca to sleep. After he dressed himself he went downstairs to the kitchen and made himself a coffee. Rebecca's phone rang and he picked it up.

"Hello – is Rebecca there?"

"Who's speaking?"

"It's her mum."

"She's sleeping, I'll go and wake her up."

"No just leave her, I was just wondering if she wants to come over for Sunday lunch – tell her to ring me when she wakes up."

"I will, bye."

Rebecca came downstairs, "Who was that, Adam?"

"Your mum, you'd better ring her back," which she did.

"Are you alright?"

"I'm fine – are you coming for lunch?"

"I have Adam here Mum, I was coming to yours about four o'clock to pick the girls up."

"Why don't you bring Adam with you, he's quite welcome to come for lunch – I've got a big joint of beef Rebecca, more than enough for all of us."

"Hold on, I'll ask him…"

"Mum wants to know if we both want to go for lunch."

"Yeah alright, tell her thanks."

"…what time do you want us there Mum?"

"Come when you like, I'm doing lunch for one o'clock."

"Okay we'll see you then Mum, bye."

"You don't really want to go Adam do you?"

"I don't mind, it'll be good to get to know your parents more and get to know the children Rebecca. I'm not planning to leave you, I'm going nowhere my darling," and he gave Rebecca a big hug.

"We're okay aren't we Adam?"

"I think so, don't you?"

"I've never felt this happy in a long time. Don't get me wrong, I adore my children but it's lovely to do things with a partner."

"Good, then you can make me a crispy bacon sarni with brown sauce Rebecca, and I'll make you a cuppa."

"Just let me have a quick shower and get dressed Adam."

"No hurry, take your time – I'll do breakfast."

After Rebecca had showered, dressed and went back downstairs, Adam took the bacon off the grill and made the sandwiches. They sat at the kitchen table eating their breakfast when there was a knock at the door.

"I'll go Rebecca, stay there," and when he opened the door Betty was standing there. "I'm sorry to trouble you, I'm Betty – a neighbour. Is Rebecca in?"

"I'll go and get her for you."

"Who is it Adam?"

"Someone called Betty…"

Rebecca went to the door, and Betty explained, "I'm sorry to disturb you, Irene has had another fall in the bathroom. I'm finding it hard to lift her up – could you help me?"

"Of course, I'll come right now…"

Rebecca closed the door behind her, and when she went into the house with Betty the two of them went straight upstairs to the bathroom. Irene was crying out in pain, so they lifted her gently off the floor and took her to the bedroom and put her gently on the bed.

"What am I like, Rebecca! My leg is killing me."

"I think it may be a good idea to call an ambulance, you might have broken it," Betty suggested.

"No you bloody well won't, tell her Rebecca – the interfering old busybody."

"You haven't lost your spirit! Nothing much wrong

with you Irene, but I do think you should get checked over – Betty's right."

In the end Rebecca persuaded Irene. The ambulance was called and came within fifteen minutes, and Betty went with Irene to the hospital.

Rebecca went back indoors. "Christ where have you been?" Adam asked.

"My neighbour had a nasty fall, she's gone to hospital poor woman. I think she needs a home-help – she can't manage on her own but she's as stubborn as a mule. I've grown very fond of her…"

"You love everyone Rebecca, you're far too soft for your own good. I'll make you a cuppa."

"Where's my half sandwich Adam?"

"It was stone cold, but I ate it – do you want me to make you another one?"

"Nah, it's alright, Mum always makes a big Sunday roast – she's a good cook."

"I was thinking we could stop at the garage down the road, they sell flowers on the forecourt – I want to buy some for your mum Rebecca."

"What a lovely thought, Adam. Mum will be over the moon, she loves flowers especially roses or lilies."

"I'm a bit nervous about meeting the girls though."

"Don't be daft, my girls are great kids. Mind you, I would say that, I'm their mum. You just have to be yourself, Adam, and they will see what a lovely person you are – I'm impressed," and she kissed Adam on the cheek.

"Which one of them takes after you Rebecca?"

"I'm not sure… my daughter Mary is a sensitive child and she's quite shy but very affectionate, whereas Amy her twin sister is full of self-confidence – she speaks her mind and will tell you what she thinks but she has a big heart."

"She sounds like you Rebecca. I thought I'd buy them both some comics to take with us or maybe drawing books?"

"Don't be silly, my mum and dad spoil them rotten – you're worrying too much Adam. I'm sure in time they will both become very fond of you, but you must understand you will never take the place of their dad, they both love him to bits."

"I understand, I would never try to do that."

"I'm glad you said that. Now can we get going, I'm dying for you to meet the girls."

"We'll go in my car – I'll bring you and the girls back home and then shoot straight off. I have to pick up my mate early in the morning from his house, he's going to help me with the work on your bungalow Rebecca."

"Okay, Adam, no problem."

Rebecca and Adam climbed into the car and on the way they stopped at the petrol station. Adam picked up a bunch of flowers from the forecourt and went inside to pay for them at the counter. He hurried straight back to the car and handed the flowers to Rebecca.

"Blimey, they look half dead Adam. I would say they are chrysanthemums, my mum calls them funeral flowers."

"Oh I don't know, there wasn't much to choose from, do you want me to take them back?"

"No don't bother Adam, it's the thought that counts. Get back into the car, let's just go."

There was a lot of traffic on the road and Rebecca could sense Adam was getting stressed so she was silent till they finally arrived at her mum's bungalow. They climbed out of the car and Rebecca took her spare key out of her pocket and let herself in.

Her mum was in the sitting room dusting the furniture. "Hello my darling, and it's lovely to see you again Adam."

"Mum, these flowers are for you – Adam bought them for you."

"How kind of you, thank you so much."

"Where are the girls, Mum?"

"They're at the park with your dad, they won't be long. I've finished dusting so I'll put these flowers in a vase and put the kettle on."

"You have a gorgeous bungalow Grace."

"Thanks Adam, but with the French doors open it gets very dusty everywhere. Bert likes all the windows open as well, he loves the fresh air coming through – you can do it when we're having lovely weather like we've had lately. Would you like tea or coffee Adam?"

"Tea please."

"Mum sit down, I'll make it," and they sat at the kitchen table drinking their tea when Bert and the girls came in.

"Dad you look knackered! I bet the girls have run you ragged."

"I'm feeling my age my girl. Put the kettle on, Grace, and make me a cuppa. It's nice to see you again Adam," and Bert shook his hand.

"Girls, say hello to Adam, he's a very good friend of mine."

Amy giggled, "Is he your boyfriend Mum?"

"Honestly, you're a little devil Amy."

Grace interrupted, "Why don't you two girls do some drawings in your new books I bought you yesterday and show Adam how creative you both are. You can do it in the garden on the table, it's a lovely day and I'll bring you both some orange juice."

"Okay Nanna, will you come Mum?" Amy asked.

"No Adam will, I'm helping your nanna with lunch."

"I'm going for a lie down for an hour Grace," said Bert, "You're staying for dinner Adam aren't you?"

"I am Bert thanks."

"That's good. Grace, don't let me sleep too long otherwise I'll be up all bloody night long."

"Get yourself to bed then, you cantankerous old sod," Grace said, grinning like a Cheshire cat."

"Ignore my mum and dad, they're like this all the time Adam, always having a go at one another. I bet your parents don't carry on like this?"

"Oh I don't know, they have their moments Rebecca."

Rebecca helped her mum prepare the vegetables and Adam was outside in the garden occupying the girls.

"What do you think of Adam, Mum?"

"He seems a nice young man. I can see you're smitten."

"He'll do anything for me, Mum, and he's so laid back."

"That's good. All I ever wanted for you Rebecca is to be happy."

"I am, Mum."

"The only advice I would give you is to take things slowly, he hasn't got kids of his own; it's a shock to the system."

"I know what you mean Mum, he was nervous at the thought of meeting my girls."

"Amy makes me smile Rebecca, she certainly speaks her mind which is not a bad thing but I reckon she has cottoned on he's your boyfriend, she never misses a trick. Anyway, when is that lovely chap of yours starting work on the bungalow?"

"I told you, Mum, in the morning."

"Is that a definite?"

"Yes he is – why?"

"Your dad says Adam will need some money up front."

"I'm sorting that out Mum. I was thinking Tuesday I could come here and we could all go together to B&Q – they sell tiles and do fitted kitchens and bathrooms. It may take 3 to 4 weeks for delivery, and Adam can give me the measurements tomorrow."

"Your dad said Pete our neighbour can do a bit of gardening for you."

"Please tell him no, Mum, it's too much. I can get someone else, otherwise Dad will be helping him and he has enough to do here with your large garden to keep it under control. That reminds me – can I use your phone Mum? I have to give Ben my landlord a ring to give him a month's notice on the house, I'm dreading this."

"You can't today Rebecca, it's Sunday, he won't be too pleased."

"I don't give a bugger, I want to get it over with," so she rang him.

"Ben speaking."

"Hi, it's me – Rebecca. I'd like to give you a month's notice Ben, starting from tomorrow."

"Oh I see, well that's okay. How are you?"

"I'm fine, I just wanted to let you know, but I must go I'm busy helping Mum in the kitchen."

"Okay – bye."

"I can't stand him Mum, thank God that's done and dusted."

"I'll finish the dinner off, Rebecca. I think you ought to join Adam in the garden with the children – they must be driving him mad by now."

"Alright Mum, give me a beer and I'll take it out to him."

Grace went upstairs and woke up Bert. When she came back downstairs she served the dinner out while Rebecca set the table. The lunch was ready so she called Adam and the girls to come in from the garden and they all sat around the kitchen table having dinner, apart from Bert.

"Please Rebecca, go and tell your dad to come down. I'm not going upstairs again, my knees are giving me gyp and his food will get cold."

A few minutes later Bert came down and sat at the table, "This look's good Grace – what's this I only have one Yorkshire pudding on my plate? Adam, you're privileged – you have two."

"Be quiet Bert and eat your dinner, you can have mine. Honestly, you're a glutton – we have a guest, don't show yourself up."

"Are you alright Mum? You look in pain."

"It's my joints; I'll take a pain killer when I've eaten."

"I think you should rest more often Grace, but she never listens to me Adam – you know what women are like."

"I'll remind you of that Bert when you keep calling me for a cuppa every ten minutes."

"Mum, Adam is good at drawing animals," said Amy admiringly.

"So are you Amy."

"But I'm not as good as him Mum."

"I can draw better than Amy, Mum, she can't draw a house properly."

"Yes I can Mary, you're being horrid."

"Girls stop arguing and eat your dinner."

"The meal was lovely Grace, I enjoyed it," Adam complimented.

"Would you like some more roast beef and roast potatoes Adam?"

"No thanks, I'm full, honestly."

"Any left-overs I can make a fry-up tomorrow Grace."

"Trust you, Bert, always thinking about your belly."

"Adam, let's do some more drawings – come on," urged Amy.

"No Amy, don't be rude. He's just finished his dinner and he needs a rest. You can go with Mary into the garden and play with your games."

"Oh alright Nanna – can I have an ice-cream cornet?"

"You two go and play in the garden and I'll bring you both one."

"Mum you spoil them."

"When you were growing up Rebecca I spoilt you too. Who wants some ice-cream and fruit salad?"

"Not for me Mum, what about you Adam?"

"No thanks. I'm stuffed."

"I'll have some, Grace."

"I thought you would Bert, why am I not surprised."

"I'll get you a beer Adam, do you want one Dad?"

"Not just now Rebecca, I'll have one later on. You have your work cut out tomorrow Adam, who's helping you?"

"My mate Tom; it'll take about ten days to knock it out and get it prepared for the kitchen and bathroom Bert."

"You'll need some money to get some materials?"

"Dad, I'm giving Adam some money tomorrow."

"I charge £120 a day normally but I'll do it cheaper for Rebecca."

"That's very reasonable – have you hired a skip?"

"Yep, it's coming in the morning."

"Dad it's all sorted, leave Adam alone."

"I'm only asking, anyway I'm on hand to oversee the work," Bert said grinning.

"Are you coming with me and Mum to look at kitchens and bathrooms at B&Q on Tuesday?"

"I'll see how I feel, I hate traipsing around shops. Where's Grace?"

"She's sitting in her comfy chair in the sitting room Dad, I think she's in pain."

"Make her a cuppa Rebecca, I'll sit with her."

"Adam will you help me with the washing up and then we'll head home so Mum and Dad can have a rest?"

"Sure, no problem. I'll wash, you dry."

It didn't take long and soon everything was spick and span. Grace was delighted when she walked into the kitchen, "You two, thanks ever so much, I would have done it."

Rebecca called the girls who were still playing in the garden and she kissed her mum and dad. "I'll pop in tomorrow after work."

"Thank you for the meal," Adam said to Grace.

"You're welcome, anytime, but I expect I'll see you tomorrow too – and thanks for the lovely flowers."

When they left the house they all climbed into the car and Adam drove off. Rebecca thought he looked tired. "Do you want me to drive, Adam?"

"Don't be daft I'm fine."

"Is Adam staying at our house tonight Mum?" Amy asked.

"No, he has a flat of his own."

"I wanted to show him my hamster Goldie."

"It's my hamster too Amy, we share him don't we Mum?" Mary said with an annoying look on her face.

"Yes, he belongs to both of you and Adam will see him another day."

"Your dad is a character Rebecca."

"Yes, he speaks his mind and can be so stubborn but my mum knows how to handle him, he's just set in his ways Adam."

"I think they're a lovely couple and your mum is a really good cook – that dinner was ace. Your girls are so sweet – I can see Amy is the dominant one."

"She is strong-willed Adam, but they are both very close and look out for one another."

"I heard that, Mum, you're talking about me."

"You don't miss a trick Amy, you shouldn't be earwigging on grown-ups' conversations."

Finally they arrived at the house and the girls jumped out of the back seat of the car and stood at the front door.

"Hey girls, where's your manners? Say bye to Adam."

They both waved and Rebecca kissed Adam on the cheek, "Drive carefully and I'll see you tomorrow," and he drove off.

When they went indoors Rebecca put the kettle on.

"Can we watch a video Mum?" Mary asked.

"I think you both should have a bath, it's school tomorrow."

"Nanna gave us a bath this morning Mum before you came."

"Oh alright, go into the sitting room and watch a video – but only one! Do you want a drink?"

"Can we have a Coke, Mum?"

"I'd rather you had an orange juice, but just this once."

"Nanna always gives us Coke."

"Does she now, well I must have a word with her, Amy, I don't think it's good for you."

"Please don't Mum, she might get upset."

"I'm only joking, now go and watch your video you two, I'll bring your drinks in for you in a minute – are you hungry? I could do a peanut butter sandwich or a ham one."

"No Mum, can we just have some crisps?"

"Amy you're a bossy boots. I want a ham sandwich Mum."

"Yes alright Mary," and Rebecca went into the kitchen and put the drinks on a tray with a plateful of ham sandwiches and a bowl of crisps and made herself a cuppa. She spent the evening relaxing with the girls watching videos of children's cartoons till it was their bedtime, then took them upstairs to the bathroom so they could clean their teeth and put on their pyjamas.

When she tucked them up in bed, Mary asked, "Mum will you tell us a story?"

"No Mary, not tonight, you've watched three videos, so don't push your luck. It's time for your beauty sleep, you too Amy. I'm putting the lights out right now and I don't want to hear a peep out of you both – goodnight, God bless."

Rebecca went downstairs and put all the lights out and made sure the doors were locked and went back upstairs to bed. It had been a long day and she felt tired and decided to have an early night.

The alarm went off and Rebecca woke up. She climbed out of bed and got dressed and went downstairs to the kitchen. When she looked out of the window she could see the sun shinning, it was a beautiful day. She called to the girls from the bottom of the stairs to rise and shine, and then went into the kitchen to make herself a cuppa and a piece of toast.

It was an exciting day for her – Adam was starting work on the bungalow and she was full of the joys of spring. Mary was the first one to come into the kitchen, "Good morning, did you sleep well?"

"I did Mum, what's for breakfast?"

"Would you like me to make you some scrambled eggs on toast?"

"I'd rather have some coco pops, please."

Amy appeared with a grumpy face.

"What's up with you Amy?"

"Goldie kept me awake going round on his wheel all night."

"Oh dear, do you want me to bring him downstairs Amy? I'll put the cage in the sitting room…"

"No Mum, leave him, moving him might upset him."

"Alright, if you say so. What are you having for breakfast?"

"I'll have the same as Mary and a glass of milk."

"I might ask Adam to have dinner with us tonight, girls – what do you think?"

"Yippee! I like him Mum. I can show him my hamster

and he can do more drawings with us."

"Goldie's mine too," Mary said frowning, "and Adam can take us to the park to feed the ducks."

"Blimey, I'm not sure about that, girls – he'll be working hard on the bungalow today so he'll be very tired when he finishes work. Anyway, we'll see. Eat your breakfast both of you, I'm just going to put some make-up on upstairs."

Rebecca put her make-up on and made the beds, and when she came downstairs she was pleased to see the girls had eaten all their breakfast and had their school bags ready to go to school.

"Mum can we go now?"

"You're keen Amy, just let me put the dishes in the dishwasher then we're off."

They all climbed into the car and Rebecca dropped the girls off at the school gates. She drove back to the house as she remembered she'd forgotten her purse. When she opened her front door the phone rang and she quickly picked it up.

"Hi it's me Rebecca, I'm at the police station."

"What's happened Linda?"

"The police put me in the cell last night for being drunk and disorderly. I went out to the pub with Gemma, a friend of mine, and we got into a fight with some blokes. I can't remember anything else."

"Where's Tommy?"

"He's with my mum, will you come and pick me up?"

"I can't Linda, I'm on my way to work – why don't you get a taxi home or ring Ben?"

"I'll sort it Rebecca, don't worry about me."

"Listen I have to go, I'll speak to you later on – bye."

Rebecca drove to work feeling stressed, she hated being late and keeping her clients waiting. When she arrived and was just about to open the salon door, Maggie her boss called her into her office, "Take a seat. I'm sorry

Rebecca but we've had an epidemic of flu with my four elderly ladies who've booked to have their hair done with you, so they've cancelled your appointments. I know it's an inconvenience but these things happen."

"I understand Maggie, give them all my regards and I wish them a speedy recovery. Can you ring me when they feel better?"

"The other ladies you've got booked for the rest of the week are fit and well, so your services are needed. You're doing a wonderful job, my elderly residents speak very highly of you. Anyway, I have to go to the kitchen now and sort out the menus with the chef. Rebecca, you must excuse me – I have a busy day ahead of me."

Rebecca was pleased she had the day free when she left the office, but what she was earning was never going to pay the bills and make ends meet. In the long run it was her savings that was keeping her afloat and her mum and dad's financial help. She knew she would have to make a decision soon to change her job.

She walked to the car park and climbed into her car and drove to the high street where she parked her car and went into the bank to withdraw £500 for Adam. She fancied a coffee and went further down the road to the café where she ordered a coffee and took it to the table. As she sat down, her phone rang and she took it out of her bag.

"When are you coming to the bungalow Rebecca?"

"You're lucky – I'm not at work Adam, there's an epidemic of flu and my customers are ill, so I've just been to the bank to get your money and I'm sitting in a café having a coffee. I'll drive straight over to you when I've finished it. Is everything okay?"

"Yep, me and Tom have made a start on the kitchen but I'll need some money to buy some materials."

"I'll pay for the coffee and I'll be with you soon."

Rebecca left the café and drove straight to the bungalow. When she went inside she could see how much work had been done – all the kitchen cupboards had been knocked out and put into the skip. "Gosh, them tiles went out with the dark ages, they are ugly. I can't breathe here, there's dust and dirt everywhere Adam, you two should be wearing masks."

"Did you get the money Rebecca?"

"Yes there's £500 Adam," and she handed it to him and he began to count it.

"Cheeky bugger, don't you trust me?"

"It's not you Rebecca, some banks make mistakes but it's all there. I'm thirsty I'd love a mug of tea?"

"I'll bring one – what about you Tom?"

"Yes please, milk and three sugars."

"Okay, I'll pop over to see Mum and Dad and bring them over for you and some biscuits."

Rebecca crossed the road and used her spare key to open the door; there was no sign of her mum and dad but their car was sitting in the drive. She put the kettle on and ten minutes later they walked in.

"Where have you two been?"

"We went with Pete to the doctor's, he was feeling rough – he has a flu virus, so the doctor gave him some antibiotics. Why aren't you at work Rebecca?"

"My customers have the same thing Mum, so I have the day free. I was just about to take Adam and Tom a cuppa – do you two want one?"

"No thanks pet, take them a piece of my coconut cake I made."

"Grace what are we running, a bloody café? Let the blokes get on with their work."

"Honestly Bert, you can be a miserable bugger. Go into the garden and I'll bring you your tea."

"I know when I'm not wanted. Rebecca your mum is a hard task master, she loves telling me what to do," and he took his jacket off and went to sit in the garden.

"Mum, I'll just take the tea over the road to the workers and I'll be back in a mo."

Over at Rebecca's bungalow, the workers soon tucked into their tea and cake.

"That cake tastes delicious!"

"Mum made it Tom, she loves baking – enjoy. Adam, do you fancy coming to my place tonight to have dinner with me and the girls? Nothing fancy, just chips and burgers."

"I thought I'd have a game of pool with my mates tonight Rebecca, you don't mind do you?"

"Don't be daft, why should I?"

"How about if I come tomorrow night to your place sweetheart? I'll come straight after work and I'll get us all a take-away pizza."

"I'd like that, what time Adam?"

"Say about six o'clock or thereabouts?"

"Okay, I'll leave you two to get on," and she kissed Adam on the cheek shyly. She saw Tom had a big grin on his face. "What's so funny Tom?"

"Nothing, I just think you two are like an old married couple."

"Piss off Tom, you're just jealous. Your idea of taking a woman out is to buy her half a pint of lager and a bag of crisps," said Adam. "He's so mean Rebecca."

"I'm not getting involved! Have you got measurements for the kitchen and bathroom?"

Adam took them out of his pocket and gave them to her. "Thanks, I'll see you tomorrow Adam," and she gave him a hug.

Rebecca crossed the road to her parents' bungalow. "Mum, I'm shooting off – are you and Dad still coming with me to look at kitchens and bathrooms tomorrow? I'll come here when I've dropped the girls off at school."

"Don't count on your dad coming but I'd love to come with you. Where are you off to now?"

"I want to do a bit of shopping and visit Valerie and Rob, I feel awful leaving it so long – the baby will be crawling before I get to see her."

"She'll understand Rebecca, you've had a lot going on lately."

"Where's Dad?"

"Next door with Pete."

"Say bye for me, I'll see you tomorrow Mum," and Rebecca climbed into the car.

The traffic was bad on the roads and when she finally arrived at the council estate she was shocked to see how it had been run down and neglected. The front gardens were overgrown and there were rubbish bins stuck out on the pavements everywhere spilling over with rubbish. Rebecca got out of her car and was careful where she walked – there was dog poo all over the grass verge to the entrance of the flats.

She knocked on the door and Valerie opened it; she had the baby in her arms.

"This is a surprise! Lovely to see you Rebecca, come in."

"I don't know how you live here Valerie I'd hate it."

"I have no choice. We've asked for a move but being behind with the rent didn't help. You'll have to excuse the mess, Rob's in the middle of painting this room."

"Let me hold Ruby – blimey, she looks like you Valerie, she has your brown eyes and chubby face, what a cutie she is."

"I have no bother with her, not like my boys when they were babies. She hardly ever cries and loves her sleep."

"Where's Rob, is he at work?"

"Yes, he's still working at the warehouse. He tries to

do as much overtime as he can, it's a struggle for us managing on one wage packet coming in. I miss my cleaning jobs – that helped pay for the food shopping."

"Gosh it must be difficult Valerie, I don't know how you cope. How much do you owe in arrears on the rent?"

"Four hundred pounds, it may as well be a thousand pounds, I haven't got it. I need to buy a cot for Ruby soon – she can't stay in the Moses basket much longer, she's a big baby."

"I was thinking what to buy her Valerie, so let me buy the cot."

"Oh no, I wasn't hinting or anything."

"Don't be daft, I know that, Valerie," and Rebecca took her purse out of her bag and gave her £150.

"You're far too generous Rebecca, I can't take that."

"Yes you can, it's my pleasure. Now how about I make us both a cuppa." Rebecca went into the kitchen but when she opened the fridge to get the milk she noticed there was hardly anything in there to feed a family with. She took the two mugs of tea into the sitting room and sat down.

"You must be hungry Rebecca, I've got some biscuits in a tin in the top cupboard above the washing machine."

"No thanks, honestly I'm fine Valerie."

"Tell me all the gossip, what's been happening to you Rebecca?"

"I'm in a good place Valerie. You know Jim, he was so controlling and suffocating as a husband and Richard was an egotistical man who hated responsibility – when I told him I was pregnant he asked me whose it was, knowing full well it was his. I was devastated when I had a miscarriage Valerie."

"Oh no Rebecca, that's heart-breaking, I should have been there to support you."

"Hardly, you were pregnant yourself Valerie – you had enough to deal with looking after yourself. I got through it with the help of my mum and dad and my neighbour Irene, they were brilliant. Anyway, as the doctor said, it wasn't meant to be."

Valerie gave Rebecca a hug, "Hey don't set me off, I've shed enough tears Valerie. Anyway changing the subject, I think I've found my soul mate with the guy I am with now. He's called Adam, he's met my girls and he's doing the work on the bungalow for me."

"You mean that gorgeous looking guy we saw in the Stag pub that night we went out together and he bought us drinks?"

"That's him Valerie."

"I'm pleased for you honey, you deserve every happiness you can find Rebecca. Good luck, that's all I can say."

"Ah thanks, I just wish my friend Linda could get her head together – she's drinking like a fish and was in the police cell last night for being drunk and disorderly. I feel sorry for Tommy her son."

"We all handle stress in different ways, look at me – I don't exercise, I eat the wrong food and everyone I meet thinks I look much older than I am."

"It's because of the frumpy clothes you wear Valerie."

"Some friend you are Rebecca, thanks a lot you cheeky monkey."

"Sorry, what I meant to say was you're always wearing black when I see you."

"That's true, I do Rebecca – it's only because I think the colour black makes me look much slimmer, not everyone has your perfect petite figure."

"Stop it, your not obese Valerie."

"Oh thanks, that's good to know."

"Do you and Rob ever get a chance for a night out together?"

"You must be joking, we're always skimping and scraping, counting the pennies and besides it's not easy trying to find a baby-sitter."

"Well I can help you there. I'd love to look after Ruby and the boys for you when you need a night out. You just call me and let me know."

"You're a good friend Rebecca."

"My mum and dad went through tough times bringing me up Valerie. They lived on some dingy estates and it took them a long time to get on their feet. They inherited the bungalow but they both worked hard. You try and get the council to move you even if it's out of the area Valerie, and into the countryside."

"Rob and the boys would love that, but I pay £10 extra on top of the rent money every week Rebecca to get the debt paid off so I can't afford to pay any more."

"That's a start, it will take about ten months Valerie – you can do it. Listen to me, you're doing a good job with the kids – they're healthy and happy, you're a great mum and anyway children look for stability and security rather than materialistic stuff."

"Rob is my rock Rebecca, he does his best, it's not his fault. He never grumbles, I can't imagine my life without him in it."

"Ah bless, that's all that matters. You're a strong woman and a close-knit family Valerie, some people haven't got that with all their wealth."

"Don't get me wrong Rebecca, I'd love a decent home for my kids and to know I could afford to give them much more than I do, but it won't be happening in the near future so I have to be realistic."

"You're such a strong woman Valerie, try to stay positive – but I have to go now, I want to do some shopping before I pick up the girls from school."

"Let's not lose touch with each other Rebecca."

"I promise I won't Valerie, we'll always be good friends," and she gave her a big hug and a kiss at the front door and walked to her car and climbed in.

Rebecca drove to the supermarket where she parked her car, but she suddenly realized she had only ten pounds left in her purse after giving money to Valerie to buy the cot. She needed to go to a cash point outside the supermarket, but when she got out of the car she looked over and saw there was a long queue so she decided not to bother – the shopping could wait for another day. There were fish fingers in the freezer for dinner, or the girl's favourite chicken nuggets, and she felt too tired to hang about so she drove straight home.

When she got indoors she made herself a cuppa and took her shoes off and relaxed on the settee; there was at least another hour before she had to pick the girls up from school. The phone rang and she picked it up.

"Hi, it's me – Linda."

"Are you alright?"

"I'm with my mum she wants me and Tommy to stay with her for a while till I get on my feet. We've had a long chat about everything and I've told her how I feel."

"I think that's a good idea Linda, just keep in touch and let me know how you're getting on. I have to pick the girls up from school now – you take good care of yourself and I'll call you soon, bye."

Rebecca knew as a friend there wasn't much she could do to help her and Linda was close to her mum, so that was the best option as her mother had the time to keep an eye on her and Tommy.

Adam and Mark

The week flew by. Rebecca had been to B&Q with her mum and she ordered white kitchen cupboards with a black Formica worktop, and a white bathroom suite, both of which were going to be delivered in three weeks' time. The tiles were in stock, and available any time, so Rebecca chose bright red ones for the kitchen and cream ones for the bathroom and paid for them.

Adam had the walls prepared ready for plastering and for tiling. Things were progressing and Rebecca was over the moon.

It was Friday evening and the girls were with their dad for the weekend. Rebecca was waiting for Adam to come from work and she had prepared a roast chicken dinner for the two of them. The doorbell rang and Rebecca opened the door, "Come in – you look shattered Adam, and filthy, go straight upstairs and have a shower!

"Bloody hell, something smells good! I'm starving Rebecca."

After Adam had his shower and got changed, he came downstairs. Rebecca had the meal ready on the kitchen table.

"Mmm, this looks delicious, I've only had a ham roll all day – I could eat a horse."

"Good, then tuck in, there's more if you want it."

"By the way, Mark my brother is staying at my flat for a few days Rebecca. I told him he could meet us at the Stag pub at eight o'clock – I gave him the directions."

"Why didn't you ring me and let me know Adam?"

"I was busy. Anyway, what's your problem?"

"I don't feel like going out, and I would have liked

some notice!"

"You're out of order Rebecca, after all he's my brother and I don't see much of him. I spent time with your kids and took them out for a pizza Tuesday night. I think you're being very selfish."

"Now you're being nasty Adam, there's no need for that."

"Okay we won't go. I'll just leave him in the pub sitting on his own."

"Christ! I'll go upstairs and get ready now Adam, I don't want an argument."

"Me neither Rebecca, for God's sake it's only one night."

So Rebecca got changed and came back downstairs.

"You look lovely sweetheart, just leave the dishes and we'll do them when we get back."

They left the house and climbed into Adam's car and he drove straight to the pub and parked outside. When they walked inside, the pub was packed with customers and they saw Mark standing at the bar.

"You managed to find the place alright Mark?"

"I did bruv, but it's a dump!"

"I'm Rebecca, pleased to meet you."

"You too. I'm buying the drinks – what are you both having?"

"Rebecca will have a glass of red wine and I'll have a beer Mark."

"Find a table you two and I'll bring the drinks over."

They managed to find a table and sat down. "Your brother looks a bit like you Adam, he's much more reserved than you I would say."

"He's alright once you get to know him, he can be a bit sarcy – he speaks his mind."

Mark brought the drinks to the table and sat down.

"How are you getting on at university Mark?"

"I've nearly finished my Masters Degree and my tutor

says I'm one of the best students he's had."

"Nothing like blowing your own trumpet, you big head."

"Shut up Adam, you're just jealous, I'm the brainy one out of the two of us. What do you do Rebecca?"

"I'm a hairdresser."

"Adam told me you've got two kids, it must be difficult on your own."

"Yes, but I have Adam now."

"You'd better watch out, bruv, she'll be asking you to put a ring on her finger next."

"Take no notice Rebecca, he's a cheeky bastard. Don't you want to get married and settle down one day Mark?"

"Yeah one day, but I'd plan it out where I was financially secure first where me and my girlfriend both worked and saved hard and have our children further down the line. My brother jumps into things too quickly without thinking, Rebecca. He's a soft shit and lets his heart rule his head."

"I disagree Mark, he's happy and contented, money isn't everything – tell him Adam."

"I'm saying nothing. My brother's a wind-up merchant Rebecca. I'll go and get the drinks in – same again Mark?"

"I'll have a gin and tonic this time, the beer is awful."

While Adam was at the bar and out of earshot, Rebecca decided to have a word with Mark.

"I sense you disapprove of me Mark, because I have children."

"My brother isn't loaded and to be perfectly honest Rebecca I don't think he knows what he wants. You have two kids, and to me getting involved with you, a divorced woman, is a mistake – that's just my opinion."

"I think you're rude and arrogant Mark, and a bully – all that education you've had hasn't given you any manners."

"That's me I'm afraid, I speak my mind."

Adam brought the drinks and could sense the tension when he sat down, "I hope you haven't upset Rebecca, what have you been saying Mark? I know you."

"I've just been honest, bruv. Getting involved with any woman with kids that are not your own is going to be difficult. The biological father will always be on the scene, sticking his oar in."

"Behave yourself! What I do is my own business Mark. We're brothers, but you cross the line sometimes, say sorry to Rebecca."

"I'm only looking out for you like I've always done, bruv. Listen, I'm sorry if I've offended you Rebecca, I let my mouth run away with me at times," Mark said with a smirk on his face.

Rebecca ignored him and turned to Adam. "I'm going home, I'm feeling really tired – you and your brother stay here and I'll order a taxi outside."

"Are you sure? I'll take you home if you like."

"No I'm fine Adam, stop fussing. Are you staying at my place tonight?"

"No, but I'll see you tomorrow. I don't want to come in late and wake you up Rebecca."

"Okay, give me a ring in the morning," and she kissed Adam on the cheek.

"Bye Rebecca, nice meeting you," Mark grinned.

"Bye Mark," and she gave him a frosty look.

Rebecca rang for a cab outside. They were always pretty frequent and one came within ten minutes. She climbed into the back seat and she felt so angry with Mark that tears welled up in her eyes.

When she arrived at the house she paid the cab driver and went indoors. The kitchen looked like a bomb had hit it, there were dishes everywhere so she washed them up and tidied up the kitchen and put the kettle on for a cuppa. What was supposed to be a quiet night in with Adam and a lovely meal turned out to be a stressful evening. 'How can two brothers be so different,' she wondered. The thought of Mark made her blood boil. 'What an arrogant, big-headed, horrible man,' she thought, she didn't care if she never set eyes on him again.

She drank her tea and put all the lights out and went upstairs to bed, and when she got undressed and put on her pyjamas she felt a sadness inside. She thought Adam would be staying the night with her and she tossed and turned all night long till she finally fell asleep.

The next morning Rebecca woke up and climbed out of bed and got dressed. She felt like ringing Adam, giving him a piece of her mind – she was angry with him too, he could have spoken up on her behalf to his brother with more conviction, especially when her children were mentioned, that made her feel furious. She put the kettle on and made herself a coffee and sat at the kitchen table.

Just then the doorbell rang and she went and opened the door. "I hope I'm not intruding Rebecca," said Irene, "I'm on the cadge – have you got a couple of slices of bread please? I forgot to take my loaf out the freezer."

"Of course Irene, come in. Do you fancy a cuppa?"

"Yes please. Where's your gentleman friend?"

"You mean Adam, my boyfriend – he's at his flat, his brother's staying there for a few days."

"Oh that's nice for him dearie."

"How are you feeling Irene after your last fall?"

"Betty pops in to see me most days, she's a real fusspot but a good neighbour. She makes sure I take my tablets every day, she's very kind to me. I've noticed lately I've been a lot more unsteady on my feet but I'm hoping to get a walking frame next week."

"That's good. You look much better in your face – you've got more colouring, not so pale Irene."

The phone rang, "Will you excuse me a minute, it's

probably Adam," and she walked into the sitting room.

"Hi sweetheart, my head is throbbing – me and Mark had a bellyful last night, he's still sleeping."

"I had a bellyful too, listening to your arrogant brother's remarks."

"He's an idiot Rebecca. I told him to keep his nose out of my business. I was thinking the three of us could go for lunch, he's going home later on this afternoon."

"You must be joking Adam, the way I'm feeling I want to give him a slap."

"I understand. I'll take him for lunch and when he goes home I'll drive to your place."

"I thought you were staying with me last night Adam?"

"Don't be ridiculous Rebecca, I could hardly leave Mark on his own in the flat when he had come to see me – unless he slept at your house, and I couldn't see that happening. I can't seem to do right for doing wrong."

"What you have to understand, Adam, is that my children and me come as a package, and if you're finding that difficult to handle you know what you can do."

"For fuck's sake Rebecca, where has all this come from? You know I'm fond of them and I love spending time with the three of you. I'm sorry if you think otherwise."

"Look, I've got Irene my neighbour here with me Adam, I'll see you later on," and Rebecca put the phone down.

When she sat back down at the table Irene could see she was upset, "What's up Rebecca?"

"It's Mark, Adam's brother, he was rude to me in the pub last night. He thinks Adam is a fool for getting involved with me because I have two kids."

"Oh dear, what did Adam say?"

"Nothing much, I left him in the pub with his brother last night and came home."

"I think your young man doesn't like confrontation Rebecca, my late hubby was like that. Are you seeing him today?"

"He's coming over later on."

"That's good. Well, if I were you I'd have a long chat with him and explain your feelings. Adam's brother's obviously upset you, I know families can be a nightmare – I never got on with my brother-in-law, we fought like cats and dogs. Adam probably feels like he's piggy in the middle. Does he see much of his brother?"

"No, not as far as I know."

"Well then, I wouldn't worry. I'm sure Adam has a mind of his own, sometimes the quiet ones are the ones to watch – I know, because when my hubby lost his temper with his brother it scared the hell out of me. By nature he was a placid mild-tempered man who avoided trouble. I must be making a move Rebecca, Betty's having a spot of lunch with me later on."

"Here's your bread Irene."

"Thanks, and don't you worry Rebecca, it all comes out in the wash, everything gets resolved eventually," and Irene gave her a hug.

Rebecca showed Irene to the door. She was very fond of her and she would miss her when she moved on as she classed Irene as a very dear friend, full of wisdom and kindness.

Rebecca suddenly felt a bit better after talking to Irene and gave Adam a ring. "Hi Adam, it's me, will you bring a bottle of wine with you and some beers when you come over?"

"Sure, no problem, is there anything else you want?"

"Only you!"

"Blimey Rebecca, that's nice to know I'm not in the dog house anymore."

"I wouldn't say that Adam. Where are you taking Mark for lunch?"

"I'm not, I'm cooking us some steak and having that with a jacket potato with cheese, and a salad."

"Sounds delicious! What time do you think you'll be coming over?"

"Well, Mark is shooting off straight after lunch, so I'll be at yours about two-thirty – is that alright?"

"That's fine, I have plenty of housework to keep me busy – see you then."

"Love you Rebecca."

"Love you too, bye."

The house was looking spic and span when Rebecca had finished. She'd cleaned upstairs and downstairs, then took the sheets out of the washing machine and hung them on the line outside in the garden. It had taken a couple of hours and when she had done all of that she put the kettle on and made herself a cuppa.

The phone rang and she picked it up, "Hi darling, what are you up to?"

"I've just done all the cleaning Mum – is Dad alright?"

"He's fine, he's over his flu, so he's gone out with Pete to the garden centre. I was thinking of popping over to see you."

"Not today Mum, I have Adam coming over – he wants us to have lunch at his local pub."

"Okay, no worries, give him my regards."

"I will. I'll see you this week sometime, bye Mum," and Rebecca put the phone down. She hated lying to her mum but she wanted to spend time with Adam on her own, and after drinking her tea she went upstairs to have a shower and glam herself up.

When she came downstairs the doorbell rang and she opened the door. Adam was waving a white handkerchief.

"Is it safe to come in?"

"Don't be daft, come in Adam," and she kissed him passionately.

"What have I done to deserve this, Rebecca?" he asked, and handed her a carrier bag with the wine and beers in.

"I'm still annoyed with you Adam, and I think your brother is a big-headed nasty bloke, but can we make a truce?"

"Rebecca don't worry, I gave him a piece of my mind before he left and put him straight about my feelings for you and how fond I am of the children. He upsets lots of people – just forget about him. Now can I have a beer?"

"Can I ask you one question Adam – do your parents feel the same way about us?"

"Now you're being paranoid, my parents want the best for me Rebecca, but with all their faults they just want me to be happy whatever choices I make in life. I told you they want to meet you and the twins."

"Fair enough Adam. Pour me a glass of wine please my darling."

When he was unscrewing the cork off the bottle, she unzipped his jeans and put her hand down stroking his penis. The sexual chemistry between them was electric and they went upstairs to bed. They lay on the bed undressing each other and made passionate love.

"Phew! Are you alright my darling, did you enjoy that?"

"Don't be daft, of course I did. Now I'm going downstairs to make us both a coffee, the sex has given me an appetite."

"Rebecca will you bring me some peanuts and crisps please?"

"Christ no, you'll have them all over my clean bedsheets Adam."

"What a spoilsport you are Rebecca. Forget about the coffee, how about we go for a walk in the park? It's such a lovely day and I need a bit of exercise."

"Do we have to Adam? I feel tired."

"Rubbish! The fresh air will do us both good. I'll have a shower first – you can join me if you like."

"I'd love to but my phone is ringing, I'd better answer it – it might be Jim ringing. You go and have your shower."

Rebecca put her dressing gown on and went downstairs to pick up the phone. "Hi Rebecca, it's me Linda – what are you up to?"

"Nothing much, I'm with Adam and we're getting ready to go to the park – why?"

"I thought I'd call in to see you, Charlie's with me, we won't stay long Rebecca."

"Okay, what time will you be here?"

"In about twenty minutes, we're in the Queen's Head pub down the road. I'll see you soon – bye."

Adam came downstairs, "Who was that Rebecca?"

"It was Linda, she's coming round in twenty minutes with Charlie."

"You're mad Rebecca, why didn't you say no we're doing something or going somewhere? I just wanted a relaxing day and from what you've told me about her she's a piss artist."

"Adam you're making me annoyed, don't be cruel, she's a friend and she told me she won't stay long."

"You win, Rebecca, I'm not going to argue with you. Go and have a shower, but don't take too long, I don't want to entertain them on my own."

Rebecca went upstairs to have a shower and Adam put some crisps and peanuts out in a bowl on the coffee table. The doorbell rang and he opened the door, "Come in you two, Rebecca's getting ready she'll be down in a minute."

"I've brought a bottle of red wine Adam. It was expensive and I've never tried it before so I hope it's good."

"Thanks Linda. What would you like to drink, we have

beer or wine – Charlie?"

"I'll have a beer. You've had three glasses of wine already Linda – she can knock them back Adam."

"Shut up Charlie. I'll have a glass of wine Adam please."

"You two go into the sitting room and make yourself at home."

It wasn't long before Rebecca walked into the room.

"Wow you look lovely!" exclaimed Linda. "Rebecca, this is Charlie my boyfriend."

"Nice to meet you. Linda's told me all about you."

"Good things I hope?"

"Well she didn't bad-mouth you if that's what you mean."

"You talk with a posh accent – whereabouts are you from?"

"I was born in Oxfordshire but we moved around a lot with my dad's job, but I did attend a private school. I had a good education."

"Wonderful I'm sure," Rebecca said in a sarcy voice. "Adam I'll have that glass of wine now please."

"What work do you do Adam?" Charlie asked.

"I'm a self-employed builder Charlie."

"I'd hate that job, sounds like manual hard graft to me. I much prefer to sit in my cosy office – I have a secretary who assists me."

"He's a bank manager Adam."

"I know that, Linda, that would bore the arse off me."

"He makes good money Adam. Tell him, Charlie, how much you earn."

"Will you hold your tongue Linda. I don't discuss my finances with anyone – that's my business."

Linda bent over to put her arms around Charlie and spilled her wine all over his trousers. "You stupid woman," he said in an angry manner and pushed her away. "Can I use your bathroom Rebecca?"

"Sure, it's upstairs."

When Charlie went upstairs Rebecca sat down with Linda.

"Have you gone stark raving mad! What the hell are you going out with him for? He's a big-headed, arrogant man, so boastful."

"When you get to know him Rebecca he's not that bad, but we've got nought in common."

Adam cut in, "I have to agree with Rebecca – you're not alike at all. He's a snobbish, ignorant geek."

"Adam please be nice to him for my sake, he's talking about taking me on holiday with him to Barcelona."

"You're a fool Linda, he looks like a player to me."

"Rebecca shush, he'll hear you, he's coming... I'm sorry Charlie you'll have to get them dry-cleaned they're stained."

"Tell me about it Linda, you should be more careful, these trousers cost me a bomb – they're expensive, made-to-measure from Savile Row tailors in London. Have you got any whisky Adam or a gin and tonic?"

"No mate, there's an off-licence at the bottom of the road if you fancy going there. I'll come with you if you like, I can get more beers in."

"Have you got any money on you Adam?" Rebecca asked.

"Yep I have, is there anything you want Rebecca?"

"No I'm fine, see you two later."

"Okay, we won't be very long."

As soon as they had left to go to the off-licence, Rebecca took the opportunity to talk to Linda on her own.

"I'm glad they've gone Linda, I thought you were cutting back on the booze?"

"I have a bit, but I've come to the conclusion it's a habit not an addiction I've got. I enjoy it but I know if I really wanted to I could stop."

"You're kidding yourself Linda, but I can't force you to stop – you need help."

"Look, I know you're thinking of me Rebecca, but it's the first time I've felt good about myself in a long time, so back off – I don't need a lecture."

"Okay you win, but don't come running to me when you screw up. Tell me, how do you really feel about Charlie?"

"I enjoy his company and have feelings for him Rebecca. Let's just say when he's nice he's fantastic – so generous and kind, but he does have a mean streak in him."

"Sounds like he's a Jekyll and Hyde character."

"Honestly you crack me up, Rebecca. What personality traits do you think I have then?"

"You Linda, I would say, are a beautiful classy woman who likes the good things in life and has a good heart but lives in a fairy-tale world, and I don't think Charlie will be your prince charming you're looking for. He's nothing like you."

"Oh shut up, Rebecca you silly cow, and pour me a drink," Linda said laughing.

"Listen, what I said earlier – I didn't mean it Linda. I would be there if you ever needed me."

"I know that, you're a good friend Rebecca even though you act like my mother at times it's so bloody annoying."

It wasn't too long before Adam and Charlie returned. "You should see what Charlie bought – a large bottle of gin, whisky and twenty-four cans of beer. Oh I forgot, and two bottles of red wine."

"It must have cost a fortune Charlie, thanks."

"You're welcome Rebecca. Can I have a whisky, I forgot to get the tonics for the gin."

"I'll get you one but I'm going to be a party pooper and put the kettle on for a coffee, alcohol always makes me feel sleepy."

"What work are you doing at the moment Adam?" Charlie asked.

"I'm working on a bungalow," Adam replied.

"I can't stand them, they have no character whatsoever. They're mostly for the elderly aren't they. I much prefer town houses or country estates."

"I was starting to like you Charlie, but I can see you're such a male chauvinist narrow-minded plonker…"

"Hey Adam, ease off, he wasn't to know it's my bungalow. Charlie I've recently bought it and I love it!"

"Awkward! Trust me to put my foot in it. I'm sorry you two, I didn't mean to offend anyone."

An hour later Rebecca could see Linda was getting more and more sloshed so she suggested to Charlie to take her home.

"Come on old girl, let's make a move. Thanks Adam and you Rebecca for your hospitality, I'll take Linda home."

"I feel tipsy Rebecca."

"You're pissed Linda, I'll ring you tomorrow."

"I think I'll take the whisky home and the gin Adam. Have you got a carrier bag?"

"Yep I've got one here – what about the beers?"

"No, you can have them."

"Bye you two, thanks for coming," and Adam and Rebecca stood at the front door watching them walk down the road. "Thank god for that, I thought he was going to take the beers with him. What a tight git!"

"He's not my cup of tea Adam, I can't see that relationship working. He's so full of himself, such an irritating man. They're different from chalk and cheese. Oh my god, I have such a splitting headache – red wine always does that to me, I need to take a paracetamol."

"I'll get you two Rebecca and make you a cuppa. You go into the sitting room and have a rest on the settee."

Getting Close

Three weeks had passed and Rebecca was getting excited, only a week to go before her and the children would move into their new home. Adam had worked his socks off and the kitchen and bathroom were completed. He spent most of his evenings with Rebecca and the children who were getting very fond of him. He occasionally dropped them off at school after staying the night.

It was Saturday morning and the girls were staying at their nanna and grandad's bungalow. Adam was helping Rebecca pack her belongings into boxes.

"I hate this job Adam. I never realized how much stuff I have."

"Don't forget to label the boxes which room they're going into. I forgot to tell you Rebecca, my landlord is selling the flat – me and my mate have to look elsewhere to rent. He's given us a month's notice."

"Oh Christ, that's a worry, if I hear of anything I'll let you know. My mum might know somewhere. It would be wonderful if you lived near me."

"I'm not moving out of the area Rebecca if I can help it. Now put the kettle on, it's time for a cuppa."

"Your phone's ringing Adam."

"I'll get it."

It was Adam's mother, "Hello son, I was wondering if you and Rebecca and the children fancy coming here tomorrow for lunch?"

"We'd love to Mum but I'm helping her with the move. Just give it a couple of weeks till she gets settled in her new home – it's silly doing the two-and-a-half hour journey there and back for one day, we may as well all come for a long weekend."

"That would be lovely Adam. Me and your dad would love that. Are you alright son?"

"I'm fine Mum."

"Give Rebecca all our love, I'll speak to you again soon – bye."

"That was my mum, she wanted us to go for lunch tomorrow and to bring the girls, but I told her we'll all go and stay with her for a long weekend once you're settled in your new home."

"Ah that's nice of her, Adam. We'll definitely do that. I'd love to meet your mum and dad – are you close?"

"I can't complain. My dad can be a pain in the arse; he was all for my brother Mark and me having a good education and could be too strict at times, but my mum was the softer of the two. I would say I was more close to her when I was growing up and Mark was closer to our dad. Mark was the brainy one. I hated school, I could never sit long enough to concentrate on the lessons, I was always messing about. Mark was studious, always handed his homework in on time and had good grades."

"Still, you've done alright for yourself Adam."

"I just wish I'd been more attentive in my maths lessons, I'm hopeless at costings on my jobs. My mate who I work with helps me, and filling in forms is a bloody nightmare – but don't tell your dad Rebecca, you know how he worries, he'll think I've overcharged you."

"Don't be daft, I know you wouldn't do that – I won't breathe a word."

The whole day was spent packing boxes and they both decided to give it a rest. Rebecca cooked some steak and chips and they sat down at the kitchen table having their meal.

"I'm knackered Rebecca, can we do more packing tomorrow?"

"I agree Adam, I feel tired myself. You've been brilliant, I couldn't have managed without you helping me."

"You may have to help me when I move, Rebecca."

"Of course I will."

"Don't be daft, I'm only joking – it's only my clothes and personal items, the furniture belongs to the landlord."

"I won't miss this house Adam, only my neighbour Irene next door but we'll keep in touch, she's a sweetheart – she's been good to me and the children. By the way, I was thinking of giving my notice in at work, the wages I get there aren't enough. I'd love to own my own salon one day but that's a pipe dream."

"I don't see why not, it's good to have goals."

"What about you Adam?"

"I would love to have the finances to buy a cheap rundown property, to renovate it and sell it. I've discussed it with my parents in the past and they said they'd give me a loan to buy a property."

"That's good of them Adam."

"I think it's because they've always helped Mark out with his university fees, they feel slightly guilty so they want to help me now. I said I'd pay them back once I've sold the property and I would share any profit I make with them, it's just finding the time to go to the auctions."

"It's a great idea Adam. You surprise me, I thought you just wanted to settle down and have kids?"

"You mean you thought I was a boring, predictable bloke with no ambition whatsoever."

"Don't be putting words in my mouth, I never thought that of you Adam."

"Woah! I'm only kidding, Rebecca, of course I'd like to get married one day like most blokes and settle down."

"Tell me Adam, are me and the girls included in your future?"

"I'll have to think about that one," Adam replied with a big grin on his face."

"You cheeky bugger! You're sleeping on the settee tonight."

"I feel like crashing out right now Rebecca, it's been a long day."

"Me too, let's go to bed."

A Future Together

The weeks flew by and Rebecca was settled with the girls in the bungalow. She loved living there, and having her parents across the road was a bonus. Adam was still living in the flat with his mate, as the landlord had changed his mind about selling the property.

Rebecca was sitting in the kitchen having a cuppa with her mum; they had just come back after dropping the girls off at school.

"What are you thinking about, you're miles away Rebecca?"

"I was just thinking Mum, what would make my life complete is having Adam move in with us so we could be a proper family."

"Don't you think you're rushing into things? As much as me and your dad have grown quite fond of him, there's no hurry."

"I see him most days and I can't imagine my life without him Mum, I do love him."

"Okay Rebecca, but make sure Adam wants the same thing as you do, he may not be ready just yet – that's a huge commitment on his part – so don't be disappointed if he isn't."

"You'd rather I was engaged or married Mum, wouldn't you?"

"You're wrong Rebecca. Me and your dad want you to be happy, that's all. A ring on your finger and a piece of paper can't guarantee that. Listen sweetheart, I'm sorry I have to make a move – your dad will be wondering where I am. I said I'd only be ten minutes, his belly will be rumbling and he'll want a cuppa and a bacon sarni. I'll see you later on, bye."

Rebecca was determined to ask Adam and arranged for her mum and dad to have the children that evening to have a sleepover. She prepared a lovely meal for Adam.

When he walked in the door from work there were candles on the table and a beef casserole dish in the oven. "Blimey, what have I done to deserve this? It smells delicious whatever you're cooking."

"Have a quick shower Adam, dinner's nearly ready."

When they sat down at the table eating their meal, Rebecca took a deep breath and plucked up courage. "I was just thinking, Adam, it makes sense to me… but you can say no if you like… I will understand…"

"Spit it out – what are you trying to say Rebecca?"

"What about you moving in here with me and the girls?"

"Oh my darling, I would love to – are you sure about this?"

"Of course I am."

"Good, because I have fallen in love with you."

"I feel the same way Adam. I can't imagine my future without you in it."

"I've told you once before Rebecca, I'm going nowhere," and he kissed her passionately on the lips.

Rebecca was filled with joy and happiness. The future looked exciting, she had finally moved on and the past was the past.